How much longer did they have to live?

L. Madison Steele had never negotiated against death. She held no power base, only concessions.

How many more times would she visit her aging parents? Five? Ten? Twenty?

Or hold her little girl in her arms before she was too big to be held? A hundred?

Or sleep with a man?

Madison propped her chin in her palm and spotted Jon in his seat several rows up. His head bowed, the even cut of his blond hair on the back of his neck made her fingers itch to test its softness. How many times would she have left to brush against his hand by accident or run her fingers through his hair on purpose?

She might have only one time left to fall in love again or to be loved or to make love. Letting those times come and savoring them, that was the best she could hope for.

Because the greatest natural resource is life, too precious to waste on "what-if's" and "what might have been's."

"We can't stop you from publishing this book."
--US Air Force Public Affairs Personnel

Also by

Lorna Tedder

From *Spilled Candy Books for Writers*
Reclaiming the Magic:
A Writer's Guide To Success

Book Promotion for the Shameless:
101 Marketing Tips That Really Work

From *Spilled Candy*
Books for the Next Millennium
Access: Book 1 of The Lorelei Files (New Age thriller)
*Gifts for the Fairies
*Magick'ly Delicious
*The Goddess Program
*Gifts for Gaia
*Waiting on the Thunder (New Age thriller)

From *Kensington Books*
Top Secret Affair (romantic comedy)
*The Cure for Shyness (romantic comedy)

From *Silhouette Books*
A Man Called Regret (romantic suspense)
(under the pseudonym Lauren Shelley)

*Coming soon

About the Author

Like L. Madison Steele, Lorna Tedder is a contract negotiator for the Department of Defense. Readers may write to her at Lorna@spilledcandy.com or c/o Spilled Candy Books, P O Box 5202, Niceville, FL 32578-5202.

ACCESS

Book 1
of

THE LORELEI FILES

A New Age Thriller

by

Lorna Tedder

Spilled Candy Books for the Next Millennium

Access, Book 1 of The Lorelei Files , Copyright 1999
By Lorna T edder

Published by:

Spilled Candy Books for the Next Millennium
Spilled Candy Publications
Post Office Box 5202
Niceville, FL 32578-5202
Staff@spilledcandy.com
http://www.spilledcandy.com

Cover art: Spilled Candy Publications
Author photo by HPM Financial Services

Electronic Release: January 1999
First Printing: April 1999
Printed in the United States of America

ISBN:1-892718-00-6 (disk/download version)
ISBN: 1-89-2718-12-X (print)
Library of Congress Card Catalog Number: 99-90314

Dedication

For Shannon, who will one day be a great writer,
and for Aislinn Eileen, my vision of light:
you are the future.

The night is far spent,
  the day is at hand;
Let us, therefore,
  cast off the works of darkness,
and let us put on the armor of light.
—Romans 13:12

PROLOGUE

In the Year 2000, the Earth spun off its axis and into the sun.

At least, that's what my lover says happened. And he should know: he was there.

It wasn't supposed to happen that way, he says. The human race was supposed to have entered a new millennium and a new age of enlightenment at the same time. It was my lover's fault it didn't. He was a great scientist, and back in the 1960's, he found the key to time travel. It was his doings that changed the course of our future.

To salvage what he could of our planet and our race, he forged a different future. As you know by now, the Earth did not spin off its axis in the Year 2000. Nor was it left untouched.

It was my lover who found a woman destined to save the world, time and again. A woman who would later become the High Priestess of the Remnants of Mankind. She was Lorelei Madison Steele, and she was my mother.

This is the story of the *first* time she saved the world and of the man who was willing to give his life to keep her safe.

—Delilah Steele
2018 A.D.
Georgia Colony

PART I

THE FAR-SPENT NIGHT

"Within the next 5 to 10 years, it would probably be possible to make a new infective microorganism which could differ in certain important aspects from any known disease-causing organisms.

Most important of these is that it might be refractory to the immunological and therapeutic processes upon when we depend to maintain our relative freedom from infectious disease.

A research program to explore the feasibility of this could be completed in approximately 5 years at a total cost of $10 million."

—Senate testimony
DEPARTMENT OF DEFENSE
APPROPRIATIONS FOR 1970
United States Senate Library

CHAPTER ONE

Tuesday, 28 September 1999, Eglin Air Force Base, Florida

"I work my ass off for you people, and you think I'm a spy?" She brought her fist down hard enough to crack the glass plate that covered her desk. Her hand smarted from the impact, but she didn't flinch. "Look, I don't understand why I'm wasting precious time defending myself to a man who doesn't know the difference between botulism and nerve gas. Why aren't you out trying to catch the real thief?"

"*I'm* asking the questions here."

Oh, yeah. Interrogation was definitely his forte. Wear 'em down, wear 'em out. And if that doesn't work, shoot 'em.

Maybe his looks were part of the plan. He was sexier than he had any right to be, especially for an executioner. Black suit. Black turtleneck. Black eyes. He could have been James Bond. The silver pen in his hand could have been some newfangled gadget designed to pierce her to the heart with a heat-seeking bullet, but the ink scribbled on the yellow legal pad in his lap did enough damage without the benefit of Space Age technology. If not an executioner, he was certainly her judge and jury.

With the precision of a metronome, Special Agent Austin Wait tapped the pen point against the pad, leaving indented dots in a symmetrical pattern. His eyes twitched, wanting to squint as they tried to look right through her. If he could strain a little harder, maybe he could see something beneath her skin he hadn't spotted in the past four hours of interrogation.

"And is it correct," he asked, leaning forward, "that your first name is 'Lorelei'?"

She winced. She couldn't do much about being just under thirty or taming her wild mane of blonde hair, but she refused to sabotage her own career with a name that better suited a porn queen. In the nine years she'd worked for the Department of Defense at Florida's Eglin Air Force Base, she'd kept her first name a secret from her co-workers. But a poorly chosen name was nothing compared to other things she'd hidden. Sooner or later, the past would rear its ugly head and people would get hurt. Again. Especially her.

"I prefer to use 'L. Madison Steele.'" There. Poise and professionalism beamed from the halo she imagined over her half-undone French braid. Proud of her smug answer, she nearly smiled but didn't. After spending the day with the Air Force Office of Special Investigations in her cramped office, she felt as if she should be in one of those annoying antiperspirant commercials that asks when a woman needs confidence most. She discreetly tugged the sides of her hounds-tooth gray suit away from her armpits. Her brand had stopped working three-and-a-half hours ago.

"You *prefer?*" The tiniest of smirks nudged the corner of the agent's mouth upward. "Why do you prefer to hide behind an initial?"

Her halo wilted. "I'm not hiding behind anything. I don't think 'Lorelei' is a serious name."

"You don't think 'Lorelei' suits you? You don't think you're a bit of a siren, luring men to the rocks?"

So much for the past rearing its ugly head later than sooner. She swallowed hard. Was he playing with her? Did he know about Tim?

Her eyes stung. Not good. She didn't cry in front of anyone, and especially not in the presence of an OSI agent who was already convinced she'd stolen biological warfare files from a locked safe in a cipher-locked room in a card-keyed, secure building on a remote Northwest Florida military installation guarded by razor wire and soldiers with machine guns.

Madison sank back into her ergonomic chair and laced her fingers tightly enough to turn her knuckles white. A bad habit, one that grew out of high-stress negotiations on missile contracts. Men twice her age would glare at her or curse her or yell at her, expecting her to crack. She never did. Usually her hands were hidden behind her desk or under a conference table, but this time Special Agent Austin Wait glanced down at her locked fingers and grinned.

Madison jerked her hands apart and, in a calculated move, smoothed the wrinkles in her skirt. Crossing her legs as if merely trying to find a more comfortable position, she kicked over one of the dozens of stacks of paperwork that littered the floor, desks, tops of file cabinets, bookshelves, and every chair in her office except for hers and the one the OSI agent sat in. Madison didn't believe in the clean desk policy.

Keep it together, she ordered herself. *You've been through worse.*

"I am a contracting officer for the United States of America," she grated out, leaning forward to match his posture as she would in any negotiation gone sour. "I am the watchdog for millions of taxpayer dollars and for making sure we have the capability to fight the next war. How seriously do you think the CEOs of major defense contractors are going to take someone named 'Lorelei'? I think not." She leaned back into her chair again, this time her fingers laced but relaxed.

Agent Wait slumped sideways, watching her, his grin gone. He raked her over with an appreciative gaze, visibly approving her tailored suit and silk blouse. If he cared to notice, he'd see that she dressed like a real businesswoman instead of the typical civil servant. Nothing polyester, Lord help her.

He nodded to himself, then cast the same inquisitive glance around her 8-by-10 foot office. Not a smidgen of table surface remained uncluttered. The computer on her desk unintentionally resembled a daisy with its overlapping yellow Post-It Notes circling the glow of its blinking to-do list. Like most bureaucrats who worked for the Air Force, she had turned the wall behind her into an "I Love Me" display, filling it with framed certificates for outstanding performance, crummy squadron plaques from previous offices that had served as her training ground, and colorful matted photographs of bombs bursting in air during official Government testing. A diploma for completing her three-year internship in the Contracting Career Advancement Plan—or COPPER CAP, for short—hung slightly askew over a diploma from an out-of-state university. Not a square inch of the wall had been left untouched, but in the center gleamed her prized possession: a contracting officer's warrant. She'd fought to get that damned certificate of appointment to the job and now would have to fight to keep it.

"I suppose you have a point," Agent Wait conceded, not bothering to hide the bitterness in his voice. "And I don't know of any lieutenants whose careers you've dashed recently. Do you?"

He knew. Damn him. He knew about Tim. And any civil servant who had been on Eglin Air Force Base seven years ago could have told him. Years of practice had taught her not to flinch.

Agent Wait ran one absent-minded hand through his jet-black hair and said nothing else. He merely watched her, probably expecting her to squirm in the lack of conversation and confess to a serial murder or something.

Oh, she could play this game. And win. As a negotiator, she knew what an effective tool silence could be. She'd used it often enough. Her adversaries could sit across the table and rant and rave, but she—a slight woman young enough to date their college-age sons—kept her poker face and her deadly silence until those superior-acting men lost their cool and started babbling. A sophisticated game of blink, that's what it was.

"Aren't you going to get that?" he asked.

"Get what?" She pretended not to hear the insistent buzz of her intercom. For good measure, she smiled sweetly. He didn't reciprocate.

"Your telephone. Aren't you going to answer it?"

She folded her hands in her lap and waited for the phone to stop buzzing. "No."

"I thought you said you prided yourself on being responsive to your customers. What was it you said? That 'good enough for Government work' should be a challenge, not an insult?"

"Don't try that Total Quality Management bullshit on me," she said softly. "And don't twist my words. Answering your questions is my top priority today. Besides, my voice mail will pick it up. If you're worried about who's calling—you know, whether it's Russian spies asking where to deposit my pay-off for the missing files on five hundred ways to annihilate the entire population of Planet Earth—well, I'm sure you're already monitoring my calls anyway."

"Don't be glib, Ms. Steele. This is a very serious situation."

"Yes, I know. You're blowing my schedule. That's definitely serious to me. I plan to award the Project Andromeda contract within the next three days. Instead of bothering me, you should be looking for whoever took those classified files from The Facility. Do you have any idea how fast cloristium botulinum toxin can kill you once you breathe it? I should be getting that contract off my desk instead of being badgered by you for no reason."

"Oh, we have reason. Keep—" He broke off in time to slant an impatient glance toward her open doorway. Frowning at the hinges, he no doubt wondered why her door was missing. Then his gaze followed Lt. Col. Gavin Ballard down the hall for the third time in the past hour, which was three times more than The Gutless Wonder had dropped by her office in the past year. Agent Wait cleared his throat and continued in a lowered voice. "Keep this attitude up, Ms. Steele, and I may have to mirandize you."

That sobered her. The absolute last thing she needed was the world's sexiest OSI agent frisking her and reading her her rights. She hadn't done anything wrong, but a good lawyer could empty her bank account—

what was left of it—in a matter of days. The Government had its own lawyers, and the U.S. Attorney over in Pensacola was no slouch. Even if she didn't land herself in jail, she'd end up destitute with what was left of her reputation in shambles. And there was always the chance they'd find out about her clandestine trips along the backroads of Georgia.

Madison closed her eyes. "I'm sorry," she whispered. If the truth wouldn't set her free, maybe humility would. Opening her eyes, she focused on Agent Wait and deliberately softened her expression to gain his good will. "I did not steal anything—classified or *un*. I am mad as hell that something like this happened on one of my programs, and I do feel responsible but I feel responsible for everything I work on, even when it's not my job to be responsible. But I didn't breach security and I don't know who did or who would."

"Ms. Steele, have you ever heard of the Sleeping Dogs?"

"Yeah, sure. You lie down with them and get up with fleas. What gives? You don't strike me as the type of man who spouts pithy sayings."

"I'm not."

She let out a long sigh that turned ragged in her throat, made her sound nervous. "Look, I'm sorry if I'm a little tense, but it's not every day my integrity is questioned. If you could give me some idea why you think I would ever sell Project Andromeda secrets to another country...."

"I'm not at liberty to say. Not yet."

"So it's none of my business why I've been accused?"

An indecipherable message whined from the walkie-talkie he had laid atop the nearest stack of papers she had yet to file. After a second burst of static, Agent Wait shrugged. "You haven't been accused of anything yet. Whether we open a full investigation depends on the answers we get."

A full investigation. God, they would find out everything! It didn't matter that they would eventually realize she wasn't guilty of disclosing classified information to a foreign government. Every little detail of her past would be bantered back and forth, whistled at, laughed at. All the secrets would come out. The investigators would go home at night and while they screwed their wives whisper, "Honey, you won't believe this case I'm working on." The things that had hurt so much would be treated with less respect than an afternoon soap opera.

"I don't understand." Madison rubbed at her unpolished thumbnail. She couldn't bear to look into Agent Wait's eyes and feel the indifference there. He was like a machine, pouring over facts and motives, not stirred by the confusion and anger caught in her throat. "Why do you think I would do something like that? Money? You think I need the money? Who doesn't? Half the people in my office are in hock up to their eyeballs. Probably most of the people who work here in Building 13."

"You're not."

Damn. So the OSI had perused her credit rating already. "I live simply. I don't need a lot." Besides, all the stores were closed by the time she left work.

"Then I'll be blunt, Ms. Steele—"

"Hasn't stopped you so far."

"Are you being blackmailed?"

Her jaw dropped before she could prevent it. "No!" Then, more softly, she repeated, "No." She hiked her chin defiantly. "Why would you assume such a thing?"

A muscle in his jaw twitched. He thought he had her, didn't he? "You're a GS-12 contract specialist grossing about four grand a month in your pay grade. Once a month, you withdraw two thousand dollars. Every month. Like clockwork for the last six years and a couple of months. A woman in your profession, with your security clearance, working on special counter proliferation programs like Project Andromeda, is highly susceptible to blackmail. Considering the kinds of technology you have access to, you're an easy target for a terrorist willing to bet you'll trade American technology for keeping quiet about some sleazy indiscretion that happened when you were a COPPER CAP trainee."

Sleazy indiscretion. The words twisted around inside Madison's throat, cutting off her breath. Leave it to the gossip mill to turn the love of her life into a "sleazy indiscretion." Since Tim's sudden transfer, she had lived her life conservatively, performed her work flawlessly. It didn't matter. Even after seven years, the brightest flag waved when her name was mentioned was the one that proclaimed "Sleazy Indiscretion."

"Ms. Steele?" Waiting for an answer, Agent Wait raised his eyebrows. When she didn't respond, he prompted with "Why don't you tell me what you've been doing with almost twenty-five thousand dollars a year in cash?"

Madison untangled a strand of blonde from her braid and twisted it around her index finger. "That's...personal."

"You might as well spill your guts while we can still cut a deal. Because I will find out your secrets. All of them. And that's a promise."

She locked her gaze with his. "It's none of your fucking business."

A little gasp from her doorway caught her attention. Eileen Rabourn held tight to the door jamb with one hand, the other palm flattened over her lips as if pressing hard would somehow obliterate the f-word from Madison's vocabulary. Eileen hadn't heard it often in the six months she'd been working for Madison's contracting team. A combination secretary, right hand, and Super Mom, a good procurement clerk was scarcer than hen's teeth.

Eileen was better than most. Madison guessed she was in her forties, but with her finely-applied make-up, it was hard to tell which side of forty-five. Eileen was always immaculately dressed, her mousy hair highlighted to fade the gray. She said "Good morning" to everyone in the office before she made her first cup of coffee, and she offered to pray for her co-workers whether they needed it or not. Eileen was never without a Band-Aid, a gum drop, or a smile. Until now.

"Ex-excuse me, Madison." Eileen glanced from Madison to the OSI agent and back. "You have a, um, visitor here to see you." She made an odd gesture with her eyebrows as if to tell Madison something without Agent Wait understanding the message, but Madison didn't comprehend it either.

A visitor? Madison had been double- and triple-booked in meetings all morning, but she'd canceled all of them at Agent Wait's insistence. She swiveled in her chair, hit the space bar on her computer keyboard, and watched her calendar materialize on the screen. Her answer to a Congressional inquiry on the Mayer-Frick and Associates' allegations was due in the policy office in a scant thirty minutes, and she'd promised to review Cathy's sole source justification document by 1:30. She didn't have anything else scheduled until 1:57 PM when the entire Project Andromeda team would gather in The Facility for a daily dose of her expertise. She'd scheduled a dry-run of their final briefing to the visiting general who would give them a thumbs-up to proceed.

"Your visitor's not on your calendar," Eileen offered, as usual reading Madison's mind as any really good procurement clerk was likely to do. "I must have forgotten to tell you. I apologize."

Eileen hadn't forgotten anything. She never made mistakes.

"I don't think Agent Wait is particularly interested in whether I get any real work done. Could you reschedule my visitor, please?"

Eileen looked stricken. "Oh, no, no. I don't think I'll be able to get rid of your, er, visitor. Besides, you've had about a dozen phone calls from Lt. Colter wanting to know when you'll be done with, um—"she inclined her head in Agent Wait's direction—"this particular priority. Oh, and the policy folks want to know where your response to the Congressional is. If you're late, the Senator in Dr. Frick's back pocket will be screaming to Colonel Kildee."

Agent Wait checked his watch, then reached for his walkie-talkie and legal pad and rose to his commanding height. "I could use a break to check in with my office and see what they've found so far. Go ahead and take your meeting. We'll resume when you're done." He brushed past her as she stood, almost grazing her elbow, then stopped in the edge of the hall. Turning his head as if to look over his shoulder, he studied the ugly orange and purple carpet instead of looking directly at her. "Oh, and Ms. Steele?"

"Yes?"

"You're not to discuss this case with anyone. Got that?"

Eileen inched backward. Her hands shook.

Madison clenched her fists. If she could have thought of a way to growl at Austin Wait without scaring the beejeezus out of Eileen, she would have. "That's a big assumption, Agent Wait."

"What is?"

"That I have the time or the inclination to discuss your questions with anyone."

A shadow of a smile flitted over his lips as if he thought she thought she'd met her match. He stalked away.

Madison let out a long sigh and plowed her palms over her cheeks, rubbing at the headache that had settled in her temples. "Thank you, Eileen. You're an angel of mercy. I can't tell you how much I appreciate this reprieve, but you didn't have to lie for me. I don't want to get you in trouble."

"I-I didn't lie. I mean, I would have if I knew what to say, but I didn't. You really do have a visitor."

"Aw, man!" Madison slammed her fist against her overflowing inbox. How was she supposed to cram five hours' worth of work into the next thirty minutes, take a visitor, answer God-knows how many telephone calls, even from the very sweet Lt. Colter? If the research and development laboratory she worked for had any sense at all, they'd figure out a way to clone her. Or at least how to get rid of her tension headache.

Eileen bit into her bottom lip. "I'm sorry. I thought you'd want to see this visitor."

"Do I look like I want to see somebody?" Madison flung her arm in a wild gesture toward the stacks of paper, each one representing some urgent project that wouldn't get done today or tomorrow or even this week, no matter how late she worked. Then she noticed the crushed expression on Eileen's face. "Sorry, Eileen. I don't mean to take it out on you. Whoever it is, would you please, please, please send them away? I don't have time to explain to another engineer how to do his job."

"I didn't want to say anything in front of the OSI, Madison, but your visitor isn't here on business."

Madison caught her breath. Tim? He wouldn't come on business. If he came at all. She twisted the thin gold band on her third finger, left hand. She'd never been married, yet she wore a wedding band. A gift from Tim. A promise he'd return and make it real one day.

"Madison?" Cathy Barner craned her neck around the door. "Could I puh-leeze have a minute before someone else grabs you? Are you going to have a chance to look my sole source document today? I can't do another blessed thing until I've got your autograph." She hoisted a thick, brown folder stuffed with neatly filed papers.

Actually, no. Madison didn't have time to review Cathy's work. Not that she ever really needed to. Cathy, a black woman in her late thirties, gave three hundred percent of herself to everything she touched. A far cry from the expectations of their racist ex-boss who had soothingly informed Madison that she would have to take Cathy on her team because Madison had a talent for getting at least a little bit of work out of the problem children.

Grimacing, Madison took the folder from Cathy and snatched up a pen from the "Beware: I'm armed and I have PMS" mug on the corner of the desk. She flipped open the folder, read the first sentence, then lifted her gaze to Cathy. "Is it right?" Madison asked.

"Hmmm. I think so."

Cathy had probably agonized over every crossed *t* and dotted *i,* making sure every word was perfect. The worst thing Madison had ever found in her files was a typo, and certainly not the kind of typo that would matter in a hundred years. With a nod, Madison scrawled her illegible signature across the page and thrust the folder back at her. "Then I think so, too."

"Madison," Eileen pressed as Cathy slipped away, "do you want to see your visitor in your office or in the conference room? I thought the conference room. At least it has a door."

Privacy. That's what Eileen was trying to tell her. She would need privacy with her visitor.

Tim. It had to be Tim.

"My office will do fine." In her job, appearances mattered more than the truth. And no one knew that better than a woman named Lorelei.

Rubbing her damp hands against her skirt, she stumbled back into her office. Hard to believe a reunion with an old lover could leave her more anxious than a day of OSI interrogation. Her knees turned to jelly, sending a quiver of weakness up her backbone. She hadn't had lunch yet, but she wasn't really hungry. Her stomach had tied itself up in knots.

She'd had seven years to learn to control her emotions, to learn to tamp down any sign of passion, to learn to overcome the past. She hadn't been the subject of scandal in all that time, and until Agent Wait's unkind reminder, it seemed people had forgotten about Tim. On the other hand, if Tim Sandusky's touch could melt her the way it had way back when, she probably wouldn't care if her office had a door or not.

"Your visitor's here," Eileen announced from behind her.

Madison closed her eyes, gathering strength. She exhaled, opened her eyes, and spun on one foot. She felt the smile on her face collapse, even before she realized her visitor wasn't Tim.

"Don't look so goddamned thrilled to see me." Jolene Steele dropped a red duffel bag to the floor. She crossed her arms and glared at Madison from behind dirty, reddish-brown bangs. She might have been sixteen by now, but the smattering of freckles on her nose and her mismatched clothes made her look younger. Still, she had a hard edge to her—like she'd been rode hard and put up wet. She wasn't wearing her wedding ring either.

Madison pasted on a smile. "Of course I'm glad to see you, Jolene. I wasn't expecting you. Is Toby with you?"

The girl frowned as if she'd forgotten her own husband's name. "Shit, no. He's still at sea. Fucking Navy's trying to break us up."

Probably the best thing that could happen to Toby, Madison mused. After her own distorted attempt at having a real life, her family had held such high hopes for her kid brother. Instead, this little gold-digger had latched onto him and within a few weeks had claimed to be pregnant. Toby—stupid my-brain-is-in-my-dick, Toby—had dropped out of medical school and married the little trollop, only to find he couldn't afford her. He joined the Navy figuring it would pay the baby's hospital bills, and then she miraculously got her period. So much for happily ever after. Madison liked to think she was better at choosing mates than her baby brother, but the truth was, she was worse.

"Jolene? If Toby's at sea, how did you get here?"

She shrugged one shoulder. "Took a bus."

"Where are you staying?"

Jolene rolled her eyes. "You get three guesses and the first two don't count," she snarled. Her gaze darted around the small room and lingered on Madison's plastic nameplate. She knew Madison as Lorelei, which was unfortunate at best. "This your office?"

"Yes."

"I thought you were some big hotshot or something."

"Or something."

She snagged her shirt on the empty hinge. "Ha! You don't even have a fucking door."

"I'd appreciate it if you wouldn't say 'fucking' in my office." Bad memories. Very good, very bad memories. "Does Toby know you're here?"

The girl shrugged again, both shoulders this time. "I dunno. I left him a message. He'll find it if he ever comes home."

"So he doesn't know where you are."

"I told you, I left him a message. If he loves me enough, he'll come find me. This is what he gets for leaving me all alone."

Madison slapped her own forehead. Geez. She was under investigation for leaking secrets that could wipe out every living organism on earth with the possible exception of cockroaches and she was listening to this adolescent drivel? God! She should be negotiating multi-million dollar contracts, not baby-sitting!

"Jolene, go home. I'll buy your bus ticket back to Jacksonville."

"Yeah? Well, who's gonna help me take care of the baby?"

"Don't try that trash with me. It may work on my hormone-driven little brother, but it won't work on me. There are only so many times you can fake a pregnancy before everybody catches on. Even Toby."

"I don't have to fake anything. I already have a baby." She knelt and dragged a blanket-laden infant carrier into the edge of the office. In the center, sleeping peacefully, lay one perfect and tiny creature, wrapped in a white, crocheted gown.

Madison's heart wrung itself out inside her chest. How much more stress could she take in one day?

CHAPTER TWO

1400 hours.

He'd dreamed about her last night. She'd been some kind of high priestess, sickle in hand, running from an unseen enemy. But it was only a dream. Nothing real. Nothing like the stuff his mother dreamed.

1401 hours.

Something was bad wrong.

Madison Steele was never late for her daily meeting with the Project Andromeda team. In the two months that Jon Colter had worked with the woman, he'd seen her face redden with anger exactly three times: once because someone had called him a "know-nothing lieutenant" and twice because people had walked into *her* meetings late. If she had to sign up to an impossible schedule to get Project Andromeda on contract by the last day of September, she insisted that every member of the evaluation team cancel their social lives and expect to work late into the night and through the weekends. And if she called a meeting for 1357 hours, military time, in The Facility, they had better not show up at 1400 hours. So far, no one had balked, and so far, she was beating the Congressionally imposed schedule by days. In the world of government procurement, bureaucratic inertia ruled except when a woman who signed her name *L. Madison Steele* charged in, took over, and worked miracles.

For the first time since Jon had met her, Madison Steele was late.

"Pssst! Colt!" Lt. Carmen Terranova, one of his two roommates, waved a hand in front of Jon's face, effectively blocking his view of the school clock that hung between a framed photograph of the President and a copy of the Wright Brothers' contract for the first airplane. "Eighty-six that infernal humming, will ya?"

Jon abruptly stopped humming and shot him an annoyed glance. Terranova—"Figmo" to his friends—was every woman's idea of tall, dark, and handsome, but unfortunately for every woman, he tended to break hearts faster than the last one could mend. Among men, he was a loyal friend, but truth be told, Figmo could be as obnoxious as hell. Under his breath, Jon uttered a curse, though he doubted any of his companions at the table heard him.

The room thrummed with a tension that had nothing to do with the urgency of getting Project Andromeda on contract before the fiscal year end's drop-dead date of 30 September. Normally chatter didn't fill the room. But then, Madison was usually in the room at this hour, presiding over them, walking from table to table to survey their penciled drafts, making sure everything went smoothly, making sure everything went right. Without Madison in the room, the thirty or so members of the team lacked focus. A group of engineers in the corner discussed the latest *Star Trek* episode too loudly. Lt. Miri Spinalli, Jon's other roommate, was in the middle of a raucous blonde joke that could have cost her the second lieutenant's bars on her shoulders. But the grandest topic of discussion was why The Facility had been crawling with security personnel since daybreak.

"Pssst! Colt! Where's Madison?"

Jon shoved a stack of classified notes to one side and leaned across the table. "Don't know," he said in a low voice. "I called her office about a dozen times this morning, and she hasn't returned my calls. She's working some kind of hot suspense."

At least, that's what her clerk, Eileen, had told him. Still, Madison was always working some kind of emergency. That didn't account for the edge in Eileen's unerringly calm voice.

Figmo frowned across the table. "What are you calling Madison Steele for?"

"No reason," he answered too quickly. He had called Madison to hear her voice and for no other reason. He dared not admit that to Madison or to anyone else. Not even to himself. "I thought she might know what was going on this morning."

"Keep calling her, Colt. You've got the inside track with her. See if you can get her tell us what really happened here last night."

The inside track? Hardly. "Ah, she won't tell me anything she won't tell everybody else."

"Colt. Use some of that sweet-talking you're so famous for. See if you can get her alone. She'll tell you everything."

"Yeah, right."

In the past two months, he'd worked fifteen or more hours a day *every day* with Madison, and he had yet to be alone with her for more than thirty seconds at a time. In the mornings, she showed up in The Facility at o-dark thirty with her tall, doe-eyed, COPPER CAP trainee in tow. At night, Jon stayed with her until the third to last person left the building. Then Madison insisted he leave, too.

Just as she had last night.

Why did she refuse to be alone with him? She seemed to like him. He made her laugh when no one else could. He listened to every word she uttered, every sigh of frustration. Yet she turned down his casual suggestions to have lunch together unless Madison's COPPER CAP trainee, Roxie, or another lieutenant joined them. Damn it, they didn't need a chaperone! Getting Madison alone had become something of a game, one he was losing.

She didn't have any reason not to trust him. In fact, she seemed to put more stock in his ideas than anyone else's. If she was scared of him, that didn't make sense either. At twenty-three, he still battled the occasional remnants of teenage acne. What was there to be scared of? He wasn't physically intimidating. At least, he didn't think so. He worked out every other morning but with his slender stature, he tended to build more endurance than bulk. His height didn't quite top six feet, and women seemed to favor his blue-gray eyes and boyish blonde hair over his other features. Besides, he was several years Madison's junior and definitely out of his minor league.

The door opened, and the entire room quieted in anticipation of Madison's arrival. Instead, the building administrator, Eugene Krueger, shuffled inside. He twisted his mouth into a pucker and, in deep thought, stared at the mauve carpet. Sinking his hands into his pockets, he bowed his balding head in defeat. He sneered at most lieutenants, and they tended to repay the lack of respect by referring to him as "Freddy," the villain from *Nightmare on Elm Street.* Jon wondered if Madison had ever been alone in a room with *him.*

Eugene cleared his throat a third time before he spoke. "I've got some bad news," he began.

Miri groaned. "Congress has cut our funding, haven't they? They said we had until midnight this Thursday. We were going to get this thing finished with a few hours to spare. I knew it. They didn't believe we could do it. I knew—"

"The problem isn't with Congress, Lieutenant. Not this time anyway." Eugene fished in his pocket for an oversized handkerchief and mopped his forehead with it. "We've had a security incident. A breach. Someone's had access to Project Andromeda."

A hush fell over the room. Engineers, chemists, scientists all exchanged discreet glances. Any one of them could have left a classified proposal in a chair or, while in the hallway between the evaluation room and the latrine, mentioned the best way to inoculate against anthrax, botulinum toxin, and even deadlier threats. Any one of them could be facing dismissal for discussing germs far deadlier than the AIDS virus. Biological weapons, or BWs, deserved their reputation for a swift, messy death.

Before his trip to Iraq a few years back when he'd been a freshman lieutenant, Jon had been shocked the first time he'd attended a classified briefing and heard about BWs. Not because of the content, but because he'd heard it all before. From his wacko mother. The day he told her he'd joined the Air Force, she'd screamed at him. Then she had cried, her whole body shaking with every sob. She hadn't spoken to him since, and he wouldn't phone her to hear how he was part of the great war machine that would fulfill the ancient prophecies and hasten forth the Apocalypse.

"How bad is the breach?" stammered Roxie. She twirled a loose strand of dark hair around a nervous finger. She'd picked up the habit from her mentor. Jon had watched with fascination dozens of times as Madison twisted her hair, always when she was stressed.

"It's bad. At this point, all I can say is that it appears someone used their access card last night between midnight and two a.m. to get into this building and steal Project Andromeda documents."

"St-steal?" Roxie paled. Even for a trainee, she realized the implications. "I don't understand why anyone would want to steal Project Andromeda."

"Yeah, and that's the problem with you contracting people." Otto Trollinger, the technical supervisor for the entire project, narrowed his bulging eyes at Roxie. In addition to his squat stature, thin hair, and whisk-broom mustache, he had a tendency to turn ugly when he didn't get his way. The lieutenants in the room didn't call him "the Troll" behind his back for nothing. "If we've had a breach, I'm holding you people personally responsible."

Jon smirked. Madison Steele always did her homework, and if Madison had been in the room, she would have eaten Otto for lunch. Not that anyone else had the balls to stand up to him.

"If you contracting people had half as much brains as you've got nerve," Otto continued in the tone he usually reserved for know-nothing lieutenants, "you'd know Project Andromeda is the culmination of everything the Department of Defense learned about biological weapons since Desert Storm and the one technology that could keep germ warfare in check. Never mind that the United Nations sent me and Colter with their delegation to dismantle the BW facility at al-Hakam. Of course, the damned Iraqis were willing to dismantle a few token bio and chemical facilities, if it meant they could sell oil. But were the economic sanctions really effective?"

Roxie shrank into her chair. It was a rhetorical question, but she tried to answer anyway. "I—"

"Hell, no. Did anybody really expect Iraq to live up to the agreement? You think they'd destroy their own weapons of mass destruction, BW facilities included?"

No one on the Project Andromeda team believed it. Not even Roxie, Jon ventured to guess. Too easy for the Iraqi government to hide their germ fermentation laboratories inside their huge, oh-so-legitimate fertilizer and pesticide production centers. Not as innocent-looking as locating such secrets beneath baby formula factories, but at least hiding BWs under fertilizer plants had some comedic irony.

"Why do I have to get stuck with trainees?" Otto asked the ceiling. "You'd think as important as this program is, I'd have a dedicated contracting team of the most experienced buyers and contracting officers." He turned to squint again at Roxie. "Not a bunch of goddamned trainees."

Every lieutenant in the room hung his or her head in gratitude. Otto's tongue could be sharp, and for once, he was berating someone outside his chain of command instead of Jon and the other junior engineers. Still, Jon felt sorry for Roxie.

"Idiots," Otto mumbled. "None of you understand how important this project is. None of you."

"Yes, sir, we do," Jon spoke up. If he didn't say something, the Troll would verbally dismantle Madison's trainee, if for no other reason than because with Madison out of the room, he could wield his power unchallenged. Jon cleared his throat. He sat so straight, his spine ached. "I think we do realize how urgent it is for us to get these proposals evaluated, get on contract, and affect a successful solution."

Otto raised his eyebrows. Jon had worked for him long enough to know the Troll was impressed by big vocabulary words. "Are you certain?" Otto sniped.

"Yes, sir. In the late 1980's, the CIA reported Iraq's capability of designing and growing biological weapons, including strange little brain cancers as well as germs that could be used for discreet assassinations. By the time President Bush initiated Desert Storm—in my opinion—the Gulf War wasn't about oil."

"And what do you think it was about, Colter?"

"It was about Iraq's overwhelming stash of chemical and biological weapons and the threats to use them. Cholera, pneumonic plague, cloristium perfingens, anthrax, and botulinum toxin could be sealed inside a warhead and lobbed at Desert Storm soldiers. Or worse."

Otto nodded. He'd tutored Jon well during their last two-week trip to Iraq. The man especially liked hearing his own buzz words tossed around "Some of the germs," Jon continued, "can be treated with relatively inexpensive antibiotics. Other micro-organisms, by the time the disease is diagnosed a few hours after exposure, act too quickly on the human nervous system to allow an antidote."

Otto pointed a long finger in Roxie's face and jerked his head sideways toward Jon. "Listen up. Maybe you'll learn something."

Roxie cringed and sank another inch into her chair. It didn't matter how much she knew about the project or understood it. To Otto, she would always be an ignorant trainee.

Otto shot Jon a withering glance. "Colter, did I tell you to shut up?"

"Uh, no, sir. I was about to say that the unavailability of antidotes is what makes Project Andromeda special: it kills biological weapons before soldiers or civilians can be exposed to them. Either allied soldiers or enemy soldiers." Jon wrung his hands under the table where Otto couldn't see them. Jon had sat in on enough classified briefings to know the spiel by heart. Heaven help him if he forgot something. "If the Iraqis learn the antidotes we plan to use, then their germ designers will simply change the BW's design enough to make the antidote useless. Or change to a slightly different design that dictates a vaccination too expensive to inoculate all the troops."

He paused but Otto didn't nod, didn't yell, didn't do anything to indicate he was satisfied with Jon's explanation. Jon expelled a deep breath and gripped the table's edge.

"Plus, the whole project is a political hot potato," Jon ad libbed. "If the U.S. bombs an underground bunker housing BWs, not only will anthrax or something worse be released, but the enemy will say the U.S. bombed *them* with BWs. And no one alive will be close enough to the target to prove otherwise. We have to have some way of holding these world-destroying germs in check, and Project Andromeda is the nearest thing we've got to a solution."

Finally Otto nodded. "And now, the best weapon against an unseen enemy has probably been compromised. Right under our goddamned noses."

"You know, Otto," the administrator, Eugene, said, wrestling the floor back from the Troll, "the OSI or our security office may question you and your team about what time your people left last night. Or if any of you saw anything suspicious."

"Whoa." Otto bounced up out of his chair two tables away and anchored his fists on his pudgy hips. "I don't have time for that. We've got a job to do here. I don't care how it's done, but I don't want any screw-ups at this point."

Everyone in the room knew what Otto meant. His promotion was only a few weeks away and he didn't care who got fried as long as he got promoted to the Senior Executive Service. If he had to choose between contracting people and technical people, he preferred contracting people do the frying.

"Aw, sit down, Otto," Eugene muttered. "I've already talked to Lt. Col. Ballard in the contracting office, and he assures me we'll be on contract within a few days as planned. He's sending over Sarabeth and Nell to finish the project."

Jon stared at the man. Sarabeth? Nell? They weren't on Madison's team. Where the hell was Madison? And whose access card opened the door after Madison had left the building?

"Mr. Krueger?" Roxie raised her hand but didn't stop shaking her head. Her ponytail swished back and forth over her shoulders. Was she begging for more abuse from Otto? "Where's Madison? And what do you mean Lt. Col. Ballard's sending over Sarabeth and Nell?"

"I'm not at liberty—"

"This is Madison's project, Mr. Krueger. She nicknamed it. You know, after that Michael Crichton book where *The Andromeda Strain* virus from outer space turns people into powder and stuff. Madison got the program this far. It's her baby. Do you mean you're taking her off the program? And me? What about me?"

Whispers buzzed around the room. Jon strained to hear.

"Roxie, my understanding is that you're staying on the project as a trainee—" An annoyed grunt from Otto interrupted him. "You're staying on, but you'll answer to Sarabeth."

"But...but what about Madison?"

"I can't say at this point."

Jon shoved back from the table, the rolling chair squawking under the fierceness of the move. "They think Madison stole the files? That's frigging crazy!" Jon's throat tightened. He couldn't breathe. Where was Madison now? She needed him, even if she didn't know it yet. Wherever she was, he had to find her. He had to get out of this stifling room and find her!

"I didn't say she stole anything," Eugene argued. "But she has been removed from the program. Until further notice, none of you are to discuss Project Andromeda with Madison Steele or allow her into this room. We will be changing the combination to this room and to the safe, and you are not to discuss either with her. Is that clear?"

No, it wasn't clear. It was impossible. Whatever had happened, Madison couldn't be to blame. He'd watched her leave. Hell, he'd followed her home.

"What have they got on her?" Jon pressed.

Eugene dug into the carpet with the toe of his shoe. "Nothing conclusive, as far as I know, Lieutenant. But it looks like she was the only one here alone."

"No, she wasn't. There was someone else here after—" Roxie clapped her hand over her mouth. All eyes on her, she sighed heavily and scrambled out of her seat. "There's someone I have to talk to. It can't wait."

Jon stared at the door as it closed behind her. He barely heard the taut words between Eugene and Otto. "Freddy Krueger" represented the contracting side and "The Troll" the technical side. Neither trusted the other—a long standing tradition. The contracting pukes saw it as their job to tie up every sophisticated technology purchase with red-tape and bureaucratic rigmarole and seemingly find a way to keep program managers from doing their jobs. The tech weenies saw it as their duty to get the technology they wanted—legally or not—from the company they liked best no matter what it cost and without letting the contracting guys know what they were doing because, of course, the contracting people would call time-out on their under-the-table deals. Contracting officers and program managers were enemies to the core. That's what made Madison different; like it or not, she brought both sides together.

And now she was in trouble.

Ignoring the debate that warmed between Eugene and Otto and knowing poor old Eugene was no match for a peeved Troll, Jon slipped out of his seat, through the cipher-locked door, and then into the hall. No sign of Roxie.

He ducked into the front foyer. She hadn't left yet. From there he could see the women's restroom. After a few minutes' wait, no one came out.

Jon tiptoed past Eugene's office and stopped abruptly at the sound of a whisper. Roxie's voice. Hidden behind a partition in Eugene's huge office, she had found a quiet place for a conversation. One of the buttons on the telephone near the door glowed an eerie orange in the dark room. Jon held his breath and listened.

"But she's been really good to me," Roxie pleaded. "I have to tell the OSI what I know. How could you ask me not to?.... All right then. I'll wait. But if things get worse, I might have to...." Her voice trailed off. The light on the phone blinked and disappeared.

"Roxie?" Jon called. No answer. She couldn't have left. He stood between her and the door. "Roxie, I know you're in here." He flipped on the light switch. The fluorescent bulbs flickered into a steady bluish light. Only their hum answered him. He had a bad feeling in the pit of his stomach. He fought the urge to open the window for fresh air. "Roxie."

She stepped out from behind the partition, her dark eyes large and wet. She was probably several years older than Jon, but right now she looked more like a child who had just realized her daddy wasn't perfect. "Leave me alone," she said in a steady voice. She'd watched Madison too carefully. Except for the tears, she had all the moves down. *Never let them see any weakness.*

"What's going on?" He moved to block her exit.

"None of your business. Now leave me alone." She tried to squeeze past him, but he grabbed her shoulders and held her in front of him. "It doesn't concern you," she stressed.

"It concerns Madison, doesn't it?" He searched her eyes. She turned her gaze to the floor. "Doesn't it?" Against his better judgment, he shook her.

Roxie broke loose and backed up. "I can't say anything, Jon. We're talking careers here."

"Yeah. Madison's. What did you see last night?"

She pursed her full lips into a tight, defiant line.

"You said someone was here after Madison was. Who?"

"I...can't say. Not yet. Look, they haven't arrested anybody. They're just asking questions right now. Let's wait and see how things go."

Those weren't Roxie's words. Whoever had been on the other end of her conversation had put those words into her mouth.

"Why won't you stand up for her?" Heat flashed in his cheeks. He had no patience for cowards, and Roxie usually wasn't one. "She'd stand up for you. She has on several occasions."

Roxie's face reddened. No doubt she knew some of those occasions.

Madison hated vicious gossip. She refused to work with anyone who uttered a word of venom. The first day on Project Andromeda, she'd kicked five people off the team for rabid speculation over Roxie's recent divorce.

"I'm sorry. I can't."

"Exactly what were you doing here between midnight and two? You left at twenty til midnight and Madison practically shoved me out the door after you. She left at ten til. What were you doing watching The Facility after you were supposed to be gone?"

"And what were you doing watching Madison after you were supposed to be gone?"

Shit. What could he say? That he'd sat on his motorcycle in the dark, hoping Madison might change her mind and offer him an invitation to her home? That he'd watched the lights go out in the building as she walked through, watched her lock the front door, watched her pause to rub the wedding band she wore to fake out guys she didn't want to date, watched her stare up at the night sky for a solid three minutes before sauntering to her old Chevy and sitting behind the wheel, dabbing at what looked suspiciously like tears?

"You're in love with her, aren't you? Well, you're a bigger fool than I am, Jon Colter. Everybody knows she's still carrying a torch for a guy who left her years ago."

A sucker punch if he'd ever felt one. "You're changing the subject."

"Ask anybody." She didn't let up. "He was a lieutenant, too. That was back when all techies were revered as crooks and any contracting officer stupid enough to get involved with one was cut up into little pieces and fed to the rumor mill."

"I'm not going to listen to this garbage." He spun on his heels and started back toward the evaluation room. In five minutes, he'd have his classified files locked away and in another ten minutes, he'd be at the door to Madison's office.

"It's not idle speculation," Roxie called after him, something primal in her voice. For some reason, she was scared to death. "They got caught. They sent him away." Her voice cracked. "A week later he was stationed at Rejavik, and she never saw him again."

CHAPTER THREE

By the time Madison walked back into the suite of contracting offices in Building 13's weapons laboratory, it was nearly 6:30. Most of the people in "The Lab" left the building promptly at 4:15 after exactly eight hours of work and one of lunch, or some combination thereof. With any luck at all, her favorite OSI agent had gone home as well.

Too bad he was the enemy. He didn't wear a wedding band and he was sexy as hell. Whenever she could drag herself away from memories of Tim in her bed, nineteen percent of her fantasies featured Special Agent Austin Wait. One percent of her fantasies were aimed at a pony-tailed inmate of the on-base Federal Prison. The nameless con tended a small rose garden outside her building and on more than one occasion had pruned a rosebud for her as she walked by. The other eighty percent of Madison's fantasies featured someone even more forbidden.

She'd been thinking way too much about sex lately. She didn't know if it was because she'd gone without for so long or if it was because her thirtieth birthday loomed a few months ahead. If she had a few years yet to reach her sexual peak, then she was in trouble already. Big time. Most likely, she'd been thinking of a man's hands on her body because for the past few weeks, she'd been cooped up in The Facility with a man who both terrified her and stirred a heat inside her she'd forgotten. One who absentmindedly hummed "Maggie May" in her presence. One First Lieutenant Jonathan Colter. His uniform looked damned fine on him, though it would have looked even better on her bedroom floor.

Madison shook the thought of him from her head and quietly closed the main door to the contracting offices behind her. She hated being gone from the office for so long, and she hated having to come back. Her gut instinct had been to stay with Jolene's baby, hold him to her chest, protect him from all the monsters of the future, and long for days that could never be.

She had met Jolene only once before—at Toby's fiasco of a wedding where the mother of the bride had turned into a sloppy drunk and put the moves on the groom. In the past few hours, Madison's theory that Jolene was a real little shit had proven itself out. Jolene had barely said ten words the whole time Madison had flitted around the house, turning the second of the two bedrooms from a junk room into a nursery. The twit had turned her nose up at it, too, commenting on the smallness and sparseness of Madison's home.

What bothered Madison most, though, was that Jolene knew nothing about the baby. Not that Madison expected a girl of fifteen or sixteen to be an expert on diapering or burping newborns, but Jolene refused to tell her the little boy's name, how old he was, or what Toby had said about having the son he'd always wanted. Only one thing bothered Madison more: Jolene could see how much Madison's fingers itched to hold the baby, but the little shit had ordered her not to touch him.

All the more reason not to work late tonight. Not at the office, anyway. Madison planned to grab the files for the Mayer-Frick congressional inquiry, plus the acquisition plan Cathy needed reviewed by tomorrow, and then head over to The Facility to see how Roxie had fared honchoing her very first team meeting. After that, Madison would haul her work home with her and find a way to hold Jolene's baby, rock him, shield him, caress him, wish.

She rounded the corner to her office and nearly skidded on the orange carpet. Mac and Beatrice, equally startled, peered up at her from their positions on either side of her doorless office. Drinking coffee and gossiping. Same as they did for more than half of every day. Mac, a teddy bear of a substitute father, could have retired years ago but still needed the money. He retained both his Scottish accent and Southern drawl. Beatrice, who brought Madison chocolate eggs at Easter and left chocolate donuts on her desk once a week, was due to retire in three years, four months, and ten days. Not that Madison kept up with such trivia: Beatrice announced the countdown every morning like clockwork. When they worked, both were solid C-plus employees and both fit into Madison's team of problem children. No one else wanted them.

"Maddie! Lass!" Mac gave her a one-armed bear hug, sloshing his coffee onto the already stained carpet. "We were worried about you. OSI's been asking all sorts of questions."

"Oh, my goodness, yes." Beatrice nodded emphatically. A clump of graying hair hung against her forehead like a pendulum. "I told them it couldn't have been you. I told them what a fine person you are to work for, too. I can't think of a finer person to work for before I retire. That I'd be proud to have you as a daughter-in-law. And that's precisely what I told that man in black."

Madison tried not to frown. Beatrice meant well. In fact, the woman was one of Madison's strongest defenders. The closest thing to a mother she had outside the state of Georgia, though the thought of another blind date with Beatrice's sniveling son turned her stomach. "Don't worry, guys. Nobody's accused me of anything yet. How could they? I wasn't anywhere near that building between midnight and two a.m. My understanding is that several dozen people are being questioned."

"Well, we're behind you, darlin'." Mac gave her a second squeeze. "Come on, Beatrice. Time we mosey on home. See you tomorrow, Maddie-lass."

Ignoring their jovial chatter as they trotted out of sight, Madison flopped down in her chair and raked her palms over her face. God, she was tired. Her computer screen blinked a schedule long overcome by events. She'd forgotten to log off her e-mail, but thankfully the system logged her out automatically after a ten-minute span of inactivity. The Mayer-Frick congressional inquiry files still taunted her from her desk top. Her in-box, already steep before her visit from the OSI, overflowed onto the floor. She might as well write "IN-BOX" on her trash can and streamline the process.

Madison picked up the sealed envelope on top of the pile, the one from Personnel. Another announcement that she'd come up on a certificate for a promotion. She'd been getting certs off and on for several years, though most of the time budgets were cut and the authority to promote was withdrawn from Personnel's grasp before interviews could be conducted. She sighed and tossed it back into the wooden tray.

The Post-it note stuck to her keyboard brought a bigger smile than any promise of a promotion. "Where ARE you?" the note read. "Need to see you. Call me." The plea hadn't been signed, but she knew who it was from: Lt. Colter. She closed her eyes and imagined him standing in her tiny office, humming "Maggie May" and hunching over her desk to scribble a frantic note. Not many days passed that she didn't see him every hour of daylight and often into the evenings. He was back at The Facility, waiting. He was always waiting. Always there. On really bad days, the knowledge that he would glance up from his work and shoot her his warmest smile was all she needed to drag herself into the office. Too bad he couldn't be anything more than her sidekick. Too bad Project Andromeda would be awarded in less than three days and the need to spend so much time with him would be over.

"Daydreaming?" The Gutless Wonder propped against her door jamb.

"I never daydream," she deadpanned, discreetly folding Jon's note and then sliding it under her keyboard. Gavin Ballard didn't need to see the one thing that could make her smile right now. The lieutenant colonel had been her division chief for nearly a year, and what he lacked in backbone, he more than made up for in his interpretation of other people's ethics. If one of the good-looking, young engineers hung around Roxie or any of the other single women in the office too much, Gavin promptly barred the transgressor from ever entering the hallowed halls of the contracting offices again. Madison didn't intend to give Gavin any reason to make her life even less pleasant.

Gavin helped himself to the only empty chair in Madison's office. He was forty-ish with a broad frame but not much of a chest under that blue uniform. Perennially pale, too. Probably because he burned rather than tanned. Madison guessed that at one time, maybe fifteen years ago, Gavin had sported a headful of brilliant orange-red curls. Only the whisper-thin waves above his ears shrouded an otherwise shiny globe.

"Did you want something, Gavin, or can I get back to work now?"

"You ever gonna clean up this place? You know I have a clean desk policy."

"Let everyone else end the day by dumping their in-boxes into their desk drawers and digging them out again the next morning. I am not a hypocrite. You want me to have a cleaner desk, you give me less work to do."

"You know I can't do that. We're undermanned as it is."

Madison gave him her best why-don't-you-explain-it-to-me-slowly-because-I'm-stupid look. The truth was, the best bureaucrats completed their stacks of work early, only to be drowned in work left unfinished by their less dependable peers who took off whenever they damned well pleased. Once a worker got the reputation for getting it all done no matter what, management would overload that employee until she never again saw the light of day. Hence, Madison's dawn to dusk schedule.

Gavin cleared his throat. "Eileen said you left the office for a while. Some kind of emergency."

"You want me to sign a leave slip?" Madison glared at him. He wouldn't dare ping her performance appraisal, not if he expected her to keep carrying his lousy ass. She was his work horse, and he knew it. "How can you ask me to sign for leave when I'm already working through lunch *and* dinner, seven days a week?"

Gavin threw up his hands in protest. "Now, Madison, who said anything about docking your time card? I thought it might have something to do with the OSI's visit."

"No. It was personal. And no, I'm not discussing it."

"That's a relief. That it wasn't about the OSI, I mean." He rested one ankle on his other thigh and leaned forward. "So what happened with the OSI?"

"I'm sorry, but I can't discuss that either. Their orders."

"They didn't mean me. For Chrissakes, I'm your boss!"

"Hmmm. You mean you didn't get your ears full the ten times you sauntered past my office?"

He tried to look hurt. "Madison. You know I subscribe to the Management By Walking Around school."

"Yeah, then try walking around when the investigators aren't in my office."

"I do, I do. But I can never get in to see you."

"Argh!" She rolled her eyes as disrespectfully as she could. "And why not? You know I have an open-door policy." She gestured at the empty hinges. He'd have to be stupider than dirt to miss her sarcasm. Just her luck, she had to get an ex-pilot for a boss, one with no experience in contracts and even less behind a desk. True, they had to put aging fly-boys somewhere, but why in contracting? "When are you going to get my door fixed anyway? You've been putting me off for the past year."

"Um, eventually."

"Eventually? Gavin, why am I the only contracting officer without a door? Lord knows, it's great not having to work in a cubicle any more, and I love having paper-thin, real walls and even one tiny window with a pristine view of a parking lot and a dumpster, but why can't I have a door? Sarabeth has a door. So do Mig and Jarvis. How am I supposed to have any privacy if I don't have a door?"

Gavin jerked his head down, suddenly a little too interested in a thirty-year-old coffee stain on the orange and purple-speckled carpet.

"Gavin? What's the deal? And don't tell me you're having trouble scheduling a maintenance crew to hang my door. That excuse has worn thin. Get me the door, and I'll have a couple of my lieutenants hang it for me."

He shrugged. "I shouldn't tell you this, you know."

"Tell me what?"

"It's not fair for you to blame me for all your troubles. It's not my fault, you know. Mr. Smith said not to be in any hurry."

Madison's heart lurched. Mr. Smith was the head of contracting at Eglin. The man didn't have time to bother with office furnishings and trivial bickering. The fate of hundreds of contracting jobs depended on him. Why would such an important man want her office doorless?

"Anyway," Gavin continued, "we've got more important things to worry about. Like Project Andromeda."

"Yeah, I know. I haven't been over to The Facility yet today. As soon as I get my papers together here, I'll run over and take a look at the briefing charts. I expect to get a thumbs-up tomorrow afternoon to award that puppy. Ahead of schedule, too."

"I've been meaning to talk to you about that." Gavin hung his head again. "You've been removed from Project Andromeda."

"What?" Madison scrambled to her feet. The Gutless Wonder rose, too, though taking his time. "You can't remove me from the project. Not now. I've broken all the records. The counter-proliferation people are thrilled with our progress. Gavin, I'm days—hours!—away from finishing up months of work." Perspiration stung her forehead. "Why?" she wailed.

"It's not my fault." Defeat shone on Gavin's forehead. Had he really stood up for her? She supposed there was a first time for everything. "Mr. Smith insisted. Sarabeth and Nell will be taking over, effective—" he glanced at his watch—"four hours ago. They'll do a decent job."

"Sarabeth and Nell do great work, but it's my project, my baby. What about Roxie? Is she kicked off the team, too?"

"No, she's a trainee. A COPPER CAP. She needs the experience. Plus, she can help transition the project to the new team."

"New team," Madison echoed, digging her fingers into her hair. Her braid tangled around her knuckles and loosened, then fell to her shoulders. "I don't understand. I can't understand. Am I being transferred to one of the weapon systems program offices? I know Mr. Smith thinks of it as a promotion, but you know how much I hate working on production contracts. I'd much rather work the cutting edge stuff we do here."

"I doubt you'll be transferred any place with prestige. As of now, you're considered a problem child, and problem children don't work on big programs. Or important programs like this one. I'm sorry, Madison. Really, I am. It's not my fault, you know."

"Yeah, yeah. I heard you."

"I do want you to give Roxie a run-down of what she needs to know to finish up the project. Tomorrow morning will be soon enough. I wouldn't want this ordeal to reflect badly on her."

"What about on me? It's okay if getting kicked off a majorly important program reflects badly on me?"

"I didn't mean it that way. You know we can't afford to blow our schedule, and with you being a prime suspect in this security breach, we can't take that kind of chance."

Madison sank back down into her chair. "Pr-prime suspect? The OSI didn't say anything to me about that."

"To me, either. But since they've got evidence you were in the building when the breach occurred, it seems that would make you a prime suspect."

"What evidence?" She shook her head. The pounding in her temples had started up again. "What are you talking about? I wasn't in the building then, so there can't be any evidence."

Gavin frowned, apparently deep in a mental debate with himself.

"Gavin? You know me. Do you think I stole something from the Project Andromeda files?" She pinned him to the wall with her most serious gaze. He couldn't stand conflict, and she wouldn't make it easy on him. "Gavin?"

He peeked around the door, checking to see if the hall was clear. "Anybody here?" he called. When no one answered, he turned back to Madison. "Looks like we're the only ones left."

"Answer me. You know how important Project Andromeda is. Do you think I'd steal classified secrets?"

He sighed heavily. "No. Not unless you were in some kind of trouble. Blackmail or whatever."

The two thousand dollars a month. It wasn't blackmail. It was an obligation. And it was none of anybody's business.

"Not even for blackmail, Gavin. I'd give up all my own secrets before I turned over military secrets. I'd destroy myself and take the blackmailer with me."

"So you do have secrets."

"And you don't?"

He stiffened. "Of course not. I'm an open book."

"Well then, Mr. Open Book, tell me what's really going on here. Why are all the fingers pointing at me?"

"You didn't hear it from me." The coward lowered his voice to a whisper. "Last night at 2:00 a.m., one of the security police noticed a very faint light in The Facility. A closet light, as it turns out. He hadn't noticed it at midnight. When he got close enough, he saw a screen was off a side window and it was open. He flashed his spotlight inside and saw the open, four-drawer safe. This morning, it was determined that one of the classified proposals had been taken out of its binder—the one we plan to award the contract for. We found the proposal and documentation concerning why we're picking that proposal on top of the photocopier. Copies had been made, too."

Madison stared at him. "Then this security breach wasn't mere carelessness. I turned off the copier when I left. And all the lights. And the safe was definitely locked. I specifically remember twirling the dial four times and tugging on each drawer to make sure I hadn't made any mistakes. Then I signed off on the security roster. I remember the time: 2345 hours." Fifteen minutes before midnight, normal people's time. A shudder rippled down her spine. She could have sworn someone had been watching her when she'd left the building. Apparently, they had been.

"Definitely not an accident. Looks like somebody surprised them, and they fled the back way instead of out the front door. Unfortunately, they can't narrow the time down any more than twelve to two, and one of your neighbors says you were home by a quarter after midnight."

"The OSI's already questioned my neighbors? I don't even know my neighbors' names." *Who the hell has time to socialize when they live at the office?*

Gavin smiled. "They don't know your name either, but they said your car runs rough and their dog barks when you come in at night and wakes them up every single time."

"Geez. I didn't know. So you're saying my only alibi hates my guts." She couldn't even remember what the neighbors looked like or if she had ever met them.

"Let's take what we can get, okay? It might be the only thing that saves your hide."

Madison raked her fingers through her hair again, spilling the long strands through her fingers and over her forehead. "That still doesn't explain why I'm a suspect. At least four other people have the combination to that safe."

"Yes, but you're the only one who has the combination to the safe, the combination to the evaluation room door, an access card to get into the building, and no alibi for midnight until a quarter after."

"Alibis are for the guilty. If I'm not going to commit a crime, I don't need to have someone by my side all the time." Okay, so she was wrong. Guilty until proven innocent. She'd learned that the hard way. "My word is good. Why would I need an alibi?"

He hesitated, mulling his next words in his mind before giving them voice. "Security ran a computer check on the access card log-ins this morning to see who entered the building at the most probable time. It turned up one *Lorelei Madison Steele* entering The Facility at five minutes after midnight."

What? "Well, it's wrong. I didn't go back in. I was dead tired. I went home. Besides, I couldn't have gotten into the safe, made copies, and high-tailed it out the window in time to get home ten minutes later and wake up my neighbors. I'd have to be a lot more energetic than I am right now."

"Then that doesn't leave many options, does it? You went back inside or someone broke in. I'm sure the OSI will want to talk more about that tomorrow." He checked his watch again. "I'm late for dinner. You know how the wife gets if I'm late."

Staring after him, Madison laced her fingers together tight enough to cut off her circulation. It didn't make sense. None of it. Someone had stolen classified secrets on *her* program, damn it, and she was offended. But she was worried, too. Someone might have betrayed National Security. How dare these people think she could be responsible! How could Mr. Smith turn his back on her when she hadn't done anything wrong?

Politics. Fucking politics. Appearance, not truth, was what mattered.

Only one thing was clear: if she'd been removed from Project Andromeda, she wouldn't be needed in The Facility until midnight tonight. She had no life outside of work, and nowhere to go but home.

Jolene! She'd actually forgotten about Jolene and the baby. But why shouldn't she? After all, being a prime suspect in what was going to prove a very nasty investigation was bound to take precedence over an incompetent teenage mother bickering with her absent husband. If only Tim were with her, he'd take her mind off the OSI. Then again, if Tim were with her, she'd have an alibi.

"Between twelve and two, Special Agent Wait? Oh, my. I believe I was in bed during that time and loving every minute of it." Yeah, that would get a reaction from Austin Wait. She grinned at the thought of it.

Madison picked up the Mayer-Frick files and the thin folder containing Cathy's acquisition plan and then stacked them on her desk. No, that wasn't right. She should have been looking for a spot on the floor or in the empty chair. There shouldn't have been space on her desk. If there was room, then something was missing.

Her office had never been neat. Contract files, documentation, memos for the file, all sorts of bureaucratic papers to be pushed comprised each heap littering the floor. But she kept the papers in each stack neatly collected. No ragged edges. No carbon copies skewed slightly out of the precise cube of paper. Until now.

Madison clenched her fists to keep them from shaking. Since she'd left with Jolene, someone had been in her office. Every stack had been sifted through and slammed back into its approximate place.

Her fight or flee instinct kicked in. With her toe, she flipped off the computer power cord and dropped the file folders onto her desk. She grabbed her purse, turned off her light, and instantly regretted it. Someone had already turned off the lights outside her office, leaving her in the dark as she stumbled into the hall.

She felt her way through the office, along the burlap-grained partitions of her coworkers' cubicles, toward the locked wooden entrance to the contracting suite. The doorknob glinted in the light of the fax machine buttons on Eileen's desk. Madison reached for the knob and froze.

The ugly orange carpet, now muted by the lack of light, stopped at the door to the contracting offices. Bare tile covered the main corridor outside. Footsteps shuffled and waited on the other side of the door.

Roxie?

Couldn't be. The doors to Building 13 where Madison's contracting offices were located were promptly locked at 5:00 p.m. That was 1700 hours, military time. The only way into the building was via the crosswalk over busy Eglin Boulevard, and one had to have both an access card and a key to the crosswalk doors to get in after hours. Contracting officers were allowed keys, but trainees weren't. If Roxie came back to the office to chat, she would have to call first so Madison could go downstairs and let her in.

The doorknob turned slowly, halfway, and stopped. Then it turned slowly the other direction, halfway, and stopped. Whoever was out there was trying the door.

Oh, crap.

Working late in The Facility was one thing. It was near the main quadrangle, well-lighted, with Base Security driving by regularly. She never minded being alone there, though she was rarely the only person in the building. Even late at night Jon, her slender, protective lieutenant, was nearby as well as at least one other team member. When the third to last person left, she ordered Jon out, too, and locked up in the next ten minutes.

But in this building, being the last one out meant walking down long, darkened hallways with nothing but the echo of her sensible low heels to cut through the silence. From there, she'd tiptoe down a dim stairwell. Once she exited the back door, she'd have to cross a pitch-dark alley to her car. She might as well have "Rape Me" tattooed on her forehead.

Footsteps shuffled again.

If a contracting officer had antennae, by now hers would have been on full alert.

Maybe she was being silly. Maybe the OSI agent had come back to finish his interrogation.

Crick! The doorknob turned again.

Confront them or stay? Madison held her breath. Negotiate or run? The same feeling she got in the pit of her stomach when a negotiation went bad flopped inside her. She wanted to sink down on the floor and hide in the dark. She wouldn't. She wasn't the type to run.

"Who's out there?" She punched the button lock on her side of the knob. She waited, listened, held her breath. Nothing. "Is anybody out there?"

On the other side of the door, the floor creaked. The footfalls whispered away from the door, as if someone were moving very cautiously, rolling heel to toe toward the stairwell. Whoever was out there was no longer at the door. Now they were down the hall somewhere, and they knew she knew they were out there.

"I'm not spending the night in here," she muttered to herself. Jolene's baby needed her and so did the baby's mother, whether Jolene admitted it or not. On the other hand, Madison didn't know who or what was outside of that door.

Feeling her way along the partitions, she found Eileen's table and then fumbled with the handset on the fax machine. Too dark to see the dial pad. Madison was familiar enough with the position of the keys to dial her temporary office over at The Facility.

"Hello?" Roxie's voice. Thin, uncertain, maybe even scared.

"Roxie? It's Madison."

Silence.

"Roxie? Are you there?"

Her trainee took a deep breath. "I'm not allowed to talk to you. And you know this phone line is monitored." Regret punctuated every word.

"I understand. But can you tell me if Jon—I mean, Lt. Colter—is still there?"

"He and Figmo left a few minutes ago."

Butterflies banged into the walls of Madison's stomach. Her reputation relied on her strength, her self-sufficiency. How would it look if she called the Security Police to escort her out of the building or dragged Gavin away from dinner with his paranoid wife? She was so goddamned tired of being strong. Just once, she wished she had someone she could be weak with.

But a woman afraid of the dark probably would be afraid to stand up to a defense contractor asking an unreasonable price. That was the perception anyway, and inside the Government perceptions were more important than the truth. Perceptions were reality. If she called the Security Police for help, given the fast-spreading belief that she'd stolen classified secrets while working in a Government building after hours, the OSI would probably lock her up and throw away the key.

If she called for help, it had better be someone she could trust. Jon was the only person she could ask to come walk her out of the building. And the absolute last person she should ask. They lived and worked in a goldfish bowl and even in an empty building, someone somewhere would see them leave together. The next week, the young lieutenant would be shipped off to Iceland.

"Madison? Are you still there?"

"Yeah. You should be going home."

"Hmmm. I've got to lock things up and pull security, and I'll be out of here."

"Okay, well, maybe we can have lunch tomorrow?" Maybe Roxie could shed some light on the security breach and why Madison was being turned into the sacrificial lamb.

"Uh, sure. Lunch sounds great."

Madison hung up and squeezed her eyes shut. Roxie wouldn't be available for lunch. Madison could hear it in her voice. Her star trainee would have something more pressing, some lousy excuse.

No doubt the rumors were already flying about Madison Steele, the contracting officer under investigation by the OSI for missing military secrets. Not that it was the first time she'd been the center of scandal. But for anyone to be seen having lunch with her or give the appearance of being a friend bode ill for her companion.

She wouldn't do that to Roxie. Roxie's splendid divorce had fueled the rumor mill for several months, and Mr. Smith had a long memory for both fiction and fact. In another three years, Roxie would be considered fully-trained and ready to sit before an oral review board and defend her knowledge of procurement regulations. Like Madison, Roxie would have to fight to prove her character worthy of signing contracts on behalf of the American public. And if Roxie didn't fight hard enough or—God help her—flinched with any emotion at all, she would be relegated to buying pencils and paper clips for the rest of her government career.

Sometimes Madison wondered if it was worth it. The long hours, the interference from Congress, the facade of living the way the old-boy network expected you to. But she was damned good at her job, and she did it better than any other civil servant she knew. Somebody had to look out for U.S. taxpayers, and by God, she was it.

Hands clenched, she stalked back to the door. If evil lurked in the stairwell, she'd beat it to death with her bare fists. She seized the doorknob and twisted it to the right.

Hey!

It didn't move. The smell of glue stung her nose.

Who the hell would lock her in?

CHAPTER FOUR

Rain! Damn!

Jon yanked off his motorcycle helmet and killed the engine. He squinted through the growing mist at the third floor window of The Lab's Building 13. The light in Madison's office blinked off.

She hadn't come back to The Facility. Nor had she called him. He knew he should have signed that note. Madison probably had no idea who had been in her office.

Oh, hell. She probably had no idea who he was either. Just some witless lieutenant who followed her around like a lost puppy, fetching caffeine-loaded Pepsi's for her before she could ask and barking at anyone who dared waste her time. He'd do anything she wanted, but he could never ask her out. She was almost seven years older and way out of his league. She was, after all, L. Madison Steele.

His cheek caught in a grimace. She'd read the note and called someone else. A boyfriend he hadn't heard about. Her idiot boss maybe. Even Roxie. Anybody but him. Certainly not a lieutenant who dreamed she was a priestess.

At the time, signing the note had seemed like an incredibly bad idea. It still did. Way too many nosy people in her office. Contracting pukes were famous for their noses and tongues. He'd thought about making up something legitimate-sounding. Like, "Lt. Colter called about Project. Respond immediately." But then he would have had Sarabeth or Nell calling back about Project Andromeda when the real reason Jon wanted to see Madison had nothing to do with business.

Okay, so he couldn't touch. Couldn't look either, except when no one else was watching. But he could be her secret guardian angel, always an inch out of sight if she needed him. As he did so many nights, he would watch her leave work, lock the door behind her, trudge to her car. He would keep her safe, and she would never know it.

But tonight? She didn't exit through the loading dock. Ten minutes had passed since the light in her office flickered to blackness. Odd. Leaving through any other exit didn't make sense. From where he perched on his now wet motorcycle, he could see her clunker of a car parked in the alley outside the adjacent Building 11. Not a glimmer of light shone anywhere else in Building 13.

He laced his fingers and held them to his forehead to keep the water out of his eyes. The mist seemed heavier, more raindrops than dew. With such dark clouds overhead, night fell faster than on the average work day. He scanned the third floor windows yet again. This time, one was open.

A shadow moved near the top of the fire escape. His heart caught in his throat. Madison! He'd recognize the silhouette of her business suit against the parking lot lights anywhere. What the hell was she doing up there?

One foot after the other, she climbed down, gripping the wet railing, her blonde hair loose and clinging to her face and neck. One step at a time. One heartbeat at a time.

Oh, Madison.

What if she fell? The railing was slippery when dry, but slick with rain? Helpless, Jon bit down on his bottom lip.

Another rung, and another. Her foot slipped. She swung wildly from the railing and pulled herself back in close to the metal rungs. She hung there in the rain, perfectly still, then started down again.

Jon realized he'd been holding his breath. His heart thundered in his chest. If anything happened to her....

She paused on the next step, pried her shoes off, and watched them tumble a long way down to the wet grass and bounce to a bruising halt. Not unlike what Madison would do if she lost her balance or her grasp.

Jon sucked in another breath. If he rushed to help, he might startle her, cause her to fall. Often enough, he'd done more harm than good.

What was she doing on a fire escape when the fire alarms hadn't sounded? Did it have anything to do with the accusations against her? Madison couldn't have stolen those files. Even if he hadn't stared longingly at her while she drove home last night, leaving The Facility and its inner secrets behind, he knew in his heart she couldn't be a spy.

Then why the dramatic exit? A woman in a business suit did not decide to leave her office via a narrow window and a grimy, slippery fire escape for the thrill of it. At least most women wouldn't. He didn't know what Madison did for thrills or if she ever had any thrills at all.

Madison dangled above the ground for a few seconds, then dropped into the soggy grass. She picked herself up quickly, brushed off her sodden knees, and squished across the grass to snatch up her shoes. She stayed close to the side of the building—maybe staying dry, maybe blending in with its shadow. Her purse slid down from her shoulder and hung at her elbow. She still carried her soaked shoes. If only Jon had a blanket to wrap up his bedraggled tigress!

At the corner of the building, she stopped and did the damnedest thing. She peered around the corner, into the dark alley between The Lab and Building 11. Then she tiptoed the length of the alley, pausing every few steps to look over her shoulder.

God. She looked terrified. The mighty L. Madison Steele was actually afraid of something.

She fumbled with the keys to her car, dropped them twice, then finally managed to open her car door. Intent on the steering wheel, she bent forward, toying with something too far away for Jon to see. Her engine whined and died.

Too much of a coincidence, Jon decided. First she came down the fire escape. Then she couldn't get her car started.

She glanced around, frustration in her raw movements. Then she tried again. The engine didn't even click.

She needs me. Whether she likes it or not.

Anticipation swelling in his chest, Jon strode down the alley. Rivulets of rain trickled down his forehead, between his eyes, dripped off his chin. He swiped his wet hair back from his brow and tried not to grin. She needed him and he was there, soaking wet but there, damn it. He knew an opportunity when he saw one.

As he neared her car, he could see her through the window, through the graying of night. With the same determination he saw in everything else she did, she wiggled the key in the ignition as if will alone would cure a dead battery.

Rain splattered off the roof. Water pooled in the potholes and filled his shoes. The mist had turned into a full-fledged downpour.

"Madison?" he yelled over the thunder of raindrops. He tugged open the driver's door and bent to face her. "Need some—Yow!"

He jumped back just in time. Madison's frenzied swipe nicked his cheek. Touching it with his finger, he felt the rain on the cut before he felt its sting.

Madison stared back at him, her keys gathered into her fist with the jagged edges pointed out. Her hand, like a bear claw, poised to do more damage if he came closer.

"Jon." Her eyes still glistened with fear. "I thought you were someone else."

"I-I hope so." He fingered his cheek again. Just a scratch but an inch higher and he might have lost an eye. Maybe she'd feel guilty about the damage and let him help her.

"Let's go," she shouted, regaining control. Before he had a chance to coax her out of the car, she scrambled out with her soggy shoes tucked under her arm.

"Go where?" He jogged along beside her, not quite sure where she was headed except that it was away from her car. How she was able to run so fast in her bare feet over the water and rocky asphalt amazed him. Like the priestess in his dreams.

"Your car. Do you have cables? I need you to jump me off."

Great. Not even a chance to suggest a course of action. Madison, as usual, was two steps ahead, thinking, planning, fixing.

"I don't have a car. I have a motorcycle. And no jumper cables."

Panting, she stopped at the alley's edge. "No car, no cables. Fantastic." Rain drizzled down her cheeks and disappeared into her blouse collar. Her usually perfect hair plastered itself to her scalp. She didn't look anything like the cool, calm, collected woman who strolled into Project Andromeda meetings every day and dared anyone to defy her. Tonight she was an ordinary woman in trouble.

"Let me take you home," Jon offered, then blushed at the suggestion. He'd use any excuse to get inside her home, but he hadn't considered the truth.

She cast a doubtful glance at his motorcycle and shook her head. "Can't. I'm a contracting officer. You're a lieutenant, an engineer. Someone might see."

Someone might see? He checked his anger, keeping his tone low and even. "Nobody's going to see. Nobody with any sense is standing out here in the rain taking notes for the gossip queens. For once, can't you accept my help?"

Madison winced. He could see the war going on behind her pained eyes. "I don't care what people say about me, but I won't have them destroy your career."

"Nobody's going to destroy my career." He gingerly caught her arm and pulled her toward his motorcycle, memorizing the feel of her elbow in his palm in case he never again had the opportunity to touch her. She was still protesting when he slipped his helmet over her head and buckled the chin strap. "You're anonymous now," he told her with a grin. "Just another motorcycle babe in a wet business suit."

Raindrops speckled her visor. With a sweep of her hand, instead of clearing her visor, she smeared the droplets. Rain misted over her helmet again.

Jon flipped up her visor and smiled in at her. "You okay?"

"I'm fine. I'm *always* fine. But you don't have a helmet."

"Don't worry about me. Daddy always said real men don't need helmets."

"That's not funny. I don't want to take your helmet and put you in danger."

"Will you stop debating for a change? If I'm in danger, that's my problem. Besides, you're a contracting officer. I'm a lowly, expendable, first lieu-ey. You're more valuable to the Air Force than I am. Now get on the bike and let's get out of here before the Security Police notice I'm not wearing a helmet."

She rubbed her lips together but didn't say anything. Rain soaked through her suit, at least as deep as her clingy blouse and probably all the way down to whatever wonderful things she wore underneath. The fabric wilted against her arms. Her wet shoulder pads jaunted up on either side of her helmet. She looked like a badly beaten football player for the junior varsity.

"I'm not sure I can get on this machine," she said with an uneasy laugh. Even dry, her slim skirt would have been difficult to get over her knees, much less up to her thighs.

"What is it you're always saying, Madison? You weren't built for comfort; you were built for speed? Speed is all I can offer tonight. Let's get you home. Someplace safe and dry."

Madison let out a long sigh and then nodded. She shimmied her narrow skirt up to her thighs until something that looked suspiciously like panties peeked from underneath the hem. Grinding his teeth, Jon turned away at the last minute, slung his leg over the bike, and then toyed with the key in the ignition. He was only playing at being a gentleman, and whereas Madison's work dictated that she was built for speed, not comfort, the glimpse of her inner thigh burned a quite different impression in Jon's mind. The woman was definitely built for comfort. The slow, all-night kind.

Jon waited while she struggled to get her feet back into the wet shoes and then threw her leg over the seat behind him. She slid her arms loosely around his chest, the heat between her thighs low on his back. He revved the engine until he thought the bike would squeal, then lurched into the wind and rain.

He cornered the intersection too tightly. He couldn't breathe, but whether it was her closeness or the squeeze of her arms and thighs against him, he didn't know.

Straining to see through the rain, he angled the bike at an access road seldom traveled by the Security Police. On at least a dozen sleepless nights, Jon had lain awake, dreaming of the day when he might take L. Madison Steele for a ride on his motorcycle. He'd imagined sunshine on her face and warm wind in her long, blonde tangles. What he got was rain and her helmeted cheek pressed softly into the back of his shoulder. On the other hand, Madison would never accept a ride from him on a sunny day when she wasn't in trouble.

But what kind of trouble? Once he got Madison safely home, he intended to find out exactly why she'd been doing acrobatics on a slippery fire escape in a rainstorm.

In ten quick minutes, Jon veered his motorcycle into the driveway of a modest home a scant two miles from the base. He was familiar enough with the neighborhood on the back side of Valparaiso to recognize most of the homes as rentals for airmen and low-earning locals. Not the kind of place he expected a GS-12 civil servant to call home, but she kept an immaculate yard. If it had been daylight, he could have admired the strange and different blue flowers bordering the house and the ivy that climbed the walls. Between the darkness and the rain, he couldn't make out where grass ended and flowers began.

Then a nervous dread twisted in his stomach. "Ah, shit," he muttered into the rain. He wasn't supposed to know where she lived. He'd taken her straight home, but he'd forgotten to ask directions.

Jon leapt off the motorcycle and reeled to face her. Without thinking, he slipped his hands under her arms and lifted her off the bike. He couldn't have her slipping off the wet seat and falling into the watery grass, now could he? Her arms twisted up around his neck—natural, automatic—as if she held onto him for dear life every night.

Good. She wasn't thinking either. As long as she wasn't thinking, she wouldn't realize he'd known all along where she lived. He wouldn't have to lie and say she told him her address back at Building 13. He wouldn't have to admit he followed her home every night, hanging behind at a discreet distance, driving by only after she'd unlocked the door and withdrawn safely inside.

He did his damnedest not to look down at her skirt, scrunched up to her thighs. Why torture himself? She would ask him in tonight. She would. It didn't matter if he spent the next ten minutes inside or the next ten hours. He had so many questions for her. Like her theories on the security breach. Like why she had been so terrified when she ran away from Building 13. Like if her eyes were naturally that blue.

Madison's feet were already walking by the time they touched the ground. Running, practically. She reached the dry porch two steps ahead of him and stood there in the glow of a yellow bug light, clawing at the strap under her chin and stepping out of her muddy shoes.

"Hold still," he ordered, taking her damp hands in his. He held them for a split second longer than was necessary. Her gaze locked with his, and he thought he saw something there. Then she stared into the distance. Odd. He reached for the buckle on her helmet. Jon had seen her stare down tough adversaries, yet she couldn't look him in the eye.

"Thanks," she sputtered, the word nearly lost in the muffle as she pulled off the helmet and thrust it at him. Tucking her shoes under her arm again, she dug into her purse and dragged out her door key. "Thanks for everything. I really appreciate the ride home." She turned her back and jammed the key into the lock.

"Madison."

She threw him a broad, anxious smile over her shoulder. The door cracked a half inch. "Thanks again. I'll see you tomorrow."

"Madison." He planted his spit-shined shoe in her door and winced when it crashed against his toes. If he wanted, he could force his way in. He wanted to, but he wouldn't. "Madison."

The door swung open. Madison stood there, frozen in time. The war behind her deep blue eyes raged.

Jon perched the helmet under his arm and plowed both hands through his hair, plastering the wet hanks of blonde against his scalp. He could turn around and straddle his bike and go home to another sleepless night. Or he could take a chance. "Aren't you going to ask me in?"

Madison shook her head. She didn't say anything, but her eyes turned sad.

"You're going to turn me back out into the rain?"

"I-I'd never do anything to hurt you. But it wouldn't look right."

Her eyes begged him to understand. He did. Appearances. If word got out he'd seen the inside of Madison Steele's house, the rumor mill would be churning by daybreak. The general public would never believe the pettiness behind the federal workforce. The bureaucracy had a funny way of taking care of its own.

"Too bad motorcycles don't come with umbrellas. Do you mind if I wait here on your porch until the storm passes?" Thunder answered his prayers with a rumble overhead.

"Geez. Come on inside." She stuck her head out the door and checked the street. One white Ford Crown Victoria across the street in her neighbor's driveway. No traffic. At least not as far as the eye could see in the heavy rain. "Hurry up before someone spots you."

Jon choked back a grin and followed her into the house. He should have known it wouldn't be what he expected. Her office in The Lab looked like a tornado had torn apart a library but inside her tiny house, everything had its place. The furniture could have come straight from Jon's grandmother's house. Not so much antique as it was old. Simple designs. Muted florals. Solid, real wood.

He caught himself humming "Tonight's the Night" and broke off in mid verse.

"Wow," he breathed out.

She cast a dubious glance in his direction. "There's nothing in here to 'wow' about."

Other than her. "It's not quite what I expected. I thought you'd have—I don't know—*stuff* everywhere."

"You mean, like in my office?" She dropped her soggy shoes beside the sofa. "Sorry. I'm never home to mess up the place."

"Obviously." He tilted his head in the direction of a small pyramid of newspapers near the front door. At least two weeks' worth, still in their rubber bands and plastic sleeves, waited to be read.

"Yeah, I know. But by the time the paper boy gets here in the morning, I'm already headed out the door." Dropping her purse next to her shoes, she peeled out of her wet jacket. Her blouse, translucent with rain, stuck to every curve. "I've thought about canceling my newspaper subscription. That and cable. I could save probably another fifty dollars a month that way. Besides, I could always check the top news stories on the Internet at work if I really care what's going on in Washington."

Jon set the motorcycle helmet down on the brown carpet and stood awkwardly, waiting, always waiting. No way in hell could this woman have stolen Project Andromeda files. He'd heard a certain expression more than once in the past few months, something about a contracting officer always going down with the ship. There was another saying, too, about security being everyone's responsibility, but in reality, the tech-weenies and their supervisors always pointed to the contracting officer, shrugged their miserable shoulders, and insisted that keeping classified secrets safe was ultimately the contracting officer's responsibility, no matter what the regulations said. No matter who had stolen those files, someone would hang for it, and Madison was the easiest target. Once he had answers to his questions, he'd figure out a way to help her.

"Madison, we need to talk."

A light thud in another part of the house caught her attention. She lifted her chin and listened like a doe caught in crosshairs.

"Someone's in the house!" He threw up a protective hand, motioning for her to stay put. A prowler maybe? Or whoever had taken the classified papers from The Facility? "Stay here. I'll take care of it."

He reached for the brass poker propped against the fireplace tile, but Madison grabbed his hand and then, just as quickly, dropped it.

"No. I've got—" She paused again, listening, nervous. "I've got company."

She might as well have kicked him in the stomach. Company. A boyfriend. Another man wrapped up in her sheets.

She frowned at him and shook her head. "Not that kind of company." She almost laughed. Was he that transparent? "My little brother's wife and her new baby. Very unexpected company. They dropped by the office while I was being interrogated by Agent Wait. Not the best time for company if you know what I mean."

Relieved, he nodded. That explained a few things at least. It didn't explain what she was doing on the fire escape.

The patter of raindrops on the roof deepened in a crescendo that threatened to drown out her words. Thunder rumbled again. Jon studied his shoes. Wasn't she going to ask him to sit down? Offer him something cold to drink and something warm to wrap up in? He rubbed the heel of his shoe with his toe. Still dripping with water, he stood in a small, wet circle.

"Say, Madison? Do you mind if I get a towel and dry off?"

"No. No, not at all. I'll fetch one for you." She came back a minute later with a towel the color of wine. "Here," she said, handing it to him. "You can take it with you. Again, I appreciate your bringing me home. That was very...kind of you."

Kind? He didn't watch her every step to be *kind.* Not that he loved her or anything like that, but he couldn't stand the thought of anything bad happening to her. He didn't worship the ground she walked on, but he did admire her, her determination, her strength, the way she defended him to naysayers, praised him to his supervisors, and spurred him with opportunities contracting officers didn't generally give to rookies.

"Madison, we need to talk about tonight."

"Uh, no. We don't need to talk."

Why was she blushing? He meant the fire escape, not the motorcycle ride.

"You can return the towel to me later. You really should be going." She dropped her gaze to the carpet. "You hang around me and you'll end up getting transferred to Iceland or some other godforsaken place."

Thunder boomed, shaking the house. He tilted his head toward the front door. "You're going to send me back out into that? I'm soaked to the bone." Then in a moment teasing, he added, "Don't you have a heart?"

She grimaced. "Well, okay. But as soon as it lets up, you'll have to leave."

"I will. I swear."

She nodded to herself as if to confirm her decision. Did she dislike him so much that she couldn't bear to be alone with him?

"Madison?" He smoothed the towel over the sofa cushions and sat down. "I'm not supposed to be talking to you about this but, rumor has it, you've been taken off Project Andromeda."

The steel came back into her eyes as she stood there. She crossed her arms and regarded him coolly. "In this case, the rumor is true."

"Rumor also has it that you're under investigation."

"I am."

"I know you didn't do it. I know you're not a spy."

She threw her head back in a hollow laugh. "What makes you so sure? Everybody else is intent on crucifying me."

"I, uh, hung around after everybody left last night. To make sure you and Roxie got to your cars all right. There's no way you could have come back and broken in."

Leaning against the wall, Madison blew out a slow sigh. Arms still crossed in front of her like a shield, she watched him with a twitch of a smile. "I wouldn't tell that to anyone if I were you."

"Why not? Maybe I can help clear you." He would, damn it. He'd find a way. He'd earn her respect.

"Maybe, but it raises too many questions. Lieutenants hanging around for no reason—"

"Hey, I had reason! Like I said, to make sure you and Roxie were okay." The temperature in the room jumped by twenty degrees. L. Madison Steele could discern a lying defense contractor three thousand miles away. If she looked into his eyes, she'd see the truth.

"Seeing us out safely is too gentlemanly a thing for anyone to believe. Even for you, Jon Colter."

He swallowed hard. "Can't you let me help you?"

"I don't want you lying to the OSI for my sake. You'll only get yourself in trouble."

"Have it your way. But my being your alibi would at least narrow the window of opportunity for you to go back into The Facility."

"I didn't go back."

"I know that." How he knew, he wouldn't say. If she knew he discreetly escorted her home every night, she'd probably kick him out of the house. Madison wasn't the kind of woman who could accept help from anyone, especially not someone younger and less experienced. "But the OSI doesn't know that. If my playing watchdog will placate them, why not?"

Her eyes narrowed, suspicion glinting as she tilted her head back to appraise him. "Was that what you were doing tonight?"

"What do you mean?"

She waited for a rumble of thunder to fade. "I mean, do you always stand in the pouring rain outside a building where you don't work while you're waiting to see if I get safely to my car?"

Heat bloomed in his face. He bowed his head to hide the tell-tale blush in his cheeks. What did she want him to say? That he didn't occasionally stand in the rain and wait for her? "I tried to call your office earlier, but you were tied up with something more important." He tried not to sound bitter, but hey, he'd called her a dozen times. "I left you a note."

A smile broke the stone of her expression. She unfolded her arms and wrung her hands out behind her back. "I got it. Thanks. I did call back to The Facility, but Roxie said you'd already left." The smile faded into a frown. "You didn't drop by my office tonight, did you?"

"No. I don't have an access card for Building 13. Why?"

"No reason."

Then why did she look so worried? "There's a reason for everything you do, Madison Steele. Why did you ask?"

"Tonight," she relented, "after Gavin left, I realized somebody had been through the papers in my office. When I tried to leave, somebody was outside the door to the contracting suite."

"And you thought it was me? I would never snoop through your office."

"Never crossed my mind that it might be you. But somebody was there. And then he—or she—locked me in."

"Ah-ha."

"Ah-ha, what?"

"That's why you were on the fire escape."

"You saw me up there?"

Jon nodded. "So somebody locked you in by accident. Probably didn't realize you were working late."

"Even if somebody locks the door from the outside, anyone *inside* can still unlock the door. This wasn't an accident. They quick-glued the strike plate, so I couldn't open it."

Dread snaked down his back. "Why would anyone shut you in on purpose? Even as a prank?"

"I make enemies occasionally. Engineers usually. Sometimes other contracting people who get jealous when I get a kudo once in a blue moon. If I hadn't gone out the window, I would've been there until five tomorrow morning when the cleaning crew comes in. By then the glue smell would have dissipated and they would have thought the door was stuck again from all the humidity. They'll probably have to call maintenance to take the door off its hinges."

Leaning into his knees, he gazed up at her as if waiting to be knighted. She wouldn't have been there all night. He would have found a way to go in after her. Especially once he realized something was wrong. "Madison? When was the last time you bought a car battery?"

"Hmmm. Last Christmas. I was up in Georgia visiting my...my parents, and I left my headlights on. Why?"

"I think somebody meant to keep you at work tonight. First you get sealed into your office, then your battery dies on you? I don't believe in coincidences. Somebody wanted to make damned sure that you didn't come home tonight."

A kitten mewled in the distance. Madison stiffened, then raced toward the hallway. Jon stood, confused, watching her disappear into a guest room and close the door.

Several minutes later, the door opened and Madison tiptoed through, a bundle in her arms and a wistful smile on her face. Her eyes misted. A baby. Unbelievably tiny.

"Shhh," she soothed. The baby turned its splotchy cheek to her damp blouse and rooted. Madison cuddled the misshapen head against her, trailing a robin's egg blue, flannel blanket over her elbow as she rocked ever so slightly from side to side. "Hush now."

"Your nephew?" Hard to tell, the way she held him. She could have been the kid's mother. Hard as rock, cold as ice, L. Madison Steele owned a gentle touch, too. Chew up nails and spit out tacks at the negotiation table, Madison had a soft side. And he was the first to see it.

She nodded. "Jolene, my sister-in-law, fell asleep. Little fella's soaked through. I think his diaper weighs more than he does right now." She eased him down onto the sofa and held him there expertly with one hand while smoothing out a disposable diaper and a wipe with the other hand. Obviously, she'd changed diapers before.

Bending over the sofa, Jon slid his forefinger into the baby's palm and watched as the tiny fingers curled around his. "What I can't figure out is how somebody used your access card to get into The Facility to steal Project Andromeda files."

"They couldn't have." She untied the drawstring on the baby gown and pushed the delicate fabric up over the baby's umbilical stub. "I always wear my access card on my jacket."

"You're not wearing it now," he pointed out. She'd peeled out of her wet jacket, leaving it haphazardly tossed over the back of the recliner and the access card clipped to the lapel.

Ripping the tape from the soiled diaper and opening the padded paper, she glanced up. "So? I always wear my jacket at work."

She did, too. He'd sat behind her during negotiations in a 100 degree room and nearly laughed out loud as one by one her adversaries tore off their jackets. Madison never did. Somehow, keeping her jacket—withstanding the heat—had been a subtle victory in the game for power and illusions.

Jon untangled his finger from the baby's grip, then crossed the room to her jacket. He unclipped the card and ran his finger over the hard edges. The numbers along the bottom corresponded with her office symbol, but the sequence was odd.

"Madison, this isn't your card." He examined the other side. The access cards didn't bear a photo or name, though the new cards scheduled to come out in October would bear the owner's likeness. "This card's newer than mine. My number starts with a five and this one starts with a six." He flipped the card over again. If she had someone else's card, then who had hers? Who was masquerading as Madison Steele to pilfer germ warfare information from a locked building?

"Madison? Did you hear me? This isn't your card."

But she hadn't heard him. She was too busy staring at the genitals of her little nephew, who wasn't a nephew after all.

CHAPTER FIVE

Wednesday, 29 September 1999, V alparaiso, Florida

Ah, this is the way it should have been.

Madison leaned back in the recliner, her eyes still closed. The delicate heat and weight of the baby snuggled against the soft expanse above her breast. This is what she had wanted with Tim. Yearned for. What she would never have. And didn't deserve.

But with her eyes closed and the scent of baby powder wafting up to her nose, Madison could almost believe she was back in time in some alternate reality. Tim was hers, the baby was hers. In this fantasy, she'd never faced the petty politics of the government bureaucracy. The working world couldn't be that hypocritical! Life couldn't be that needlessly restrictive! Why couldn't they live and let live, or why couldn't she make it not matter?

Opening her eyes, she tilted her head out of the warm sunshine. The lieutenant asleep on her sofa was Jon Colter, not Tim Sandusky. The baby in her arms wasn't hers either. The only thing Madison had to look forward to was another grueling day filled with petty rivalries, bored rumor-mongers, mounds of paper, and—oh, yeah—intrigue. Another day of Special Agent Wait's prying questions and not-so-subtle hints about her part in Tim's exile. Another day of keeping the past in the past and keeping the future safe.

The baby girl mewled, struggling to lift her slightly pointed head, turn it away from the sunlight, and drop her tiny cheek back to Madison's chest. The baby's face still carried bruises from a difficult birth. The dark spot on the right cheek looked more like a birthmark than a bruise, but even in the span of one night, hues of yellow had mixed with the purple and promised to fade completely. The heat where the baby's cheek met Madison's chest had left a damp circle on Madison's aging, red T-shirt. Instinctively, Madison smoothed down the spiderweb-fine, black hair damp from body heat.

Jolene has some explaining to do, provided she ever got her butt out of bed. Granted, after such a difficult birth, traipsing across the State of Florida to antagonize Toby hadn't done the girl any good and she needed the rest. Had the girl lied about the baby's sex for kicks? Or could there be a softer side of Jolene, some misguided notion that she could protect Madison from being hurt again? No, Toby would never tell a soul, not even a wife, about what had happened all those years ago.

"You're a natural."

Both Madison and the baby startled. Jon Colter had a voice as soft and lyrical as any deejay's, but she hadn't expected him to be awake. He didn't move except to slant a blurry pair of blue eyes at her. Shushing the baby, Madison rocked the little bundle against her thundering heart. "I thought you were asleep," she muttered, feeling stupid. She wouldn't look at him. His electric gaze would only catch hers and tempt old demons back to play.

"Couldn't sleep. I didn't realize you live under the flight line. Every F-16 that lands at Eglin comes right over your chimney and jars my teeth down to the fillings."

"Fighter jets. The sound of freedom." She smiled and outlined the baby's ear with her fingertip. On those rare lunch hours when she could escape the office, she liked to take a sandwich out to a grassy knoll near the flight line and watch the powerful Falcons zoom overhead. The joy of flight surged through her every time. "I guess I'm used to the noise. I don't even hear it anymore." She stole a glimpse of him and then studied the baby's cheek. "Anyway, you're the one who's a natural. Thanks for helping out last night."

"If I hadn't been able to earn my keep, you would have thrown me out in the storm." He paused, worrying over his next words. "What I can't figure out is why you let me stay here all night, alone with you."

"We weren't alone. One or the other of us held this baby all night long. Besides, Jolene was in the next room."

Jon sat up and leaned forward, bracing his head in his hands. He pushed his long, slender fingers through his hair. He had beautiful, young hands. Finally he angled his gaze up at her, hurt shining through. "I don't understand you."

She smiled back humorlessly. "Join the club."

"You don't have to be afraid of me. Don't you trust me?"

"As much as I trust anyone. It's not you I'm afraid of. You're taking this whole thing too personally."

He snorted and shook his head. "I can't figure out if you like me or hate me. Or merely tolerate me."

"I don't hate you."

"You can't stand to be alone with me in the same room."

She shifted in the recliner. She desperately wanted to reach out and squeeze his hand. Instead, she stroked the baby's cheek. "You've got it all wrong."

"Do I? How many times have I worked side by side with you all day long until it ended up being you, me, and Roxie? Then the minute Roxie headed out the door, you ordered me to leave, too. I would have stayed. Every single one of those nights, I would have stayed and helped you. Aw, you probably think I'm some goof-ball lieutenant who can't even tie his own bootlaces."

"That's not true. You're young, but you're bright. And whatever you lack in experience, you more than make up for in enthusiasm and hard work."

"What? Did you lift those words right off my evaluation? Get real."

"I am real. It's because I like you so much that I can't spend time alone with you." That and the secret fear she would touch him too long, too tenderly, too often if given half a chance. "If I spend too much time with you, it won't matter what awards I write you up for or what a good job you do because everyone will assume you're getting praise because we have a personal friendship. You know how the grapevine is. Hanging around me will only discredit your strengths."

"I don't care what people believe about my work. If I know that it's good and you know it's good, what does it matter? I don't care what other people say about me."

"I care."

"You shouldn't. Why can't we all do our jobs, be friends with whoever we want, and be happy? Is that so much to ask?"

Madison laughed. "You don't know how often I've asked that question myself."

"You've got more serious things to worry about than gossip."

"More serious, yes. More important? That depends. Gossip is like feathers in a windstorm. Tickle some, choke others. But no matter how hard you try, you can never get all the feathers back into the bag. In the end, people believe what they want to believe. Bureaucrats aren't very creative except when it comes to gossip."

"You know, it wouldn't hurt you to be a little less cynical sometimes."

"And it wouldn't hurt you to be a little more realistic. But you're right: there are more serious matters for me to worry about than the rumor mill. Our country's best defense against biological warfare got stolen on my watch. For all we know, the Project Andromeda proposal is already in the hands of the Iraqis. Bad enough this happened on my watch, but it sure looks like I did it."

"The question is, if somebody used your card to get into The Facility to steal those BW files, whose card do you have?"

"You're thinking I've got the culprit's card, aren't you? I don't know, Jon. Doesn't feel right." Gut instinct was one of those things you couldn't document in a negotiation memorandum, yet it was more reliable than the thousands of pages of cost data that formed the Government's official negotiating position. "Besides, I'm not in the habit of swapping access cards with my co-workers."

"Never? Maybe you loaned it to someone who needed to go to the snack bar and didn't have their card with them. Happens all the time in my office."

"No. Never. That card stays in my possession at all times."

"Except for once. Face it, Madison: somebody took your card. Somebody used it to get into The Facility. Somebody who knew the combination to the evaluation room and the combination to the safe." Pausing, Jon blinked, then frowned. "And if they knew those things, they probably had access to Project Andromeda already. Can you think of anybody who would intentionally set you up?"

A set-up. Madison hadn't considered that. She could see an external threat, commonly known as a "spy," duplicating an access card and cracking a couple of combinations to get at BW secrets, but why would they bother to bury her in the process? Jon was right: this reeked of something personal.

"It's my job to say no, but I'm sure I've pissed off somebody."

"Enough to frame you for treason? Spreading rumors about somebody's personal life is one thing, but we're talking national security here."

"We're talking *lives.* If the information in that proposal gets leaked or sold to the wrong people, we're putting the entire population of this planet at risk. It'll be as bad as the biblical Armageddon."

"You sound like my mom, the High Priestess of Fruitcakes. She spouts End of Time garbage in every other sentence."

"This isn't garbage. This is real. The threat was there before the Gulf War, and it's still out there. Project Andromeda is our best bet of seeing—" she glanced at the baby on her chest and a sob caught in Madison's throat—"of seeing our children grow up."

She had to find out who had framed her and stop them before Project Andromeda was used against the children of the world. She eased one hand around the baby's fragile head and laid a palm across the breadth of the baby's back. Madison held the baby's life in her hands, both literally and figuratively. If she didn't find the thief soon, Jolene's baby would never know the sweet taste of success or the spicy touch of a lover. She would never grow up to hang college degrees from her office wall. She would never make a valedictory address at her high school graduation. She would never play piano sonatas in the school recital. She would never bake Christmas cookies with her mommy. If some newfangled germ didn't kill everyone instantly, the feeble, the frail, and the children would die first. Madison, of course, would be among the last. By sheer will, she would survive the early stages of the deadly strain, only to bury everything she loved before succumbing herself. No one would be left to bury her.

An image flashed in her brain: Madison leaning in heavy defeat onto a shovel, preparing to bury the newborn girl wrapped in a flannel blanket and laid in an empty dresser drawer that once had held satin underthings and rose sachets.

No, that wasn't right. She wouldn't desert this child, too. If bio-warfare struck, she'd take Jolene's baby and flee to Georgia to save what little family she had left. She'd find a way. Somehow.

"Are you okay? You looked a million miles away."

"Not a million," she said. "Just a hundred and fifty." In a place in Georgia so rural that the town would willingly hide your secret.

Funny. Small towns were notorious for everybody knowing everybody else's business, yet some people could be trusted to handle certain matters discreetly. Especially when it was in the best interest of a child. In a small town, favors were preserved for generations until one day, out of respect for a long-dead founding father, a neighborly doctor might risk his profession to alter official records and make private arrangements for a hometown girl in need of a miracle.

She brushed her lips against the baby's forehead, kissed it. Jolene had no business with a kid. The little twit was hardly more than a child herself.

It wasn't fair.

The baby in Madison's arms would be raised by an absent father and by a mother who regarded the child as insurance against ever having to get a high school diploma. Toby on his ship, thousands of miles away in the Persian Gulf or as nearby as the coast of Haiti, would discover his daughter through photographs and letters while on his long treks away from home.

And Jolene? What kind of mother would she make? She was too immature to care about anyone other than herself. Too selfish to think of a husband as anything more than a meal ticket to carefree days of gawking at TV talk shows and late nights hazy with alcohol and sweet smoke.

It wasn't fair.

Madison and Tim were intelligent, talented people able to afford a child financially, emotionally, in every way that mattered except one: politically. But a child should grow up with two parents, not with only a mother who spends her quality time making apologies. Madison had made the right decision. Anybody could be a better mother than she could, but not anybody could do her job for the Department of Defense. How often did she tell herself that in hopes she'd one day believe it? Six years ago, it had seemed right. She had had a job to do, a job no one else could do as well. Since then, Madison kept herself too busy to think very much about her choice. It was safer that way. And saner.

The baby's rosebud-shaped mouth quivered with breath. Madison blinked furiously. Damn it. She hated it when the yearning caught her unawares. Next thing she knew, she'd be singing lullabies, and word would get out she had a soft heart. Instead, she yawned and settled against the recliner.

"Sleepy?" Jon asked from the sofa, then yawned and laughed. They had shared baby duty all night, each taking two-hour shifts while the other slept and while Jolene snuggled down in the guest bed and pulled the pillow over her head so as not to be disturbed by the occasional cries.

"Sorry. It's not the company. Honest. I don't think I slept at all last night."

"You did. Some." A frown plowed its way across his forehead.

"What's wrong? Did I snore or something?"

"No, but you must have been dreaming. Did you know you cry in your sleep?"

"You were the one dreaming. I never cry."

"Don't get mad at me. If I were in your shoes, I'd be crying, too. The past few days have been rough on you, haven't they? Oh, that's right. You wouldn't admit it if they were."

Madison managed a slight smile for him. He understood her better than he thought.

"You should be going home now." She glanced up at the clock. "It's nearly—oh, shit!—nine o'clock. I guess I overslept. We'll both be late for work. What are you going to tell Otto?" L. Madison Steele was never late for work, and especially not late with a lieutenant. Not anymore.

"I'll come up with something. All I need's a shower."

"Your roommates. What will they think?" And what would they think if they knew he'd spent the night in his contracting officer's house?

"Figmo's got two girlfriends. One gets him on odd nights and the other on even nights, but they don't know it. His room's a mess so neither woman will sleep over at our place. And Miri's engaged and so gaga eyed that she doesn't have any idea what's going on around her."

Must be nice, Madison mused. Three young lieutenants sharing a house, two men and one woman. All single. All platonic. Perfectly acceptable in the world of government procurement. Of course, they were all engineers, and everyone knew that engineers had no integrity to jeopardize.

"But what would they think about you staying here all night?"

"They'd think I got lucky." His face flushed the moment he said it.

Heat bloomed in her cheeks, too. The idea of Jon Colter sleeping on her sofa didn't satisfy her. Jon Colter not sleeping in her bed sent an involuntary shiver down her spine. What if he did spend the night—no Jolene, no baby, no worries about security breaches—and what if they both got lucky? Who would make the first move? And who would take the lead in lovemaking? She was older, maybe more experienced. All this time she'd watched him working at her side, wanted him. Except for last night's motorcycle ride that had left her tingling for hours, she had not once touched Jon Colter. Geez, she deserved a medal.

"Don't worry, Madison. I won't tell them it was you I was with."

She nodded, suddenly somber. Once upon a time, she'd heard the same words from Tim. He'd been called before his colonel and asked to explain his frequent, friendly visits to Madison's cubicle. Hard to believe that a few short years ago, "teamwork" was not one of the Government buzzwords connected with every piddling project conceived. At the time, Federal employees stuck strictly to their functional areas—engineering with engineering, finance with finance, contracting with contracting—and never any two to mingle. Inside the government walls of bureaucracy, fraternizing with "the enemy" was looked upon with less regard than interracial marriages in a backwoods, Southern town. Then one night when the recall roster had been "activated," Tim had been ordered to report to work within five minutes. He'd breezed out Madison's back door, damp-haired and smelling of sex. "Don't worry," he'd told her, grinning over his shoulder, "I won't tell them it was you I was with."

A determined knock on the door shattered the silence, casting a stone into the deep, still waters of memory. She blinked and looked up.

"You sure no one knows where you are?" Madison eased herself out of the recliner, careful not to disturb the baby's slumber.

"Nobody would think to look for me here."

Madison squinted through the peephole and gasped. Special Agent Austin Wait stood outside in his black suit. One of his black suits. Doubtful he wore the same suit to work every day, yet she'd never seen him in anything other than his executioner's black. She whirled to face Jon. "Quick," she whispered. "Hide!"

Jon laughed. "You've got to be kidding. You don't really have a husband, do you? Everybody says your wedding band is just for show."

"Get in the closet. Now!"

He frowned. "You're serious, aren't you?"

"As a heart attack."

His eyebrows knit in indignation. Surely a guy as pleasant on the senses as Jon Colter had hidden from jealous husbands. "I am not about to hide in some closet while some boyfriend of yours—"

"It's the OSI," she drawled with less patience than a kindergarten teacher. "Now get in the closet and don't hum!"

Jon scrambled off the sofa. He yanked open the closet door and made a face at the boxes of junk she'd stashed haphazardly inside. The rest of the house was spotless, but the closet was the equivalent of a rug to sweep things under. He shot her a helpless glance, shrugged, then closed the door behind him.

"Just a minute," she called out for the benefit of Special Agent Wait. Still holding the baby close to her chest, she scampered back to the guest room. "Jolene?"

The lump under the bedcovers moaned.

"Jolene? I want you to listen to me. We have a problem."

The girl lifted her head enough to glare over her shoulder at Madison. Jolene's reddish-brown tangles fell into her eyes. The girl had slept in her clothes. Judging by the expression on Jolene's face, Madison might as well have rolled in the contents of the baby's diaper.

"The OSI's here. They're going to want to speak to me. I'll keep them from talking to you if I can, but you must stay in your room and do not—do you understand?—*do not* come out unless I call for you."

"The who?"

"OSI. They're like...military investigators."

Terror clouded Jolene's sleepy eyes. Good. Jolene needed to be scared. Asking nicely wouldn't help. Jolene was the kind of prankster who would ask Madison in front of the OSI where she kept her marijuana and stolen TV's. Given half a chance, Jolene would gleefully end Madison's government career.

Madison tiptoed back to the front door, unlatched the two chains, twisted the deadbolt, and cracked the door enough to slide her knee and shoulder through but keep the baby hidden on the other side. "Why, Agent Wait," she said with sarcastic sunshine. "Whatever brings you to my humble abode? Just in the neighborhood?"

He twisted his strong jaw to one side and appraised her. Typical. Always watching, observing, waiting for a mistake. "Hello, Ms. Steele. I didn't expect to find you at home."

"Do you always visit people you don't expect to be there?"

"I checked with your office. They said you were AWOL."

"AWOL! The work day doesn't start until 7:15 officially, and I've got two hours to report in so I believe I have a few more minutes yet before I'm AWOL."

He shrugged. "Only reporting what they said. Are you always this defensive?"

"Hey, just because I'm usually working at o-dark-thirty, doesn't mean that's the official start of the day." And yes, she was always this defensive when her ass was on the line.

"That your bike out there?" He gestured toward Jon's motorcycle, parked in a deep puddle.

"Belongs to a friend."

"Aren't you going to ask me in?"

She stood on her tiptoes to see if he was alone. Good. Only one gray-suited man in a white car on the other side of the street. Worst case, Wait would have had five or six fellow agents behind him for backup. Her stomach twisted. "Do you have a warrant?"

"No. Do I need one?"

"I don't think so." She stood back, opening the door as she did and waiting for the shock to register on his face when he saw the baby against her chest.

If the sight of her with a child unnerved him, he didn't let it show. "Looks good on you," he commented.

Her knees nearly buckled under her. The thought of a baby looking good on her was too much a luxury. "Th-thank you."

She swallowed and took another step back, wavering and almost toppling. He grabbed her arm and steadied her. His hand was warm, confident.

Warm hands, cold heart?

He used the gesture as an excuse to squeeze past her in the doorway, leaving her to close the door behind him. Austin Wait entered her home as if he owned it. He surveyed it the same way he surveyed her legs. Deft, analytical, precision strike. In some ways, he was like Jon, but older, jaded, without the idealism. Precisely the kind of man she worked best with.

Except that he was her enemy. No, not enemy. *Adversary.* He might systematically annihilate her, but it wasn't personal.

"If you're staying home today," Austin Wait said, helping himself to a barstool near her kitchen counter, "you should probably go ahead and call into your office and let them know."

The baby stirred on her chest. The rosebud mouth opened, searched, wanted to suck. Madison claimed a bottle of soy formula from a pan of warmed water, tested it on the inside of elbow, and plopped the nipple into the baby's mouth. Thank goodness Jolene had had enough bottles of soy formula in her diaper bag to prevent extra trips to the grocery store. Small eyes unlike Toby's or Jolene's stared intently at her. Air gurgled up through the bottle sweeter than a hundred champagne bubbles. Madison fought back a smile. It was almost as if the baby filled an empty spot in her heart. Almost.

"I'll call in after I feed the baby. Thanks to Mr. Smith, I've been taken off Project Andromeda, so there's no need to rush into work this morning. Besides, I have plenty of comp time."

Agent Wait smirked. "I don't think your procurement clerk knows that."

"Eileen? Eileen knows—"

"Raynene," he corrected.

That explained it. Raynene had a policy: if you screw up the work badly enough, you'll never be asked to do it again. The woman couldn't—wouldn't—take a telephone message. Somehow she always managed to transpose at least two numbers, but which two was anybody's guess.

Raynene didn't know anything about Madison's comp time, mainly because it was all under the table. Personnel had some stupid rule that any unpaid overtime had to be compensated within the same pay period. That wasn't practical for contracting officers. Source selections sometimes went on for months, and it wouldn't do her a bit of good to work an eighteen-hour day on a Monday and take off Tuesday to make up for it. She was needed there every day from dusk until dawn and until the job was done. Project Andromeda alone had netted her twenty-three weeks of comp time, all of which Gavin had agreed to let her take when and if her workload ever let up. What a joke.

"Great. You take Raynene's word over mine. Raynene, who asks me after the fact if I wanted that letter faxed or shredded."

Austin Wait laughed. "There's one in every office." Then he sobered. "Did you say Mr. Smith took you off Project Andromeda?"

"Yeah. Happy now?"

The agent turned his head to curse. "I explicitly told him I wanted no changes at this time."

Had she heard him right? The OSI didn't want her taken off Project Andromeda? "But you said I was under investigation."

"You are."

"And you still want me to work the project?"

"I have my reasons."

She settled onto the recliner and jostled the baby against her chest. Sweet little thing wanted nothing more than a mother's love. Something Madison had never been able to give. "Reasons you won't share with me?"

"Not yet."

"Oh, that makes perfect sense. Especially from a man who drops by to see me when he doesn't expect to find me at home."

Grinning, he nodded. "This from a woman whose car was at work and she wasn't?"

"Dead battery. In the rain, too."

"Long walk home?"

She didn't take the bait.

"Did you call a taxi?"

"No." She drew the word out and prayed Austin Wait would let it go. The last thing she wanted was another scandal, another lieutenant shipped off to a distant country to separate him from the siren of Federal acquisitions. "A friend gave me a ride home," she murmured.

"Does this friend have a name?"

"Just a friend, all right?" Next thing she knew, he'd be jotting down Lt. Jonathan Colter's name on a yellow legal pad, only to become part of an official report that would end up crucifying her favorite engineer.

"Ms. Steele? Do you have an alibi for last night?"

"Last night? I thought it was the night before last you were interested in. Monday night."

"Now I'm interested in last night."

"My brother's wife and baby stayed here all last night." She nodded toward the baby, half-finished with the bottle and gazing intently at Madison's knuckles. "I was here from about eight o'clock on. At work before then."

"Would your brother's wife testify to that?"

Oh, God. She was in serious trouble if her freedom depended on Jolene. "She's asleep in the guest room."

"Call her out. I'm going to need her statement."

"Not a problem." His tone dared her to question him. She shifted the baby into the crook of one arm and rose from the recliner. She could only hope Jolene understood the seriousness of the OSI's questions and answered them truthfully. Madison leaned close to the door but didn't open it. "Jolene?"

No answer.

"Jolene? Come on out and meet Special Agent Austin Wait."

Jolene didn't answer. The little twit was going to make Madison come in after her.

"Jolene?" Madison pushed gently against the door, enough to peer through the crack at the lump of blankets and pillows too flat disguise the shape of a lanky teenage girl. Her own pulse rang in her ears, yet Madison kept as calm as she always did under pressure. No sense in alerting Special Agent Wait to her fears. "Jolene, it's okay, honey. You can come on out now."

"Any day this year," Austin Wait muttered from behind her.

"Jolene!"

No one answered the stage whisper.

Madison bumped the door open another notch and gasped. Damn her hide! The little weasel had fled through the open window.

The OSI agent reached over Madison's head and nudged the door completely open. She didn't have to say anything. He could see that the window had been shoved haphazardly up, the blinds and curtains hanging out as if Jolene had pitched headfirst through the gap and tangled her feet in the window dressing. He strode to the window and peered out at the sunshine.

"She was here a few minutes ago," Madison offered, her defenses rising. She was in enough trouble without having to explain the antics of a surly teenager. "Just ask your man in the white car. And while you're at it, ask him why he didn't stop a girl sneaking out the window."

"What man in a white car?"

"Your partner."

"I don't have a partner." Wait frowned at the baby in Madison's arms. "Is that her kid?" the agent asked.

Madison nodded. The baby had stopped sucking and closed her delicate eyes in contentment. Her eyelids were so thin Madison could see the capillaries threading through the skin.

"Kid can't be more than a few days old. Why would she run off and leave her baby?" he wondered aloud.

Good question. Madison would never leave her own baby. Unless, of course, she counted leaving her child in more capable hands than her own. Maybe that's what Jolene had done. Lord knew, the girl wasn't emotionally equipped to be a mother.

Madison hugged the baby to her chest and shrugged. "Maybe you scared her."

"Me? I hadn't even talked to her yet. Why would she be afraid of me?"

Madison shrugged a second time. She'd told Jolene to keep quiet unless she was needed. She'd told Jolene the OSI—military investigators—were on her doorstep. Why had the girl bolted?

Special Agent Wait glanced around the room, quickly assessing the unmade bed, the duffel bag spilling blue jeans and dark green fingernail polish onto the floor, the shiny dental retainer on the night stand. "Do you think she'll come back?"

Half of Madison wanted to rant that the girl had better come back and start acting like the responsible parent she claimed to be. But the other half of Madison ached for any excuse to keep the baby safe—from Jolene, from the world, from crazy, foreign dictators with buried bunkers full of anthrax, botulism, cholera, and the Good Lord only knew how many other deadly germs.

"I'm sure she'll be back."

"I hope so. You might need that alibi."

Madison sucked in her breath. The less said, the better. "For what? I didn't do anything. I was at work until 7:30 and then I came straight home to be with Jolene and the baby."

"And no one besides your missing sister-in-law saw you?"

Madison looked away. If she'd been in a billion-dollar negotiation, she would have met her adversary's gaze straight on and answered with a cool, staccato "No." But this was different, personal. Jon had been with her. All night. In her house. Not in her bed, but if knowledge of his presence got out, it wouldn't make any difference. No one would believe that L. Madison Steele had spent over twelve platonic hours with a sexy lieutenant. Not with her reputation for lieutenants.

"Ms. Steele?"

She lifted her gaze to his and discreetly wet her lips to buy herself time. "Other than my runaway house guest, I don't have an alibi for last night. Why would I need one, anyway? It was night before last—Monday night—that Project Andromeda was stolen."

Agent Wait closed the distance between them and bent down to look her directly in the eyes and make his point. "If you can think of anyone else who can verify your whereabouts last night between 7:30 and 8:00, I need to know. Right now."

Madison studied Agent Wait's black eyes. Tempted as she was, she didn't cast her gaze toward the closet where Jon waited. If anything, she stiffened unnaturally. She wouldn't allow her body language to lean toward the closet or do anything that might give away her lieutenant's hiding place.

"All right then." The man in black blew out a long sigh. He didn't believe her. She could almost see the wheels turning inside his head as he tried to figure out who owned the motorcycle in the driveway. "But you should realize that you might be charged with murder."

Madison's jaw dropped. She clung to the baby. "M-murder?"

The closet door opened, and before Madison could screech for him to stay put, Jon stumbled out. Austin Wait startled, then collected himself instantly as if embarrassed to have been caught off guard.

"I was with her," Jon blurted out. "The whole night."

Agent Wait cocked one eyebrow and crossed his arms. Silent, he surveyed Jon's wrinkled blue uniform and the stain of baby spit-up on his shoulder. A slow grin spread across his face. "Do you always hide in a closet, Lieutenant?"

"She didn't want you to jump to the wrong conclusion."

Wait roared with laughter. "The wrong conclusion? You stepped out of a hall closet. What the hell is the right conclusion?"

Madison eased in front of Jon to shield him from Wait. Not that he physically needed her protection. "The right conclusion is that I didn't want an innocent bystander dragged unnecessarily into your investigation of me."

The agent appeared to consider her explanation, then grunted his approval. "So Lieutenant—" he squinted to read Jon's name on his uniform—"Colter, would you be willing to swear you were with Ms. Steele all night?"

"No," Madison began.

Jon elbowed in front of her. "Hell, yes."

"Really? All night? Maybe you fell asleep, and she slipped out like her sister-in-law?"

Madison edged in front of Jon. She couldn't let him do this. He'd be giving up his career. His reputation. For her. For nothing.

"I didn't fall asleep." Jon stepped forward, dead even with Madison in the narrow hallway. He wasn't willing to be protected. "We were both up all night."

Wait whistled. "Well, Lorelei, you got yourself a stallion this time, huh? I'd heard about Lorelei's Lieutenants' but I'd never met one until—"

"Shut your goddamned mouth!"

In a flash, Jon lunged for Wait's throat. The agent caught Jon's wrist and slammed him against the wall before the echo of Jon's howl faded.

Madison saw the flash of silver, heard the clink of handcuffs. God, no! Her worst nightmare. She'd ruined another lieutenant. And with a baby in her arms, there was little she could do.

Wait clamped Jon's face against the wall. Blood trickled from his nose and caught on his lower lip. Jon squeezed his eyes shut and opened them. His breaths came heavy and fast, like a trapped rabbit's. Didn't he know he was too young and sweet to ruin his career defending her honor?

"Down, boy," Wait commanded. "Feisty one, too."

Madison clutched the baby in her arms. Her alternatives were limited. If she hadn't had the little thing cradled against her chest, Madison might have challenged Wait herself, not for her honor but for his brutal response to Jon's gallantry. Wait was bigger than either of them and no doubt could easily subdue Madison if she chose to pummel him, but Madison wouldn't go down without a fight.

That wouldn't save her favorite lieutenant.

"Agent Wait." She kept perfectly still, except to jostle the baby once in her arms. Her practiced tone meant business. It meant, too, she wasn't afraid of Austin Wait and the whole OSI combined. There was no hurt he could inflict on her that she hadn't already endured a thousand times over in her memories. He held Jon at bay but gave Madison the courtesy of his attention.

"Ms. Steele."

"Too bad you didn't bother to ask, instead of baiting my friend with insinuations that would best be reported to the Social Actions office." She paused to let her subtle threat sink in. Even the OSI was afraid of sexual harassment lawsuits. She noted the flicker of understanding in his expression and continued. "Had you asked, you would have learned that Lt. Colter and I have been up all night taking care of a newborn while her mother slept. A scared teenaged mother whom, I remind you, took off when you showed up and has now left me with an infant in my care until she feels safe enough to come home."

Wait screwed his jaw to one side. Taking his time, he unlocked the handcuffs and stepped back.

Jon reeled to face the older man. The lieutenant looked as if he might lurch forward and repeat his earlier mistake. Instead he stayed by Madison's side and glowered. A rivulet of bright red trickled down his chin. Madison stifled the urge to press a damp cloth to his wounds. Though he rubbed at the dark red welts on his wrists, it was his ego that had been bruised the worst.

Wait nodded at Jon. "That so, hotshot? You and Ms. Steele babysat the night away?"

"Yeah."

"That your bike outside?"

"Yeah."

Poor Jon. He'd tried to fight for her honor and lost. If there'd been a rock close enough and large enough for him to crawl under, he probably would have.

"What time of night did you pick up Ms. Steele? I take it she did ride home with you?"

"Yeah. She did. Around 7:30. It was about dark. Just before the rainstorm set in."

"I had a dead battery," Madison emphasized. "It was raining cats and dogs, and Lt. Colter was good enough to give me a ride home. By the time we got here, the lightning was terrible. Absolutely terrible. I couldn't send him back out into weather."

Wait smirked at Madison. "No, of course not. Methinks you do protest too much. And before dark? Where were you then?"

"At work."

"You always work so late?"

"Usually later," Jon interjected. He blushed again, though Madison couldn't decipher the reason. "I work with Madison on Project Andromeda." He glanced at her. "It's okay if I tell him that, isn't it?"

"It's okay." She smiled back at him, but he didn't seem any more at ease than he had a few seconds ago. Poor kid. And he did look like a kid now. A kid with a bloody nose. One bested by a bully with a gun and handcuffs.

Yes, Jon knew how late she worked every night. He ended every work day by her side, only to have her send him home. And then there were those nights like last night when he wondered aloud if she would be okay and offered to take her home. He'd never been to her home. How was it last night he'd taken her to her meager little house under the flight line yet she'd never told him where she lived?

"I've already talked to your division chief," Wait said.

"Gavin?" The Gutless Wonder.

"Yes. He verified he left you alone in the office but he couldn't be sure of the time. Anyone else there with you?"

Madison didn't answer. For some reason, the question felt like a set-up.

"She wasn't by herself," Jon grumbled. "Somebody locked her in her office. From the outside."

Wait's eyes widened. He looked from Jon to Madison. "The door to Contracting had to be taken down this morning. Some kind of fluid had been squirted into the strike plate. So you couldn't get out. That true?"

She cuddled the baby against her chest. She'd have to have a long talk with Jon about when to open his mouth and when to keep it closed. "It's true."

The OSI agent pressed his lips together and leaned against the door jamb. "Ve-wy in-te-westing. Dead battery, too, you said?" She nodded. "Sounds like somebody didn't want you going home, Ms. Steele. In fact, sounds like somebody wanted to make sure you stayed put for a while. Perhaps—" he jabbed a finger in Jon's face. Jon took an annoyed half-step backward. "Perhaps it was one of Lorelei's lieutenants."

"You idiotic—" Jon leaned forward, his body yearning to retaliate.

Another two seconds and he'd get himself into trouble again.

"It wasn't Jon."

"And what makes you so certain, *Lorelei* Madison Steele?"

"Because I heard their footsteps, and I know Jon's footsteps."

Jon hiked his chin. "You do?"

"Whose footsteps were they?" Wait pressed.

"I don't know."

"But you know they weren't Colter's."

"That's right." She kept her jaw set. Okay, so the secret was out. She knew Jon's footfalls and no one else's. Him. Her lowly lieutenant. The only other footfalls she'd ever recognized were those of a lieutenant named Tim Sandusky. She hadn't heard those footsteps in seven years, the day they'd walked out of her life.

"Besides," she added, trying to salvage what was left of her privacy, "after I realized someone was outside my door, I called over to The Facility and asked Roxie to send over Jon or somebody and she said he'd just left, so it couldn't have been him."

"You morons should be trying to find out who stole that classified proposal," Jon insisted, gathering his courage. "You ought to be out there finding out who's harassing Madison rather than harassing her yourself. She could have broken her neck crawling out the window of her office last night."

Wait straightened to his full height. "You're a big talker, Lieutenant. Tell me: who was at The Facility when you left it?"

"Um, nobody. Just Roxie. Figmo and I—I mean, Lt. Terranova and I—had helped Roxie finish shredding a bunch of evaluation drafts. She was going to pull security and head home. I got on my bike and headed over to Building 13 to make sure...um." He stumbled over his own words. "To make sure, um, Madison was all right."

Madison's lips curved into an involuntary smile. Did he check on her every night? Or was he her guardian angel with a bloody nose?

"Roxanne Daniels was alive when you and Lt. Terranova left The Facility?"

"Of course, she—" Jon broke off.

Alive when he left...? Oh, God. Agent Wait had said something about a murder. Madison swallowed her wail. "Not Roxie! Roxie's dead? Somebody killed Roxie?"

And what about Project Andromeda? Who would handle the contract now that Madison had been taken off the program and Roxie was dead? She couldn't let herself think of Roxie as really dead. Missing, maybe. Absent. But not dead. It didn't make sense. It wasn't real.

"How?" was all Madison could think to say. She wished tears could come but at the same time, she refused to believe.

Wait hesitated as if debating with himself how much to tell her. "The security checklist we found in her hand gives us a good clue of the order of events. According to the Standard Form 700, last night at 7:30, civilian time, she turned off the shredder. At 7:35, she locked the four-drawer safe. At 7:40, she turned off the computers. At 7:45, she turned off the coffee pot and popcorn machine. She hadn't locked the walk-in safe."

"That was last on the list," Madison whispered.

"This morning at six, Eugene Krueger opened The Facility and found Roxanne Daniels locked inside the walk-in safe." Wait lowered his broad-lashed eyelids as if to give a moment's silence to the weight of his words. "Suffocated. Safe wasn't equipped with oxygen."

Madison shook her head furiously. Krueger kept the safe filled with boxes of papers to be shredded in his free time. Without the stored documents, the safe was bigger than most walk-in closets, but with the boxes stashed inside, there was barely room to turn around. Certainly not much air. Queasiness roiled in her stomach. She'd shared air with Roxie every day for months months. "Couldn't have been an accident."

Jon paled. "Sweet Jesus. The phone was ringing when we left. Must have been Madison calling. Figmo walked out the door right ahead of me. About 7:30. That means...that means I was the last person to see Roxie alive."

"No," Wait said. "Her killer was the last person to see her alive."

A shudder ripped down Madison's spine. Definitely not an accident. Walk-in safes were equipped with emergency oxygen tanks. Just in case. The tank had been there the night before, the night of the break-in, when Madison had pulled security.

Madison fingered the fuzz over the soft spot on the baby's head. Such a delicate creature. In the wee hours of last night, the baby had still been growing accustomed to the art of breathing while Roxie had been struggling for air.

"Agent Wait? Do you think whoever shut me in my office was responsible for locking Roxie in that safe? If so, he—or she—must have done it after gluing me into my office. If that's the case, if he was working alone, he would have had to use an access card to get inside The Facility."

She knew. By the look in Special Agent Wait's eyes, by the feel in her gut, she knew.

"The computer shows an access card was used to gain entrance at 7:45. Ms. Steele? It was your card."

CHAPTER SIX

"Hey, Colt! What happened to you?" Figmo glanced over his shoulder from his position at the urinal.

"I was defending a lady's honor," Jon muttered. He folded the wet, paper towel one more time and pressed it against his battered nose. He checked his face in the mirror over the lavatory. The scratch from Madison's keys had nearly healed. His nose was sore, but not broken. A little bruised and swollen. He'd seen worse in junior high school.

Then again, in the fifth grade, he hadn't been standing in front of Madison Steele. Damned OSI agent. Jon hadn't leapt to Madison's defense to impress her. His response had been automatic. How dare anyone make such a smart-ass remark to her! Yet it was Jon with the bloody nose. The bastard had baited him, and he'd ended up looking like a fool in front of Madison.

"So what does the other guy look like?" Figmo joked.

"About six inches taller and fifty pounds heavier."

Figmo zipped up and sauntered over to the lavatory next to Jon. "You missed the final briefing this morning. Why weren't you there? You were supposed to brief the bidders' performance risk, remember? Otto corkscrewed himself right up into the ceiling wanting to know where you were."

"Got tied up with the OSI." He dabbed at his nose again. Handcuffed, actually. But Figmo would have thought that was too cool.

"Come to think of it, where were you last night? Some babe on the side you haven't told me about? All this time Miri and me thought you were working late at The Facility. Where were you, man?"

"Out. What happened at the final briefing?"

Figmo sucked at his front teeth, snarled into the mirror, and then ran his tongue over the outer edge of his bite. "They gave us the go-ahead to let the Project Andromeda contract. Sarabeth's already sent up the congressional notification of the contract award. They said she can sign the contract tomorrow after four o'clock, five o'clock Eastern."

Jon slammed his fist against the tile wall. "That is so frigging unfair! Madison was the one who worked all this time to get Project Andromeda going. And Sarabeth steps in, takes over, and claims credit."

"Yeah, well. Them's the breaks. Nobody ever said life was fair. Just look at Roxie."

Jon nodded. Best he didn't tell Figmo about the OSI's visit to Madison's house. He'd spent the afternoon doing a little "research" that Otto wouldn't have approved of. Jon wadded the napkin into a ball and flung it at the overflowing trash barrel. It bounced off the lid and onto the floor. "I heard. What's the scoop on that?"

"Somebody locked Roxie in the safe after we left. I can't believe it. You know, I asked her out once, but she's got—I mean, had—some mystery dude on the side."

"Any idea who did it?"

"No. But there's talk."

"There's always talk."

"Maybe her ex-husband. Maybe this dude she was messing with. I figured he was married 'cause she never would talk about him much. But who knows? Hell, several of us thought maybe it was the mighty Madison Steele."

Jon scooped the errant paper ball off the floor and spiked it into the trash. Figmo didn't understand Madison. He came from a long line of male chauvinists who couldn't understand strong women if they read the how-to guide and paid for tutoring. And because he couldn't understand her, he couldn't appreciate her except in the purely physical sense. He resented women who could give orders. Ball-busters, he called them.

"Madison didn't have anything to do with Roxie's death, and you know it. I hope you stuck up for her."

Figmo shrugged. "She *was* kicked off Andromeda."

"That doesn't mean anything."

"Hmmm. Maybe not. You know, Colt, OSI's been all over kingdom come this morning asking questions about where people were last night. I went straight over to Belinda's house—it was her turn. And you, you got on your bike and rode off." He winked, his mouth twisting into a playful smile. "Come to think of it, where did you ride off to last night?"

"Don't worry about it. I have an alibi if I need one."

"Sly dog. Who was she? Come on, man. You can tell me. I won't tell too many people."

Figmo could be trustworthy, Jon knew, but only if told something was a secret and to keep his mouth shut. Idle speculation was most likely to turn into common knowledge. If Jon bit the bullet and confessed his crush on Madison to Figmo, his pal would give him hell in private but go to the wall for him in public. Or at least, if Figmo liked the woman, he would. Jon wasn't so sure how loyal Figmo would be where Madison was concerned.

"Tell me something," Jon said. "Is that secretary down in Security still sweet on you?"

Figmo made a face. "Too sweet. I went out with her twice, and she thinks we've got a relationship."

Yeah, Jon thought, and Figmo wasn't looking for anything more serious than a little exercise when he couldn't make it to the gym.

"Why?" Figmo pressed. "You want her?" Then his upper lip curled. "You're not saying it was her you were with!"

"No, nothing like that. I wanted her to do me a favor, and I thought she might be more willing to do you a favor than me." Jon had already visited the Security Office to get an access card from her and been yelled at for requesting one so close to the release of the new cards. He needed the card if he was to find out who in Building 13 hated Madison enough to frame her.

"What kind of favor?"

Jon dug into his pocket and brought out the access card Madison had had pinned to her jacket. Back at Madison's house, he had started to tell that OSI agent about the card, about his theory that someone had switched cards with her. Madison had shot him one of her subtle "shut-up" looks. Like a kicked puppy, he had obeyed. Madison liked to talk about how negotiations were always a matter of who had the power base, yet Jon had stood there with his bloody nose and bruises on his wrists and had known who had the upper hand in the investigation.

He thrust the access card at Figmo. "I need you to find out who this belongs to."

Figmo took the card, frowned at it, turned it over, frowned at it again. "Why?"

"Just do it, okay? Ask your friend in Security who it belongs to."

"What am I supposed to tell her? I'm not supposed to have anybody else's card."

Sheesh. "Make up something, all right?" Why did Figmo have to pick now to have a conscience? The self-proclaimed stud didn't usually have any problem lying to women.

Fifteen minutes later, Figmo emerged from the Security office with a smug grin. He joined Jon in front of a bulletin board sprinkled with "Roommate Wanted" and "Boat for Sale" notices.

"Well?"

"Hey, buddy, you owe me big time," Figmo joked. "She's invited herself over tonight. Now what am I supposed to do?"

"What you usually do. Give her something to laugh about. Now, what did you find out?"

"Un-huh. You first. Who were you with last night? Was she sweet? Or spicy?" He chuckled and slapped Jon on the back.

"Sweet. Definitely sweet." Jon smiled to himself, guessing what Figmo was thinking. "I got roped into baby-sitting a newborn all night long."

"What?"

"Yeah. Madison's niece. And let me tell you, Madison's sister-in-law is one scary chick. Precisely your type." Not that he had actually met the surly teenaged mother who had refused to come out of her room all night to care for her own baby. No harm in letting Figmo think more people had been in the room than Madison and the baby.

"You're pathetic. You know that, Colt?" Figmo kicked at the base of the block wall with his spit-shined black shoe. "Pathetic."

Yeah, he knew. After Special Agent Austin Wait had worked him over, Madison probably thought he was pathetic, too.

"So what did you find out?"

Figmo handed the access card back to him. "Depends. You gonna tell me what you're doing with *her* card?"

"Her who?"

"Celeste Oschlager."

"Celeste? Celeste." The name sounded familiar but it wasn't the prize he'd hoped for. He expected the name of somebody on the Project Andromeda team. A co-worker with a grudge. Someone with something to gain.

"Yeah. You remember. Celeste. That secretary in the contracting office."

Jon blinked. "Madison's secretary?"

"Yeah. Don't you remember? Itty-bitty thing, built like a brick house. Last time I saw her she was maybe a hundred pounds, and twenty of it was baby."

Ah, that did it. The pregnant one. He did remember. Jon slipped the access card back into his pocket. Celeste had given birth to twin boys at least a month ago. She wasn't sure if she wanted to come back from maternity leave, according to Madison. Gavin was holding her clerical position open while the new mom made up her mind. How long had Madison had Celeste's card?

"Thanks, Figmo."

"You wanna thank me? Go get laid, then come tell me all about it."

***

No way in hell was he going to let Madison take the fall for this mess. Roxie's murder, the stolen classified proposal, the switched access card, Madison's dead battery, someone locking her into her office. Any idiot could see the whole deal was squirrelly. It was a set-up of some sort.

But instead of anyone doing anything to help, they were all spending their time, wasting their energy, standing in the halls and around the water coolers, running their mouths about "did you hear?" and "do you think?" Once upon a time, Madison had accused him of being too young and idealistic. Maybe he was. But he still believed in standing behind people he cared about. He'd thought it didn't matter—and it didn't, as far as he was concerned. He knew Madison was innocent, but still, it hurt to hear people who knew better wonder out loud why she'd been ordered to stay home.

The truth was—as if the truth really mattered—she hadn't been ordered to stay home. Mr. Smith had taken her off Project Andromeda. Everyone knew that. But when Madison's sister-in-law had disappeared, leaving her alone to care for a baby too young for its eyes to focus properly, Madison had called her division chief to tell him she was taking some of the comp time he owed her. Lt. Col. Ballard had agreed without hesitation, which in itself was odd. Yet Jon knew Madison well enough to know that had she not been so caught up in the child abandoned to her care, she would have walked into Building 13 today with her head held high and her backbone straight.

Somebody had to stand up for her. She fought for everyone else, but when she needed someone to take a stand for her, they took the easy way out. They weren't willing to risk their professional reputations or be tainted by association with the accused.

Well, damn them all. Madison Steele was about the find out that a certain first lieutenant might be bloodied, but he wasn't beaten.

Jon rounded the corner to the suite of contracting offices, then stopped abruptly. Except for his visits to Madison's office, this place was unfamiliar territory. He'd heard tales of how, years ago, the people who worked in the contracting offices hated program managers. The program managers were technical types, usually engineers, sometimes business majors, sometimes scientists. Officially, they were responsible for pulling together all the resources necessary to manage certain projects. In the case of the Laboratory, those projects usually fell within the arena of research and development of non-nuclear munitions.

Program managers, according to Madison, were notorious for dealing under the table with defense contractors and forgetting to tell the contract administrators about their gentlemen's agreements which invariably ended in dispute when the program manager left the Government, got transferred, or had a simple change of heart. The long-standing feud between contracting and program management must have hit its peak six or seven years ago. Madison seemed irrationally attuned to it. The general public, however, never saw the pettiness or viciousness in the underbelly of the Federal workforce.

Jon paused at the clerk's station and tried to think of a lie for being there. He could say he'd come to see Sarabeth and Nell to see how things had gone at the final briefing, but they'd chastise him for not attending the real thing and then say they couldn't discuss it because Project Andromeda was still "source selection sensitive."

He could say he'd come to see Madison and then pretend he didn't know she was at home. Someone had switched Madison's and Celeste's access cards, even though Celeste was out on maternity leave and Madison swore her access card never left her jacket's lapel. It made sense, didn't it, that someone in the contracting office might have an idea how that had happened? It made even more sense that one of her snippy coworkers might be behind the switch and the theft of bio-warfare secrets. His wacko mother would have called it a "feeling" and lit a dark blue candle to aid her psychic awareness. Jon preferred to think of it as a hunch.

Today, the office was unusually quiet. Not surprising, he supposed, since one of their number had died mysteriously in the night. Roxie had been one of their more vibrant forces. Young, fun-loving, frequently joking except in the past few days. She had held more promise than most civil servants. She'd been with the Department of Defense for a little less than a year, all of which she'd spent in The Lab under Madison's tutelage. She had been a freshman in the COPPER CAP training program, which was a special three or four-year internship designed to lure the so-called best and brightest into Federal service. Like other COPPER CAPS, she'd probably signed documents that proved her high college grade point average, her viability for a security clearance, and a mobility agreement that would force her to move to wherever the training headquarters at Randolph Air Force Base needed a graduate of the program.

But she hadn't signed up to die in an air-tight walk-in safe. If Roxie hadn't been dead, Jon might have gone to her for answers. She'd seen someone at The Facility Monday night. She'd known. She'd left questions with no answers.

Why had she been hanging around outside The Facility so late? Why had she been terrified to admit it? She'd known the person who'd gone into The Facility after Madison had left.

Was that why she was dead? Because she knew something? And if it was, that meant she knew her own killer.

"Can I help you?" A woman he knew only as Raynene swaggered toward him and ground her knuckles into her wide hips. Not that he knew most of the people Madison worked with, but Raynene was predisposed to fluorescent stretch knits, two-inch long fingernails, and make-up applied with a trowel. Best he could tell, she'd never met a Twinkie she didn't like.

"I'm looking for Madison Steele," Jon said. He slanted a discreet glance at the sign-out board above Raynene's shoulder and hoped he'd recognize a name.

"What about?"

"Huh?" What was wrong with her? He wore a military uniform. It wasn't as if he'd wandered in off the street and asked to see Madison's office filled with the trade secrets and salary data of huge, international companies. Unlike many of the visitors to the contracting offices, lieutenants didn't require escorts.

"Why do you want to see Madison?"

"Excuse me?"

"What do you want to talk to her about?"

He couldn't point out that it was none of Raynene's business. The woman had already decided she had a right to know the subject of his visit.

"That's private," he grated out.

"Oh. You mean, it's personal?"

"No. I mean it's private."

"Which is it? It is personal or is it business?"

"Business." As far as Jon was concerned, clearing Madison's name counted as business.

"Then why don't you tell me what business you're here to see her on, and I'll see if she can see you today."

"Aw, Raynene, give the lad a break." Behind the clerk's station, an older man shoved a thick volume of bound regulations into a bookcase. He walked forward to give Raynene a bear hug. "Just tell the lad. Maddie's not here today."

Jon stepped around Raynene and extended a hand. "Jon Colter. You must be Mac. Madison's told me a lot about you."

"Good, I hope. Mac McNeely." He pumped Jon's outstretched hand with the enthusiasm of a politician. "Come on back to my cubicle and sit a spell."

An opportunity was an opportunity. Jon followed the older man down a narrow corridor lined with a hodge-podge of salvaged partitions alternating orange, purple, gray, and puke green. Probably one of the program offices had upgraded to top-of-the-line modular furniture and the contracting office had taken their cast-offs.

Mac's office was about the size of the bathroom Jon shared at home with Miri and Figmo. Mostly salvage-quality furniture, a small but coveted window, and a collage of grandchildren's photographs. Sad that a man of his age and probably twenty-five or thirty years of government service would end his career in this minuscule space.

"Have a seat, have a seat." Mac gestured at a guest chair at least as old as Jon and then Mac himself flopped down in a comfortable chair he'd probably brought from home.

Jon had heard a little about Mac, though not as much as he pretended. Jon could usually size up the career civil servants who had been with the Federal government since God was a baby. They'd all bought ties in their early years, and as the old-timers aged, their ties grew shorter. Or at least, it seemed that way. In actuality, their bellies grew rounder until their ties rested at a forty-five degree angle, leaving a wide expanse of shirt between the tip of the tie and the belt buckle. Mac's tie couldn't have been more than six inches long.

According to Madison, Mac blended his Scottish heritage with several decades in the Deep South, but his true nature was closer to that of a great, big teddy bear who talked too much. Way too much. Not a secret Mac wouldn't tell if he had the right motivation. Exactly the person Jon needed to see.

"You know, lad," Mac said, leaning forward and adjusting his tie, "you should learn not to be so obvious."

"Obvious about what?" That he'd decided to investigate every contracting officer, contract specialist, and procurement clerk in the building?

Something about Mac reminded Jon of his own grandfather. Back before his mom went off the deep end, Lydia had dreamed of the old man's death. After that, everything in Jon's childhood had fallen apart.

Mac chuckled. "You're being obvious about Maddie. Madison Steele."

"Um, what about Madison?"

"I can't blame you, lad. Not one bit."

"For what? Trying to prove she didn't steal anything classified?"

"No, lad. Though I don't blame you for that, either. You're as transparent as I've ever seen a man."

"Who? Me?" Jon squirmed in his chair. Whether the back wasn't firm enough or the seat was missing a spring, he couldn't sit still.

"You walk into a room with Maddie, and I can feel the temperature jump by ten degrees. And she doesn't even know you're alive, does she?"

Shit. Never mind the temperature of a room. No matter how discreet he tried to be, too many people watched Madison for errors in judgment. Not that they ever saw her do anything wrong, but when Jon came close to her, all they saw was a love-sick lieutenant. He had to learn to hide his feelings better. Like Madison.

"She's your contracting officer, right, Mac? You work for her."

Mac's chuckle faded quickly. He gave a curt nod.

"But you're old enough to be her father. Doesn't that bother you?"

"Damn, lad. Cut to the quick, why don't you?"

Jon shook off the surge of guilt. Mac had unintentionally embarrassed him, but Jon remembered his grandfather well enough to recall conversations about the young Turks taking his place when his glory days were spent.

"Don't you think sometimes, Mac, that you should be the one barking orders and Madison should be the one taking note?"

Mac stared out the window at some distant spot, losing himself in thought. He blinked to clear his vision, then looked back at Jon. His pale lips curved into a thin smile. "Sometimes. But if I have to answer to somebody, I'd rather it be Maddie than some old coot my age. Hell, son. I could have retired three years ago. But why would I want to stay at home and draw my pension? Who needs Geritol iron when I can get my daily dose of Steele?" He chuckled again.

Jon willed himself not to blush. A man didn't have to be sixty years old to appreciate Madison's slender body, long legs, or defiant tilt of her nose.

"I've heard the rumors in the hallway," Jon continued, zeroing in on what he'd come for. "I bet you have, too."

"Shoot, there's always a rumor in the halls. Always has been, always will be. Way of life around here."

"But these rumors are about Madison."

"That's what I mean. Always have been, always will be. The forerunners in any army are going to take the most arrows. She does things her way, and people can't take it. As long as I've worked for the government, I've never known anybody to get in trouble for not doing work. But do things differently, and you got alligators all over your ass."

"Yeah, that sums it up." Not that Jon had come for Mac's war stories or tidbits of advice from one generation to another, but at least they saw Madison in the same light. The original out-of-the-box thinker. Give her a knot to undo, and instead of untying it, she'd cut it in two and move on to the next challenge.

"I don't see why she puts up with people here," Mac continued. "She could go anywhere, be anything she wanted. People here are so blamed nosy. If I was her, I'd tell 'em to f-off, and I'd leave. Those idiots up in the Front Office won't even give her a door to her office."

Budget cuts, Jon had heard. "Madison said they had some trouble getting maintenance up here to fix it. I offered to hang her door myself."

"They're not going to get maintenance up here, and they got no intention of getting her a door."

Jon shook his head. Madison conducted telephone negotiations, sensitive acquisition planning, employee counseling, and even personal career advice for lieutenants from her doorless office. Fortunately, Madison's soft voice didn't carry well in intimate situations, but between the paper-thin walls and missing door, she couldn't keep anything secret. "A contracting officer needs a door."

"Dang right she does! But ol' Smitty Smith and them don't trust what she might do behind a closed door."

"Why not?" Jon asked in a conspiratorial whisper. He wanted to scream the question, but so far, all he'd heard was innuendo. Even from Madison herself. He knew from Roxie—God rest her soul—that certain subjects were taboo to Madison. He knew there had been a scandal with a dark-haired lieutenant and Madison had been at the heart of it all. Jon liked to think of himself as too honorable to ask anyone who knew her for the sordid details and too sensitive to ask Madison herself about things he knew still carried such deep hurt. But he wanted to know. How could he help her if he didn't know?

"She hasn't told you?"

Jon shook his head again and hoped his wide-eyed curiosity wouldn't betray what he needed to know and what Madison wouldn't tell him.

"If she hasn't told you, I reckon she doesn't want you to know."

"Has she told anybody, Mac? Did you ever think that maybe she can't bear to tell it herself?"

Mac sighed heavily and dug a pocket knife out of his desk drawer. He flicked open the sharp blade and proceeded to carve a point around the broken lead of a yellow pencil. "I imagine you're right, son. It would be a hard thing to tell. For her to tell. Hard thing to live down."

"Tell me. You know I'd never hurt her. Don't let me be the only one who doesn't know."

Mac brushed the pencil shavings from his pants leg and went back to carving a sharper point. "I remember it when it happened. Better than I remember what I ate for lunch today. Maddie was a trainee. A COPPER CAP. Or COPPER *Crap,* as us old fogies call 'em. She was working for a weak-kneed contracting officer on a missile program. The program manager was a lieutenant colonel, and it was a well-known fact he was in bed with the contractor. Under the table deals made all the time. The contracting officer had to have emergency surgery and ended up being out for a few months. They put Madison in charge."

Jon smiled at the thought. Madison in charge for the first time. To him, it seemed she'd always been in charge, probably from the time she could march her imaginary friends into kindergarten and set them to work.

"With the contracting officer out of the way," Mac continued, "Madison decided to do something about the kick-backs she thought her contracting officer had been papering over. It took her less than two weeks to gather all the evidence to turn the case over to the OSI. Course, she had a little help. There was this lad who worked under the lieutenant colonel. A lieutenant. Can't recall his name. What Madison couldn't find, he could. The two of them were a lethal combination. To the lite colonel, that is. As much to each other. Back then, Madison played by the rules. She came and talked to me about it. I was kind of her mentor in those days."

Mentor. Madison hadn't worked for Mac, but she'd been a trainee relying on his advice. How did the old timer feel about his former protege taking his place? Jealous? Would he frame Madison to get even?

Instead, Mac smiled. If he resented Madison, he didn't show it.

"I told her to take the evidence directly to the OSI. But she felt like she had to take it through channels, first. You know, in case she was wrong and might make her department look bad. I warned her what would happen, but like I said, she played by the rules back then. She said that protocol dictated she take it through her chain of command and let our division chief pass it to legal counsel and the OSI. That right there was her mistake."

Jon grimaced. "Let me guess. Her division chief was another gutless wonder." Not her current gutless wonder, but there were enough of them still in the Air Force. Too many of them were promoted to lieutenant colonel and knew they'd never graduate to colonel but were satisfied to retire to golf courses and beaches on the nearby Gulf of Mexico, provided they didn't rock the boat and get themselves transferred back to Dayton, Ohio or Los Angeles, California.

"More or less. Our division chief sat on her report for about two months. Meanwhile, he decided that if Madison didn't have anything better to do with her time than to do the OSI's job for them, she obviously didn't have enough work to do. So he piled it on. It was before appraisals were due. He set her up to fail. He gave her so much work, she couldn't possibly do it all. And if she couldn't get it done, she stood to get kicked out of the trainee program she was in. Back along that time, I wanted to spend my afternoons in the vegetable garden, so I'd come in here about dawn and there she'd be, nose to the grindstone. Late at night, too."

"Not so different from the way it is now," Jon mumbled.

"A lot different. That young man of hers, that lieutenant, he knew what they were trying to do to her. We all did. He was in here before work every morning and after hours at night, helping her out. Running photocopies, typing labels. I guess you could say things just developed between them. Madison's one smart cookie, but you have to remember, she is a young woman. A passionate young woman. That can sometimes make a woman not so smart."

Jon swallowed hard. He wanted to hear all about this lieutenant who had broken through Madison's walls. Who knows? Maybe back then, Madison didn't have walls. She still carried him so close to her heart. Damn it.

But he didn't want to hear it.

"You remind me of him."

Jon jerked his head up. "What?"

"He did things for her, too. Brought her a sandwich when she worked through lunch. That sort of stuff. Like you do."

"What happened to the evidence they gathered on that lieutenant colonel?" Jon asked, shifting the subject away from himself as fast as he could.

"'What evidence?' That's what her division chief said. 'What evidence?' He said he didn't remember them talking about it. Couldn't find the material either. I'd told Maddie to make a copy." He shook his head. The blade of his pocket knife whipped down the long edge of the pencil, shaving off needle-like splinters. "Back then, she followed the rules. Trusted people. You learn soon enough. You will, too, lad."

"We were talking about Madison."

"Everybody talks about Madison. She didn't let them break her down. No matter how many hours she put in. She always got the work done. Night after night, her young man showed up to help her. After a few weeks of that, seemed like they were inseparable. You could see something in Maddie's eyes. I don't know if it was gratitude or lust, but you could tell she wanted to be with him. I wasn't the only one who noticed. Other people did, too."

Jon watched the knife blade sliver off small chunks of wood. Mac hardly noticed. He stared out the window instead. Jon bit his lip to keep from stilling the man's hands. The old guy would cut himself if he weren't careful.

"Maddie got called into the Front Office. Smith wanted to know if something was going on between her and that lieutenant. To tell you the God's honest truth, I don't think there was anything going on at the time. Smitty had heard about how corrupt that program office was. With Madison being so close to the lieutenant colonel's right hand man, that had Smitty speculating that Maddie was as dirty as the rest of them."

Hadn't Madison warned him that the truth didn't matter? Appearances. Perception was as good as reality.

"Mr. Smith didn't know about Madison's investigation and what she was doing with that, um, lieutenant?"

"Nope. Our division chief got his appraisal from the lieutenant colonel's boss. Spineless jackass." He sliced through to the pencil's core. The pointed end snapped into the air and landed at Jon's feet. "Word got out those two kids were spending so much time together in Maddie's office at night. Poor kid didn't have any social life. Only lad she saw at all was the one who was helping her every night. Kinda natural, I think, that she should fall in love with him. Him being the most supportive person in her life back then. And then they got caught and all hell broke loose."

Jon's stomach twisted itself into knots. He didn't really want to know how they got caught, did he? Or what they got caught at.

"Yep. Our division chief, that lieutenant colonel, and Smith. The three of them stormed into Maddie's office late at night. I swear they'd been waiting for it to happen. Lad got caught with his pants down. Literally."

Jon didn't want to hear this. God, he didn't want to hear this. In his heart, he knew—*he knew*—Madison had had lovers in the past. He wasn't so naive as to think no man had ever touched her heart or body. The thought of her with another man. What did he look like? Was he taller than Jon? Was he tender? Did he ever get rough with her? Make her beg? And what was she willing to do for him?

"So now you know," Mac said. He folded the blade back into the pocket knife, then bent to retrieve the severed half of the pencil.

Jon bowed his head and plowed his fingers through his hair. "Yeah."

"You won't tell her I told you, will you?"

"I won't tell her I know." Jon expelled a long breath and leaned back in the rickety chair. "Whatever happened to the lieutenant colonel?" Maybe he was a candidate for whoever was putting Madison through this hell.

"Him? Oh, he got promoted to colonel and transferred to Dayton to Wright-Patterson Air Force Base. Probably retired by now."

"And her division chief? The one who covered up everything?"

"He got promoted, too. Last I heard, he was at the Pentagon playing flunky to the four-star generals. And her lieutenant got sent to another base in less than a week. Rejavik, Iceland, I think." Mac shook his head. "I could have killed them for what they did to Maddie. She's the gutsiest little girl I've ever known and the one of the most beautiful women."

Why hadn't Jon seen it before? The way Mac's eyes twinkled when he talked about Madison. He could have retired years ago, but he stayed on to be near Madison, a woman young enough to be his daughter. Forget the money. Mac was in love with Madison.

"Mac, you remember how they pinned everything on Madison and made her look dirty? I'm afraid they're going to do it again unless I can stop them. I've got to find out who really stole that proposal from the facility and who killed Roxie."

Mac shook his head. "I can't believe that little girl's dead. One of my girls is dead and the other's in a whole mess of trouble. I'll help you anyway I can, lad, but I don't have any idea how."

Jon shrugged and pretended not the notice the tear Mac wiped away. "Keep your eyes open. We both know Madison didn't steal anything. Roxie knew, too."

Suddenly, Mac seemed very old. The lines in his face burrowed deeper than before. His wrinkled pale hands trembled as he reached to fidget with a government-issue fountain pen that no doubt could be whittled to shreds if Mac was of a mind to. According to Madison, Mac was never without a joke or a hug. Yet today, he was as solemn as the rest of the office. Solemn, drained, and numb.

Jon knew the feeling. He had liked Roxie, too. Her death would hit him soon enough, but for now the idea that someone had purposely locked her inside a walk-in safe to silence her seemed unreal.

"If those investigators had half a brain, they'd realize it couldn't be Maddie. They don't know her the way we do, but any thinking person can see Maddie wouldn't kill the one person who could clear her. Roxie knew who did it."

"She told you?"

"Not exactly." Mac glanced up sheepishly. "Roxie came tearing in here yesterday afternoon like a bat out of Hades. Said she had to see Gavin, but he wasn't in. She left him a note in the seat of his chair." He cleared his throat. "I peeked."

"And?" This was no time to pass judgment.

"It said she had to see him right away. That she knew who stole the files and it wasn't Maddie."

"What did Gavin—I mean, Lt. Col. Ballard—say about the note?"

"Nothing."

"Not a word? This is significant. Don't you think?"

"Yep. But I'm still around because I learned a long time ago not to question politics."

Jon bolted to his feet. Somebody had to do something. Sitting on your butt for thirty years and avoiding speaking your mind might mean keeping your job, but that wasn't a job worth having. "You don't question politics, but I do. I'm going to Lt. Col. Ballard about this!"

"He's not in. Hasn't been in since early. He's taking this thing with Roxie pretty hard." Mac paused, his huge Adam's apple bobbing up and down. "We all are."

Jon kicked at the base of the partition. He caught his bottom lip between his teeth and concentrated hard. Gavin Ballad was a typical middle manager and third-rate human being. As long as his stats looked great, he'd work his people into the ground. He was more interested in briefing beefed-up lead-times and workload miracles than in giving his employees the resources they needed to do the job. Hell, half the time they didn't even have paper for their one lousy laser printer. But if he'd gotten Roxie's message, surely he would have turned it in to the OSI.

Unless he was the one behind the plot to ruin Madison.

"Mac, are you sure he got the note?"

Mac twisted his jaw to one side, then the other, his brow furrowed deep in thought. "I went in later to get him to sign a leave slip—you know how it is at my age when I've got plenty of use-or-lose leave—but I don't remember." He hesitated, thinking back. "At my age, I can't be sure."

"Could anybody else have, um, peeked at that note?"

"Anybody in the office. Gavin has an open door policy."

If Gavin Ballard knew Roxie's message cleared Madison of any suspicions, why hadn't he said anything to the OSI? Either he never got the note or he was somehow involved in what looked more and more like a conspiracy against Madison.

"They found your note, though," Mac informed him.

"My note?" Jon wasn't a note-sending kind of guy. If someone had found a note he'd written, then it had to be—argh!

"Yep. They thought it was yours."

Maybe it was something completely innocent. Maybe somebody else had written her a note. "What note?"

Mac smiled. "'Where ARE you? Need to see you. Call me.'"

Crap. Jon had left the note in plain sight on her desk yesterday. And he'd been worried that Madison wouldn't recognize his handwriting.

"Who's 'they'? Who found my note?"

"Sarabeth. She found it under Maddie's computer keyboard."

"What's Sarabeth doing nosing around Madison's office?" He'd ask Sarabeth that same question as soon he found her and wrung her neck.

"Sarabeth's in charge of Project Andromeda now, you know. She's also our office's security monitor. One of her extra duties. After her briefing this morning, Security told her to tear Madison's office apart looking for the classified stuff that's missing."

"That's-that's crazy." But very possible. The Security office was run by a different group from the OSI, and not nearly as thorough in his humble opinion.

"Somebody called Security this morning and told them Maddie could hide all sorts of documents in plain sight in her office. That's what Sarabeth told me they said."

In plain sight. Madison's office had never conformed to the clean desk policy. She knew where everything was, even if nobody else did. She kept reams of paperwork stacked on her desk, her floor, on tops of file cabinets. According to one story he'd heard, her office was mistakenly identified as having been damaged back when Hurricane Opal ripped through Northwest Florida in '95. But if she wanted to hide classified information in her office, she could do so without any worry of it being found.

The thought struck him like a hammer.

Or someone else could hide classified without her finding it for weeks!

Jon pivoted and ran for the doorless room on the far side of the suite of offices. He stopped short of the door frame and pumped his fists. Capt. Jarvis Barton stood in the hallway outside Madison's office and patiently examined the back of the Arnold Schwartzenegger *Terminator* poster that Madison had had thumbtacked to her crumbling cork wall. Jarvis was supposed to be Madison's immediate supervisor, but he was a weakling. Were all the men Madison worked with wimps or did they just seem that away compared to her?

"Can I help you?" Jarvis asked, not looking up.

"I doubt it," Jon grumbled. Stepping around the fluorescent orange traffic cone which indicated classified work inside the room, he peered inside Madison's office. Most of the stacks of paper had been removed. Nell—he knew it was Nell because of her strong Cherokee features—sat on the floor, sifting through one of the stacks.

"Found another one," Nell said without looking up. She picked a page with *SECRET* stamped across the top and laid it on a small pile of similar pages.

The other occupant of the small office had to be Sarabeth, the contracting officer who'd taken over Project Andromeda. Maybe thirty-two, Sarabeth dressed and carried herself like a much older woman. Her face was still unlined, yet she looked downright matronly. Her blonde hair had been sprayed into a helmet, her white pantyhose gave her plump legs a deathly pallor, and she would probably leap out the window if she broke a fingernail. About as opposite of Madison Steele as possible. The woman didn't even glance up. She was too intent on the note she'd found taped to the back of picture frame that held Madison's certificate of appointment as a contracting officer.

"Listen to this, will you?" Sarabeth cleared her throat. "'The future is bright. Never hesitate to walk through the door—wonderful things and people and experiences may be on the other side. I love you. Tim.'" Sarabeth glanced up to say something to Jarvis, then saw Jon and snapped her jaw shut. "Hello, Lt. Colter," she said sweetly, eyeing his name tag to jog her memory. "We missed you at the final briefing this morning. You'll be pleased to know the general gave us the go-ahead on Project Andromeda. We should have it awarded within hours."

He barely heard her. All he could think of was the mess on Madison's floor and how they were going through personal tidbits she'd hidden around her office to remind her of happier times. If she knew how they were invading her privacy, the OSI would be arresting her for murder, and not Roxie's.

"You stupid bitch," Jon erupted. He couldn't control his voice. He could barely control his fists. "How could you call yourself her friend and then fuck with her like this!"

"Hey, you're out of line," Jarvis said from behind him but did nothing.

Sarabeth's chin dropped. She stared back at Jon, big teardrops welling in her eyes and then spilling down her cheeks. Another gutless wonder in the making. "Lt. Colter, I don't approve of that kind of language."

"And I don't approve of what you're doing to Madison!" He jerked the picture frame out of her hand, then tore off the note and stuffed it into his hip pocket. "You know she didn't steal anything. Are you part of this frame-up, too? Are you jealous of her? Is that it?"

"I know you don't want to believe she stole anything," Sarabeth began, "but we've found nineteen pages of a classified proposal in her things. I think maybe she fooled you, too."

"No, Sarabeth, you're the fool—"

"Shut up," a familiar voice ordered. "Just shut up."

The crook of an elbow clipped him under the jaw. Jon fell backward, struggling against the larger arms, struggling for air. He heard the picture frame crash to the floor. The security cone toppled and rolled in a semi-circle. Jon's assailant half-dragged, half-carried him into a nearby office and flung him inside. Jon caught the corner of the executive style desk to keep from sailing across the room. Even before he turned to fight, Jon knew he'd find Special Agent Austin Wait daring him to pounce.

"Sit!" The OSI agent slammed the door behind him. "I said, sit down!"

Heart pounding in his chest, blood racing through his temples, Jon considered it a moment. Austin Wait had handcuffs and a gun. All Jon had was a temper and a protective streak. Defeated, he flopped into the managerial chair behind Jarvis' desk.

"Good boy." Wait stood over him, equally winded. His eyes narrowed in anger. "I get the impression you don't like me. Is that a fair assessment?"

"I'd say it's right on the money."

"For what it's worth, I don't like you either. You're too young, too hot-tempered, and too stupid for your own good. For Madison Steele's own good, too."

"What would you know about Madison's own good? You're too goddamned lazy to go after the real thief. You're like everybody else—too willing to sacrifice her to keep from having to do any work."

"And what are you doing to help her? Sacrificing yourself by challenging authority?"

Jon shrugged. He had always fought authority, and authority had always won.

"You really want to help your girlfriend?"

"She's not my girlfriend."

Wait rolled his eyes. "If you say so. Would you do something for her?"

"Anything." He meant it. Jon relaxed into the chair. He'd do anything for Madison. As long as he didn't lose her.

"Then stay out of the investigation."

"But you're missing things," Jon protested. His voice came out in a squeak. "Important things."

"We haven't missed anything."

"Roxie left a note for Lt. Col. Ballard saying she knew who broke into The Facility and that it wasn't Madison. Did you know about that?"

Wait didn't answer.

"See? I told you you were missing important stuff."

"Give us a little credit, Colter. If we weren't so thorough, I swear I wouldn't have left your girlfriend sitting at home rocking a baby. She'd be in custody."

"I don't get it." Did Wait believe in Madison? And if he did, why was he letting everyone treat her like a criminal?

"You're not supposed to get it. You're supposed to stay out of it and let me do my job."

Jon shook his head emphatically. "You expect me to walk away while you let them ruin her reputation. Un-huh. I'll go to Congress. I'll go to the media. I'll tell them everything."

"Listen." Wait leaned across the desk and beckoned Jon closer. "This security breach is bigger than you. It's bigger than me. It's bigger than Madison Steele's career. Even bigger than a dead COPPER CAP."

Jon flinched. "I don't trust you."

"No? Then you go home tonight and turn your TV on to CNN. Check the past few weeks' worth of newspapers. You'll see some real interesting connections if you're willing to look for them."

"Yeah? Like what?"

"A daycare center near the Air Force's Phillips Lab reported a flesh-eating virus two weeks ago. Nearly every parent who works in the lab missed several days last week because the moms and dads were too terrified to leave their kids in any daycare center anywhere."

Jon had heard about it from a couple of secretaries in his office, but he didn't have kids in daycare so it hadn't made that much of an impression on him. "So? What's that got to do with Madison?"

"So panic paralyzed a significant percentage of Lab employees that week. Their level of output went way down."

Jon shrugged. He still didn't see what the daycare situation in Albuquerque had to do with Madison.

"Near the Navy's facilities at China Lake, three people died last week from eating hamburger meat infected with e.coli bacteria. Significant absenteeism this week."

"Bad things happen everywhere. Look at the e.coli epidemic in Japan."

"Yeah, look at it. Too many bad things are happening these days, Colter. Turn on the TV when you get home tonight. You'll see a news story that focuses on how the buildings we work in are 'sick.' They'll miss the real point. Did you know that in the past five days, ten romance novel editors in one Manhattan building have died? Sudden, hopeless, mysterious illnesses."

"Now you've really lost me. The connection between an Air Force laboratory and China Lake, I understood. They both employ military and civil service workers. For the Department of Defense."

Wait leaned forward, his voice dropping to a whisper. "Those editors worked on the floor below a tiny Manhattan firm involved in one of the Pentagon's top secret projects. Their water cooler was contaminated—after the jug had been opened." He paused for effect. "The autopsies found traces of cloristium botulinum A toxin."

Impossible. Jon went limp.

"I see you made the connection. When your focus is on staying alive and keeping your kids healthy, you don't pay much attention to what's going on at work. It's a quick way to paralyze the enemy."

Jon nodded. He'd watched a newborn baby paralyze Madison's get-out-of-my-way-or-be-run-over way of conducting business. Were it not for an abandoned baby, she'd be knocking heads left and right.

"We believe it's a terrorist group called The Sleeping Dogs. And right now," Wait said, "they're only experimenting."

Botulism, e.coli, flesh-eating bacteria? What next? Anthrax? Plague? Ebola? Marburg? Dengue fever? Seemingly random occurrences, but not random at all.

"Germ warfare terrorists," Jon whispered back. "Think what would happen if they released a BW cloud over the Olympic Games or the Super Bowl or Disneyworld. Forget pipe bombs. Deadlier than popping a nuke."

"You're more familiar with the technology than I am. Can this stuff wipe out whole cities? Colter?"

"Whole cities and more. Remember the Black Plague? Killed two-thirds of the population? In some places, it wiped out entire cities. Ever read about the plague of 1665 and what it did to London? God." Jon squeezed his eyes shut. He'd never looked for clarity, but now he couldn't stop it. Answers flashed through his brain faster than he could accept them. Images from history or imagination, he couldn't tell. "Nostradamus, the Mayans, the Bible, ancient prophecies. The unleashing of plagues. That's the only way the prophets knew to describe germ warfare."

Wait laid a hand on Jon's shoulder. "Sit down, Colter. You don't look so good."

Jon hadn't realized he was standing.

He had to get to a phone.

He had to talk to his mother.

CHAPTER SEVEN

Finally, it was sinking in.

Not Roxie's death. That would come later.

At first, Madison had been indignant. The very idea of someone stealing classified secrets on her watch! Then she'd been pissed. From the looks of it, she was being framed for murder and treason. Her. The little-known protector of the free world.

"I'm scared," she admitted to Jon over the telephone. Terrified. Almost two days had passed since the break-in at The Facility. The winning Project Andromeda proposal might have prevented the widespread, agonizing deaths of millions of people, but by now the proposal was likely in the hands of the Iraqis. The enemy would know the U.S.'s best defenses long before biologists and scientists completed their work.

"Yeah. Me, too."

Madison hugged Jolene's baby against her chest and rocked a little harder. Her neck ached from holding the portable phone between her ear and shoulder.

"God, Jon. This is more than a major setback. What if the U.S. gets caught up in another war—one with something deadlier than nukes—one with chemical and biological weapons? What if it happens before the Project Andromeda group comes up with a new counteragent to the deadly micro-organisms?"

The child wouldn't stand a chance. As if anyone would.

The list of deadly germs studied, grown, and manipulated in Iraq's secret underground fermentation laboratories had stretched on for three or four pages. Some of the germs bore familiar names, though the CIA intelligence she'd perused contained the fancier terminology: bacillus anthracis, salmonella typhi, eschericia coli, clostridium tetani, clostridium botulinum type A, plague bacillus, clostridium perfingens, francisella tularensis.

Then there were the strains of microorganisms she'd never heard of. Dozens of them. All deadly. All in need of a Project Andromeda to render them ineffective from the moment of human contact. Or before.

"Madison, we need to talk."

"Then get over here. You know there's only so much I can say over an un-secure line." She couldn't talk about classified, and she wouldn't talk around it. Listening devices were surprisingly accurate and cheap and readily available through ordinary mail-order catalogs. Any run-of-the-mill spy or defense contractor could be monitoring her conversations. Not to mention the OSI.

"No," Jon persisted. "I need to talk about something else."

"What else is there?" Didn't he get it? They were talking about the existence of human life on Planet Earth. "This is important. We're in real danger. The whole world is. Even people not involved in these asinine disputes between different countries."

Not that the average American knew it. Or wanted to know it.

During the Persian Gulf War, the general public had ooh-ed and ah-ed over the surgical strikes of the Patriot missiles and the GBU-28 Bunker Busters. Americans sat glued to their television sets while the media greeted U.S. soldiers' stealth invasions with lights, cameras, and less sense than a dead pig in sunshine. The viewing public later witnessed reporters' obvious panic at the sound of chemical warfare warning sirens.

Idiot journalists. They couldn't seem to get their gas masks on fast enough. Nothing like the threat of death up close and personal to make them forget about winning awards and making careers.

The folks back home wrenched their hands over the threat of chemical weapons, but at least chemicals could be detected in time for the soldiers—and reporters—to grab their masks and pray. Real-time detection and advance warning systems did not yet exist for biological weapons. If anyone had bothered to explain that to the news crews, the Gulf War would certainly have received less coverage.

"Stupid media."

"What? You're not making sense, Madison."

She was tired, so tired. Couldn't he understand? She jerked her head up and out of the pull of sleep.

"You're not thinking of going to the media?" Jon asked.

"Never. Lord knows, they blow minor news out of proportion and gloss over the important stuff. Just look at the Gulf War. The reporters were more interested in our soldiers' spiffy desert-camo uniforms and the price of oil than in what was really in Iraq."

"I've been to Iraq. Been to Babylon."

"Yeah, that would have been a real story. But the journalists missed it. Our own troops didn't know what was over there." Madison squeezed her eyes shut and rocked almost hard enough to tip over. What was it Jon had said? That he'd been to Babylon? "When you went with the

U.N. to Iraq, did you have any shots?"

"Some. The standard stuff."

"Anything out of the ordinary?"

The strongest warnings for Desert Storm soldiers had been in the form of experimental, or "investigational," unlicensed vaccines. But how many soldiers really understood the implications? The U.S. Secretary of Defense had quickly approved a biological defense program to inoculate for anthrax and botulinum toxin. The program had included half a million individually packaged antibiotics, bulk antibiotics for one million, botulinum antitoxin for thirty-five hundred, anthrax vaccine for a hundred thousand, and botulinum toxin vaccine for another thirty-five thousand.

"No," Jon answered wearily. "Nothing unusual. Madison, I need to ask you something."

"Nothing unusual. Good. Good." Jon was safe. For now. She'd think of some way to keep him off any upcoming United Nations invitations to inspect Iraq's underground chem and bio bunkers. He was still young enough to believe in his own immortality. Still young enough to believe everything he was ordered to believe.

During the Gulf War, soldiers had been given a sugar-coated explanation of the drugs they were offered. Antibiotics, given in time, could counteract anthrax, but botulism required repeated vaccinations and if a soldier was indeed exposed to the botulinum toxin, he or she might be given the antitoxin but likely with little success. Soldiers were asked to sign voluntarily that they had read the information about the botulinum vaccine and were willing to try it, but the notice sounded like any other Government document—written in third person and completely benign. With the benefit of hindsight, Madison had reread the explanation given to soldiers and found herself cursing. Not that anyone had lied. Every word was the truth. Especially if she read between the lines.

The explanation had blandly mentioned that soldiers were at risk of exposure to botulism. Gee. How many people did the average soldier know who'd actually died of botulism? Botulism. How bad could that be? Somewhere between chicken pox and mumps? Until Madison read the reports, she'd always thought of botulism as something you wouldn't get as long as you washed your hands after peeing or didn't eat deviled eggs and potato salad left out too long at family reunions. Something you could be careful of and not really worry about.

"Promise me something, Jon."

"Anything."

"You'll always question things done supposedly for your own good."

"Okay," he drawled. "Any particular reason?"

Poor kid didn't understand. How could he? He'd been a high school kid during the Gulf War. Probably tasting beer for the first time. Not so much younger than the boys who headed for Saudi and Kuwait. And all of them so willing to take the word of authority.

The vaccine notice had gone on to list a few of the symptoms of botulism but led the reader to believe the likelihood of severe paralysis and death could be avoided, thanks to this wonderful, experimental vaccine. Buried in the text was a startling bit of truth: treatment after exposure was "primarily supportive" and soldiers would do best to rely on their chemical protective masks and over garments. Yeah, the mere two suits of chem gear that couldn't be used twice. The notice should have been framed and honored as the sleekest bureaucratic bullshit she'd ever seen.

"Madison?"

She barely heard Jon's voice. Clenching the phone to her ear, she stared ahead. She had to do something. She was in deep. The whole world was.

Forget the chemical attacks. Some of the biological weapons were ten thousand times more deadly than the nerve agents the panicking reporters ranted about. Iraq had filled forty warheads with anthrax, botulinum toxin, and maybe other germs and hidden them, buried them in the ground. Some germs could be released in the water or food supplies of soldiers' encampments or, for that matter, civilian populations. Others were best spread through spray devices, aerosol generators, or lobbing them in the general direction of the enemy army.

On the battlefield, air samples could be taken routinely to monitor the protein levels of microbial cells in the environment, but by the time the testing was done at a field laboratory and the soldiers notified three or more hours later, what was the point? Unlike warning alarms for chemical attacks, biological weapons couldn't be detected with field equipment. No country in the world possessed the capability.

Without Project Andromeda, no country would.

The baby in her arms let out a shriek. Madison startled, then shushed the infant. She hadn't realized how tightly she had been hugging the little thing to her chest. Madison rocked harder, even after the baby fell asleep again.

"Madison? Madison, are you all right?"

"I have to find an answer. I've always been good at solutions. The best."

But now, with a tiny baby in her arms, she was as helpless as the child. What could she do to protect her daughter?

And how could she save the baby in her arms if the threat became real?

Anthrax wasn't immediate. Exposure to anthrax usually meant breathing in anthrax spores. One to six days later, a mild fever and fatigue. Hell, that was most days after a grueling day at work. Next, after the fever and fatigue, a temporary recovery. Then sudden respiratory distress, followed by death in less than a day. If caught in time, anthrax could be treated with antibiotics.

Botulinum toxin was a different story. Symptoms began six to twelve hours after inhalation. Dizziness, progressive muscular weakness, difficulty swallowing and talking, death. By the time the symptoms developed, the patient was already dying.

"We'll figure something out," Jon promised over the crackling line.

"Don't the hate-mongers understand? They have to stop playing around with creating and manipulating diseases. Once Pandora's box is open, then what? They can't keep this stuff penned up. Other countries will get access to it. Nut cases who don't mind blowing up Federal buildings and daycare centers—they'll love this stuff. Right now, the only lock to Pandora's box is Project Andromeda, and it's probably circled the globe a dozen times since Monday night."

"Look, I'm going to finish up here and come right over. You haven't had enough sleep, have you?"

"Hmmm. I had forgotten about napping when the baby naps. I'm tired." Her mind flitted out of control. She couldn't focus. All the terrible possibilities swirled in her brain.

"I'll come over, and you can get some sleep, okay?"

"I don't have time to sleep. Time enough to sleep in the grave."

"And that's exactly where you'll sleeping if you don't start taking care of yourself."

Poor Jon. He sounded so worried. Sweet of him.

"There are more important things than taking care of myself. It's my fault Project Andromeda's been compromised. I'm responsible for seeing the project through, for protecting its secrets." For saving the world as she knew it. Her daddy had been right about her having a God complex. Madison only hoped she wouldn't have to sacrifice her own child to save mankind.

"Madison, it's not your fault."

"It's my responsibility."

"Have you thought of anybody who could have done it? Maybe I can help you come up with a few suggestions when I get there. I gotta go. Okay?"

"Okay." She punched the off button and eased out of the rocker long enough to slip the phone back into its cradle. She was so tired, so sleepy. But if she slept, she'd only feel guilty. She should have been working or at least figuring out who had stolen her card.

Snuggling the baby against her, Madison rocked hard. Jon could be on her doorstep in another ten minutes, but she didn't want to wait that long. If patience was a virtue, she'd been damned for years. Someone had stolen Project Andromeda from under her nose. Maybe under her nose was the best place to look for the culprit.

"Okay. So who had access?" she whispered to the baby. Babies liked to hear soothing voices, even when they couldn't understand the words.

If she wanted the baby girl to sleep all night, Madison could always read to her from the Federal Acquisition Regulations. That would put Madison to sleep real fast. But for now, talking out loud, softly, kept the child asleep and Madison awake.

She nodded to herself, determined to clear her head long enough to think through the problem logically despite her lack of sleep. "Let's see. The thief had my access card—not an easy thing to snatch—plus knowledge of The Facility. The thief knew the combination to a cipher-locked room and the combination to the safe. Those combinations are even harder to steal than my access card." On the other hand, almost every safe combination she'd ever seen was 80-40-80 or 50-25-50 or something equally predictable. In general, Government employees had no sense of creativity.

Hundreds of people had access cards, which were needed to gain entrance to a handful of technical and contracting buildings on base. The thief could have had his or her own card. Since possession of an access card was the only way into The Facility, the thief had had to use somebody else's card, one that wouldn't give him away. But why Madison? Plenty of engineers and scientists could be counted on to be careless with their cards, lending them to their favorite contractors' local reps or leaving the cards atop the urinals while they tended to personal business. Someone had gone to a lot of trouble to steal a contracting officer's card.

Not everyone had access to the cipher-locked room. Maybe twenty people on the Project Andromeda source selection team. Madison believed in small teams. Fewer people to argue and get wound down in bureaucratic inertia. Her source selections always broke records, each one faster than the last. Other than her team, only a handful of policy review people, legal counsel, and small business advocates knew the combination to the evaluation room. Plus Eugene Krueger, who ran The Facility.

"Okay," she told the baby, "so we've narrowed it down to thirty people. Including myself and Mr. Smith."

But the combination to the safe, that was the distinguishing factor. The culprit had to know it. Unless he was a professional safecracker. Breaking into a secure building and playing with possible combinations until the safe opened was too risky.

Madison, of course, had the combination. As a contracting officer, she had to have it. Ultimately, she held the responsibility for every piece of classified that came into their evaluation room. Technically, specific people named in the source selection planning documents were in charge of security matters. Morally, everyone was responsible for security matters. But when it counted most, when something went wrong, the techies always pointed at the contracting officer. The planning documents were ignored, the moral obligations forgotten, and the contracting officer was stripped of her appraisal rating and made to teach the standard security briefing to the population of The Lab at the next Commander's Call.

Just in case, Madison had given the safe combinations to Roxie. Trainees weren't normally afforded that privilege, but Roxie was good, and Madison had the right to give the combination to her contract specialist, or "buyer" as they were affectionately called. Having Roxie open the safe in the mornings was a small thing, but it saved time in the long run. Besides, more often than not, Gavin forgot the combinations, and Madison wasn't always available to tell him.

Gavin, the Gutless Wonder, had been told the combinations at least twenty times and still couldn't remember them. As the contracting division chief, he assumed responsibility for Madison's efforts—unless something went wrong—and liked to be on the periphery of the action. As long as he could pop in and look over documents, suggesting a comma here and a capital letter there, he felt useful and stayed out of Madison's way. Besides, she ignored all his suggestions.

Eugene Krueger knew the combination, too. No choice there. Eugene took care of keying the new safe combinations and instructing any source selection team in The Facility on how to create fancy charts for their final briefings. Eugene had never run a source selection on his own, though his attitude didn't betray him. He clearly enjoyed the power of his position, the tangling with defensive contracting officers, and the ritual of making popcorn every afternoon at 2:00 p.m. sharp. Madison couldn't conceive of him as a spy. The man simply didn't have enough imagination to lead a secret life.

Otto Trollinger was the only technical type to know the combination. Roxie had called him "the Troll," though never to his face. Personality-wise, Otto was a good candidate for a thief. Lt. Miri Spinalli had offered a time-saving suggestion in Madison's and Otto's presence. Within two days, Otto had claimed credit for his subordinate's idea and been awarded a few hundred bucks in the total quality incentive program. Par for the course, according to Jon. Otto made a habit of filing patents in his own name, whenever his lieutenants brought him a new idea.

If anything went wrong, Otto would gleefully blame someone in the contracting office. He didn't care whom he sacrificed as long as his upcoming promotion wasn't in any danger. Yes, he could have been the thief except for one thing: as program manager for Project Andromeda, Otto Trollinger had more to lose, career-wise, than anyone else. He'd invested fifteen years of his life in the biowarfare technology. If the need for the technology faded, he could be transferred to another job, outside his area of expertise, where he would find himself a good fifteen years behind his colleagues. And then his chances of promotion, too, would fade away.

That left one person who knew the safe combination: Lynette. Lynette Thomas had worked for Madison for over two years, but she never seemed to make it into the office anymore. When Lynette wasn't in the office, invariably she had an excuse from a local psychiatrist. Insomnia. Depression. Stress. When she did come to work, she spent her eight hours whining about her workload. Lynette wanted the important assignments, yet when Madison fought to get her the programs she wanted to work on, Lynette complained that they were too hard, too stressful, too...upsetting. On the first day of the Project Andromeda source selection, Lynette had startled everyone by going into a screaming, conniption fit and slinging classified files at the walls. The doctor sent a note back later, declaring Lynette unfit for such stressful work for the next ninety days, claiming worker's compensation benefits of 100% pay, and sending the woman to her bed for a good rest and three months of tabloid TV.

What could Madison say? The contracting career field was stressful, all right, even for people who seldom did much work. With a few exceptions, everyone Madison knew worked overtime, unpaid, and still had to put up with asinine questions about $600 hammers from morons who thought you could buy jet-repairing tools from your local hardware store or that a twenty million dollar airplane ought to be held together with two-cent screws from the lowest bidder. Still, her job was more demanding than most, and with the contract specialist on such a major program as Project Andromeda on "stress leave," Madison's own workload had turned twice as stressful. Thank God, she'd had Roxie to fill in the gaps and help keep the source selection on schedule, because Lynette wasn't of much use to anybody and somebody had to pick up the pieces and ignore the stress when co-workers bailed out, and that someone was Madison.

"I doubt it was Lynette," she murmured, smoothing down the baby's curls. "Last time I saw her, she claimed walking into Building 13 gave her anxiety attacks. No, if she wants to get her own whiny little way, she'll stay as far away as possible from anything vaguely resembling work."

This wasn't working. Damn it. She was good at solving problems. Well, everyone's but her own.

None of the handful of people who had the safe combinations seemed likely candidates for intrigue. Of the others who had been in and out of the evaluation room, the young engineers and scientists were pawns in Otto's office. The full-bird colonel in charge of The Lab, Col. Kildee, seemed angrier that someone had screwed up his 458 days without a security incident than he was upset that Project Andromeda may have been compromised. Mr. Smith, who had been a dragon before he made his last promotion and allowed politics to dictate his position on truth and appearances, spent his concern on keeping Col. Kildee happy without giving up any job slots and at the same time gently requesting computer upgrades for Madison's office so they could work with something a little faster than their slow-as-molasses-in-wintertime 386-processor computers.

Her contracting coworkers who weren't on the Project Andromeda team were unlikely suspects, she supposed. Still, they bore consideration. Mac was a crusty old teddy bear whose worst sin was that he hugged too many women. Beatrice, a mediocre worker at best, was like a second mother to her, always bringing her little odds-and-ends meant to cheer her up. If Cathy hated Madison, surely it was because Madison cut more corners than made Cathy comfortable, but Cathy's work was so good, it didn't require more than a cursory look.

Capt. Jarvis Barton, Madison's supervisor on paper, was about as harmless as they came. He'd been granted a supervisor's slot because he needed the experience if he ever hoped to make "Major Barton." Their roles were often reversed, with Jarvis asking Madison for advice. Fortunately for the government, he spent his days tinkering with the computer system, which was probably the best way he could spend his time.

The other team supervisor's role belonged to Capt. Miguel Melendez. Competent and competitive with Jarvis, Mig handled personnel matters and workload assignments, which wasn't exactly fair since he tended to overassign dog contracts to Jarvis' team, with Madison getting the brunt of the dogs. Mig's team was clearly the chosen few while Jarvis' team had all the problem children.

Sarabeth, the other contracting officer, epitomized every wholesome quality the higher-ups craved. She was a strong church-goer, junior-leaguer, and perfectionist. As if that wasn't annoying enough, she talked too much about Christian diets and urged her co-workers to listen to scripture while exercising and to read inspirational text instead of eating something sweeter than a rice patty.

Maeve was a laugh a minute, no matter who was the butt of her jokes. Always competent and well-dressed, she openly admitted she was in hock up to her eyeballs but still bragged about the cost of her boat, hot tub, European vacations, and luxury car she traded at least once a year. A loud-mouth comedienne by nature, Maeve made everyone's business her own and everyone else's. Thank God, she'd been away on business to LA for the past week. Sleeping on the other side of the continent was alibi enough.

Nell was good, too. Very steady, knowledgeable, and the office's token Native American. Nell kept to herself. Outside the office, no one really knew anything about her personal life. But then, why did they need to know?

Dougie spent his time trying to impress Mr. Smith with barbecues and informing the women in the office that they were all inferior to men. Dougie and Roxie had a running battle over cubicle space. Though all the buyers were supposed to live in identical square footage, Dougie started every day with a cup of coffee and shoving his moveable walls out at least a quarter inch more than the day before. After three months, Roxie's cubicle was roughly a third the size of Dougie's. Much to his disgust, Madison had caught on and bulldozed Dougie's cubicle back to its original perimeter. Given the sniping that had ensued, Dougie was definitely a candidate for the I-Hate-Madison club.

Deacon was another COPPER CAP. A black man with a shaved head and multiple earrings. He did good work, but Madison never could get beyond the obvious nipple rings bulging beneath his starched shirts.

Eileen was the goddess of all procurement clerks, Raynene was the scourge of the earth, and Celeste was home on maternity leave.

Madison couldn't see any of them as having the brains, initiative, opportunity, and guts required to pull off the theft of Project Andromeda. Someone wasn't what he or she seemed to be.

The telephone shrilled. Madison held her breath until she was sure the baby hadn't startled awake. As long as she was in Madison's arms, the tiny creature slept through the constant barrage of fighter jets practicing their landings, Madison's slightly country-sounding lullabies, people calling from work to ask how to handle problems on their contracts, and Jon's incessant humming of "Forever Young." If Madison put the baby down, she'd wail before she could figure out how to open her eyes.

If only Madison knew what to call the child! She could call the baby "Rhiannon," but did she really want to wallow in pain? Having a newborn in her arms again brought back too many awful memories. Awful, wonderful memories. This baby wouldn't substitute for the one she had given up out of obligation. Madison couldn't make that up to anyone, especially not to herself. Tim, the baby—she'd sacrificed everything for her career.

Amid the soft shrills of the phone, Madison laid the baby gently on a blanket on the floor and rolled her onto her tummy. She patted the fabric down around the baby's mouth and nose, then lightly rubbed her back to soothe her back into slumber. Madison tiptoed across the room and picked up the telephone.

"Lorelei?"

"Toby?" It sounded like Toby. His voice had deepened since she'd called him last month to wish him a happy nineteenth birthday. Besides, only people back home called her by her god-awful first name. "Where are you?"

"I can't say."

He didn't have to. Far away. That was enough. Though she'd bet he was somewhere off the Persian Gulf. His ship was somewhere on the other side of the planet, stopping in exotic ports her farm boy of a brother had never imagined. Jolene had trapped him into marriage and destroyed his chances of becoming a doctor or of much else. Thank God, Uncle Sam had wanted him. He'd learn more in the Navy than he would eking out a living in the red clay of Georgia. Maybe everything would work out for the best and their father would finally have a child who could make him proud. Lord knew, Madison had tried and failed.

"How are you, Toby?" She realized she was shouting into the phone to bridge the distance.

"Great!" He sounded homesick.

"Any chance I'll see you this Christmas?"

"Possibly Thanksgiving. Looks like I'll be out to sea til then. If it's longer, send me some fruit cake."

"Deal." Toby was the only person she knew who liked fruit cake. Probably, he liked the alcohol content best. In most places, he wasn't even old enough to drink.

"They said I can't talk long. They said you've been trying to reach me all day. They said make it quick. Mama and Daddy okay?"

"Fine." At least he'd remembered to ask. Not all men were that thoughtful, especially when they were only nineteen. He probably knew she'd give him hell if he didn't show a little concern for their aging parents.

"Then what's wrong? You never call just to call. You always have a reason."

Madison sucked in a breath and frowned over at the baby on the blanket. "Jolene's here. Or she was."

Toby yelped. His tone turned ugly. "What did she tell you? I didn't kick her out."

"She, um, didn't give me that impression."

"Well, whatever she said, it's a lie. Don't you say a word to Mama and Daddy about this. Promise?"

And watch them agonize over Toby's future? "Promise."

"I'm divorcing her butt when I get back to Florida."

Good for you, Madison wanted to say. Toby had finally seen the light. About time, now that he'd loused up his career choices in the name of hormones. "What about the baby?" Would Toby be able to get custody as long as he was in the Navy? As immature as he was, Toby would still make a better parent than Jolene. "I'll do what I can to help you get custody."

"What baby? What are you talking about? She didn't tell you she was preggers again, did she?"

"No." Madison drew out the word.

"Good. Did you know she lied about being pregnant when I married her?"

Madison didn't answer. She didn't have to be an obstetrician or a psychic to figure that one out.

"Um, Toby, have you talked to Jolene recently?"

"Yeah. Last week. I called home and one of her boyfriends answered." Toby's voice held a bitterness she didn't remember. At nineteen, he was growing up fast, the hard way. "Told her to hit the road. She threatened to go to Mama and Daddy and tell them she was pregnant again and get them to take her in. Or give her money. Lorelei, don't you let her do that. You know how Mama and Daddy are. They see somebody they think is in trouble, and they open up their bank account."

Not in all cases. But with other people's problems, they were generous to a fault. Funny, how they could forgive everyone's sins but hers.

"You hear? I can't talk much longer. Don't let Jolene sucker Mama and Daddy. And don't tell them we're splitting. Not unless you absolutely have to. Not yet anyway."

"I won't." As usual, everyone in the family counted on Madison to fix things. No matter what the catastrophe, she had to be the pillar of stone while everyone else could freely fall apart. Just once—*just once*—she wanted to be the one down on her knees, sobbing her heart out. But that was a luxury she wasn't allowed.

"Good. I've got to go."

"Wait! Toby." How could she ask? Maybe he didn't know. It would be so like Jolene to empower herself with deception. "Toby, Jolene took off this morning, but she left your daughter with me."

"My what?" His voice cracked.

"Your baby."

"What baby?"

Oh, geez.

"Toby, you've got to do something. I've got to get back into the office. All hell's broken loose at work, and I can't stay here with a newborn until Jolene decides to act like an adult—even if she isn't—and comes back."

Static crackled over the long-distance line, but Toby said nothing.

"Maybe I can take the baby up to Mama's until you can make arrangements. Is that what you want me to do? Toby?"

"I don't know what you're talking about. I don't have a daughter. I can't have a daughter. Lorelei, when I got on my ship over four months ago, Jolene wasn't pregnant."

That sinking feeling was back with a vengeance. "Then whose baby do I have here?"

"I don't know. But it ain't Jolene's. And it sure as hell ain't mine."

CHAPTER EIGHT

At 4:00 central time, Jon watched with a grimace as Sarabeth drew a black line through the *L. Madison Steele* typed on the bottom of the contract and penned in her own name. Her signature constituted the award of Project Andromeda, a sixty-two million dollar program won by The Cameron Institute, which resided in a large, windowless building on Colorado Springs' Garden of the Gods Road. TCI's winning features included its strong past performance record, world-renown microbiologists and chemists, and its in-house laboratories suitable for testing artificial bio-warfare germs. They were definitely not the lowest bidder, but then, Project Andromeda wasn't intended for buying paper clips.

At 4:30, the whole team—minus Madison and Roxie—headed over to the Officers' Club to celebrate. The beer was flowing, Otto was buying, and nobody really cared about a dead COPPER CAP or Madison's ruined career as long as the contract got signed on time and Otto could get his back patted by a couple of Senators and four-star generals.

At 4:45, Jon climbed back onto his bike for a hard, fast ride into the countryside where he could clear his mind and mourn Roxie in his own private way. Sometimes when he closed his eyes, he could almost hear Roxie's labored breaths, her whimpers, her fists pounding against the cold vault door.

The group celebrating Sarabeth's signature felt only exhilaration. Let them have their party. They'd worked hard for it, the ones who'd been on the team from the start. The celebration didn't mean anything without a woman with the odd name of Lorelei. How could they celebrate with Roxie dead and the whole project stolen and jeopardized? How could they discard their worries when the Sleeping Dogs lurked in quiet country towns and centers of power?

Sometime later, Jon careened through a fast-food restaurant. Then he headed to the one place he wanted to be.

By the time Jon turned down the narrow lane to Madison's house under the flight line, the sun had painted the sky a deep pinkish-purple and the first constellations had begun to pierce the coming canopy of night. Hunkered over on his motorcycle, he passed Madison's house with its blue flowers muted and fading into the evening shades. The lights were on low in the living room, which meant she was home, and the drive was empty, which meant she was home alone. Tomorrow, he would retrieve her car from the alley next to Building 13.

Jon made a U-turn and headed back to Madison's. The neighbor's—he assumed it was the neighbor's—white Ford was still parked across the street where it had been when he'd brought Madison home last night, but other than that, he was the only thing on the street. He swerved into Madison's drive and then veered around the corner of the house and parked in back, amid more blue-flowering shrubs, as the last rays of sunlight faded.

"Hi," he said, when she answered his tapping at the back door. "I hope you don't mind me parking around back."

She took her time answering. She wouldn't mind, would she? Maybe she'd even appreciate his effort. If what Mac said was true, she'd suffered enough scandal once because of an overzealous lieutenant. Jon Colter was smarter than that. He could be discreet. Even when nothing romantic was going on, he could be discreet. But if nothing romantic was happening or going to happen, why did he feel as if he were standing in quicksand?

"It's okay for me to park back here, isn't it?"

"I wish you wouldn't."

She stood behind the closed screen door and didn't offer to open it. Shadows under her eyes made her look tired, but even in her ragged cut-offs and faded blue T-shirt that clashed with the depth of her eyes, she melted his heart. He didn't usually see her in casual clothes. At work, she played the part of the consummate professional, neatly pressed and unruffled.

Tonight, she looked ruffled.

"Then where should I park?" He hooked his helmet onto the knob of the porch railing and tucked the warm paper sack of food under his arm. Any second, she'd open the door. He'd spent one night in her home. If he played his cards right, he'd spend another. And maybe another.

"You shouldn't park here at all. You shouldn't be anywhere near me. Austin Wait will come back sooner or later, and I'd rather you not be here."

"I don't care what he thinks."

"I do. I don't want your name in some stupid report."

"I talked to him already today. I don't think he cares." Not enough to make a stink about who slept on Madison Steele's couch anyway.

"You did? What did he say?" Still, she didn't unlatch the door and let him in.

"You want me to repeat all that standing out here?"

"It's not raining."

He glanced at the darkening sky. "So?"

"I had a good reason to invite you in last night. The thunderstorm. Tonight, I don't have a reason."

Jon sighed and squelched the desire to ring her pretty neck. "How about because you want to?"

She wet her lips. "Not reason enough. Sorry."

At least she didn't deny she wanted him there. "How about because I want you to?" A little braver but as far as he dared. The hint of yearning in her eyes deepened, but she didn't give in. The air between them thickened. "Or because I brought Chinese take-out to entice you?" He held up the sack that stifled him with the scent of sesame chicken and eggs rolls and made a goof-ball face at her. She rewarded him with a smile and unlatched the door.

"How did you know I hadn't eaten?"

"Wild ass guess," he lied. Not much guesswork to it. Too often, he'd watched her work through her lunch hour or get so caught up in her work that she forgot to eat. She took care of everyone but herself. Fine. He'd make it his mission to take care of her. Wasn't that what that other lieutenant had done? Jon could do it better.

She popped open a couple of cans of Pepsi while he arranged the plastic forks, oversized napkins, and thin cardboard boxes of food on the table next to the day's mail. A small town newspaper he didn't recognize, a phone bill, a letter addressed to Tim Sandusky and returned to sender.

Tim. The note taped to the back of her contracting officer's warrant had been signed "I love you, Tim." Her other lieutenant? Was that his name?

Jon let his gaze linger a bit longer than necessary, then busied himself with fishing two fortune cookies out of the sack. Part of him wanted to know everything about the man who had once stolen Madison's heart. An equal part of him ached not to hear it. His curiosity would do him no favors.

Madison slipped into her chair, brushing her wild tangle of blonde from her forehead. Without a word, she draped a napkin over her bare thighs as if she might drop a crumb into her lap. Jon took a deep breath and reached for his Pepsi. He'd chase any crumbs she'd give him.

"Where's the baby?"

"Sleeping." She smiled. "Finally. I got a few hours' sleep, too. Until you knocked."

"Oops. Sorry." Why hadn't he noticed? Her eyelids were heavy with sleep, not yearning. "I'll watch the baby tonight, and you can sleep." *And I can stay the night.*

"That's okay. I can handle it."

No, she couldn't. He'd be there when she realized it.

"Did you get any calls today?" Jon tested the waters. Surely someone had told her the latest.

"A few." She bit into an egg roll and nodded her gratitude. "Beatrice and Mac called to check up on me. Cathy called, wanting to know if I'd reviewed her sole source files yet, and the review committee called to find out if I'd answered the Mayer-Frick Congressional inquiry. And Nell had some questions on the Project Andromeda files. She called two or three times."

Jon set the drink can down with a thud. If there was any fairness in the world, one day they'd be sorry for the way they treated Madison. "I don't believe those people. They kick you off the team and then have the gall to ask for your help."

Madison shrugged. "I'm not exactly thrilled about it either, but Andromeda's too important for egos. Everyone's saying that Sarabeth's doing a great job with getting the award notice to Congress and getting the file ready to sign."

"Everybody who? And what's there to do? She orders Nell to put a letter *you* wrote on the fax machine to Air Staff. She didn't even have to sign the letter. Then she gets the call-back saying TCI's congressman's been notified so he can act like he had something to do with who got the contract and hoof it out to TCI for a photo-op. All Sarabeth has to do then is sign her name on the dotted line. Big fucking deal. Everybody but you gets credit, Congress included."

"At least it's getting done." She regarded the egg roll with an obvious loss of appetite. "Beatrice says they'll make the award on time. She called on her lunch hour. That was sweet of her."

Beatrice. Why Madison liked her, Jon would never understand. He wasn't allowed to mutter an ill word against the woman, even though it seemed clear to everyone but Madison that Beatrice hated her. The older woman brought in chocolate chip cookies baked especially for Madison. Sometimes, she brought in little gifts. Miniature Easter baskets best described as "cute" or souvenirs from frequent four-day weekend trips. She fussed over Madison's eating habits, lack of sunshine, and long hours, and mothered her sore throats with warm lemon water.

As soon as Madison left the room, Beatrice's complaints began. Heaven knew, Beatrice spent enough time hanging around Otto's secretary's desk a good twenty feet from Jon's cubicle. Madison had been all of three years old when Beatrice's civil service stint began, obviously a burr under Beatrice's saddle. To Madison's face, she took orders enthusiastically. To Madison's back, she resented the younger woman's higher rank in the contracting office food chain. Beatrice wasn't patting Madison on the back to comfort her—she was looking for a spot to stab. But try telling that to Madison, and he'd get his head handed to him on a platter.

Maybe it didn't matter whether Madison liked her underlings or not. Maybe she felt compelled to protect them from higher management and always sided with them. How could a woman like Madison Steele see so clearly yet be so blind to the faults of the people under her?

"Um, Madison? They awarded Project Andromeda this afternoon."

"Oh." She dropped her egg roll into her rice and hung her head. He might have guessed how disappointed she'd be. She'd given her all for weeks, yet Sarabeth would step in and take credit, merely because it was Sarabeth's signature in the bottom right-hand corner of the contract cover page. No matter how much work Madison had put into Andromeda, Sarabeth had officially let the contract.

"Did Beatrice say anything about Roxie?" he asked.

"Just the usual. And that the funeral service is Thursday afternoon."

But nothing about cause of death. Funny. Beatrice seemed to know everything else and didn't mind passing along anything new. "You're going?"

She took an unenthusiastic bite of the egg roll and glanced up. "I hadn't considered *not* going."

He wished she wouldn't. The rumor-mongers would have a field day. Half the people in her office were convinced that since Sarabeth and Nell had recovered the missing classified pages, Project Andromeda was now safe and sound. The wadded note from "Tim" irritated his skin through his pants pocket. The dogs of the past were close on her heels.

"Mind if I go to the funeral with you?" He stirred his fried rice but didn't eat.

"I don't think that would be a such a good idea."

"You need someone with you."

"I'll have the baby with me."

"Baby?" He laid down his fork and shoved away the box of food. "Can't Jolene watch her? I mean, it *is* her baby."

"No. It's not." Madison rested her head against the back of her chair and studied the ceiling. "I talked to my little brother today. Jolene doesn't have a baby." She paused to let the news sink in.

"Then whose baby have you been staying up with half the night to take care of?"

"I don't know. Jolene hasn't come back. I don't think she will. She must have thought the OSI was looking for her. That's why she bolted."

"Madison?"

Instead of answering, she stared at the lamp and shook her head. Her eyes glazed over. He'd lost her—to Tim, to memories, to something far away either in distance or time. He'd seen a different side of her in the past forty-eight hours. Her steel veneer hid a thousand invisible cracks, and he was watching one of them sprout crevices big enough to fall into for the rest of her life.

"Madison, you've got to call the police. Or HRS. Whoever looks after missing children. Somebody."

"I can't." She lowered her gaze to meet his. Her eyes swam with tears. None spilled down her cheeks.

"You have to. How is this going to look to Austin Wait? What about all the gossips at work?"

"I don't want to talk about this."

"Why not?" he asked, at the risk of having Madison castrate him. She was used to having her word taken for law and not some smart-ass lieutenant questioning her. "Don't you think the baby's real mother is worried sick?"

"I can't give her up again."

"Again?"

Madison sniffed and looked away. "I'll think of something tomorrow morning. I need to sleep on it. Maybe Toby's wrong."

Jon nodded. "Maybe." He supposed this was the worst possible time for her to call the police to her house. The OSI would be on her in a heartbeat. Then she'd have to contend with stolen babies and security breaches at the same time. More rumors. He understood now. Appearances, not truth.

"Madison? I could take the baby to HRS. I'll make up something. Tell them I found the baby. I don't know. It would keep you out of more trouble."

"She's my responsibility. I'll take care of it."

"No, she's not. She's—"

"Look." Her eyes came back into focus. Her jaws clenched in her usual don't-question-me expression. "I believe everything happens for a reason. The responsibility for that baby was thrust on me for some greater good. I've been given a second chance. This time, I'm not going to blow it." She twisted the fake wedding band frantically. "Anyway, I'm waiting for Jolene's mother to call me back. I want to get at the truth before I call in the authorities, you know? I have to be sure. What if I'm wrong? My parents would never forgive me if I caused Jolene and Toby to lose their baby."

"Okay." He nodded. He wouldn't push. At least not tonight when Madison was dead on her feet from lack of sleep. He'd think of a way to fix things to keep her out of trouble. "Okay. Then we should get someone to baby-sit so you won't have to drag the baby to the funeral."

"No. No, I am not leaving her."

"She's not your baby."

"She's my responsibility. For now."

The fire and water in her eyes told him arguing was useless. He'd seen the stubbornness too many times before. Someone had laid a problem at her feet, and she was determined to find the solution all by herself or die trying. If she'd only ask for his help. If she'd only accept his help.

"Did Beatrice say anything else?"

"Like what?" she asked, rearranging her fried rice with her fork.

"Like they ruled Roxie's death accidental?"

She stared back. "That's impossible."

"You want my professional opinion? Cover-up."

"Why would anybody cover up the truth? Is the base commander worried about how this will look to the press if it gets out?"

"Don't know. I think the OSI's behind it. But if nothing else, it gets you off the hook."

"I don't want to be off the hook. I want to find Roxie's killer. I have to."

No, she didn't. But he did. Regardless of what Austin Wait said. The OSI had its own agenda, and that didn't necessarily include saving Madison Steele's quavering career. At least she wouldn't have to worry about the media getting hold of the official list of murder suspects. If that happened, the TV networks would crucify her faster than they had that security guard at the Atlanta Olympics, the one suspected of planting a pipe bomb responsible for deaths and injuries. It didn't matter what kind of hero a person was, everyone had secrets, blotches on their records, even if it was nothing more than too much ambition and zeal for God-knows-what. Her entire life, including the scandal of Lieutenant Tim, could be laid bare to the whole world for their jeers. Better a person be a natural born killer than an innocent wrongly accused.

"I spent most of today asking questions," Jon said. "God knows, nobody else seems to be interested in finding the real answers. And they won't be now that Roxie's death has been ruled an accident."

She eyed him warily. "Did you learn anything new?"

"Nothing," he answered automatically. "Nothing new."

It wasn't true. He'd learned all sorts of things. He fidgeted with his cellophane-wrapped fortune cookie. Half an hour ago, he'd been hungry. Not any more. Jon had made a little progress in his own personal investigation, but by far the most startling revelation was Mac's recollection of Madison's interrupted rendezvous with her lover. Like a man with a guilty conscience, Jon had mistaken her question. Or had he?

"I suppose I did learn a few things." He ventured a glimpse of her face, recognized the hidden panic, and then busied himself with crushing the fortune cookie. "About Roxie," he added quickly.

"About Roxie," she echoed.

"For example, I know that Sarabeth refused to take on Roxie as a trainee."

Madison nodded. "Roxie didn't know it though. I never wanted her to find out. I always end up with the problem children."

"Roxie wasn't a problem child."

"Oh, but she was. She was wonderful. Very sharp. Hard worker. Unfortunately, she came into our office with a sullied reputation, and that's why I got her. Her divorce was final a few months back. The rumor mill was vicious. Supposedly she left her husband for another man."

Jon flicked the fortune cookie crumbs away from a wrinkled strip of paper that bore miniature red print. No wonder Madison had taken Roxie under her wing. Madison didn't mind the scandal-ridden past. She'd been there, done that.

He wanted to take the love note from Tim out of his pocket and fling it onto the table. He couldn't. She'd be crushed if she knew her coworkers had torn her office—and her past—apart.

"So? Did she?" he asked.

"Did she what?"

"Leave her husband. For another man."

"I don't know. I never asked."

"Why not?" Madison and Roxie had been close. As close as he'd seen Madison to anyone. They'd shared breakfast, lunch, and dinner for the past few months. Roxie had even managed to get Madison out of the office at lunch every Wednesday to play tennis.

"Why should I? That was her personal life. I never mess around with my buyers' personal lives unless it effects their work. And Roxie's work was always outstanding."

"Your coworkers' personal lives might hold the key to finding who stole Andromeda and pinned the breach on you."

"Hmmm. Maybe. I don't care as much about who stole it as I do finding out where it is now."

"Uh...yeah. You're not going to like this." He hated being the one to tell her, but she'd find out soon enough. And she'd find out he knew and be angry if he didn't tell her. Damned if he did.... "They found all of the missing pages today. In your office."

Blood drained from her face. "In my...? Sheesh. Why am I not surprised? I suppose Austin Wait will be dropping by to arrest me."

The OSI had its agenda. Austin Wait definitely had his own. Not that Jon knew what it was. He smoothed out the crumpled fortune and frowned down at the words.

IT'S LATER THAN YOU THINK.

What the—? Earlier today, his mother had said the same thing. The paper felt hot in his hands.

"Jon?" Madison sat up abruptly, reached across the table, and clasped his hand. The warmth of her touch sent a shiver of yearning down his spine. "Are you okay? You're pale. Maybe you're coming down with something."

"No. Today's been, er, disturbing."

Scary was more like it. His hand trembled in hers. He laid his other palm on top of hers and squeezed. God, her touch felt good!

"Jon? What happened?"

"Nothing."

"You're holding back on me."

"I—" Pulling away, he wrenched his hands and looked up. "Madison?"

"Yes?"

"Remember I told you I had to ask you something?"

"Vaguely. What did you want to ask?" She had that look, the one that worried about the depth of the question. She probably thought he was going to ask about Tim.

"If the country were caught up in a germ war, would you stay here or go into hiding?"

A hollow laugh escaped from her throat. "You think there's a place to hide?"

"Hypothetically speaking. Maybe an underground bunker with a good air conditioning filtration system. Would you go?"

"Hypothetically? Hmmm. I don't know. Could my family go, too?"

"Yeah, sure. Hypothetically. So? Would you go?"

She didn't hesitate. "No. I'd send my family. Then I'd come back here and do everything I could with Project Andromeda to give them a fighting chance at having a world to come out to."

"Even if it killed you?" Someone had to protect the protector.

"We're all going to die sooner or later. If I have to die, I might as well die fighting."

He smiled. In his dreams, he saw her in purple robes, conducting ancient rituals of life. Lydia Colter had startled him by with her own dreams. "My mom says you were a warrior in another lifetime. In many, many lifetimes. But she's a little nuts."

"A warrior, huh?" Madison paused to contemplate it. "I can see that. Somebody has to fight for what's right. I think I like your mom."

Figured. He hadn't spoken to his mother in over two years. He'd written to her, sent her postcards from his trips to Europe and Asia, sent her gifts for Mother's Day, Christmas, and her birthday. Still, his mother refused to answer his letters or take his calls. Something about the Universe being out of balance and him being part of it. He'd wondered at one time if maybe she'd moved and he was dialing the wrong number, but he'd checked it out and found that yes, her Los Angeles telephone number was indeed working, even if she didn't answer the phone.

This morning, she'd answered.

And before he could say a word, she'd said, "Hi, Jonathan. I knew you'd call."

He hated it when she did that. Couldn't she at least pretend to be a normal mother? Growing up in her home had been worse. Other kids could get away with skipping school and lying to their parents, but not Jon Colter. Even when he sweet-talked his way out of punishment from his teachers, he would come home, walk through the front door, and hear, "You're grounded, buster!" Other mothers had eyes in the backs of their heads. Jon should have been so lucky.

"Jon? What's wrong? Your hands are shaking."

Madison would notice that, wouldn't she? He clenched his hands into fists. "I talked to my mom today."

"Is she okay? Is everything all right back home?"

He shrugged. "I'm not real sure how everything is at home. I hadn't talked to Mom in a long time. Years." She gave him one of those famous L. Madison Steele glares, the same one she reserved for people who kicked pregnant cats. "Hey, it's not like I haven't tried to talk to her."

"I'm sure if you wanted to talk to her," Madison said coldly, "you could have found a way."

"Not when she won't answer the freaking phone!"

"What did you do to tick her off?"

"I didn't do—" Jon bit off the words and lowered his voice. "I didn't do anything."

"Parents don't usually forsake their children without a reason."

"Yeah? It was her reason, not mine. My mom's kind of weird."

"Yeah? And if you were my parents' child, you would have gotten your jaws popped for saying that. No matter how old you are."

"But she *is* weird. Different."

"Some people say I am, too."

"You're always unusual, Madison." He chuckled. "But you make sense. Mom's a little off kilter. She's one of those New Age gurus. One of those tree-hugging, white witches. She thinks the whole world would be a bright, shiny place if we'd only get rid of all the soldiers."

Madison's expression softened. "Okay, so I don't suppose I would get along that well with your mother. Then again, she's not my mother. Still doesn't give you any right to show disrespect."

"It's not disrespect. I love my mom! She fits right in in Southern California, but anywhere else in the country, and they'd have her locked up. I'm talking straight-jackets here. Not that my dad's much better. He's one of those anti-Government militia leaders who doesn't believe in paying taxes and sneaks out in the middle of the night to wrap machine guns in oily rags and stuff them inside PVC pipe and bury them in the middle of a cornfield because you never know when the 'New World Order' will take over. The whole time I was growing up, they both threatened to disown me if I ever, ever joined the military."

She laughed. "I'll bet you raced down to the closest recruiting office."

"I hadn't planned on it." He rubbed his thumbnail. Maybe he was young and idealistic, but his days of innocence had died with Sam. "My college roommate graduated a year ahead of me and joined the Air Force. He went off to the other side of the world on a peacekeeping mission. Mom would have liked that part. Except that he got himself killed by a terrorist car bomb." His voice caught.

"I went to his memorial service and sat there the whole time looking at a stupid white wreath. Nobody ever told me that when you lose someone to a bomb, there's nothing left to bury." The familiar lump in his throat shoved upward from his chest. "I was so pissed off. It was a matter of honor and protection and I don't know if you understand—"

"I understand."

"—But Sam thought he was immortal. Why wouldn't he? He had everything to live for. And then at the memorial service, they had four F-15's fly over. Ear-splitting. The jets flew almost over us and then one jet pulled away from the other three and shot straight up until it disappeared into the clouds."

"Missing man formation," Madison whispered.

"It got me. Right here." He crushed his fist against his chest. "That's when I first knew my purpose in life is to protect. When I told my parents I'd joined the Air Force, Mom screamed and then cried and cried. Said the war machines would destroy the world. Said she'd seen it herself. Nothing I could say would change her mind. She said for her own mental health, she never wanted to see me again." The muscles in his neck tightened, choking him. No child should ever have to bear a mother's rejection. "I didn't realize until today how much I'd missed her."

Madison offered him a faint smile. "I'm glad you changed her mind about talking to you."

"I am, too. I think. All these years, I thought my mom was a fruitcake. Now I'm not so sure."

"What did she say?"

"The usual. Stuff I'd heard a hundred times before. I guess I'd blocked it out. I never realized what she was saying. But she's convinced the Apocalypse is coming. And that we're part of it. You especially." And especially a child Madison would one day have.

"M-me?"

"Yeah. You're some kind of high priestess of something. The Remnants of Humanity?" He'd dreamed of her barefoot amid glowing stones, but it had seemed like long ago, not a premonition of the future. "Said you were just starting your spiritual journey." He feigned a cough.

"I don't have time for spiritual journeys. I have to work."

"I think it happens whether you pencil it into your schedule or not. My mom's...a little...psychic. She's, um, a spiritual counselor. Not the kind with a tent and a crystal ball either. She has an office with an oak desk and leather chairs and a receptionist. Psychology and counseling degrees on her wall."

Madison started to say something, but he interrupted. "Don't you breathe a word of it around work. I don't want Otto thinking I'm a lunatic like my mother." Sometimes he had feelings he couldn't substantiate. Glimpses of truth. It didn't mean anything.

"I won't." Madison ripped open her fortune cookie, read the fortune, and quickly tossed it and the remnants of cookie into the trash can. "Go ahead."

"If you've ever been to L.A.—"

"Many times."

"—You might recognize her name. Lydia Colter. She calls herself a hypnotherapist. She does past life regressions." He paused to see if Madison would laugh. When she didn't, he continued. "She also does future life progressions. I know this sounds like something straight out of *Star Trek*, but she says time isn't linear. It's circular. Like a funnel. Or a tornado. She says our souls remember. That we can go back to previous incarnations or to future reincarnations."

"I see."

"I told you. Weird stuff."

"And she says I was a warrior in a past life? Maybe I should dig out the fencing foils I had back in college. I suppose I was famous, too?" She sipped her Pepsi, then grinned. "I'll bet your mom gets a host of Shakespeares and Cleopatras and Abe Lincolns."

"Actually? No. Most people regress back to mundane existences. Ordinary people in everyday lives of drudgery. Farmers, servants, tradesmen. Nobody famous. Nobody you'd consider important in history. But then, if this kind of stuff is for real—and I'm not saying it is—it would make sense that our past lives would be boring and mundane. Most peoples' lives are that, aren't they? How many of us are really famous or important in our own times, let alone in the grand scheme of the universe?"

"Are many people warriors?"

"Soldiers, yes, but not warriors. Conquerors. Mom says *you* are important. You always have been. She said if it came down to it, I should—" he swallowed hard—"lay down my life if necessary to keep you safe." He felt the heat rise in his face and looked away. A woman like Madison had certainly heard better lines than that from married men in singles bars. "Like I said, my mom's off her rocker."

"No. No, go on."

Madison reached across the table, hesitated, then laid her hand on his forearm. He closed his eyes for a moment, basking in her touch. He didn't want her to stop. Ever.

"My mom puts people in hypnotic trances and—and—" God, he felt silly talking about it. Madison would probably declare him as insane as Lydia Colter and laugh him out of her house.

"Go on."

"She takes them—well, supposedly takes them—into the future a couple hundred years. I hope you don't it's un-American of me to repeat this, but she says the future's a socialist society with pockets of people, men and women, living together in barracks. Colonies of artists near the sea. People in spaceships. But mainly small pockets of civilization. She doesn't know what happened to all the people."

Madison's grip tightened on his arm. "What does your mom think happened? I mean, happens. You know, hypothetically."

"She doesn't know. Or if she does, she won't say. But there aren't as many incarnations in the future as there are now. That means not as many people. Madison, she's done this with about two hundred people. Taken them into future incarnations, that is. Maybe a dozen or so come back in another two hundred years. So far, only one's been reincarnated—or will be—in the next hundred years."

Madison searched his face. "Maybe...maybe...maybe that person lives a very long life. Maybe all the other souls are resting." Her eyes widened, the possibilities winding like gears inside her head. Damn, but she was taking this more seriously than he had, and he'd heard it all his life.

"She progressed this woman into the year 2053. The cities were empty. Buildings were still there but no people. Only wind blowing litter down the streets and rocking children's swing sets back and forth. No people. Only wind."

Madison shuddered, then receded into an uneasy posture. "What did the woman say happened? Nuclear war?"

"Mom couldn't get the woman to go back again. The woman said it was too lonely in the future. I know this is going to sound crazy, but my mom thinks that all the prophecies are going to come to a head soon. The religious fanatics think the Rapture's going to take place the last night of December 1999, as if their calendar is the only correct way of marking time. Some people already believe that the Anti-Christ is out there right now. Probably in the Middle East."

She nodded. "I haven't been to church in years, but I grew up Southern Baptist. Believe me, I can quote scripture with the best of them."

"Some prophecies say the world as we know it will end on the twenty-first of December, 2008. The Mayan calendar accounts for twenty-six thousand years. Madison, it ends in 2012. Technology turns against us. That's what the prophecies say."

"Technology," she murmured. "*Which* technology? The kind that destroys every living thing with bio-warfare weapons?"

Jon stared at the fortune on the table between them. He could still feel its heat on his skin.

IT'S LATER THAN YOU THINK.

CHAPTER NINE

Thursday, 30 September 1999, V alparaiso, Florida

How could a five-day-old baby render her powerless?

L. Madison Steele brought together the most onerous people on the face of the earth with a common goal of getting any number of important projects on contract. They looked up to her as the only contracting officer who could work miracles. To them, she could do anything—or she'd die trying. And yet, with a child in her arms, she couldn't steal even one lousy shower without Jon watching the baby for her for five minutes. No wonder women throughout history had never matched men in roles of leadership—mothers throughout time had turned a cold shoulder to ruling kingdoms in favor of one teenie-weenie nap.

She hadn't slept well while caring for the baby. The little thing woke up every two or three hours, and Madison had forgotten the old adage about napping when the baby naps. She had to snatch sleep whenever the baby would let her, and even then, her respite was riddled with nightmares. Not of the Apocalypse, but of Tim.

The dreams of Tim had started with Jon's presence in her home. Probably something about Jon's brashness of youth had triggered buried memories. She preferred staying awake, stumbling through the days, to dreaming of Tim. The dreams were awful. They left her with a sickening heartache swelling into her throat and choking off her breath.

Last night's dream had been the worst in years. Madison had arrived at an empty auditorium where she'd once trysted with Tim, where he'd first confessed his desire for her, called her the greatest love of his life. This time, the auditorium wasn't empty. Dozens of her old co-workers and enemies filled the seats in anticipation. Madison took a seat on the sidelines on a hard, wooden bench and watched as Tim perched center stage on a stool, a twelve-string guitar in his lap and a too-cute, too-thin, too-smiling brunette at his elbow. He avoided Madison's eyes as he spoke to the crowd of finally finding the love he'd always searched for. And then he sang the sweetest of songs, a song he'd written and sung for Madison so long ago, but now he sang it for the woman at his side. One hand clasping the guitar and the other caressing the brunette's tearstained cheek, Tim ended his performance with a sloppy, passionate kiss. The crowd cheered.

With a sigh, Madison slumped into the rocking chair with the baby. It wasn't that she didn't want Tim to be happy. She wanted him to be happy *with her.* He'd promised to come back for her. He'd given her a wedding band and sworn to make it real on his return. But seven years had passed. Maybe the dream was really a wake-up call to tell her Tim wasn't coming back. He was starting—or maybe already had—a new life. One that included cute, thin, adoring brunettes. One that didn't include her.

"Well, Ms. Steele?" Austin Wait towered over her, looking every bit the candidate for the next James Bond movie and flirting twice as boldly. "You're not saying much."

"What is there to say? You're here to handcuff me, aren't you?"

He laughed. "I'm not allowed to talk about personal fantasies, remember? You'll turn me in if I do. Maybe when this case is over with, we can get together and you'll feel a little less hostile toward me. I want that."

"Yeah, and people in hell want ice water. If you're going to arrest me, let's get it over with. I don't like being played with. Or threatened with a date."

He winced. "I have no intention of arresting you, *Lorelei.* But I do need your help."

"Roxie's dead, and you expect me to believe it's an accident? There's nothing I can do for you. Nothing."

The OSI agent glanced around for a chair, noted the pile of laundry to be folded taking up every square inch of the sofa and the stools beside the breakfast bar, and finally sat cross-legged on the floor. She knew negotiation strategy when she saw it. She'd been in her share of negotiations where her chair was a good six inches shorter than her adversary's, or she had to debate an opponent with the glare of the sun in her eyes, or the man across the table casually mentioned every ten minutes that he'd been negotiating with Uncle Sam longer than Madison had been alive. Austin Wait was just as obvious. He was taking the supplicant's position. For some reason, he wanted her to feel empowered. All the more reason to feel nervous.

"Why don't you start by calling me 'Austin'?"

"As opposed to 'son of a bitch'?"

He kept his poker face. Hmmm. A worthy adversary, if an unpopular one.

"For you," he said, "I suppose that's a start."

"Then why don't *you* start by going to hell?"

"You know, you're probably the only one who can do anything for me, Lorelei. You're the key to this case. There's more going on than you think."

"Jon told me everything."

"I knew he would. Loyal little cuss, isn't he?"

"Yes, but he's my loyal little cuss."

"You know what I think? You're a decade older than he is—"

"Six years."

"Okay, six. I think he's a short-tempered punk who needs someone to kick his ass for him."

"And you think I'm it?"

"No, *I'm* that. I think he's got you confused with his mother."

She pretended not to catch his Oedipus insinuations. "I'm nothing like his mother. You know those people who walk around with signs that say the end of the world is near? Jon says that's his mom." She cringed. She'd promised not to say anything, and now she'd let it slip out.

"She'd get along fine with your dad. He's a religious nut, too, isn't he?"

Madison froze. How much did Austin Wait know about Lydia Colter? About her father? "What are you talking about?"

"Every time your dad meets someone new, he lets them know we're living in the Last Days."

"Ever think maybe we are?"

"Lately? Too often."

She'd heard about the Last Days for as long as she could remember. Most recently from her sweet, disbelieving lieutenant. Threats of the end of the world were nothing new to her, but in the past few days, they'd become a little more genuine.

Madison had had the Book of Revelation ingrained in her since she was first dragged to the Baptist Church at the age of six weeks. It seemed that every other year was destined to be Judgment Day, according to the string of preachers she'd listened to all her life.

She could still recall the red-faced evangelist at a crowded tent revival, yelling about fire and brimstone, pointing at the hazy moon above, and declaring that man had now walked on the "lamp of the earth." God would surely rain down judgment on them all. She'd found that preachers chose any number of incidences of godlessness as evidence of the coming Apocalypse, whether it was homosexuality, gang warfare, small wars in third world countries, rock music lyrics, or the state lottery coming to Georgia. Any of these many things was proof that the Great Tribulation was upon them all.

The alignment of planets in 1977 was to have caused the great earthquakes foretold thousands of years ago. The arrival of Haley's Comet in 1986 was to have been the "bearded star" falling to the earth. Then there was the Shoemaker-Levy Comet and one after that in 1996. The same was said of the Hale-Bopp Comet in spring of 1997. Comets had been a universal bad omen since the beginning of prophecy.

Awful lot of comets these days.

The preachers who didn't yell tended to be monotoned. Their sermons were so boring that Madison had spent her childhood Sundays doing one of two things: either staring at the pulpit without blinking until she saw visions—real or imaginary—of Armageddon or entertaining herself by reading the more prophetic books of the Bible, the only type of reading allowed during church services.

Madison hadn't been to church in years, but the scriptures were still ingrained in the back of her head. Maybe that's why she'd been so uneasy about some of the technologies she'd worked with in the past nine years on the Air Force base. Not that she minded being the one to buy bombs and missiles for the American war machine. Other women might be disturbed at the prospect of buying weapons of mass destruction, but Madison never had been.

She smiled to herself. Perhaps it was because she'd been a warrior in many lifetimes and knew the price of freedom.

But some of the contracts she negotiated made her uneasy when she should have been enthralled. A couple of million dollars—a minor purchase as far as Madison's career went—for a souped-up computer algorithm that would allow real-time diagnosis of breast cancer genes and save the lives of thousands of young women. The same technology that would find disease-inclined cells in children and allow their doctors to prepare nutrition and exercise regimens to reduce their chances of illness. The same technology that could be used to excise "bad" genes of any type in the embryo stage. The same technology that could allow designer babies with blonde hair, blue eyes, and right-wing Republican tendencies. Didn't anybody pay attention to history? The more man struggled to control his environment, the more the environment fought back. Given the past hundred years, man was in for one hell of a punch.

"You know, Agent Wait, I've always thought that life should be anything but boring. If we are living in the last days of this earth, I can't think of a less boring time to live in."

"Then you're not afraid?"

"For myself? No. But for the children..." She sighed heavily and reached to finger the baby's soft curls. If her past long hours spent under Austin Wait's interrogation were any evidence, her words of concern were Greek to the cold-hearted OSI agent. "What would you know about it?"

"I know I want my children to grow up and grow old. Without some crackpot spewing a BW cloud over their school."

She stopped rocking. "You have kids?"

"Three. The youngest started first grade in August."

First grade. Madison sucked in her breath. She eyed his ring finger and found nothing. Not that a wedding band meant anything to a man, married or not. "I didn't know you were married."

"I'm not. Not anymore. I guess it's too much to expect a spouse to put up with the late nights and all my chances of getting shot."

"Yeah, I guess." Late nights? She could sympathize. Getting shot? That, too. A contracting officer's job wasn't quite as dangerous as an OSI agent's but the possibilities were there.

"They live in Iowa. My ex used to accuse me of not being much of a husband and father because I was always off on the job. Now she accuses me of not being much of a man because I let myself lose contact with them. I keep trying to take time off to see them, but...you know how it is."

She knew. God, she knew. Austin Wait had sacrificed his wife and family for his career. All he had left was the job. No wonder he was so intent on getting his man. She'd disliked him because he was a kindred spirit.

Somewhere out there was a child learning to read without both parents. The little boy probably came home from first grade with all sorts of wonderful stories, and Austin wasn't there to hear them. She knew exactly how Austin felt.

Unless he was lying. Maybe he wanted to appeal to her sense of guilt and long list of obligations, all in the name of solving his case. She wouldn't put that past him.

"What do you want, Austin?"

He raised his eyebrows. "Can you act? I want you to play a part."

"What kind of part?"

"I want you to be a bad girl."

Madison squirmed in her seat. She hadn't had a shower all day, he'd teased her with talk of bondage fantasies, and now he wanted her to pretend to be a bad girl. Whatever that meant. One day, she promised herself, she'd tie Special Agent Wait to her four poster bed and make him lose that damned poker face.

"Go on," she said.

He grinned. "Somehow I knew I wouldn't get much of a rise out of you, Lorelei."

"Why don't you tell me what you really want before this baby wakes up and I make you change her diaper."

"I want you to help me catch a spy."

"Glad to. So who is it? Make my day and tell me it's Otto Trollinger."

"I don't know who it is. But he—or she—is still out there, and they're counting on seeing your head roll."

"Well, that narrows the field of suspects to a few hundred," Madison joked. "Got a motive?"

"I was hoping you'd be able to help."

"Two days ago, you were ready to crucify me. You grilled me for four hours. Wouldn't even let me go to the bathroom. Why the change of heart? And don't lie to me. You know something I don't."

"Let's hope so. That's my job." He rearranged his lanky body on the rug in front of her and leaned forward on one wrist. "We're both professionals. I'm sure you won't hold it against me."

"Don't insult my intelligence with that line of bull."

He laughed, though whether it was genuine or well-practiced, Madison couldn't tell. "You have to admit," he urged, "a couple of nights ago, you did look guilty. You've got too many secrets for a woman in your position. Sooner or later, your past is going to catch up with you."

Madison nearly swallowed her own tongue. That's what her fortune cookie had said: *YOUR PAST WILL SOON CATCH UP WITH YOU.* She'd lied to Jon about what it said. "'You will succeed in business,'" she'd told him later. The fortune could mean anything to anybody. The interpretation was hers alone.

"Sooner or later, Lorelei, your past is going to come out. That makes you a prime target for an intelligence threat."

He was right, of course. Madison had another six months before she came up for her ten-year security review, and she'd been dreading that for the past seven years. With a few damning exceptions, she'd been terribly careful to walk the straight and narrow since she'd joined the Department of Defense.

Back in college, before her employment with the Government, she'd smoked exactly five joints and snorted cocaine once. Smoking was a filthy habit, she'd decided, and snorting was the most un-ladylike, unglamorous practice she'd ever encountered. Worse than chewing tobacco or spitting on sidewalks. While she tolerated casual drug use among her college pals, she hadn't needed it herself and stayed far from it for almost ten years. She liked not needing drugs to get through her day.

She liked not needing anything—or anybody.

She'd met the occasional man in the occasional city while on temporary duty, or TDY, to a kick-off meeting or a program review at a contractor's plant and, after taking several days to get to know the man, had invited him up to her hotel room on the last night of the business trip. But they were never men she worked with or men who worked for the contractor she negotiated against. She was always discreet and gave them a call whenever she flew into town. They knew her only as "Lorelei," not Madison Steele. Her refusal to tell them anything other than the fact that she worked for the government left them suspecting—most unfortunately now—that she was a spy. Yet for whatever reason, they were willing to accept the relationship on a first-name-only basis. Their trysts were sweet, passionate, and brief, and they were as much as Madison could hope for.

She was still a woman, a woman with needs and feelings and yearnings to be touched. Those things might count against her in an FBI file check, but they weren't any more incriminating than the short-term liaisons she'd witnessed among the various married men she'd worked with. All of them still had their clearances and their wedding rings. They'd rolled through their security checks without a hitch, so why shouldn't she? Probably none of them had a little secret stashed away in rural Georgia. And if they did, they certainly didn't bear any of the stretch marks to show for it.

Austin cleared his throat. "I know what happened to your friend. Tim Sandusky." He paused for her reaction, but she didn't give him the satisfaction. The only evidence he might have spotted was the involuntary tightening of her jaws.

"I thought at first that maybe somebody was blackmailing you to keep the facts about Sandusky from coming out, but then, everybody knows, don't they?"

She didn't flinch but felt her eyes narrow.

"So," he continued, "I figured, what's the big deal? You were an unmarried woman, he was an unmarried man. No commitments to anybody else. I suppose if you're going to get caught in the act, your cubicle at work is not the best place for that to happen. But other than that, what's the big deal?"

"Why don't you ask the gossips that?"

"You go back to Georgia, spend a year in long-term-full-time training, and when you get back here, you've got your master's degree in public administration and most of the furor has died down. Your reputation's shot, but you've still got your job. You have to scramble, but you manage to land on your own two feet." He clapped his large hands. "Bravo."

"Thank you," she choked out. Who the hell was he to compliment her?

"But that's not enough reason to sell out your country. Okay, so you're paying off somebody to the tune of twenty-five grand a year. What for, I haven't been able to figure out. But I will, Lorelei, I will."

Heaven help her if he did.

"Then I wondered if maybe you were willing to sell off Project Andromeda to pay for whatever other dirty little secrets you're being blackmailed for."

"I'm not being blackmailed."

"Really? When you take two thousand dollars out of your paycheck every month like clock work for six years and don't sink it back into any, um—" he glanced around the living room and curled his upper lip— "visible assets, it sure looks like blackmail to me. When I was interrogating you, as far as I was concerned, you were guilty as hell."

"Then what changed your mind?" she grated out. He'd been picking at her scars for long enough.

"Three weeks ago, someone tried to bribe Otto Trollinger to turn over Project Andromeda for a cool quarter million."

Madison laughed. "And Otto didn't take it?"

Austin smiled back. Apparently he'd heard about Otto's warped sense of ethics. Otto had a pricey house on the ninth fairway at a country club resort. A cheap bribe wouldn't do for him, but Madison would bet any day that he'd be Andromeda's best candidate for pond scum.

"I'm not sure Otto Trollinger is the paragon of virtue he pretended to us, but he did report the contact in less than half an hour. He gave us a shitty description of the woman who contacted him. Other than the fact that she had an accent Otto couldn't place, his description sucked. I suspect he was afraid to give an accurate description of the woman. His description was something like: 'medium height, reasonably pretty, and some kind of accent.'"

"That sounds like Otto. Not exactly the most observant of men." In fact, she'd had the whole Project Andromeda team roaring with laughter for more than a week. Every time The Troll stalked into the evaluation room, Madison hummed Darth Vader's theme. Not that Otto was nearly as tall as the helmet-wearing villain of the *Star Wars* movies, but their single-minded ambition bore close resemblance. Eventually, Eugene Krueger tipped him off, and Otto flung himself into the expected rage.

"Fortunately," Austin continued, "the next person she tried to bribe was Lt. Carmen Terranova."

"Figmo?"

"Lieutenants are considerably cheaper. Ten thousand dollars and sexual favors."

What could she expect from a guy nicknamed for the apathetic attitude of soldiers on their way out of the military: *Fuck-It-Got-My-Orders?* Madison groaned. "Figmo would screw a snake if it would hold still."

Austin laughed until his eyes glistened with tears. "He didn't screw this snake. I suppose the boy showed remarkable restraint. You should have heard his description. We sat around the office and laughed for half a day about how we were ready to go out arrest this Miss Centerfold because, well, that's the kind of woman he described. Legs up to her neck, hair down to her butt, and a good double handful of, um, well, you know what I mean." He cleared his throat.

Madison nodded. She knew all right. Figmo's second favorite pastime was describing the women who peopled his nights. "Wait a minute. You're saying Otto and Figmo were both approached by a spy—a Penthouse Pet kind of spy—for money and sex *and they both turned her down?"* She shook her head. "I guess I have to give them more credit for integrity than I'd thought. Gee, though, I almost feel disappointed. Nobody tried to buy me. Should I feel hurt for being left out? Or maybe this woman only does men?"

"Hard to say yet. Her name is Giselle Villemaire." He opened his jacket and plucked a sheath of papers folded lengthwise from his inner pocket. He opened them face out and held them up for her to see. Still too far away for her to read the typing, but the black-and-white photo didn't make Figmo out to be a liar. The woman was dropdead gorgeous. Even in a candid shot. In a disgustingly unreal, super model kind of way.

"Hmph. I have to agree with Otto. She is reasonably pretty."

Austin smirked. "Reasonably dangerous, too. Calls herself an information broker. Does most of her business out of Montreal and Quebec City, but she's a French operative."

Madison jerked her head up. "French? I thought we were looking at the Iraqis. Does the French government know?"

"Oh, they know. She works for them. Among others. Possibly the Sleeping Dogs or other terrorist organizations. Just because we're not at war with the French doesn't mean they're not interested in what we're doing."

Why hadn't she thought of that? Of course, the Iraqis would be interested in Project Andromeda technology. After all, it was their underground bunkers that Project Andromeda was designed to counteract. Iran would be interested, too, as well as Libya with its chemical-loaded bunkers. And China. China was always a contender.

And then there were the "safe" countries. The ones most Americans thought were their friends. Israel, Canada, United Kingdom, France. The cold war was over, and no one worried about Russia any more. But the big thaw spread to every country, whether they were purported to be friend or foe. America's allies were smart enough to keep gathering discreet tidbits here and there. Hard to tell where the lines of friendship might be drawn in the next world war. Or in a biological catastrophe.

Austin folded the papers and stuffed them back into his jacket pocket. "You haven't seen her, have you?"

"No. No, and I'd remember her. You think she stole my access card?"

"Or switched it?" he asked. "Oh, yes. I know. Your card and Celeste's card were switched. Lt. Terranova's girlfriend in Security thought we should know. Next time you and Colter withhold information from me, I'm gonna let you two bunk together in the county jail for interfering with an official investigation."

"Leave Jon alone. He was doing what I told him to do. You want to arrest anybody? You arrest me."

"You two are something else, you know? You take complete responsibility for him, and he takes complete responsibility for you."

Madison blinked patiently. "I asked if this Giselle-person was the one who took my card."

"I doubt it. We know she recruited someone else on the Project Andromeda team. We don't know who."

"Somebody on my team? You're positive?" She gave a little grunt of indignation. Somebody on her team had actually betrayed a government secret. For money. For sex. For whatever. She resented it. Damn, did she! Not that she had any control over Otto's lieutenants or that she was legally responsible for everything they did, but it was her team. Hers. And if the weakest link in her chain broke, she took it as personal failure.

"Positive."

"So what you're saying is that somebody on my team sold us out."

"That's right. Somebody who knows Celeste well enough to get into her home while she's on maternity leave and take her access card. According to Celeste, everybody in your office except Dougie and Deacon have dropped in to see the new baby. And a number of the Project Andromeda team have stopped in, too. And it's somebody who knows you well enough to get close enough to you to exchange the cards."

A shiver wound its way down her spine. "You mean you think somebody actually switched the cards while I was wearing my jacket?"

"I don't know. It's a possibility. You said yourself you wear that card at all times. Unless somebody got into your house while you weren't wearing it. I assume you don't sleep with your card clipped to your nightgown. Or any other body parts."

Madison didn't like that option either. Somebody in her house? While she slept?

"Here's how it plays out. They use your card to get into The Facility. They either already know or have found a way to get the combination to the cipher-locked evaluation room. Plus, they either already know or have found out the combination to the safe. They watch The Facility, wait until you send out Roxanne and Colter, and then you yourself leave.

You and Colter leave to go home. For whatever reason, Roxanne doesn't go home right away. She sees someone she knows enter The Facility."

"Roxie stayed? You're sure of that?"

"The Security Police reported seeing her sitting on the hood of her car at midnight several times the week before. Waiting for her ride, she told them. Anyway, that night she watched someone she knew let himself into The Facility. Roxanne had tried to report it to Lt. Col. Ballard. Left him a note. But then, you know that already. Courtesy of Lt. Colter."

She nodded. Jon might be playing amateur detective, but he was half a step ahead of Austin.

"Whoever borrowed your access card wanted everyone to know there had been a security breach. They left lights on, they left the safe drawer open, they left the photocopier lid open with classified paperwork hanging out. Classified pages were strewn everywhere. Most breaches are accidents. People leave documents on top of the safe when the fire alarm goes off or classified papers get caught underneath the bottom drawer of a safe. Even if the perp screws up and then tries to hide the breach, he covers it up so it takes as long as possible to discover the breach. Whoever stole those classified pages made sure the paper trail led to you."

"They found out Roxie knew the truth and killed her, too."

"While you were locked in Building 13 without an alibi. Did I mention maintenance had to take the hinges off the door to the contracting suite? Someone glued the strike plate and the hinges. From the outside."

"Then I was right. Roxie's death wasn't accidental." Madison stopped rocking. "Oh my God. They could have killed me, too. Instead of locking me in, they could have walked right in and blown me away."

"Then they couldn't frame you. Whoever stole Project Andromeda did it for more reasons than money. According to the profile I've worked up, they had personal reasons, too. And you, Lorelei, framing you for it was the bonus. Someone with a vendetta."

"But how did you know it wasn't me? When you interrogated me day before yesterday, it didn't matter what I said. You'd already made up your mind I was guilty. Nothing I said made any difference to you."

"You're right. But I spent a good portion of Tuesday night going over every electronic mail message you've sent in the past two weeks."

"My e-mails?" Uh-oh. What had she written and sent out over the Internet? Nothing incriminating or fraudulent. No recipes or chain letters or personal mail like some people. But she did sometimes mention the nice weather in her chattier e-mails to Federal employees in Ohio, and occasionally she engaged in a little risqué banter with some of her engineers. Her e-mails wouldn't get her fired and probably not reprimanded, but she wasn't altogether comfortable with the OSI peering over her shoulder.

"Two very interesting messages were in your electronic folder called 'Andromeda.'"

"I don't have an electronic folder called 'Andromeda.'"

"You do now. Both messages said the same thing: 'Mission accomplished. Please forward payment.'"

"What?"

"We found a message sent on Tuesday morning, before I came by your office to question you. Sent at 7:35 a.m."

"That's impossible. I was in a 7:30 meeting with Cathy."

"I know. That's what Cathy told us. And the second message was sent at 1:55 p.m."

"I was...let's see..." She was used to checking her scheduler. Without it in front of her, she could barely think. "It couldn't have been me. I took Jolene home around that time."

"Yes, I know. I followed you."

She should have known. He had said he needed to check in with his office, but in truth, he'd lain in wait for her. If she were a spy, he might have caught her in a mistake then instead of watching her run home and set up house for a teenage guest who hadn't stuck around for the hard part.

"Do you log off your computer when you leave your desk?" he asked.

"Yes! No. No, not always. Sometimes I get called away too quickly. And I don't log off to go to the bathroom. Besides, it logs me off automatically if I'm away from my desk longer than ten minutes."

Austin crouched beside her, his posture uncomfortably intimate. "Lorelei, someone sent messages from your computer within those ten minutes after you and your sister-in-law left. Whoever's doing this is very close to you. At least physically."

Ten minutes. "You can't walk from The Facility to my office in ten minutes. Anyone in the evaluation room Tuesday afternoon couldn't have done it. Unless they win a lot of races."

"Right. The bad news is, we don't know who Giselle Villemaire ensnared to steal Project Andromeda. The good news is, all the classified pages that were missing were found in your office and they've been accounted for. We double-checked the copy-counter to make sure, and then verified it with a light exposure test. Our traitor decided to frame you by stashing the classified documents in your office when they thought they'd be caught."

Someone close to her. Physically. Someone she worked with every day. She'd been betrayed in more ways than one. "What else did the emails say?"

"Nothing else. It was enough. Very incriminating stuff. They were addressed to Giselle but the address was phony. Those messages were designed to bounce back through the system administrator for lack of an adequate address. Whoever did this was at your desk long enough to see the message bounce back to your computer and then transfer the message to your electronic folder. So you wouldn't see it, but we would. Someone wanted those messages to be found. They wanted you to take the blame."

"I guess they fooled you, didn't they?"

"Just the opposite. They tried to plant evidence on you at the exact time I was watching you and your sister-in-law drive into your front yard. Bad timing on their part. Otherwise, it might have sealed your fate."

Someone who knew her—someone she knew—had tried to set her up. She wouldn't take it lying down. On the other hand, what else could she do?

"So you want me to help you catch a spy. How am I supposed to do that?" A week ago, she would have done it without his help. But now, with the baby....

"I want you back at work."

"*I* want me back at work." Though why, she didn't know. Bunch of ingrates. "I'm home on comp time right now, but I've been checking in with the office eight to ten times a day, giving directions, answering questions. I haven't been avoiding work." Avoiding sleep was more like it. She made herself available to her buyers and program managers no matter how little sleep she'd had.

"I realize you're trying to keep up with your work here at home. Home doesn't count. I want you at your desk. Or at least in the building. Someone's using your office to set you up. I think they'll try again. So I need you to be at work but at your desk as little as possible."

"That shouldn't be too hard. I'm always in a meeting."

"We'll rig your office with cameras. We'll see what he's got up his sleeve this time."

"He?"

"Or she. If you're at home, he—or she—won't be using your computer or planting false evidence in your office while you're away from your desk. If he had your account and password, he could send the messages under your header from any computer, but our acquisition security folks could trace it to the specific machine. He had to do it from your computer. If you're at work and he can make you look guilty, I think he'll go for the bait."

"Bait. That's what I am to you." To a man who'd given up his family for his job. A man who had nothing else to live for but his work and didn't particularly care who else got hurt is he could get his man.

Austin shrugged. "I suppose."

"And then what? We all live happily ever after?" All except Roxie.

"Sure, we do. We'll catch our murderer and spy. By then, everyone will know you cooperated with us. Your reputation will be restored. We might even catch Giselle and the Sleeping Dogs."

Madison nodded. Her reputation had been through worse. She'd shake it off and come out stronger. Again. "And Project Andromeda isn't compromised and soon we'll have effective counteragents to biological weapons. That's probably as close to happily ever after as I can wish for." Fairy tales weren't intended for her.

"I suppose we could have been a lot worse off," Austin noted. "There was only one hard copy of the winning proposal inside the safe. If there'd been more than one, whoever did this could have taken an entire copy instead of trying to photocopy a few pages."

The baby opened her eyes wide, and Madison bent to kiss the bridge of the baby's nose between her eyes. "That's because I streamline my source selections," she said in a sing-songy voice for the baby's amusement. "Years ago, we told our contractors to send us ten or fifteen copies of their proposals if they were interested in doing work for the Government. That was ridiculous. Two hundred pages of technical stuff in each copy and then sometimes thousands of pages of spreadsheets per copy to show how they came up with their price. Nowadays, I ask for one signed original for the contract file and one copy on disk."

Austin's face went blank. "There was a disk?"

CHAPTER TEN

"Our Father, Who art in heaven," the elderly minister prayed in a tremulous voice. He closed his eyes and raised his worn face to the sagging ceiling of the green tent. The storming sky pelted against the other side and nearly drowned his words.

The prayer should have been soothing, healing. Instead, Jon felt numb down to his toes.

"We know that sometimes we cannot understand Thy will," the old man droned. "We look upon these dark days and think that truly, Thou hast forsaken us. Yet, it is not for us to know. Only for us to have faith that it is Thy will. For now we do not see beyond the veil. Rather, Lord, Thy truths are kept secreted away until that day in the not too distant future when Thou shalt reveal those blessed secrets to us, Thy humble servants.

"And Father, we implore You to quiet the despair in our hearts. For we know that Thou hast taken this child to be with You and all Thy angels in the realm of glory. She has returned unto Thy bosom.

"Now Father, we commit this body to the ground, but not her spirit. We'll still witness the warmth of her smile in the faces of those who knew her best. We'll still hear the echoes of her laughter in the halls where she worked. We'll still see her influence as the work she gave her life for comes to fruition.

"Now Heavenly Father, let us not say good-bye. Let us say 'good night.'

"'Good night, Roxanne. We'll see you in the morning. Bright and early.' Amen."

Several men standing both in the rain and under the tent murmured their amens, echoing the minister's interment prayer. The crowd began to stir again, most of them raising their heads, some racing for their cars. Others sidestepped Roxie's pink carnation-draped casket to clasp the hand of each mourner in the front row of metal folding chairs.

Jon hunched closer to Madison, his big black umbrella shielding Madison, the baby, and his left shoulder from the spitting rain. He ignored the pain between his shoulders. He was at least half a foot taller than Madison, and sharing the umbrella meant slumping for the past half hour. Madison, safe and dry beside him, cuddled the baby against her chest and stared at the casket with lackluster eyes.

"Roxie would have been proud," he whispered above the softening rain. "She had a fine turn-out today. Especially when you consider the weather."

Madison gave him an almost imperceptible nod. If her eyes focused on anything at all, it was on the black space between the casket's edge and the perimeter of the grave. Jon dared to slip his arm around her shoulder and squeeze. They could have been a family there, the three of them. Anyone who didn't know better might have mistaken them for a young couple and their baby. But everyone knew Madison Steele, and no one made the mistake of thinking Madison was anything other than the cutthroat negotiator she was.

Jon had caught a few people in the crowd—others who hadn't bowed their heads and closed their eyes like they were supposed to—stealing glimpses of Madison standing next to him and holding the baby. He had noticed Beatrice right away. Madison refused to hear anything bad about the woman, even though Beatrice had shared some disturbing speculations with Figmo and Miri. Disturbing musings about where Madison had been for the year after Lt. Timothy Sandusky had been transferred to Iceland. She claimed to know something about Madison no one else knew. Something she'd learned long ago. What would Beatrice gossip about next?

Don't answer that, he told himself. Jon already knew he'd be the next name linked with Madison's. Just as she'd fretted about so often. He'd thought her sweetly paranoid. He'd been wrong.

"Look at them," Madison said, tilting her head in the direction of the little groups of people huddled together to exchange lies. "Mr. Smith declares it a down-day, requisitions a military bus, and tells everybody in contracting to try to make it here to Roxie's service. Look at them all. Just look at them. Given a choice between working and attending a funeral, they show up here. To pay their respects. Can you believe it? Respect. It's too late now. They didn't respect her when she was alive, so how can they respect her when she's dead? Fucking hypocrites."

"Shhh." He squeezed her shoulder again.

Sarabeth stood on the opposite side of the funeral tent and, although she walked the straight and narrow with more self-righteousness than the law allowed, she hadn't bowed her head either. Dressed in black except for her pearl necklace and designer earrings, Sarabeth clutched her designer umbrella overhead with one hand and with the other, dabbed at her eyes with a lace handkerchief. Then, as she patted either raindrops or teardrops from her cheeks, she peered over the lace hanky at Madison.

Jon knew he should remove his arm from Madison's shoulder. The rumor mill would be chugging away within hours. But Madison seemed to stop shaking under his touch, and comforting her was a viable excuse for holding her so close.

"What are you thinking?" he whispered.

She gritted her teeth and inhaled through her nose. Maybe L. Madison Steele didn't cry, but she did struggle for composure. "I was thinking that—" she slanted a gaze up at him—"that what if Roxie was one of the lucky ones?"

His heart skipped a beat. "What do you mean?"

"I mean, there are worse ways to die. Earthquakes, starvation, war."

"Comets plunging into the earth," he half-joked. "Aw, don't let my mom's so-called visions scare you."

She ignored his attempt at wit. "Plagues." She dropped her cheek to nuzzle the baby's head.

"I don't know. I think suffocation is a lousy way to go, too. She knew what was happening to her. She clawed at the vault and—" He cringed at the image. He could see it. Roxie in the dark and dust of the walk-in safe. "Roxie screamed for help. But no one came. Figmo and I hadn't been gone but a little while. Whoever did it must have watched us leave." He glanced around the cemetery. The stone markers dotted the landscape for as far as he could see. Mourners scattered toward distant cars. "Have you thought that someone here today probably killed her and tried to frame you?"

"Like returning to the scene of the crime?"

"Not quite. But a killer would have to be careful not to arouse suspicion. They'd be here, no matter how much water they had to wade through to be at this funeral."

Jon peered at the spot where Sarabeth had stood in her in her unmuddied, winter-white pumps, but she was gone now. Not even the imprint of her shoes remained in the thick grass.

He watched the line of mourners bend to shake hands and offer condolences to Roxie's family on the first row. Roxie's mother leaned into her younger daughter, both of them clutching at the other and sobbing loudly. Another sister, maybe nineteen or twenty years old, stared at a circular arrangement of roses and white carnations and chewed her fingernails to the quick.

Did they know what had happened? Or did they think Roxie had somehow closed and locked a safe door on herself?

Roxie's step-father, a distinguished man with silver at his temples, shook every hand without a word and acknowledged each condolence with a curt nod. He looked pale and lost.

Beside him sat Roxie's ex-husband. The rumored raging anger of a few months ago had been replaced by the plastered-on smile of a man who'd suffered the emotional equivalent of a lobotomy.

Beyond the casket, without an umbrella, Lt. Col. Gavin Ballard stood in the muddy grass with his hands sunk deep into his uniform pockets. The pain in his eyes, the hopelessness, the grief gnawed at Jon.

"Hey Madison? Take a peek at your fearless leader. How did he and Roxie get along?"

"I don't think Gavin killed Roxie, if that's what you mean. They rarely spoke to each other. Every time some good-looking lieutenant came around, Gavin ran him off. I think she was mad that he kept her from having a social life."

"You don't read people very well, do you, Madison? Outside of negotiations anyway. Maybe there was another reason he didn't want guys hanging around her."

"Like what?"

"Look at him. Does he look like he slept to you?" Gavin's eyes looked bloodshot and swollen, dark circles underneath each. Granted, the few people who had been close to Roxie were either taking her death very hard or refusing to let themselves believe it at all, but Gavin Ballard was taking the death of a trainee he supposedly disliked far harder than he deserved. "I think maybe we've found Roxie's mystery man."

"Oh, I don't think so. Gavin's a married man."

"Madison."

Realization dawned in her eyes. "Oh!" She made a face. "No, couldn't be. I thought Roxie had better taste than that. I mean, she could have had anybody. What would she want with a spineless weasel like Gavin Ballard?"

"Makes sense though. That explains why Roxie was hiding her boyfriend's identity."

Tuesday afternoon in The Facility, Roxie had sounded so strange on the telephone, pleading for permission to tell what she knew about the break-in. She must have been talking to Gavin. He was the type to tell her to wait it out, see if Madison got arrested, before risking his career. Coward.

On the night of the break-in—Monday night—Roxie had left The Facility right ahead of Jon. Outside, Jon had stayed in the shadows to wait for Madison. Roxie had waited in her car for Gavin. Then Jon had followed Madison home, and Roxie, still waiting to tryst with her married lover, had seen someone she knew enter The Facility. And that someone had killed her the following night.

Madison made a sound of disgust. "I wondered why he kept dropping by to check on Project Andromeda. He said he needed to keep an eye on such a high-viz project. Should have known it was too good to be true. He doesn't generally take much of an interest in what I'm working on. He hung around to be near Roxie. That's why he always shooed guys away from Roxie's cubicle, too. Afraid they might steal her away from him."

"I'll bet he met up with Roxie every chance he got." Jon held the umbrella a little closer to Madison. She smelled misty in the rain. In a weird sort of way, he could understand why Gavin Ballard would find any excuse he could to spend time with the woman he couldn't have.

"No. Not openly. But come to think of it, I have seen Gavin on base late at night, near The Facility. I thought it was pretty strange because he makes a point to be home in time for dinner with his wife and kids. I wonder what excuse he used with them to come back to work."

"Roxie knew who set you up, but Gavin wouldn't let her say anything. He was too afraid the truth would come out. She was too afraid he'd get shipped off to Iceland like—"

Too late, he bit off the words. Sometimes he could be so stupid. He held his breath. He'd really screwed up this time.

Madison slowly cut her gaze toward his in her usual, careful display of control. No emotion. Not even a twitch. But from what he'd heard, she'd had plenty of practice by now.

He gave her a little shrug. "Sorry," he said. "Sorry."

She blinked at him and said nothing.

Ah, well. What the hell. He dug deep into his pocket and brought out the crumpled note that had been taped to the back of her framed contracting officer's warrant. He slid it into her palm. She must have known what it was because she curled her fingers tightly around it and held it to her chest.

"I hate to be the one to tell you, Madison, but when you get back into the office—whenever that may be—your office will look a little bit different. Sarabeth and the others, they went through all your stuff. Somebody tipped off Security that you had the proposal photocopies hidden in your office. Sarabeth found this. I thought you might want it back."

Deep fierceness flared in her eyes, but she said nothing. She couldn't have lost the will to fight. Maybe she was filing away yet another transgression against her into her long memory. One day, she'd destroy them all. For now, he watched her swallow the lump in her throat.

"Sorry," he said again. He knew that she knew that he knew about Tim. That there was at least a kernel of truth in the rumors.

"Thank you," she mouthed.

"I liked what it said," he stammered. "It's a lot better than that stupid fortune cookie from the other night. 'The future is bright,'" he quoted. "'Never hesitate to walk through the door—wonderful things and people and experiences may be on the other side.'" He left off the I-Love-You-Tim on the note.

She nodded. "I used to read that all the time when I felt a little down."

"Then it's time to read it again. I think it's important to keep a positive attitude."

She rolled her eyes at him. "And how, pray tell, Lt. Pollyanna, am I supposed to keep a positive attitude? I'm here at the funeral of one of the few friends I have, I've been betrayed by someone else I work with, everyone else thinks I'm a spy or a slut or both, a newborn's been abandoned to my care, the disk that has the electronic copy of Project Andromeda is missing and probably in enemy hands, and according to your mother and all the prophecies, the world is coming to an end. Forgive me for not counting my blessings, but what the hell good would a positive attitude do me?"

There she went again. The cynic. The old Madison with the sharp mind and the sharper tongue. The one who'd stepped aside to make room for the mothering instinct.

"Not much I can do about those other things," he told her, "but as far as the world coming to an end, I don't think we have to worry about that for a long time. I wasn't going to tell you this. I talked to my mom again this morning, and she had a message for you. It was kind of weird. She said your child will be a great writer, and she'll keep the record of the new history after the world as we know it ends. So see? You don't have a kid. We've got plenty of time before you have to worry about the end of the world."

Madison stared right through him as if he were some kind of ghost.

Jon glanced up and groaned. "Now there's something you should worry about."

Austin Wait in his god-awful black suit and matching umbrella nodded at Madison and strode toward them through the light drizzle. "Good to see you, Ms. Steele." His gaze flickered over Jon, but Wait said nothing, whether he saw Jon as a nuisance or a rival. The shield of unmistakable dislike slammed down between them.

Madison actually smiled at the S.O.B. "Hello, Austin."

Austin? *Austin?* Since when had she gotten on a first name basis with the son of a bitch?

"I see you're still taking care of your niece. Her mother hasn't come back yet?"

"Not yet."

Madison had spent most of last night trying to get in touch with Jolene's mother, the drunken slut. When she finally reached the woman and asked her if Jolene had a baby or not, the best response Madison had received was that if Jolene said she had a baby, then Jolene had a baby. On the other hand, Jolene's mother hadn't been able to provide the simplest information. Like the baby's name or age. Or sex. Madison's guess was that Jolene's mother was either too drunk to recall the most basic information or their conversation was the first the woman had heard of a grandchild.

"Let's hope your sister-in-law comes back soon so you can get back to the office."

Yeah, right. Like Austin Wait cared about Madison's reputation.

"I'm looking forward to it," Madison replied.

It was absurd, of course, but sometimes Jon got the feeling something was going on between Madison and the OSI agent. Like they weren't telling him something.

Wait jerked his head in Jon's direction. "I suppose you've already told him everything," the OSI agent said to Madison. His way of talking about Jon as if Jon weren't present—or worse, as if he were a child too young to understand the implications—was annoying at best.

"You told me not to tell."

"What 'everything'?" Jon demanded. "What didn't you tell me?"

Madison ignored Jon and jostled the baby against the soft bodice of her black dress. "I believe your exact words were 'Breathe a word of this, and I'll lock his butt up.' Sound familiar?"

Jon had the urge to jump up and down in front of her. He tried to edge in between them and got a collar full of rain for his trouble. "Breathe a word of what?"

Madison kept her eyes on Wait. Probably a wise thing to do. "Jon, Austin knows I didn't take Project Andromeda. He's on our side."

Jon choked. "Austin Wait's not on anybody's side but his own."

At that, Wait bothered to look at him. His nose twitched as if the smell of cemetery dirt offended him. "You're right, kid. It so happens that this time my side and Lorelei's side are one and the same." He turned back to Madison and clucked his tongue. "I didn't expect you to keep a secret from the boy."

"Did I pass your test? It was a test, wasn't it? To see whether you could trust me?"

"Trust you about what?" Jon interjected. They both ignored him.

"You passed," Wait said. "When are you going back to the office?"

"I don't know." She shifted the infant in her arms to keep the spatter of rain off her cheeks. "I can't. I have to take care of the baby."

"You've got more important things to do than take care of that baby.

This investigation is at a stalemate now. Without you in that office, Project Andromeda is lost."

She winced with guilt. The world's best solution to biological weapons, and she was too busy with baby-sitting! Maybe what Wait had said about family crises as a nation-crippling strategy was right on the mark. The working parents with children in a daycare infested with flesh-eating bacteria chose to stay home with their babies and toddlers rather than go into work. Even those military members and "essential" civil servants ordered into government buildings to keep things running weren't giving their country a hundred percent when their minds were elsewhere. In times of crisis, family takes priority.

"I've already called around," Madison said. "I can't get the baby into a daycare until she's at least six weeks old. Jolene's missing and Toby's at sea."

And denying paternity, according to Madison.

"What about Jolene's mother?" Wait suggested. He swiped his damp hair out of his eyes. "Can't she watch the kid for a few days?"

"No." Madison shook her head furiously. "She's a drunk and an addict. I wouldn't let her watch my dog."

"You have a dog?"

"No."

"What about your parents? Can they watch the baby?"

Her eyes widened as if she hadn't thought of it and wouldn't dare think of it. "My parents are almost seventy years old. They're not able to stay up nights with a baby. To tell you the truth, I'm not sure I am either. Not sure I could do it without a little help from Jon."

"Yeah, I noticed Colter had moved in with you."

"I have not," Jon protested. "I'm spending the night on the sofa."

"Yeah, whatever you say."

"I am!"

If he'd slept with Madison, he'd sure be willing to take credit in front of Austin Wait. The truth was, he hadn't seen the inside of her bedroom. Yet. And the way things were going, he never would. He'd spent three nights inside her house, and every night had been under protest. From her, of course. She hadn't wanted him there, hadn't wanted his help. At least she'd said she hadn't. Her eyes always had betrayed her. L. Madison Steele wasn't the kind of woman who accepted help, not easily anyway. And she wasn't the kind of woman who would ever ask for help.

He wasn't exactly happy to have to share her with a newborn who cried for practically no reason but thankfully slept most of the time. When Madison could fall asleep during the day, people at work wouldn't leave her alone long enough to let her nap. She refused to take the phone off the hook in case someone found out something about the missing Andromeda disk or Roxie's murder. If he came straight home from work, Jon could bring her dinner—or maybe eventually make her dinner—and send her to bed by 7:00 p.m. Then she could get up by one in the morning, feed the baby her soybean milk, and nap with the baby in her arms until daylight when the calls began again. Neither of them got enough sleep that way, but it seemed the only way to keep Madison going.

A week ago, Madison had been hell on wheels. Nothing could have stopped her then. Somehow the child had drained all her power. Madison still wanted the same things, but with lack of sleep and lack of time and no lack of worry over the baby and her missing mother, she'd become an impotent warrior.

"Have you called HRS?" Wait asked. He stared down at his muddy feet as he studied the problem.

"I am not calling HRS."

"Why not? The girl's abandoned her baby."

"That's because of me. The least I can do is make sure this baby is taken care of until her mother comes back."

"Suit yourself. On the other hand, it's nice to know you've stopped blaming me for her disappearance. A few days ago, you said it was all my fault."

"It is all your fault. But somebody has to be responsible."

"If you call HRS, they'll take the baby and we can get you back into the office."

"I am not calling HRS. If they were to take this baby away from my brother and his wife, it would be all my fault." If the baby really was Toby and Jolene's. "Can you imagine what my parents would think of me if I caused them to lose their granddaughter?"

Wait shrugged. "Have you thought about a sitter?"

"She's too young for a sitter."

Jon had the strangest feeling Madison was looking for excuses to keep holding the baby. And as long as she had the baby, he could stay close to her, but not close enough. "I could probably take off from work a few days," he suggested. "I've got plenty of leave."

"No. No, you need to be at work."

"So do you. More than I do. Like Wait said, you're the key to this whole thing."

Though he was determined Madison wasn't going back to work alone. Jon had already volunteered to Col. Kildee to work on a special employee morale booster "extra duty" in Building 13. Once Madison was back in her office, he would use the special project excuse to be within a few dozen feet of her. Someone who knew her, someone who worked with her every day, had betrayed her, set her up for a security violation and a murder rap. They'd killed once, and they'd probably kill again. He wouldn't walk away from Madison like he'd walked away from Roxie minutes before she'd been locked inside that walk-in safe. If it was the last thing Jon did, he'd find out who had set up Madison.

"Look, Lorelei, we've got to do something," Wait said. "The clock is ticking. We're going to get you back into that office if I have to hire my own mother to baby-sit."

Or, Jon thought, if he had to call HRS himself. She'd never forgive him if she knew, but the mothering instinct left Madison far too constrained. How could she save the world with a baby in her arms?

The morning rain had evened off to a light mist, barely peppering down on their umbrellas. Roxie's family had left the tent. The mourners and gossips had gone home. The employees of the funeral home unlatched the crank on Roxie's casket and began to lower it into the rectangular hole.

A lump ballooned into Jon's throat. That could as easily have been Madison.

Madison whimpered. She covered her mouth. "I think I'm going to be sick," she whispered.

A white Crown Victoria splashed through the mud puddles along the cemetery's perimeter. Jon squinted at the driver. A sandy-haired man. Mid-thirties. Gray suit. Jaw tight with determination. Jon had seen the same car before, the same man, parked across the street from Madison's little house under the flight line. The car had been close by since the night he'd watched Madison climb down the fire escape. The night he'd taken her home in the rain, and she'd pressed her body tight against his on his motorcycle. The night Roxie had died.

Jon grunted. "Your back-up man over there doesn't seem to have anything to do. Maybe he could watch the baby."

"What back-up man?" Wait gingerly closed his umbrella and then fumbled with the snap. He patted the bulky walkie-talkie on his belt. "My back-up's right here."

Jon tilted his head toward the man in the car. He couldn't see the man's face. The driver had raised a pair of binoculars to his eyes and stopped the car. "The guy in the white Ford. If you really believe Madison isn't guilty, why do you have that goon watching her house all the time? Or is he supposed to be some kind of bodyguard?"

Wait craned his neck. "I don't have a guy watching her house. But maybe I should."

Madison twisted to look. "It's him! It's the same guy who watched Jolene crawl out my window. The guy I thought was your partner or something."

"He's not my partner," Wait said through gritted teeth, "but I have a feeling he could answer a lot of questions. There's a convenience store up on the corner," he spat out, rapid-fire. "Take the baby and go up there. There'll be plenty of people around. I'll have someone meet you there in a few minutes. Colter!" He jabbed one finger into Jon's chest. "You stay with Lorelei, but don't do anything stupid. You're protection, not a hero." In four ball-splitting strides, Wait had hurled his umbrella toward his black sedan and taken off in a dead run after the Ford.

"Come on. Hurry." Jon ushered Madison toward her car. He pushed her along too fast for her to look back. He glanced over his shoulder in time to see the Ford spin away, spewing a wave of mud in its wake. Wait turned and ran back to his sedan, all the while blasting orders into his walkie-talkie. Before Madison could get the baby properly installed in her car seat, Wait had gunned his engine and headed out of the cemetery. Wait didn't manage to slam his door until his tires met the asphalt on the adjacent street.

Madison tried to peer over her head rest. "What happened back there?"

"We'll find out later. For once, I think Austin Wait is right: I need to stay with you, and we need to get you and the baby out of here."

"But the man in the white car!"

"Madison, if he's not one of the OSI's goons—if you believe Austin Wait when he says that guy isn't his back-up man—then there's no telling who the guy in the white car is or who he's working for." Sleeping Dogs, maybe? Jon filled his lungs with a nervous gulp of air. "Or what he might have done if I hadn't spent the past few nights with you."

She seemed to consider his words, then gave him a quick nod.

"I think it would be a good idea if we found another place for you to stay until this mess blows over."

"I'm not leaving my home. What if Jolene comes back? What if my parents try to get in touch with me? No. No, I'm not leaving."

"Then you'd better get used to having me on your sofa every night." He looked at her again, and she didn't argue. If she knew him at all, she knew he wouldn't take no for an answer. Not this time.

Jon wheeled into the convenience store's last empty parking spot and killed the engine. "Let's go."

"Inside? We can wait in the car for Austin."

"And have some guy with a gun take potshots at us while we're sitting here? Come on. Lots of people inside. He won't try anything in there." Jon hoped.

He jumped out of the car and made it around to the passenger door before Madison could unbuckle her seatbelt.

Would life ever be back to normal? He couldn't stop looking over his shoulder. Not a white car in sight, but he still couldn't relax.

"Come on, come on. Hurry up."

She picked up the baby too quickly. It started to cry. Madison tried to pat it, but she couldn't rise fast enough, couldn't get the right rhythm. She grabbed a four-ounce bottle of soy formula from the dashboard.

Jon hauled her out by the elbow and guided her through the swinging glass doors. The baby broke into a full-fledged cry that sounded more like the bleating of a wounded animal than the crying of a baby.

He cornered Madison on the far side of the store, between the candy bars and the racks of the *National Enquirer,* recipe magazines, and newspapers. Madison sank the nipple of the baby bottle into the baby's mouth. More angry than hungry, the child didn't take the bottle at first, but with a little prompting, she closed her lips around the rubber nipple and tugged hard.

Madison herself had turned pale. Her hands trembled as she directed the bottle at the baby's mouth, yet her jaw was as stony as ever. If she was afraid, she didn't intentionally let it show. He and Madison were probably wishing the same thing—to be in the heart of the action rather than relegated to the sidelines.

A teenage girl at the cash register frowned up at them. Madison shifted on her feet. "We should—I don't know—buy something. We look like we're casing the joint."

Jon laughed. "We could always take this opportunity to buy a few more diapers or formula."

So far she'd sent Jon out to run those errands, citing the fact that the baby was too young to go out. Of course, funerals didn't count. Madison had had to attend Roxie's funeral, and she wasn't about to leave the baby with someone else.

She sidestepped Jon and pretended to look over the rack of scandal sheets boasting crazy news of UFOs, mind control, and time travel.

"Oh, no." She glanced from the local paper to Jon and back. "There was a hurricane?"

"He read the headline over her shoulder. "Several weeks ago. Up the coast. coastline. Our local utility companies are sending linemen up to help out."

"Oh. I knew it hadn't come near here, but I didn't know where it'd made landfall. If it had come up the Gulf, Eugene Krueger would've had everybody in The Facility on drills."

Jon chuckled to himself. Stacks of newspapers, still in their plastic sleeves, guarded Madison's front door. During the long hours of source selection and the wee hours of taking care of the baby, Madison had lost track of the world outside. She was too caught up in saving the world to know what was going on in it.

"Jon! Jon, look at this!"

He took a step forward, close enough to feel the heat of her body through her black dress. She nodded toward a small photo and a two-column story in the lower corner of the front page. "Desperate Father Offers Reward for Missing Baby," she read. "A baby girl." Madison spun on her feet and gazed up at Jon. "Are you thinking what I'm thinking?"

Austin Wait, breathless and panting, nearly skidded between them. His eyes were wolf-like and wild with determination. "Lost him. The guy in the Ford. Car's stolen, obviously. The plates check out to a man named Owen Plummer."

Madison cuddled the baby. "I don't know any Owen Plummer."

"Course not. I had our database double-checked. This clown surfaced about three months ago. He's using Plummer's birth certificate to set up phony bank accounts, credit cards, driver's license, everything. Gun permits. And now he's keeping a close watch on you. Lorelei, listen, I don't want you going out of town."

"But I already have plans for the weekend. I have to go out of town."

Jon stifled a twinge of hurt. He'd practically shared every breath with her for days now, and she hadn't mentioned any trips. Where did she plan to go? To find Jolene? Her brother, Toby?

"Not this weekend you don't," Wait warned. "This Owen Plummer pretender is probably affiliated with Giselle Villemaire or one of the BW terrorist groups we talked about. Maybe the Sleeping Dogs. I want you close by in case he makes his move."

"What about the real Owen Plummer? Who's he?"

"Scientist. Special projects for the Pentagon, according to the record. He led a top secret project during the Kennedy administration. *Enoch's Gate.* Other than that, his record's been wiped clean. Funny that our pretender would pick him."

"But what about the real Owen Plummer? Does he know his identity's been stolen?"

"The real Dr. Plummer died before you were born. At this point, I don't know if our guy is related to the missing Andromeda files, but believe me, I'm going to find out."

Jon swallowed hard. "You think the impostor's the one who killed Roxie?"

"Possible. But I still think he had help from one of Ms. Steele's colleagues. Someone she knows well enough to switch her access card."

But what Austin Wait really meant was that Madison's enemy was most likely a trusted friend.

CHAPTER ELEVEN

Friday, 1 October 1999, V alparaiso, Florida

For the third time in the past hour, Madison picked up the telephone handset and then dropped it back into its cradle. No, she couldn't do it. She couldn't place one simple phone call. Not as long as the slimmest chance existed that she could be wrong.

What if the baby really was Jolene's and Toby's? What if Madison was making a mistake?

Again.

L. Madison Steele had to be Superwoman, trying to do everything for everyone. Trying to save the world. But this child, this fragile baby, was her kryptonite. She didn't want to save the world from bio-warfare terrorists. She didn't want to think of Project Andromeda. All she wanted to do was sit in her rocking chair and snuggle the baby against her bare breasts, pretend she was in another time and place. She had work to do, but the baby brought back too many paralyzing memories. Until Jolene had shown up with a baby in need of a mother, Madison had been comfortably numb to the past.

Again, Madison reached for the telephone, then drew back. None of her usual modus operandi fit her situation. If she couldn't be good at the game, she didn't want to play at all. When it came to hard decisions, she made them and walked away with no regrets. Let the chips fall where they would. At least someone was doing something, and action was sometimes more important that the consequences.

This time was different.

She paced in circles in her tiny kitchen. She stopped once to check the baby's formula, warming in a pan of hot water. She had fed, diapered, and bathed the baby, who now slept soundly on a cushion on the living room floor. But the moment the little thing woke and wanted to nurse, Madison would be ready with the bottle and two loving arms. Maybe Madison didn't want to make the phone call because she actually enjoyed taking care of a baby, even with the grueling hours. Having the baby in the house was like a second chance, one she didn't want to lose.

Everyone else was so ready for her to give up the child. Jon, Austin Wait, Toby. Somehow it seemed only right of her to refuse. Especially since last time she had been the one so ready to give up her own flesh and blood. Tim's flesh and blood.

Everyone else had such good reasons for her to give up the baby Jolene had left in her care. Good reasons. Logical reasons. Perfectly acceptable reasons. Toby knew the baby wasn't his and knew what a burden Jolene's latest antics had become to Madison's career. Austin Wait saw the baby as a hindrance to her job and to national security. And Jon—bless him, he was sound asleep on her sofa—had only her happiness in mind. He wanted her to be safe. Protected. He knew the baby had taken the edge off her and he wanted her back the way she used to be—angry, taking charge. If that meant calling the HRS to come get the child, so be it.

All good, valid reasons, but Madison's reason for giving up the child went far deeper. She had been Rhiannon's mother and for that reason alone, no reason was acceptable for giving away her baby.

Madison walked past the kitchen table and fingered the unfurled newspapers that were nearly as old as the baby. Jolene's baby. Not hers.

Not Jolene's either.

Sheridan Cashwell's baby, according to the papers.

Sheridan Cashwell hadn't neglected his paternal duties. According to the papers, his fiancée' didn't want their baby, but he did. He'd been willing to raise it alone if necessary.

Damn him. Some men could be so noble. Maybe if Tim had known, he would have stuck around, too. Or come back sooner instead of leaving Madison to wait for him for seven years with only an unconsummated wedding band for a souvenir and a child she couldn't keep.

The media had made Sheridan Cashwell out to be both a hero and a victim. His girlfriend had been adamant: no children. Not good for the career. Maggie Blanton was a specialist in environmental law and on the fast track to a partnership in a law firm. Having never been a child herself, she didn't particularly like children. The papers had made her sound absolutely awful for not wanting to be a mother.

Though Cashwell had been too impatient for protected sex, he later agreed to take on the financial and emotional role of parenting if Maggie would only carry the child to term. He'd come out the hero. Public opinion was nearly as strong against the missing baby's mother as it was against the kidnapper. Madison didn't have to hold the mirror very far away to see how the rest of the world would see her if they only knew the truth.

Why was it that men got hailed as heroes for doing all the things women naturally did as mothers but were condemned as mothers if they failed to do any one of them?

According to the papers, Sheridan Cashwell had taken his one-day-old daughter home from the hospital. His decision to keep his own daughter was lovingly accepted and supported by family, friends, and colleagues at his engineering firm. Relatives rushed to help out on the first night home, and throughout the second day, they brought over food so he didn't have to worry about cooking. They took turns with the baby so he didn't have to worry about catching a nap whenever possible. No one stopped to visit his now former fiancee' before she left the hospital. The woman slipped quietly away. Everyone seemed to agree she should get out of Cashwell's life quickly, and not one of Sheridan Cashwell's family dared to think the mother might have taken her own child.

On the third day at home, little Bronwyn Cashwell had become so irritable that no amount of hugs could comfort her. Right away, Cashwell had called his pediatrician—like any good mother would—and got a walk-in appointment for late that morning. The doctor immediately declared Bronwyn's tummy troubles due to her milk-based formula and switched her to soybean. The doctor had filled her diaper bag with soy formula samples in four-ounce glass bottles, exactly as Jolene had had in her bag, and sent father and daughter home.

Then it had happened.

The relieved father had walked out to the car, opened the passenger door, and set the baby, carseat, and diaper bag onto the front seat.

Then he'd walked around to the trunk to rearrange a baby stroller that had rattled the whole way to the doctor's office. When he returned to the passenger door, Baby Bronwyn, her carseat, and her diaper bag were all missing. He'd sworn he hadn't taken his eyes off the baby for more than ten seconds, though by the lengthy description of how he'd repacked the trunk, it sounded more like minutes. Cashwell's well-to-do parents had dropped a quick ten grand into a bucket of reward money for anyone having any information leading to the safe return of their little princess.

Madison walked back to the telephone, lifted the handset, and fingered the keys. Could she risk being wrong? She slipped the handset back into its cradle. This baby wasn't hers to risk.

If only Jolene would come back. Maybe if Madison knew more about the Cashwell baby, she'd be able to determine whether or not the baby sleeping in her own arms every night was in fact the same child. From the description in the papers, Jolene's baby and Bronwyn Cashwell could have been twins. Then again, the newspaper photograph, taken at age one day, was as useless as any other newborn photograph. Babies changed by the day, and already Jolene's baby had grown chubby enough that the armbands of her dress were tight against the creamy flesh of her upper arms.

Maybe if Madison talked to Sheridan Cashwell himself, she could find out something more. Some distinguishing characteristic that would tell her Jolene's baby definitely wasn't a Cashwell. But how? She could call the number in the newspaper—the one that offered a reward for information—but she knew better. Phone calls could easily be traced or, at the very least, by punching up a few numbers, Sheridan Cashwell could retrieve the telephone number that had dialed his last. Then he'd know exactly where to find her. He and the cops.

Maybe she could disguise her voice, wear shoes two sizes too big for her and rubber gloves, and trot down to the nearest pay phone to make the clandestine call. But could she get out of there before the cops showed up? Doubtful. She could send Jon to make the call, but she'd never put him at that kind of risk. Never.

Madison paced the length of the kitchen one more time, pausing by the table to study the newspapers. An ad for a furniture store's going-out-of-business sale caught her eye. The words, *FINAL DAYS*, had been stamped across the ad. Of course, they meant the final days of the furniture sale, but to Madison, it served as a reminder of the end of the world and the part she supposedly played in the scheme of the universe. She had to find out what had happened to Project Andromeda and reverse the damage, but first, she had to get back into the office.

With renewed purpose, she marched back to the telephone, lifted the handset, and began to dial. Not Sheridan Cashwell's number, but another.

"Who are you calling?" Jon roused from the sofa and ran one sleepy hand through his tousled blond hair. He let his cheek rest in his palm as he gazed up at her.

Madison stared down at her bare feet. She was about to say something she couldn't remember ever saying before. "I need help. I can't do this alone."

"Ah, Madison." Jon bolted up off the lumpy cushions and closed the distance between them. He laid a strong hand on her shoulder. "I'm right here."

"I'm in over my head."

"Anything you want, anything, I'll do it."

"You can't." She tried to smile back.

"I can. I will. Just tell me what it is you need done, and I'll find a way to do it. Call HRS? Is that it?"

"There's nothing you can do, Jon. I've been fooling myself. I've always known I couldn't do my job and hold a baby, too. Maybe other women, but not me." Butterflies banged into her stomach from the inside. "I can't afford to make another mistake. If I'm wrong, my brother loses his daughter. If I'm right, I've got a hell of a lot of explaining to do."

"I'll take care of it. I'll take care of everything. Just say the word."

"I can't trouble you with this."

"Madison." He gripped her shoulders. *"Trouble me."*

The telephone stopped in mid-ring. On the other end of the line, a receptionist cleared her throat. "Austin Wait, please," Madison said. Jon flinched as if the name itself had stung him. He dropped his hands to his sides. "Yes, tell him it's Madison Steele. It's urgent. Tell him I—" She inhaled and then expelled it slowly. "Tell him I need his help."

Jon squeezed his eyes shut and shook his head, blond mane falling forward. He walked away a few steps and then wheeled to face her. "How could you ask *him* for help?"

"Shhh." She motioned for Jon to be quiet and turned a cold shoulder.

"Afternoon, Ms. Steele." Austin sounded as cool and debonair as ever. "Wasn't expecting to hear from you so soon after the funeral. Everything okay? Any sight of our Mr. Plummer?"

"No, it's Jolene's baby. I don't know who else to turn to. I don't think the baby's Jolene's." From somewhere behind her, Jon let out a ragged breath.

"Has your sister-in-law come back?"

"No, and I don't think she's going to. The baby's been here three days. My brother denies it's his. Are you familiar with the Cashwell baby that's been in all the papers?"

"Shit." Apparently he was. "That complicates things."

"You're telling me."

"Last thing we need is media attention."

"That's why I'm calling you. I want to find out if this baby is really Jolene's or if it's the Cashwell baby. And I don't know how to do it without getting myself in deeper." Her voice wavered. She damned herself for it.

"All right. I'll make arrangements for some tests. Quiet tests. You bring the baby to my office."

"Now?"

"Yesterday, if you can get here that fast."

"I'll be right there." She slipped the handset back into its cradle. Did she dare turn around and face Jon? She wrung her hands and slowly turned to meet his wounded gaze. "I had to turn to someone," she said.

"Turn to me!"

"There's nothing you can do."

"You haven't given me a chance!"

"Jon." She reached to brush his cheek, lingered too long, and knew she'd risked her soul to touch him. Her hand dropped like lead to her side. "Don't you know how hard it is for me to ask for help?"

"Yes! I do. But why did you have to ask Austin Wait? You finally ask for help and you ask him! He doesn't care about you. He doesn't care about anybody as long as he catches the bad guys. Why couldn't you ask me for help?"

She could give him any number of logic-laden excuses, but none of them would take away the pain in his eyes, faded blue and hurting.

"Why couldn't you ask me?"

In a blur of movement, he pressed her against the wall, knocking the breath out of her. He pinned her there with his body, rock-hard and closer than she'd imagined in the best of her dreams. She'd never feared him before. Maybe she'd pushed him too far. His breath came out hot on her cheek. His eyes searched hers, then lost focus in a half-lidded yearning.

"Ask me, Madison. Ask *me.*"

She wanted to wrap her arms around his neck and her legs around his hips and beg him never to let go, but she knew better. If she didn't know him so well, if he were a stranger in a faraway city, if she knew she'd never see him again. But she worked with him every day. Too much to risk. Not for her but for him. She cared too much to let him make the same mistake she had with Tim.

Jon bent closer. His tongue traced the outline of his upper lip. "I should be the one you turn to. Austin Wait doesn't care about you like I do. He doesn't love you like I do."

Before she could ask herself if she'd heard him right, his mouth descended on hers, hard and wanton and desperate. There was nothing tender in the kiss, yet it swirled with a passion she'd not felt in years. His touch burned a quick fuze to the pit of her stomach and if she'd been a weaker woman, her knees might have failed her. She broke the seal of his kiss.

"Jon."

He would have had to be a complete idiot to miss the way her body responded to his, the way her lips didn't want to part with his, the way she struggled against becoming the aggressor and turning her sweet predator into her prey. Part of her hoped he recognized her bravado as a facade, if only to spare him the sting of rejection when she didn't want to reject him at all. She steeled herself against the damnation in his touch and squirmed out of his embrace.

"Please excuse me."

***

If Jon wasn't at her house when she returned, she had no one to blame but herself. He'd been by her side for months, always willing to help, always ready to give if she'd only ask. Part of her wanted to accept his help. She'd done it all by herself for so long. She'd always been the strong one, the pillar of stone, while those around her crumbled. Just once, *just once,* she'd like to be the one crumbling in someone else's strong arms.

Jon's arms.

But being the strong one exhalted a heavy price, and she wouldn't put that burden on him. If she let herself feel ever again, then Lt. Colter might be a likely candidate. But it was too late for that. Love, for her, was history already, a habit she'd formed long ago with another lieutenant. One who would one day come back for her and make the ring on her third finger, left hand real.

A door slammed behind her and she startled, looked up. Austin Wait stood in front of her, crossed his arms, and leaned against the desk. With a patience she hated, he studied her. She met his gaze and looked away nervously. His office was the exact opposite of hers. She filled every corner with stacks of paper to be filed or copied or answered. Not a speck of paper littered his freshly vacuumed carpet. His desk and file cabinets had been dusted and polished. The reflection of Austin's tall silhouette shimmered on the surface. Half a dozen manila file folders neatly crammed full cascaded across the left-hand side of the desk. Except for a combination name plate/pencil holder and a pot of ivy on top of a file cabinet, the rest of the room was bare, anonymous. Unlike the clutter of Madison's office. The man was obviously crazy.

"They'll be done with the baby's tests in another fifteen minutes or so," Austin said. "You gonna be all right?"

"I'm always all right."

"And if the baby's test results match up with the Cashwell baby's?"

"Then I don't know. I'd have to talk to her father first."

"Even if we find the baby's Cashwell's beyond a doubt?"

"The baby's in my charge for the moment. I won't give her up unless I'm sure she's in good hands." Like last time.

"Even if she's not yours to give up?"

Madison didn't say anything, but she set her molars against molars until her jaws hurt. Until she physically, willingly surrendered the baby to Sheridan Cashwell, it was her responsibility. And until then, the child in her care would substitute for the one she couldn't have and paralyze any chance of Madison saving the planet from bio-warfare terrorists.

"You've got that look on your face," Austin said.

Her head popped up. "Which look is that? My eat-shit-and-die look?"

"No. Like you want to make a confession."

"Confession," she sputtered. "I told you, I don't have anything to confess. Not to you."

"But you will. One day you'll tell me. I still haven't found out what happens to that two grand a month in cash you take out of your salary and where you blow it."

"I don't blow it."

"Well, whatever it is you spend it on, I will find out."

"Why are you doing this? I didn't come here to talk to you about my personal finances."

Austin smirked back at her. "Hey, you're the one who asked for help."

Exactly why she usually didn't ask for help. Accepting help meant owing a favor, sometimes a favor she wasn't willing to return.

"You're right," she countered. She didn't have to accept any answer he gave her. For Lord's sake, she was a top-notch negotiator. "I did ask for your help, but you asked for mine first. And the only way I can give you that help is if I get back into my office. And getting back into my office means finding out where that baby belongs."

The baby didn't belong to her. She could pretend and dream only for so long. Already, her arms ached to hold the child. Giving up a baby after holding it in your arms had to be the worst withdrawal pains a woman could go through. Instinctively, Madison knew it was coming. Again.

"Yeah, okay," Austin conceded. "You've got a point."

"Of course I have a point. If you want my help in catching a spy, that is." How nice to be the one owed a favor, even though she rarely collected. "Any more guesses on who our spy is?"

"Nothing."

Yeah, right. Like Austin Wait would tell her everything. He'd string her along with a few hints here and there. Not so much as to jeopardize his investigation, but enough that he could pretend he'd made her a partner in his search for truth.

"What about Owen Plummer?" she asked.

"Again, nothing."

"There's got to be a tie between him and Giselle Villemaire and whoever their connection in my office is. Maybe Dr. Plummer isn't dead. Maybe our guy's the real thing."

Austin shook his head. "This guy's about thirty years too young to be Plummer, but he does bear a resemblance to the photos I've seen."

"His son?"

"He didn't have a son. He died childless. Like I told you before, he was a Government scientist under the Kennedy Administration. Special projects. Top secret clearance. Most of his official record has been wiped clean, but as always I do have my unofficial sources."

"Maybe his widow could shed some light on the connection."

"Not possible. His wife committed suicide in 1960. After that, Plummer buried himself in his work. Fanatical."

"So you have looked into Plummer's role."

Austin smiled. "I leave no stone unturned. You should know that. Unfortunately, I can't find many stones on Plummer." His smile faded. "So far, I've hit a dead-end. No pun intended."

Something niggled at the back of her brain. "How did Owen Plummer die?"

"Explosion. We didn't have the same technology back then as we do now, so we don't know what caused the explosion. Whether it was a bomb or maybe one of his experiments went awry."

"Maybe that's the tie-in. His experiments. Maybe Plummer was working on something related to Project Andromeda. A pre-cursor, maybe? We had scientists back then working on chem and germ warfare. The technology's been around since the '30's or before."

"I suppose. What he worked on, we'll never know. Those projects were highly classified. Who knows what this Enoch's Gate project was about, anyway? Maybe dealing with the space program. That was its heyday, remember? Around the time we put man in orbit, before we put man on the moon. Plummer was a brilliant physicist, but he was nutszoid, according to my sources. Eccentric is too nice a word. Before he started working for the Government and they forced him to restrain his wild ideas, guess what he gave lectures on?" Austin laughed. "'The practicality of travel through time and space.' Isn't that a hoot? Too bad he didn't live another few years to see the original *Star Trek* series. He would have loved it."

Time travel, space travel. Where no man had gone before. *Then.*

"I'm disappointed, Austin. I was kind of hoping we had the original Owen Plummer on our hands and that maybe he was some kind of microbiologist or chemist working on nerve gas or bio-technology, ultraviolet countermeasures, and the like. If he was involved with pre-Project Andromeda technology, that would have made sense."

"If anything about this case made sense, I guess that would have been it."

"So the guy who's calling himself Owen Plummer, are he and Giselle Villemaire partners? Strangers?" She shrugged. "Lovers?"

"Strangers, I doubt. Lovers? Who knows? Partners? Maybe. I did find out something interesting."

Madison leaned forward and waited. No telling what Austin might eventually tell her if she hung around long enough.

"According to my sources—"

"Sheesh. How many sources do you have?"

"Not nearly enough. According to my sources," he continued, "Giselle Villemaire isn't necessarily exclusive in who she works for. She has a few buyers lined up for the BW technology she's brokering. The Iraqis, the French, at least one anti-Government paramilitary group in Louisiana, and an international terrorist group, the Sleeping Dogs. She's already been paid twice for an exclusive sale."

"Twice and it's exclusive? She can't do that."

"Oh yeah? Giselle steals information on a black technology that could wipe out every unprotected man, woman, and child on the planet, has you set up for murder, and she's supposed to have enough integrity to negotiate fairly among her customers? I don't think so."

"Won't they smell a double-cross? I mean, if you know, then somebody else knows, right?"

"Worse. She doesn't have the technology yet."

"But Project Andromeda was stolen five days ago. By—we think—somebody she recruited."

"If she had the technology in her hot little hands, she would have transferred it by now. That's what she does. Buy information and sell it. Get in and get out quickly."

Thank God. Madison sighed. Her shoulders relaxed for the first time in hours. The classified files she felt responsible for hadn't circled the planet a hundred times as she'd feared. "So whoever took the proposal disk and tried to frame me hasn't turned it over yet. Why not?"

"Waiting for the right moment, I guess. Maybe the investigation's been too close for comfort. Maybe they're waiting for things to cool down at your office. I have had my investigators crawling all over your building."

"You know, if I were the culprit, I'd be pretty antsy right now."

"Yeah? You've been antsy from the beginning."

"Yeah, but for a different reason." Not that she'd tell him. She had way too many secrets ready to burst out and destroy her career and the lives of people she loved. She wouldn't have the OSI questioning her parents or people in her hometown. Or Tim Sandusky, wherever he was.

"There's that look again."

"What look?" Geez, but Austin Wait could be annoying!

"Like you're in love with something you can't have. You wouldn't be thinking of me, would you?"

"Not in this lifetime." Then remembering what Jon's mother had said about reincarnation, she added, "Not in any lifetime."

"It's that kid, isn't it?"

Her breath caught in her throat. Austin Wait had more sources than a reporter for a tabloid newspaper. She had a bad feeling he knew more about her personal history than he let on. "What are you talking about?"

"Colter."

Whew. *That* kid.

Austin picked up a pencil and tapped the eraser's metal band against his teeth while he visually dissected her. "I don't know why you let it worry you so. If you want him, take him. He's a lieutenant. You have a reputation for that, don't you?"

"Hey!" She bit off a string of obscenities on the tip of her tongue. It wasn't like her to give in to outbursts of emotion. It didn't matter what defense contractors on the other side of the table called her during missile contract negotiations. They could curse her. They could weep. It didn't matter. They never got a rise out of her. Then again, they didn't know about Tim.

"I don't know what you're talking about." She did and so did Austin Wait, but her denial came out as a taut warning.

"Sure you do. You'd have to be blind not to see that the boy's in love with you."

"I should be the one you turn to. Austin Wait doesn't care about you like I do. He doesn't love you like I do."

She'd had adoring lieutenants before, not counting Tim. They followed her around like lost puppies because, unlike their civilian supervisors, L. Madison Steele gave them guidance, whether it was providing them with samples of proposal evaluations, tutoring in graduate school courses designed to enhance their military careers, or instructing them not to sabotage their girlfriends' diets by buying them chocolate. Jon was like the rest of them—an appreciative young thing who knew Madison was too old for him, too jaded for him. And if Jon Colter made frequent appearances in her midnight fantasies, no one would ever know but her.

"We're just good friends," she said.

"Yeah, right. Good friends with benefits."

"I'd appreciate it if you wouldn't ruin my lieutenant's reputation based on your idle speculation. There is nothing going on between us."

Austin shot her an amused glance. "Maybe you haven't acted on it yet, but there is definitely something going on between you two. Though I can't imagine why a woman like you would be interested in a kid like that."

"What's that supposed to mean?" And why did Austin bring out the defensive worst in her?

"You've been around."

"And what's that supposed to mean? I was waiting on an explanation, not for you to stick your other foot in your mouth."

"It means you're not some starry-eyed, seventeen-year-old innocent who might be impressed by the antics of a punk twenty-something like Colter. Do you know how many times I've physically had to restrain him? Admit it: the boy has no self control."

For months now, Jon had been at her elbow for hours every day. He'd been as close to her as a guardian angel every time she'd needed help. Since Tuesday night, he'd spent every night locked inside her home with her, sleeping on the sofa only a few yards from her bed. With the sole exception of a single frustrated kiss, Jon Colter hadn't reacted at all to Madison's dubious charms. Given her cold response to him, she'd probably never know exactly how much self-control he had.

A knock resounded at the door, and before Austin could swing his feet off the desk and sit upright, the door opened. A nurse strolled into the room, the baby in her arms. "We'll have a preliminary report tomorrow," she said as she bent to arrange the baby in Madison's outstretched arms.

The wild ache of motherhood started in Madison's fingertips the moment she touched the child and worked its way up into her shoulders, down her back, and into the pit of her stomach. Maybe it wouldn't be true. Maybe Jolene really was the baby's mother and Toby the father, and maybe just maybe if they couldn't care for the child, she could adopt it herself. Anything to keep from giving this one up. She couldn't bear to go through that again.

Madison cleared her throat in an effort to loosen the lump that choked off her breath. "I suppose I should be going home now. I'm still hoping Jolene's mother will come to her senses and call me back with the truth."

"Fine." Austin stood and stretched. "Just remember: I don't want you going out of town. As long as you're in Valparaiso, I can keep an eye on your house in case Owen Plummer decides to share your street with you again."

She couldn't go out of town anyway. Not with the baby. Her parents would be fit to be tied if she showed up in Georgia with a week-old infant. They'd think she'd repeated history. On the other hand, she was due in Georgia by noon tomorrow with an envelope crammed with one hundred twenty-dollar bills. In six years, she hadn't missed a deadline.

Austin walked her to the door with his hand planted firmly at the nape of her neck. His touch was steady and confident, but somehow lacked the passion of Jon's touch. No, Tim's. She meant Tim's. She didn't know what Jon's touch was like.

Austin mumbled something about being careful, but she didn't really hear it. Halfway across the parking lot, on the hood of her car, sat a long-legged lieutenant dressed in his camouflage BDU's and lace-up black boots. Chin cupped in his palm and elbow bearing into his knee, he hunkered forward and twirled something purplish-blue between his fingers. She couldn't help but smile as she walked toward him, faster by the second.

He must have heard the scruffing of her shoes on the asphalt because at that second he raised his headful of tousled blonde hair falling out from under his camouflage-print cap. The sun struck his eyes. He squinted against the glare, but his eyes were as ferociously blue as they had been a few hours ago when she'd lost herself in their depths, when he'd pressed her against the wall and she'd almost wished that he would force himself on her to keep her from having to take responsibility for her want.

He slid off the hood and waited for her to close the distance between them. "Hi." His lips caught between a smile and a grimace.

Damn, he looked good. Maybe because she'd fully expected him to walk out of her house and her life after she'd slammed her soul shut in his face.

"Hi," she said back. "I didn't expect to see you again. Um, so soon."

"I, uh, wanted to make sure you were okay. There's a murderer out there, you know. And friends don't let friends drive around alone when there's a murderer on the loose. We are still friends, aren't we?"

"You bet." Friends, and nothing more. Damn it. But even that was better than losing him.

"I couldn't stand the thought of you being in danger."

"I'll be all right." It was an automatic response.

"Look, Madison, I'm really sorry about what happened back at your house. I don't care who you turn to for help as long as somebody somewhere helps you." He twirled a trio of purplish-blue irises, then thrust them at her. "Here. I know how much you like blue flowers."

Tim was the one who liked blue flowers, though she wouldn't tell that to Jon. She'd imagined for seven years that Tim Sandusky would come back for her, see the blue gardens at her doorstep, and know she'd carried a torch for him all these years.

"They're beautiful." She shifted the baby on one arm and took the flowers from him. "I have some like this in my...hey, you didn't pick these out of my yard, did you?"

Jon winced. "I didn't think you'd mind. I didn't know where to find blue flowers except at your house." He shuffled his feet, anxiously awaiting her approval. No one had ever brought her blue flowers before, least of all out of her own garden. "The ivy reminds me more of you, though. Irises wither almost as soon as they're cut. Ivy survives almost any heat or cold."

"Jon." She was tempted to take his face in her palm but she wouldn't. "Did you mean it when you said you'd do anything to help me?"

"With all my heart."

"Good. Because there is a favor I need."

"Anything. Name it."

"It's very important. You have to understand: I'm desperate or I would never ask this of you." She could tell by the hard planes of his chest that he held his breath. "Jon, there's no one else in the world I would trust with this."

Her lieutenant grinned. "Then I'm your man."

CHAPTER TWELVE

Saturday, 2 October 1999, Southwest Georgia

His butt had been numb for the past forty-five minutes. Would have been worse, Jon supposed, if he hadn't stopped at a roadside park on the Florida side of the Chattahoochee River to study the map Madison had given him.

The early autumn morning was hotter than he'd expected, the road longer than he'd imagined, and the idea of owning a motorcycle instead of a car as being fun was a distant memory. Madison had offered to lend him her car, but that would have left her without a way to go and he could tell she was worried that the baby might get sick or something might happen and she would need transportation. The car would surely have been more comfortable for him.

Unless he'd taken another wrong turn and gotten himself lost a third time, Jon would reach his destination within the next fifteen minutes, deliver Madison's envelope to someone named Buford, and hop back on the motorcycle for the two-and-a-half-hour ride back to Madison and the baby. He didn't relish the idea.

He'd left Madison on the front door step and the baby inside asleep on a cushion on the floor. Madison had wrung her hands and fretted and twisted her blonde hair into ringlets. She still needed his help with the baby and as much as she wanted Jon by her side, she needed him to run this errand for her more than she needed his presence. Plus, Austin Wait had convinced the local cops to patrol her street more fervently than usual and be on the lookout for a white Ford Crown Victoria.

Why had she been so anxious over his leaving? Not for her own safety, he was certain of that. Something about the errand had turned her into a basket case, but what? It wasn't as if he'd headed for a distant planet or a dangerous mission. Then again, if she'd asked him to do either of those things, he would have. And his butt wouldn't have been as numb from either one.

Leaving Madison behind felt strange, even if he was going off like a knight on a quest. He'd spent four nights on her lumpy sofa, listening to her sob in her sleep, and while he saw little chance of spending the night in her bed, being near her wasn't a bad consolation prize. At first, she'd been determined not to let him stay. She'd been so worried about rumor-mongers. But she'd been exhausted and needed help with the baby, and then she'd been worried about Owen Plummer and Roxie and Project Andromeda. With every night, he insisted on staying to help, and she put up less of a fight.

He liked to think of the romantic possibilities being close to her held, but he knew it was much more than that. "Stay close to The Falconer," his mother-the-fruitcake had said of Lorelei Madison Steele. "She's saved your life before. She'll save your life again." His mom had babbled for another ten minutes—with him paying the long distance charges—about how Madison had saved his life in many lifetimes, even to her own detriment. That her purpose in lifetime after lifetime was to protect. That in this lifetime, she would watch the end of civilization, rule over the remnants, and recreate the world in the name of a Higher Power she had yet to meet. And that in this lifetime, if she was to fulfill her mission, Jon would have to be the protector.

How could he believe in such psycho-babble? Except that his mother's words had in them the ring of truth.

Madison saw herself as the protector of everything from bio-warfare secrets to lost children to bloody-nosed lieutenants to the world itself. She was the kind of woman who wouldn't think twice about laying her life on the line—supposedly in other lifetimes, too—to save ones who mattered most to her and ones she'd never met.

Jon had laughed when his mother called Madison a "warrior queen," yet when he let himself think about it without the prejudice he bore New Age babble, he could almost see Madison astride a war-horse, broadsword in her hand, a pagan cross painted on her brow. Fighting for a lost cause. Fighting to save her people. Fighting with him by her side.

He'd made the mistake of mentioning his dreams to Lydia Colter, particularly the ones in which Madison had been a sickle-bearing priestess. His mother had offered to hypnotize Jon, to take him into a past life regression. He might learn something there that would help him protect his protector. Jon had refused, of course. Not because he didn't really believe in such things—he didn't—but in the back of his mind resided a fraction of doubt. Just in case there was such a thing as reincarnation, he didn't want to risk regressing and finding out his mother's perceptions about Madison were wrong. Far too much fun to let his imagination run wild.

He saw the sign too late to signal a right-hand turn and instead leaned the bike almost into the pavement to make a right-angle down the county line road. A few seconds later, he slammed on brakes. He'd missed the winding dirt road turn-off to his left. He backed the bike up.

Against the lush green of late summer and beyond a bumper crop of yellow bitter weeds and goldenrods, the tin-roofed buildings of a small farm shimmered in the mid-day sunlight. He'd found it.

Jon lifted the visor of his helmet and sniffed the freshly-turned soil in the adjacent fields. The earthy scent of raw peanuts assaulted his nose. Across the pastures of swaying grass and lazy cows, the hum of farm machinery and the clatter of birds migrating south for the winter echoed in his ears. No place else on earth could have been as different from the electricity of negotiations over missiles and bombs and the latest technology tax dollars could buy.

Not that he had time for peace and tranquillity. How little this simple country life knew of the dangers lurking in the world. How quickly death could wipe out everything with a weapon the size of a petri dish. The sooner he finished his errand, the sooner he could get back to Madison and the baby and Project Andromeda.

Jon revved the engine, then roared down the winding road. Somewhere up ahead was a man named Buford, Jon's point of contact on this mysterious mission. He was to hand Buford—or whatever his real name was—a fat envelope Jon carried in his denim backpack, deliver the message that Madison was stuck working on urgent business, then turn and get back on his bike without another word.

"There's no one else in the world I can trust with this but you," Madison had told him. She'd told him precious little else. She'd refused to tell him what was in the envelope, or what it was for, or even if it was legal for him to transport across the state line. He knew Madison well enough to know she wasn't delivering drugs or—how could he even think it?—top secret information. Still, not knowing brought out the uneasiness in him and reminded him of the summers he'd spent with his dad at the compound in Montana. No matter how much or how little Madison trusted him, it was Jon who had to do the trusting now. For all he knew, he could be hiring a hit man.

The old farmhouse with its peeling white paint peeked out from under the shade of the two biggest oaks he'd ever seen. Branches too large for a man to stretch his arms around sprawled the width of the house and beyond. Moss covered the limbs like hair on a lumberjack's forearms. Roots a good foot-and-a-half off the ground snaked across the yard, dwindling to nothing under an aging, fruit-laden fig tree. In spite of the dense shade, flowers of every color except blue thrived in rectangular beds that sharpened the corners of the farmhouse. Whatever hands tended them had left a garden hose trickling into the flower bed.

Angling for the fig tree, Jon killed the engine, pried off the helmet, and then secured it to the handle bars. He waited and listened. Only the hum of distant farm machinery answered him. Something was wrong. The birds had quieted.

"Hello?" he called.

Not even his echo answered.

He tried the screen door at the front entrance, but the door wouldn't budge. Locked, he supposed. The grass near the steps looked unworn. Of course. The front door was for company, if anyone lived there at all. Judging by the spectacular display of flowers, he doubted the residents ever left their garden for more than a day. More than likely, all traffic entered and exited the house through the back door. And so would he.

"Hello?" He flexed his fingers, still curved and aching from their four-hour hold on the handlebars. "Anybody home?"

Acorns crunched under Jon's boots as he gingerly rounded the corner of the house. Exotic orange lilies on long stalks fell across his path and brushed against his knees like anxious kittens. The scent of dust and sunshine rose from the back yard as he made his way across the narrow side yard. In the shade of the mighty oaks, the grass had withered to little more than sand.

He started around the corner into the back yard, chin in the air as he regarded the limbs above him and wondered at their age. Probably seventy-five years, maybe a hundred. So few people planted trees any more. In another hundred years, would any trees like these still shade the earth? Or would they all be saplings too small to hold up a child's rope swing? He frowned away a glimpse of a future where he planted trees in the name of the Goddess and in the name of L. Madison Steele.

He barely saw the movement out of his right eye before he ducked instinctively. The butt of a deer rifle missed his temple by inches.

Oh, shit. Jon raised his hands before his eyes could focus well. His father had been an excellent teacher, but Jon been too busy thinking of high school girls to learn the most important survivalist lesson: pay attention. He followed the cold lines of the gun barrel up to a pair of small hands, worn and wrinkled and too feminine to belong to anyone named Buford. Staring down the sites as if they were needed to find their target was a woman old enough to be his grandmother. Something about her looked frighteningly familiar. The stony cut of her jaw and brow told him she meant business.

"What are you doing sneaking up on a poor, defenseless woman?" she demanded. Her voice shook almost as much as her hands. She'd probably shoot him, drag him half way through the back door, and then claim self-defense. Given the unsteadiness of her age, she'd probably be absolved of any wrongdoing, too.

"I wasn't sneaking up," he said, then cleared his throat and repeated himself. She was hardly defenseless.

"Your kind's not welcome here."

"And what kind is that?" He rose slowly to his feet. Any sudden movements and for sure, she'd put a bullet in his brain.

"Motorcycle-riding hoodlums trying to steal an old woman blind, that's what kind."

"I am not a hoodlum, um, ma'am, and I've never stolen a thing in my life."

"Oh, decided to start with me, did you?" She shook the rifle barrel in his face.

"No, ma'am. I'm looking for someone named Buford."

She squinted at him. "What do you want with Buford?"

"I'm to deliver a package to him. And a message."

"A package? We haven't ordered anything."

"It's from a woman named Madison Steele."

"Madison?" The word came out in a whisper. The old woman blanched.

"Yes, ma'am. I promised her I'd give this package to Buford himself." He lowered one hand and, with two fingers, reached very carefully inside the pocket of his denim backpack and extracted the long, fat envelope. Using only his index and middle fingers, he handed it to the woman. "If you'll tell me where I can find Buford, I'll be on my way."

"You're lying to me. She wouldn't have anything to do with a hoodlum like you."

She? Madison?

"I am not a hoodlum, ma'am. I'm a lieutenant in the United States Air Force. I'm stationed at Eglin Air Force Base, about a hundred and fifty miles southwest of here."

"I know where Eglin Air Force Base is." The woman slanted a downward glance at the signature scrawled across envelope. She could hold both the rifle and letter but neither competently. "You don't look like a soldier to me."

In his jeans, denim jacket, boots and under-eye circles, he supposed he didn't look much like America's finest. On the other hand, the military uniform made everyone look, well, uniform, and he prided himself on having his own unique sense of style when he wasn't on duty.

"You got any proof you are who you say?"

"Yes, ma'am. It's in my wallet."

"Get it. Slowly."

Jon fished his wallet out of his jeans pocket and held it open for her. She snatched it away. The deer rifle wobbled against her feeble shoulder. She tried to hang onto the envelope and flip the wallet open at the same time. Finally she coordinated her efforts enough to scowl at his military ID. She could tell by the crisp military haircut—though his hair was a bit longer on top now that it had been when he'd had the picture made—and by his stiff blue uniform that he spoke the truth.

"Jonathan Colter," she murmured as if trying to place the name.

She glanced uneasily at his photo, at Jon, at his photo again. Instead of returning the wallet, she focused on the photograph opposite his ID. It was a color photograph of Madison accepting an award for something—he'd long since forgotten what. He'd snitched it from a bulletin board in The Lab before the photo could be thrown away and replaced by the next quarterly award winner's snapshot. Jon had trimmed the photo to fit his wallet and safely tucked it away. Not even Madison knew he carried it.

The woman tossed the wallet back to him. He caught it with one hand. "What are you doing with a picture of my daughter?"

"D-daughter?"

No wonder the woman looked so familiar. Madison's mother. He should have guessed. Taller but stooped with age, she had eyes the same hue as Madison's. Their noses were the same, too. And hands. Not much else was familiar. The woman had to be in her late sixties or more, and it was hard to imagine Madison ever being that gray and frail, though he could well imagine her at that age, still fiercely protecting the world around her, deer rifle or not. Had the woman in the faded flower duster once been the pillar of strength Madison now was? He squinted, trying to see the resemblance, but instead, he saw something else. Madison's mother bore an uncanny likeness—physically, at least—to Beatrice.

So that was it. Madison's blindness to Beatrice. She saw her own mother in the woman and that made Beatrice's incessant whining and snooping bearable.

"Madison's your daughter?"

"Madison." The woman made a face as if she'd stepped in dog shit. "'Madison' was my maiden name. I never expected her to use it, but the nurse said she ought to have a middle name, so I gave her the one I'd given up. Why does she have to call herself that when I gave her a name as pretty as 'Lorelei'?"

Because the Loreleis of the world aren't taken seriously, he wanted to tell her. And an androgynous name like "Madison" tended to counteract her blonde ringlets and full lips. Out of respect for Madison's mother—and reverence for the rifle in her hands—Jon said nothing.

"You didn't answer my question. What are you doing with a picture of my daughter in your billfold?"

"I work for—" No. Not officially. "I work with your daughter. She asked me to deliver that envelope to Buford. That's her father, isn't it?"

That made sense. She'd sent him to deliver a package to her father. Of course, it would have made more sense if she'd told him that the mysterious Buford was her father, that he was about to trespass on her family's farm, and that her mother might meet him with a gun.

"Buford's running the peanut-picker for a sick neighbor. You can leave the envelope with me. It's money, ain't it?"

"I don't know, ma'am. She didn't say."

"Sounds like you don't know my daughter that well after all."

"No, ma'am. I don't. But I think I know her as well as anyone."

The old woman lowered the rifle barrel. "You may be right. She's never sent anyone in her place before. Is she all right?"

"Yes, ma'am. She's fine." *She's always fine.* Physically, at least, she was. A little stressed from lack of sleep and too much worry. Eventually worn down but still refusing to show it. As far as Madison's mother was concerned, Madison was fine.

He gradually lowered his hands to his side and kept them still at his thighs. Even though the cold in Madison's mother's attitude had thawed considerably in the past few seconds, he didn't want to give the woman any reason to blow his balls off.

"Your daughter wanted to be here this weekend," Jon explained, choosing his words carefully, "but something came up at work. Something very urgent."

"Something always does. Something always has."

The woman arranged the rifle under one arm to get a better grip on the envelope. She slid a long, unpainted fingernail under the flap of the envelope, ripped it open, then blew into it. Squinting down into the envelope, she gave its contents a curt nod of approval. The flutter of green inside looked like a stack of twenty dollar bills.

Jon swallowed hard to keep from leaning forward to peer into the envelope himself. There had to be a couple thousand dollars inside! If Madison was sending money to her parents, surely she could have written them a check or wired them the money. Why cash? And why not confess her good deed to Jon if she meant for him to carry a small fortune so far?

What if he'd been robbed? Or dropped the package somewhere on the highway at 80 miles per hour? Or what if he'd opened the envelope against her orders, counted the money, and headed to the riverboat casinos in Louisiana?

No wonder she lived like a pauper. Madison Steele was sending every spare penny to her parents.

"You'll see that Buford gets that envelope, won't you?" By now, Madison had probably twisted her mess of curls into corkscrew ringlets, all the while pacing the front porch, waiting on him, making herself a target for Owen Plummer's spy ring. He needed to get back to her. Even if she weren't in any danger, he needed to see her again. "She made me promise I'd give that envelope to Buford."

The ice in the old woman's eyes melted. "I suppose if Lorelei trusted you to bring the money to us, then maybe you ain't a hoodlum on a motorcycle like I thought you was."

"Oh, no, ma'am. I would have driven up on the car." Madison's car. "But I wanted to make sure your daughter had a safe way to go, so I came up on my old motorcycle." The bike was six months old, give or take a few weeks. "Keeping your daughter safe was more important than a long, miserable ride in the autumn dust." And that was the God's-honest-truth.

The old woman chuckled. "Well, why didn't you say so to begin with? Come on into the house, Jonathan. Buford will be in from the fields in a minute, and I'm just getting something on the table to eat. I'd love to hear all about what you and my daughter are working on."

"Thanks, ma'am, but I can't stay." Madison had instructed him to give the envelope to Buford and not say another word. No questions, no excuses. Just go. Deliver the package, then get on his motorcycle, and high-tail it out of there. Well, two out of three weren't bad.

"Sure you won't stay and have a bite to eat before you head back to Florida? It's a long ride."

"No, ma'am. I—"

"Mommy?"

The sound of a child's voice, sweet and melodic and full of promise, jangled in his soul like old wind chimes. He should have turned, should have walked away, should have run. The voice sounded too much like Madison's but without the huskiness that came with giving orders.

The tattered screen door to the back porch banged shut, and a little girl scampered, barefoot, into the yard. Her dark hair fell in wild tangles to her shoulders. "Mommy? You said to let you know when the biscuits got brown. Well, they're kinda black on top."

Mommy. He mouthed the word. "Madison never mentioned a little sister." Or that her mother must have given birth around her sixtieth birthday.

"They're not really sisters."

"Oh?"

"We adopted Delilah when she was a tiny thing. We never could have any more children after Lorelei and Tobias."

Jon caught his lower lip between his teeth. He couldn't think of a delicate way to ask why a couple in their sixties would adopt a baby. A week ago, he might not have thought twice about it, but now, after learning firsthand what it was like to stumble through the day with little or no sleep and wish to God that the sixteen-plus hours of sleep a newborn averaged were consecutive hours instead of one twenty-minute catnap after another with ten-minute bursts of hungry cries. How could the old couple handle it? And how could any adoption agency choose an aging couple like the Steeles as suitable parents?

Jon forced himself to smile. "It was very generous of you to take on a small child."

The woman smiled back, and he could see Madison in her smile. "The heart is a big thing."

The little girl scurried up beside the woman and wrapped her arms around the old woman's flowery waist. The kid stared up at Jon, eyes wide and full of blue, as though she'd never seen anything like him. She probably hadn't.

"She's been a real blessing for us." Madison's mother gave the child a quick squeeze.

Curiosity niggled away at the base of his brain. He didn't need his fruitcake mother's psychic ability to know that something wasn't quite right. Why would an old couple like the Steeles take on the responsibility of raising someone else's child? And why, if the little girl was adopted, did she look exactly like a little Madison Steele with black hair?

"You know," Jon said, eyeing the child, "I think I'll take you up on that meal."

CHAPTER THIRTEEN

The child wasn't hers.

And no matter how hard Madison might wish it, the baby Jolene had abandoned would never be hers.

"You're sure?" Madison gazed up at Austin Wait. She wanted to hate him, but he'd merely done as she'd asked. "You're positive the baby isn't Toby's?"

Austin crouched beside her rocking chair. He touched the baby's rosebud mouth and smiled when the lips changed into a pucker. Madison twisted in her seat, holding the baby closer in her arms and farther away from him. "The preliminary reports show that the baby and Sheridan Cashwell share the same genetic markers. That doesn't prove Cashwell is the baby's father, but it does make it very likely. To be absolutely sure, we'd need to take a blood sample from your brother. Then, if he's excluded from having the same markers, we'd know for certain that Toby isn't the baby's father."

"Toby's on a ship somewhere. Getting a blood sample doesn't sound very likely. What about footprints? They still take newborns' footprints, don't they?" The image of another baby girl—red-skinned, plump, smeared with blood and mucous—flashed through her brain. Madison winced.

Austin blew out a long breath. "That was the next point on my list to tell you. We ran a computer comparison of the Cashwell baby's footprint and the print we took from this baby yesterday. They match."

She shook her head feverishly. "You're sure? Maybe there's some mistake."

"Computers don't make mistakes."

"Bullshit. I work with computers all the time. They malfunction, they lock up, they accept bad data."

"Stop it." He didn't bat an eyelash. Cool, calm, and reasonable, damn him. "I think it's time you face it. The baby isn't your brother's. Your sister-in-law's either. I checked with the Navy hospital where she was last seen six months ago. She'd insisted on a pregnancy test. It was negative. That baby in your arms is not three months premature."

"No." She shook her head. Her arms ached. "No."

"I thought this was what you wanted."

To give up a baby again? Just hand her over to someone else?

"You wanted to get the baby back to her parents' arms so you could get back to work, didn't you? Don't you want to catch whoever stole Project Andromeda and set you up for espionage and murder?"

"Of course, I do!"

"Then don't wimp out on me now."

Wimp out? If she hadn't had the baby in her arms, she would have wrapped her fingers around Austin Wait's throat and choked the living daylights out of him. She'd never wimped out in her life.

"Sheridan Cashwell and his mother are waiting outside in their car. You want me to take the baby out to them?" He reached for the child but she twisted sideways, raising a fierce shoulder to him.

"I want to meet Sheridan Cashwell."

"Good grief. Why?"

Because the baby in her arms was still her responsibility and if she gave away her baby—no, not her baby—if she gave away *the* baby to someone who wasn't good enough, wasn't worthy enough, then what was the sacrifice for? Austin Wait would never understand.

"I need to know if he's a good man."

Austin rolled his eyes. Apparently he wasn't used to women arguing with him. "What does it matter what you think? For Pete's sake, he's the kid's father, okay?"

"I have to know I'm doing the right thing!"

The baby startled at Madison's voice and began to cry. Madison shushed her and rocked her until the frown creasing her tiny forehead smoothed out.

"You are doing the right thing," Austin whispered. He squeezed her elbow. "You are."

"How can you be so sure? What if I'm making a mistake?" She'd told herself for over six years that she was doing the right thing, but after holding another baby close to her heart for a few days, she didn't know any more. She felt as lost as she had the first time she'd left Georgia to go home alone.

"You're not making a mistake. The Florida Highway patrol picked up your sister-in-law last night near Tallahassee for underage drinking. She thought she was being picked up for kidnapping and spilled her guts. Blamed it on you, of course. Said if you hadn't insisted she come visit, none of this would ever have happened. They thought she was rip-roaring drunk and didn't make the connection until I talked to them. She'll do time probably, but given her age, they'll go a little easier on her."

So it was true. Jolene had wanted a baby desperately, thinking that somehow a child would force Toby to give up the Navy and come home to her. If Jolene weren't such a whiny brat, Madison might have felt sorry for her. "She's just a kid," Madison muttered. "Just a stupid, lonely kid."

"A kid who caused a lot of grief. How about I bring in the Cashwells now?"

Madison nodded. Austin stalked to the door, gestured quickly, then opened the door wide for a thin woman, fiftyish with a permanent worry line on her forehead. She wore a designer pantsuit that hadn't come from a thrift shop and glittering rings on every finger. She never once looked at Madison or the baby clothes strewn across the sofa. Her gaze fell intently on the baby, and Madison fought the urge to cover the baby's face and flee. Austin picked a cigarette out of his pocket and picked that moment to step outside for a smoke.

"Ohhhh." The woman's face twisted. Tears rolled down her cheeks. "She looks like Sheridan when he was a baby."

Sheridan Cashwell stepped around his mother, reached for the baby, then stopped cold. Tall with thinning blond hair, he blinked at Madison as if she were an angel. The low arch of his eyebrows matched the baby's. His outstretched hands bore the same knuckle pattern as the little hands she'd so often rubbed her thumb over.

"May I?" he asked and held his breath.

Madison swallowed, squeezed her eyes shut, then nodded. "Yes," she croaked. "She's yours."

His hands awkwardly scooped the tiny body out of her arms and held the baby to his chest. Just that quickly the weight in Madison's arms was gone. The utter aloneness of her soul shivered down her spine. As if to protest, Bronwyn fretted and bumped her forehead against her father's shirt pocket. He glanced at his mother as if he didn't know what to do.

"Here. Let Grammy do that." Sheridan's mother practically wrenched Bronwyn from his arms. "Of course, hers crying. Hers cold. Let Grammy wrap hers up in hers blanket."

Madison ignored the baby talk and handed the white flannel square dotted with panda bears and spit-up to the baby's grandmother. Sheridan Cashwell looked about as lost as Madison felt.

"Thank you," the baby's father said through unabashed tears.

"Thank you," Madison had said years ago. She'd been dry-eyed. The stitches between her legs had still burned. She'd refused even the mildest of painkillers. The muscles in her arms had ached from grasping the bars on the side of the bed for traction as she'd pushed again and again and again. A close call, the doctor had said. The baby's father must have been a big man, he'd said to no one in particular.

"You're sure you want to do this?" Dr. Barrett had asked a third time.

"I have no choice. I have a job to do."

"I could lose my practice for this, Lorelei."

She'd clenched the sheet over her deflated stomach, her legs still limp in the stirrups and a heat lamp aimed at her bare and bloody bottom. Dr. Barrett had delivered her in the same hospital twenty-three years earlier.

"This is how it has to be. I have to be back at work in two months. No one else can do it but me."

Dr. Barrett had cast a disapproving glance in her general direction, though whether he disagreed with her rushed recovery or her decision for her child's future, she hadn't known. He had started filling out the paperwork for the birth certificate that would list Agnes and Buford Steele as the natural parents of a baby girl born at 2:59 in the morning.

"Put down her name as Rhiannon Sandusky Steele," she'd told the doctor as he penned in the blocks on the form.

"Your father already gave her a name. 'Delilah Steele.' He said if you're going to give up your child to him, then the baby's his as of now. If you want me to forge this document, Lorelei, then you've got to understand that you will never be this child's mother."

Madison had turned her face to the window and stared out at the distant sickle of a moon. "I understand."

"Miss Steele? Did you hear me?" Sheridan Cashwell stood before her in earnest.

"Wh-what?" They were alone, the two of them. She could see Bronwyn Cashwell's grandmother on the front doorstep, bragging to Austin Wait.

"I really have to go now. You understand, don't you? I'd like to spend some time with my baby."

She nodded, the ever-present lump in her throat. "I understand."

"You'll never know how much I appreciate this. I'll never be able to thank you enough for what you've done."

"I did what I had—I mean, what I have to do."

"There's a reward, you know. Ten thousand dollars. My parents were offering it. I'll get you a cashier's check on Monday when the banks open."

"I don't want your money." The saliva in her mouth turned bitter. Her voice rose with every word. She couldn't stop herself. "I didn't turn in my sister-in-law because I wanted to get rich quick. I did it because it was the right thing to do."

"Really, Miss Steele, it wasn't my intent to upset you. I meant that the reward is yours. You deserve it."

For giving away a baby that wasn't hers. A baby that could have been Jolene's. Was there a minuscule chance the tests were wrong and the baby was her niece after all?

"I told you, I don't want your money."

"Okay, then."

He chewed at his bottom lip and cast a quick glance around the room as if the question the reasonableness of her decision. Ten grand could buy decent furniture or a down-payment on a small house that didn't have its windows jarred by every fighter jet landing at Eglin Air Force Base. The man was disgustingly easy to read.

"You deserve something for what you've done. I'll talk to the reporters down at the *Daily News*. You'll be on the front page, and every newspaper in the country will pick up the story. You'll be a hero, Miss Steele."

"I don't want to be a hero."

Being a hero meant sacrifice, and she's sacrificed enough already. What she really wanted was a quiet place in the country with the man she loved and a baby girl to share her blissfully sunny days.

Unfortunately, she was destined for more.

"If you change your mind, you'll let me know, won't you?"

"Sure."

He glanced down at the ring on her finger. "I didn't know you were married. Mr. Wait said you were single."

"I'm not married. Never have been." *Never will be.*

He brightened. "I wouldn't mind getting to know you a little better. Maybe you could come visit Bronwyn and me sometime?"

Bronwyn would probably miss her. Madison would certainly miss Bronwyn. "I'd like that."

"Or maybe I could cook you dinner. I'm not a particularly good cook, but I get by. My ex used to tell me I'm outstanding with a grill. Get it? *Out* standing with a grill?" He laughed at his own feeble joke.

"I get it."

"Or maybe I could drop by your office and take you to lunch sometime?"

"Mr. Cashwell, I really don't think that's a good idea. You shouldn't confuse gratitude with something else. Besides, I'm really too busy for a relationship. Of any kind."

"Yeah, I used to say that, too. I let all my relationships around me die. It wasn't until Bronnie disappeared this week that I realized how important friends and family can be. Please say that we can be friends."

Jon had asked the same of her. "We can be friends. Sure." Unlike with Jon, the most she wanted from Sheridan Cashwell was friendship.

"Why don't you drop by Democratic Headquarters next weekend? I volunteer down there every Saturday. I'll have Bronwyn with me," he added as if that alone would entice her.

Bronwyn's father was likable enough, Madison decided, but there was no chemistry between them. And was it really a good idea for her to be around Bronwyn again? Wouldn't breathing the baby's scent only make the withdrawal pains linger?

"You are a registered voter, aren't you?"

"Independent," she said. "I tend to vote for the man rather than the party."

"Oh. Well, I hope you'll vote Democrat next time. We're already planning our next campaign."

She shrugged. She hated politics.

"The Democrats have done a heck of a job," Sheridan Cashwell bubbled as if he'd forgotten the baby girl waiting for him outside. "Don't you think so? Aren't you better off than you were when the Republicans were in office?"

She gave him a one-shouldered shrug. "About the same, maybe a bit worse. Locality pay's nonexistent, cost-of-living increases are a joke, and I could be making probably fifty thousand a year more in my career field as a beltway bandit in Washington. Then again, I'm probably lucky to still have a job. Government contracting offices are so undermanned that my sanity's in much more danger than my job. And Congress has closed down a lot of military bases but they haven't closed down Eglin yet, so yeah, I guess I'm about the same."

"Did you hear the speech the President gave on CNN the other night?" he asked, oblivious to the economy's effect on her life.

"I don't watch much TV." She liked to form her own opinions.

"It was really good. He was talking about what a good job he's done taking care of us these past few years and how the next decade will only be better. The Democrats will make sure the Government takes care of our seniors and our children, and everybody who wants to can go to college and everybody who wants a job can get one and— What's wrong?"

Jon's words echoed in her ears. *"My mom puts people in hypnotic trances and...she takes them...into the future a couple hundred years. I hope you don't think it's un-American of me to repeat this, but she says the future's a socialist society with pockets of people, men and women, living together in barracks."*

"Miss Steele? Did I say something wrong?"

Oh, God. It was starting already, and she hadn't seen it. Why hadn't she seen it? She'd been too busy doing her job every day to see what was going on in the world, what was happening right in front of her!

The Government was already taking care of people. Americans expected it. The Government took care of the children to make sure they were fed and clothed and schooled to the same low standards. The Government carried generations on welfare. The Government doled out Social Security and Medicare and Medicaid and all the other entitlements.

Entitlements. She hated the word. Like some people expected others to owe them a living.

And didn't everyone feel they were owed something? If the "have-nots" didn't get it, then the "haves" would be typecast as insensitive or racist or sexist or inhuman.

Schools tossed aside grading systems and passed everyone, even kids who couldn't read their own names, all in the name of self-esteem. Competitiveness had become an ugly word, both in academics and in sports. The political correctness movement put everyone on the same level, socially, politically, and intellectually, and filled the world with blandness and boredom and sameness.

Why hadn't she seen it before? The country was fast moving toward guaranteed jobs and guaranteed wages, with guaranteed homes and guaranteed healthcare. Guaranteed equality. Guaranteed sameness.

How much longer before the Government seized everyone's property and put people in Government housing with Government jobs and Government doctors and Government meals that met the nutritional minimum and Lord help you if you wanted to swap your serving of yellow-green lima beans for a second helping of mashed potatoes because everyone had to have the exact same damned thing?

Socialism. The prophecy was already taking shape.

"Miss Steele? Are you okay?"

"I know this is going to sound crazy, but my mom thinks that all the prophecies are going to come to a head soon."

"I'm fine. I'm always fine." She was fine. It was the rest of the world that worried her.

***

As she wheeled into the driveway at her parents' farm, Madison didn't even brake. She'd always been something of a lead foot, and today—thank the good Lord in heaven—she hadn't seen a single patrol car on the highway.

Barely two hours ago, she'd nearly shoved Sheridan Cashwell out her front door. She'd thrown a toothbrush and a change of clothes into a gym bag, wrote Jon a long note explaining that she'd be out of town until late Sunday and she was sorry she'd missed him, and then hopped in the car for what was normally a two-and-a-half hour drive to the farm.

She'd never driven like a bat out of hell into her parents' back yard. She never knew where little Delilah might be playing. On the other hand, the only thing she had to worry about in the front yard was her mama's sprawling azaleas. They never allowed Delilah to play in the front yard as Madison had done as a child. Too much danger in the world these days. Too likely that a six-year-old might be stolen from the front door step. Thank God, her parents were as protective of Delilah as they had been of her.

Out in the country like this, there really wasn't much need for locked doors and car alarms. The farm was miles from the nearest town and only in the past few years had the occasional house sprung up on the rolling farmland. Georgia was like that. The northwestern corner taken up by Atlanta and its suburbs, rolling hills to the northeast, the splendor of Revolutionary and Antebellum South around Savannah, and nothing but swamp and dry farmland covering the rest of the state. This was the part of Georgia that most favored the frontier land of nineteenth-century South where soldiers had marched away to defend the confederacy. Plantation owners had taken the fertile soil near the river and left the common man to eak out a living in the dry dirt, in the winters trapping wildcats and boars in the dense forests. Those had been her ancestors. Not the rich gentlemen in their mansions, but the common men fighting to the death to be left alone. Maybe she'd been here in another life, too.

Oh, no.

The motorcycle parked between the fig tree and a bank of blossoming pink camellias had to be Jon's. He'd left early in the morning. How could he still be here? And, she thought with a sinking feeling, what had her father told him?

She killed the engine, scrambled out, and then slammed the car door behind her. A smattering of blackbirds in the mighty pecan tree behind the house took flight. The rush of their wings sent a shiver down her spine before the birds fluttered and settled into the tree again. The smell of fried chicken wafted through the late afternoon sunlight and called her home.

She lifted her face to the old farmhouse. Despite its need for a good coat of paint and a month's worth of minor repairs, the place was still home and always would be. She hadn't meant to let Jon so close to her secrets.

A curtain fluttered and a few seconds later, the back screen door banged shut. "Lorelei!" a soft voice squealed long before Delilah bounced around the corner of the house, trampled a stray tiger lily, and bolted for her.

Madison's heart leapt to her throat. She dropped to her knees. God, the kid was great. She was barely six years old and already reading at a third-grade level. Her first grade teachers raved about her math skills and analytical abilities. In the past month, the kid had grown at least an inch, and if Madison looked hard enough, she could catch a glimpse of how Delilah might look in another ten or fifteen years: happy blue eyes, a slender frame, and a wild tumble of black hair like Tim's.

If the world was around in another ten or fifteen years.

"Lorelei, I missed you!" Delilah swooped into her arms and squeezed Madison's shoulders.

"I missed you more." Madison hesitated only a second before wrapping her arms around Delilah's body and pulling her close. She was warm and wiggling, and Madison's hands perfectly cupped the miniature shoulder blades. Madison inhaled, trying to hang onto Delilah's scent and not exhale the one sweet thing she had of her child. She closed her eyes and prayed the moment would never end.

"Ow. Lorelei, you're hurting me. You're hugging too tight."

"Oh. Sorry."

Madison loosened her grip, but her arms wouldn't let go. She opened her eyes. Jon stood at the corner of the house, studying them with a strange intensity. He didn't question or pass judgment or argue. He wasn't an angel, but without a doubt, he was the next best thing.

CHAPTER FOURTEEN

Sunday, 3 October 1999, Southwest Georgia, wee hours

Long before he saw her in the starlight, Jon heard the soft crush of acorns and oak leaves under bare feet and knew by the stealthy pattern of footfalls that Madison had come to find him. He kept right on humming "Broken Arrow" and waited, picking out her scent among the night breezes. He willed her to sneak up behind him, cup her hands over his eyes, and whisper, "Guess who?" Anything to have her put her hands on him. At times like these, she was truly his lorelei: luring him to the edge, singing him to madness, stirring him with wishes he knew would never come true.

"Care to join me?" he asked, still gazing skyward. He could have slid over another two or three inches on the wooden swing to make more room for her, but he didn't dare. He wanted her as close as possible.

After a pause, she settled down snugly onto the swing beside him. "How did you know it was me?"

"Who else could it have been?"

"I don't know. Owen Plummer, maybe?"

Jon laughed politely at her joke. "You don't sound like an Owen Plummer." He inhaled and relished the fullness in his chest. She didn't smell like an Owen Plummer, either.

"How do you know what Owen Plummer sounds like? You've never heard him speak. Any chance you're actually a French operative in cahoots with Giselle Villemaire?"

He ignored her teasing, rare as it was. "No, I have never heard Owen Plummer speak, but I'm pretty sure he's not a contralto. What brings you out here this time of night?"

"Oh, nothing. I got up to check on Delilah."

He knew. He'd seen her. Madison had perched on the corner of the rocking chair in Delilah's room full of pink ruffles. Elbows on her knees. Chin cupped in her hands. Trapped in a lovelorn gaze and watching the rise and fall of her little sister's sleeping chest. Why had Madison felt the need to check up on Delilah? The child hardly looked as if she'd a nightmare. If anything, Madison seemed to long to be immersed in the child's sweet dreams.

"And then," Madison continued, "I checked in on the guest room and saw the door open and that you weren't there and so...and so I came looking for you." She had that note of concern in her voice as if by some chance she feared he'd left in the night. "So what are *you* doing out here? Besides humming Rod Stewart songs. Making wishes on stars?"

He smiled. "Something like that." They were alone together on a cold swing after midnight, with a sky full of stars above, her denim-covered legs against his and both of them with bare feet. Every gentle rock of the swing forced them to touch. For now, this was as much as he could have wished for.

"Actually," he told her, "I'm watching for falling stars. Want to help me look?"

"Fat chance. I haven't seen a falling star in years."

He took a chance and slipped his arm around her shoulders. "When was the last time you looked up?"

"Okay. So it's been a while. Every now and then I see the moon when I'm on my way home from work late at night, but I don't remember seeing any stars."

"But that's in town. Too much light pollution. Between the streetlights and the glare of the moon, it can be pretty hard to see what's really out there. Shame that we've forgotten it, too. Think how many generations past have looked to the sky for answers. We've turned our backs on it. We've conquered it. We're so superior, aren't we?"

A spark shot across the sky and disappeared.

"Look, Madison! There's another one!"

Wide-eyed, she searched the studded black heavens. "Another what?"

"Falling star. Didn't you see it? It's the second one I've seen since I've been out here. There's a meteor shower going on between now and the end of October, maybe a little longer. You need a clear night like this to find it. It's coming from the direction of the constellation Orion. My mom says it's going to be spectacular."

"You talked to your mom again?" Apprehension edged her voice. Her back straightened to the rigidity of a broomstick.

"Yeah, she called me before you got here."

"She called here? I asked you to please not tell anyone you were coming here. Anyone."

"I didn't."

"Then why did you give out my parents' phone number? It's unlisted. No one but family's allowed to have it."

How could she think he'd ever betray her? "Madison, I didn't give out your parents' number. I don't even know it myself."

"Then how did she know you were here?"

"Like I told you before, my mom has these, um, feelings sometimes. Flashes. Glimpses, she says. I don't know. She's been doing it ever since I can remember. She's plugged in to me somehow. We've had this weird connection since I was born."

Madison let out a long sigh. The stiffness seemed to fade from her body. "I forgot. Your mom's psychic."

Easy for her to say. How could Madison accept all this mumbo-jumbo so readily when he still—after twenty-plus years of living with a mother who knew every carnal thought, every hidden report card, every ill-conceived prank a boy could dream up—had problems acknowledging what his mother referred to as a "gift" and he, the brunt of her unusual perception, considered a "curse"?

"Why did your mother call here? To tell you to watch for a meteor shower? That's it?"

His mother had called to tell him not to let The Falconer out of his sight. "Find any excuse to spend the night," his mother had said. "Her soul is awakening. These are difficult times for her and if you are not there to help her, she'll forget her purpose in this life, and everything will fall to ruin." Melodramatic as usual, his mother had closed the conversation with an instruction to tell her not to worry because her child would become the most important writer of the new millennium and of mankind's new history.

Jon shrugged. "Mom and I haven't talked much over the past few years. Maybe she's trying to make up for lost time."

"You're not telling me everything."

He twisted to face her in the dark. "Neither are you."

What about the kid? he wanted to ask. Delilah.

Few women gave birth in their sixties, even in these days of high-tech medicine. But how else could he explain Madison's adopted little sister who looked exactly like her except with dark hair? Neither of Madison's parents had been dark-haired, though they were now gray with age. Several dusty, framed photographs on the mantel over the fireplace portrayed them as young and blond and looking very much like Madison herself.

On Madison's unexpected arrival, Jon had followed Delilah out the back door and, at a dead run, around the corner of the house in time to see the little girl fling herself at Madison. The look on Madison's face had crossed the line beyond sisterly affection. He had the strangest feeling. He couldn't explain it. He dared not ask her to.

As far as Jon could remember, he'd seen that look on a woman's face only once before. The mix of relief and joy and utter desperation. He'd been five or six years old, no bigger than Delilah. He didn't remember when or why they were there, some sort of family vacation in the mountains with his mom and dad back when they were still married. He'd sneaked away and tried to cross a raging creek, stepping from stone to stone until he ran out of stones and perched on a fallen tree limb jutting out from the opposite bank.

His mom must have had another of her so-called psychic visions because she'd come running out of the woods the moment the rotten wood under his feet gave way and plunged him into the icy mountain water. She had leapt barefoot into the creek, her dress wet and wrapping around her thighs and weighing her down. He'd watched her slip and struggle up again, seizing a small limb no bigger than his wrist and thrusting it at him, snagging his belt, holding him above the gush of water until his father managed to fish them both out an eternity later. They'd both caught the awfullest colds after that, but he'd never forget that look on his mother's face when he was safely back on solid ground and in her shivering arms.

The day Lydia Colter had risked everything for her son, she'd looked exactly as Madison Steele had looked in the late afternoon light. How could any face other than a mother's contort into something so full of love and fear?

Maybe Madison was really.... No. No, that was crazy thinking. Given the efficiency of the rumor mill at work, if L. Madison Steele had given birth, every amateur gossip in the State of Florida would have heard about it by now. Mr. Smith would have buried her in the supply-buying dungeon, and she would have spent the rest of her Government career buying paper clips and enduring the permanent stain on her professional character.

She blinked up at the stars. Even in the darkness, he could discern the strong and quivering outline of her jaw, the flutter of lashes. He could press it, he knew. And he could lose her forever.

"So," she said, as if trying her voice for the first time, "did you get your bike fixed?"

"No, but I'm sure I'll get it running again tomorrow. Good of your folks to put me up for the night."

"Rare of them, if you ask me. I'd appreciate it if you wouldn't get too buddy-buddy with Daddy."

"Why not? He's already insisted I go to church with the family tomorrow." Not that Jon was that enamored with stringent Baptist beliefs, but it was a chance to learn as much about Madison as he could. "I think your dad really likes me."

Madison groaned. "I know. That's what bothers me. When I was in high school and college, Daddy hated every boy I ever brought home."

"Maybe that's it. You're not 'bringing me home.' I think you've made it clear to your parents"—painfully clear—"that I'm a colleague and nothing else."

"I don't want my father hurt."

Stung, Jon pulled his arm from behind her and crossed it over his chest. "I would never hurt your father. I can't believe you'd think I would."

"Not on purpose. But he likes you, and you're not going to be around for him to get attached to."

There she went again, protecting the world. "In case you haven't noticed, your father's a grown man."

"He's an old man, Jon. He won't be around much longer, and there's nothing I can do to save him. He was already in his forties when I was born. Time's got the best of me, hasn't it?"

It's later than you think, according to the fortune cookie. No more Chinese take-out for him.

"Jon, I have to do everything I can for him. I owe him that much. No one deserves the disappointments he's known."

"We all have disappointments."

"His are worse."

Worse than yours? Jon wanted to ask. She'd fought for justice at work, only to be ambushed by her boss. She'd suffered the public humiliation of being caught in a compromising position and the only person who cared enough about her to take a stand had been transferred to an Icelandic career slot that couldn't have been as cold as the climate in Northwest Florida. She'd struggled to salvage her reputation and continue her fight for the best war-fighting technology at the best price, and for her trouble, she'd ended up the prime suspect in both a security breach and a murder investigation that the OSI was content to have look like an accident. Given those disappointments, how could Madison find anything good in life? Even him?

Madison cleared her throat and for the first time, let her body relax against his. Not in a comfortable sort of way, but not uncomfortable. "Daddy's had a rough life. His mother abandoned him when he was young, and he's never gotten over it. He tried to compensate by having a large family but it took my parents almost fifteen years to have me and it was a sheer miracle my brother was born so late in their lives. Daddy has really high hopes for Toby. Or at least he did until Toby dropped out of med school this year." She squeezed her fingers, then alternated hands. "Daddy's spent his whole life with a ball of hurt in his gut, and he'll leave this world that way, too. He's given so much in this life and asked for so little, and everything he's asked for has failed him. And everyone he's ever loved has failed him."

"Except you."

"Especially me." A wild shake of her head brought the ringlets down to her shoulders.

Jon slipped his arm back around her shoulders and drew her against him. "I can't imagine anyone ever being disappointed in you. Know what I think? I think you're harder on yourself than all the fathers in the world combined. I don't know why you have the weight of the world on your shoulders. What have you got to feel guilty about?"

She smiled, and for a second, he thought he heard a sniffle. "Plenty of things," she whispered.

"You have a list?"

"Part of me wants to stay right here—forever—but I can't."

Right here? "Right here" in his arms or "right here" in the country away from the pressures of the office? He prayed for the former. Both would do. She had surrendered her young charge to Austin Wait, she had plenty of use-or-lose leave, and Project Andromeda had been snatched away from her. Maybe he could arrange for a little time off, too.

She shook off any hint of concession. "As much as I'd like to spend time here with my family, I need to get back to the office. I still have a spy to catch and a murder to solve, and if I don't hurry up and track down Project Andromeda, there might not be anyone alive in another decade to watch stars fall." She sighed heavily. "Plus, I've probably got an in-box that's six feet deep by now."

He covered her hand with his and patted it in a way that could be misunderstood as friendly comfort. "I wish I loved my job the way you do."

Madison snorted. "Where did you get that impression?"

"The way you work. You thrive on it. It's obvious you enjoy what you do."

"Not really. I hate it. I didn't always, but I do now. Hate it...and love it."

"You're joking, right? You're the only person I know who's so fired up to get to work every day. Always taking on the wild-and-woolly new projects. You should see the look in your own eyes when you're working, Madison. You're so alive."

She laughed. "Now you're the one who's joking."

"If you honest-to-God hate it, why don't you quit? You could do so many things, be anything you want."

"I can't quit. Who else would do the work?"

"I don't know. Somebody. It's a job, not a life." He kept his hand over hers as if he'd forgotten it was there.

"See, that's where you're wrong. It's more than a job. Look, lots of people could step into my job and do okay, but I can do it better."

And she was right, too. "I think you have a god complex."

"I know I can stand up to the heat," she added. A hint of defensiveness crept into her voice. "Not everybody can. That's why it has to be me. Other people crumble. I don't."

Not visibly at least. He wanted to wrap his arms around her and let her crumble against him. No one else had seen the cracks in her exterior. It was up to him. He'd wall her in, protect her. Save her.

She squinted up at the night sky. "Do you know what it's like to have every supervisor in your chain of command trying to talk you into signing something illegal? No support in sight. If they had ordered me to sign it, I would have refused. But they knew how to manipulate me."

"You can be manipulated only if you don't know you're being manipulated."

"Okay, then. Yes, I knew what they were doing, but still they knew the right buttons to push."

"You signed something illegal? I don't believe it."

"No, of course not. But the pressure.... At first it starts with The Gutless Wonder telling me if I don't sign the document—which he won't sign, by the way—then Mr. Smith will get a contracting officer from one of the high-fallutin' weapons systems program offices to sign it and if that happens, Mr. Smith might as well close down the contracting office in The Lab because we're not supporting the mission, and I should think what that would mean to the jobs of the fifteen people working in my office and how they'll probably end up on a surplus list somewhere."

"You're kidding." Program managers routinely lied to their contracting officers. That was a fact of the life. Otherwise, people like Madison wouldn't let people like him get what he wanted. But for such frigging ridiculousness to come from contracting people above Madison?

"And then Col. Kildee gets involved and tells me to sign it or The Lab isn't supporting the mission and The Lab might get closed down, and I should think about what that would do to the hundreds of engineers and scientists working here in The Lab."

Christ. What a wheelbarrow load of shit.

"And next I'm told that if I don't sign it, then the future of the whole Eglin Air Force Base depends on my signature, and if this base gets cut in the next realignment study Congress orders, then the entire surrounding community will become a ghost town. And presto, the livelihood of tens of thousands of people in Northwest Florida depends on my signing one document. One document that happens to be blatantly illegal."

"Wait a minute. Do all those tens of thousands know they're depending on you? Maybe we should have a Madison Steele Appreciation Day."

"That's not funny. I'm serious."

"So am I. That's not really fair, is it, to make you and you alone responsible for our community's economy?"

"No. But like I said, they know which buttons to push. But it's not about the economy. It's about hanging me out to dry so some big shot who's made a deal under the table can cover his butt long enough to get promoted or to retire to the local golf course resort. And I won't cross the line for that kind of crap. Someone else would. That's why they need me. I'm strong. I'm—" She slumped on the swing. "I'm tired. I'm tired of slaying dragons every day, but who else is going to do it?"

He pressed her hand into his. "Burn out."

"What?"

"It's got to happen sooner or later. How long do you think you can work twelve, fifteen, eighteen hours a day every day of the week and its effect not show?"

She shrugged. "I can't afford not to. Lots of contracting officers cave under pressure. I don't." Disappointment prickled in her voice. Someone somewhere hadn't lived up to her expectations.

"You're under a lot of stress. Stress is as much a plague as leprosy or Black Death, except the decay is on the inside."

"Stress is what I get paid for."

"But balance is what you need. Your life centers around work, and your work centers around stress. Have you ever considered talking to somebody about it?"

"A psychiatrist? No way. I have a security clearance. If I talked to a shrink, it would show up on my record, and I could get my clearance yanked. Do you have any idea how little it takes to lose your security clearance? Evidence of mental duress, unpaid debts, financial counseling, unexplained income, drugs, promiscu—" She stopped short.

"I meant, have you ever considered talking to a friend about the stress you're under?" She didn't have many friends. At work, she judged the value of a person not by who they were but by the work they produced. People had to earn her respect, and once she was convinced they were indeed hard workers and worthy of her attention, she was willing to give them the time of day.

"No," she answered slowly. "The only people at work who might understand are in the same boat. The others only think they are. And people who don't work for the government surely don't understand. They see us all as lazy, overpaid bureaucrats. No, Jon, there's no one."

"There's me." He was close enough to kiss her, even if she didn't hold still. Close enough to feel the warmth of her skin a thumb's width from his cheek. He could brush against her accidentally on purpose.

"You?"

"Yeah, me. You can talk to me all you want."

"You are easy to talk to," she conceded. "That's what makes it so dangerous."

"What's dangerous about talking?"

"Talking has a way of leading to not talking."

Well, hell. He couldn't argue with that, but if he had his druthers, she wouldn't say another word. Except maybe "Yes."

A shimmer of fire skimmed the dark skies in the upper periphery of his vision. He was looking at Madison, and she was looking up. He felt her awe even before he saw it in the glint of her eyes.

"Oh God," she breathed. She peered upward. "That was a falling star, wasn't it? Oh, God. I never thought it could be this close or that beautiful. It must have been huge to have gotten so close to the earth before it burned up in the atmosphere."

"I told you the meteor shower was spectacular," Jon preened. Come to think of it, his mother had seldom been wrong. Whether he liked it or not.

"I can't believe I've been missing this! You know where we should go?" Madison twisted in the seat beside him and laid a hand on his thigh. Her touch felt warm in the chilling air. "There's this runway we use for testing live bombs. It's way out on the Eglin reservation away from all the street lights and condos and hotels. I'll bet we could see every star in the universe out there. I know where the access roads are. I'll find out what the bombing schedule is and maybe we can sneak out there one night when it's clear."

Madison under the stars. He liked that idea, but the idea of being in the wrong place at the wrong time didn't particularly appeal to him. Bombing schedules were known to change. Surely there was some place they could stargaze together without risking bodily harm.

He laid his hand over hers in what might have been an accident. It wasn't. "You're like those shooting stars, you know."

"I burn out quickly?" she joked.

"No. Look at them. The stars. They're all so magnificent. Even the faint ones. But if you look up at all the millions of stars, it's the ones that move that catch your eye."

"That's not always the easiest thing. It's sorta hard to be anonymous when you're a shooting star."

"So did you make a wish?" he asked.

"I didn't have time. I was too busy admiring the sparks. How about you? Did you make a wish?"

If he told her what he wished for, she'd probably slap his face. "No, I didn't have time to make a wish either. You know what you need? You need your own wishing star."

"What's that?"

"A special star for you. One that stays still long enough for you to wish on it." One that would have her thinking of him, too, every time she wished on that star. He pointed beyond the rim of where the meteor had first sparked. "There. There's your star."

"Which one? There are so many." She leaned in close to his arm, trying to site the star herself.

"There. In the constellation Orion." He pressed his cheek against hers, lifted her arm with his, her forefinger on top of his. He aimed at the glittering pinpoints of light. "See those three stars? The ones in an almost vertical line? Look to the side of them so you can see them better. That's Mintaka, Alnilam, and Alnitak, the stars in Orion's belt."

"Uh-huh."

His skin prickled against hers. Her breath sounded heavy in his ear.

"Okay, then. Imagine the vertical line is in the center of a rectangle. The rectangle is anchored by four stars. On the upper left, there's a faint blue star, Bellatrix. It's actually Orion's left shoulder but at this latitude, at this time of night, the constellation is on its side instead of standing. See it?"

"Yeah."

"Then below it is Orion's right shoulder. That red star, that's Betelgeuse. See it?"

"Uh-huh." Her answer came out a little louder than a whimper.

"Now, Orion's feet. His right foot is white star, faint. I don't recall its name." He pointed her finger up one notch. "Orion's left foot, the blue star that anchors the warrior, that's Rigel. That's your star."

"Rigel," she whispered.

"Think you can find it by yourself?"

"If I have to, yes."

She started to say something else, turned her cheek, brushed her lips against his. A little gasp escaped her throat. She drew back. She searched his face, an odd mix of fear and doubt and...something else creasing her brow. Without a word, she dropped her gaze to his mouth. Her chin quivered.

Want kicked at his gut. He'd been this close before but this time, she didn't make excuses and run away. Slipping one hand into her wild mass of impossible curls, he drew her face closer. He dipped his head and tasted her lips. She didn't run. Instead, she matched his kiss with a tenderness that could destroy her reputation as a cold-hearted negotiator and with a passion that nailed the truth in the rumors that she was a wanton.

It was he who pushed away and gulped for air.

"Do you realize," she whispered, her eyes searching his face, "this is the first time you and I have ever been alone together? No Roxie, no baby, no Austin Wait, no Owen Plummer."

Uneasiness prickled at the back of his neck and wound down his spine to his knees. All those years he'd ridiculed his mother. How could he have been so wrong?

They weren't alone. He could feel it.

Someone was watching.

Delilah.

CHAPTER FIFTEEN

It was all Jon's fault she was about to fall asleep in the mashed potatoes as she sat at the Sunday dinner table with her parents, Jon, and her beautiful Delilah. Jon's support, his presence, his touch had reached down into her soul and dredged up some ancient yearning. In her dreams, the possibility of wanting Jon had metamorphasized into something older, darker.

The heavy knot of dread writhed in her stomach. Until this week, she hadn't dreamed of Tim in ages, yet out of nowhere, the disturbing nightmares were back. Disturbing as much in their content as they were in the fact she was again dreaming of Tim.

Two dreams in one night after saying goodnight to Jon. It had to mean something.

She knew what it meant. That this yearning for Tim would never die. Ever.

In the first of the two dreams, she'd been in some distant city on business, and Tim had called out of the blue and begged to meet her. She'd spent hours readying herself for him, for his touch, for his kiss. He'd arrived late and hardly given her a second glance. Of course not. He'd been too intent on the woman he'd brought with him. A black woman, thin and exotic and everything she wasn't. His lover. The woman had raised her eyebrows in smirking contempt but nothing more.

In the second dream, Madison had sat in Tim's condo on a sunny, California beach she'd never seen and gazed up at him. His dark hair was thicker than before, the style different now that his days in the Air Force were over. But he was as sexy, as magnetic, as charismatic as he'd always been. She'd wanted to embrace him but the best she could do was study him with undisguised desire. He caught the silent wish with his gaze and looked away. His wife—younger, blonder, thinner, more petite—cleared her throat and tried to hide the pitying glances at the woman in her husband's past. Tim always did like his women anorexic.

Madison pushed her plate away. She wasn't hungry.

"Think you'll be coming 'round this way again, Jonathan?" Fresh out of his Sunday suit and back into his favorite pair of work pants, Buford Steele shifted in his chair at the head of the table. He didn't bother to hide the anxiety in his shaky voice.

"I doubt it, sir."

"Sir?" What a suck-up. Madison rolled her eyes at Jon, but he didn't seem to notice.

"Lorelei?" Her daddy put down his fork and directed at her the you'd-better-do-as-I-say expression she'd inherited. "Bring him back any time you want. He's obviously had a good influence on you."

Out of the corner of her eye, she saw Jon nearly choke on his iced tea. She was the one who did all the influencing. She'd taught him nearly everything he knew about program management and the world of Federal acquisitions. She'd taught him to stand up for himself and that appearances can be far deadlier than the truth. What could a green, first lieu-ey teach her?

“Stop it, Daddy. You’re embarrassing Jon.” And her. “Jon and I are not involved.” So they’d shared two kisses. So what? The first time she’d walked away. And last night, he’d pushed her away with the excuse of common decency. Maybe she’d spooked him. Maybe that was it. He swore Delilah—or someone—was watching them, even though the little girl was sound asleep in bed by the time Madison had checked on her.

“Figures you wouldn’t like this one,” the old man muttered. His shirt sleeves revealed the thinning arms and loose muscles that shook when he sawed the roast with his knife. When had her daddy changed from the thick-haired man who could swing her onto his shoulders into the husk of an old man?

“You finally find a clean cut boy who seems to care about you and you’re not interested,” he continued. He curled his lip as if the roast had turned bitter. “You only want the ones who treat you like dirt.”

“Daddy, please.” Not in front of company. And not in front of Delilah with her wide eyes of Steele blue and her firm Sandusky jaw. The little girl munched silently on a biscuit but hung on every word her grandfather uttered.

Buford Steele had never met Tim Sandusky, and if Madison had told her father that Tim knew nothing of her pregnancy, he would have tracked her lover all the way to Iceland and insisted he “do the right thing.” Instead, she’d kept quiet and let her daddy think the love of her life had abandoned her. Maybe he had. Seven years had passed and still he hadn’t called, not once, to see how she’d survived the aftermath of their affair.

Madison bowed her head and pretended not to notice that Jon was watching, watching, always. What a shame she hadn’t known him then and that he hadn’t been older. If it had been Jon instead of Tim, he would not have gone willingly to Rejavik. Certainly he wouldn’t have gone quietly. Probably he would have gotten himself thrown in jail. But that was Jon: a fighter. Tim was more of a diplomat. One who looked forward to the new experiences change brought.

Her daddy swigged his sugar-sweetened tea. “You’re a good influence on her, boy. Today’s the first time she’s been to church in at least seven years. Maybe you can talk some sense into her.”

“Sir?” The word caught in Jon’s throat. He swallowed it.

“Take her to church. Every Sunday.”

“Uh, sir, I, uh....”

“If you care for my daughter, you make her go to church.” As if Jon could make her do anything.

“Ah, yes, sir.”

“I’m worried about her immortal soul.”

“Now that I’m home, Daddy, my soul’s fine.” She smiled across the table at Delilah.

She’s so pretty. So pretty. Madison couldn’t take her eyes off the kid. *She's so pretty and so smart. What a boon for the next generation. If I've done nothing else good in my life, she's it.*

"See? You're so far gone, you don't even realize it. You haven't been to church since before Delilah was born."

"Daddy!" Madison almost shrieked. One more word, and he'd let the cat out of the bag. What would Jon think of her if he knew she'd given away her baby? "Okay! Okay, Daddy! I'll go to church more! Whatever you want! Just drop it, okay?" She reined in her outburst and slumped back into her chair. "Besides, it's always the same sermon. Hellfire and damnation. Same as last time I went to church with you. Always makes God look like an ogre. I wish you'd get a new preacher or he'd get a new sermon."

"Judgment day's coming, Lorelei. Better get your house in order. I don't want the circle broken when we all get to heaven. You got to prepare. Like the good Lord says, if you're neither hot nor cold but lukewarm, He'll spew you out of His mouth."

"Aw, Daddy. Let everybody eat. Stop with all the talking about spewing stuff."

"Lorelei!" He banged his fist on the table. Silverware skittered sideways. "I'm serious, girl! The end of the world is coming. I don't want you to come up here to visit your mama and Delilah and me and find out we've all been taken up in the Rapture and you've been left behind."

"Oh, God. Not this again." She'd heard it since she was a little girl, usually immediately after expressing a viewpoint contrary to Buford Steele's.

"You look to the Good Book. There'll be wars and rumors of wars."

"Yes, Daddy, I know. I buy bombs and missiles to fight those wars."

"And it doesn't bother you a bit, does it?"

"Doesn't bother me that there are wars or that there's a need for weapons? It's my job, Daddy. Nobody does it better than me. Nobody."

Jon touched her wrist and urged her back into her seat. How long had she been standing? Her pulse throbbed in her temples. "Honor thy father and thy mother" echoed in her ears. One of many lessons from Sunday School. She sank down onto her chair.

"Mr. Steele?" Jon ventured. "I think you're absolutely right about the end of the world coming. If it makes you feel any better, a farm is good place to be. If you can hang onto it."

Ah, Jon. What are you doing? If he was trying to redirect Ol' Buford's anger, it wouldn't work. Jon would find himself on the bad side of the elder Steele.

"Farm's free and clear," Madison's daddy answered gruffly. Her parents had never bought anything on credit. They'd worked out three hundred acres, acre by miserable acre, and the debt—not their children—had turned them gray. "What's farming got to do with tribulations? Other than the obvious."

"There was a prophet back in the 1940's. Edgar Cayce. He said there's a time of famine coming, and those with farms will be better off. At least you won't starve."

The old man sharpened his bony shoulders, shook off his frailty for a moment. "Bible prophecy's the only prophecy that counts."

"You walked right into that one," Madison muttered.

"Then sir, it might interest you to go out and take a look at the meteor shower tonight. It was awesome last night. The Bible talks about falling stars, doesn't it?"

The lines in her daddy's brow deepened. "Bible says stars the size of talents will fall out of the sky. Do you know how big a talent is, son? Seventy-five pounds. How many meteors did you see hit the ground last night? Any that weighed seventy-five pounds?"

"Uh, no sir. Not yet anyway. But it may interest you, too, to know that there are plagues to be unleashed on mankind."

"Seven of them, yep." If he'd had a Bible nearby, he would have thumped it.

"Then it may interest you to know that your daughter is working on a project right now that will prevent those plagues."

Her daddy shook his head. "You can't stop it, Lorelei. Don't you know anything? You can't stop any of it. All you can do is prepare."

Prepare? God—her God at least—gave her a will to fight. She was going to use it. Even if it meant going straight to hell.

The phone rang in the next room, and Madison practically jumped out of her chair. "I'll get that."

Saved by the proverbial bell. At this point, she was willing to let a vinyl siding salesman with random digit dialing talk her ears off for the next fifteen minutes.

Madison snagged the handset on the wall near the fireplace and leaned against the empty corner. "Hello?"

"Mrs. Steele? Mrs. Steele, this is Jolene. Toby's wife. I need your help something desperate!"

Jolene. Stupid, child-stealing twit. Madison bit into her lower lip. Jolene tended to pull everyone in her path into her vortex of lies and upsets. Mama didn't need that kind of trouble. The Jolene kind. Besides, people often confused Madison and her mother on the telephone, especially when Madison was in a kind-hearted mood.

"Mrs. Steele, you're never gonna believe this, but I'm in jail in Tallahassee."

Madison let out a sigh. She had Austin Wait to thank for the warning. And for helping little Bronwyn Cashwell safely back to her father so that Madison could be free to go to Georgia and so happen to be at her parents' home when Jolene called. Otherwise, Jolene's pathetic little song and dance would have had the elderly Steeles burning rubber all the way to Tallahassee. They were soft-hearted to a fault to anyone who was in trouble as long as it wasn't her. It would be so like them to bail out their ditzy daughter-in-law, spend every penny of their retirement savings on attorneys, and take the girl in because—heaven forbid—something might cause Toby to lose a night's sleep. Ah, well. Madison couldn't blame them. They fully expected a girl with Jolene's neglect-filled childhood to make massive mistakes all over the globe, and they knew those mistakes would rub off on Toby, whom they deemed too young to marry. Other people were allowed—hell, *expected*—to make mistakes, but her parents had always insisted Madison be perfect.

"It wasn't my fault," Jolene continued, blubbering. "I never would have gone clear 'cross the state if Lorelei hadn't called me and begged me to go see her right away."

A lie. A blatant lie. Jolene couldn't even take responsibility for playing petty games of blackmail with her absent husband, let alone take responsibility for the hell she'd put the Cashwells through. Madison could only hope the girl would get the kind of counseling she needed to overcome a mother who urged her to fabricate whatever story necessary to find a man to marry her and take care of her.

"And when I got there, this black-haired woman handed me a baby and said I could have it. Wasn't none of it my fault, Mrs. Steele. The police came to Lorelei's, and I thought they was after me and I ran." Jolene paused to blow her nose loudly, though that was probably an act, too. "Mrs. Steele, you've got to get me out of here. I'm in trouble, deep."

"Yes, you are."

"You need to know how much it's gonna cost to get me outta here?"

"No."

"Then you'll come get me? Right now?" At last the ring of sincerity. The girl wanted out. She didn't care how much it cost anyone else as long as she had her freedom. Typical of Jolene.

Madison kept her voice as low and even as her mother's. "Do you want me to call Toby for you?"

"No! I don't want him to know I'm here. 'Sides, he don't have enough money to bail me out. If you could help me out, he wouldn't even have to know I got in trouble."

Biting her tongue to keep from screaming at the girl for thinking she could hide an arrest for kidnapping from her husband, Madison sank down onto the floor. The last thing she needed right now was her mother or Delilah checking up on her because she'd been on the phone too long.

"Jolene, we know you and Toby have separated."

A pause. "Who told you that? Lorelei? That's a bald-faced lie. Toby and me's real happy together. And I may be six weeks pregnant."

With Toby at sea? Brilliant thinking. Every time Jolene and Toby had a fight, she held onto him with promises of pregnancies that never happened. And Toby—Toby who was supposed to have been in medical school until he dropped out to spend more time between the sheets—was the world's slowest to catch on. He wanted a baby. Desperately. A son to carry on the Steele name before Buford left this earth. Maybe that's why he was so willing to put up with Jolene's long history of miracle pregnancies and unexplained and painless miscarriages.

Poor, stupid Toby.

"Jolene?"

Sniffles. Undoubtedly fake ones. "Y-yeah?"

"Do not, under any circumstances, ever call here again."

Madison stood and quietly dropped the phone into its cradle. She'd be damned if she let Jolene or anyone else take advantage of her parents. If Toby had to marry an idiot girl, why not one with simpler motives? A love struck teenager who wanted Toby for his good looks or awkward swagger. Anything but a conniving little bitch who wanted a quick ticket to Easy Street.

Madison hadn't been anything like that as a teenager. She'd been the girl who got straight A's in math without cracking a book. She'd been the girl who rarely dated, and not because her father interrogated her dates at the door for a solid thirty minutes. She'd been the shy library assistant during study hall, though the cheerleaders all mistook her reticence for snobbery. No matter how hard she tried, she'd never fit in anywhere, never belonged, never felt comfortable with herself. But she'd never been a troublemaker like Jolene.

Somewhere along the way, Madison had lost the shyness though she still didn't waste her breath on small talk. These days, she somehow managed to stir up trouble wherever she went, but only because she knew a better way than the time-worn rules. She'd learned to make a man's pulse race and use men willingly as pleasure points in her life. But for all the changes she'd endured in the past ten years of growing up and old, she still didn't feel she belonged anywhere.

Madison paused in the doorway of the kitchen and watched her mother swish water in the kitchen sink in preparation for hand-washing dishes. She'd bought her parents a state-of-the-art dishwasher two years ago, but they'd never been able to justify using anything so modern. Empty chairs sat askew at the table. Wet circles where glasses of iced tea had stood during the meal marked the hand-hemmed tablecloth. A white, plastic medicine bottle that smelled of bubble gum lay between the salt and pepper shakers. Madison picked it up and studied the label. "Delilah's on antibiotics?"

"Hmmm. Ear infection last week. She's better now."

"Then why is there so much pink stuff still left?" Nearly two-thirds of the bottle.

"Like I said, she's better. She doesn't need it all."

"Mama!" Blood rose in Madison's face. "She has to take all of her antibiotics. Didn't the doctor tell you that? Every drop until it's gone."

Agnes Steele arched a single eyebrow. "Don't get uppity with me, Lorelei. I raised two young 'uns already. I know what I'm doing. What was good enough for you and your brother is good enough for Delilah."

"Things are different now, Mama. Germs can get resistant to antibiotics if you don't take the whole dose or you take them all the time for no reason. In another decade, we may not have antibiotics strong enough to wipe out the mutated germs." Already in Europe, cows were stuffed with feed treated with vancomycin—the world's most powerful antibiotic and the drug of last resort—and slaughtered for their beef. Scientists raged about the long-term effects on human consumers, yet nothing was done. Another plague waiting to happen. "Promise me you'll make her finish her medicine and then keep her off it when you can. Mama?"

"Oh, all right."

"Where is everybody?" Madison joined her mother at the sink and reached for a dish towel.

"Buford took your friend out to show him how the peanut picker works. Delilah went out to feed the birds."

"Oh." What was her daddy telling Jon? He used to finish his date-night interrogations by asking the boy if he'd ever had any part of his body amputated and suggesting that it was an appropriate method of birth control if the boy didn't have a good understanding of what abstinence meant.

"Who was that on the phone?" her mother asked. "Your office?"

"Solicitor." Really. Jolene was a natural at begging for money.

"Oh, I hate those calls. They just don't know when to take no for an answer."

Madison smiled. Her mother probably had never said no to anyone outside the family. Not the polite thing for a Southern woman to do. Mama would have been horrified if she'd ever listened in on one of Madison's smart-bomb negotiations and heard the adamant refusals occasionally sprinkled with profanity. If anyone had an image of where Madison fit into the world, it was Agnes Steele.

And Lydia Colter.

"Mama?" Madison said as she rubbed a dishcloth over the damp plate. "Jon and Daddy were talking about falling stars and plagues and stuff. Do you believe in prophecy?"

"I sure do. The Bible says—"

"No, not just the Bible. Other prophecies, too. Nostradamus, Cayce, the secular prophets." She scrubbed at an obstinate splotch of food on the next plate, then rinsed it.

"No, I'm like your daddy about that. Those prophets aren't real."

"Just the ones mentioned in the Bible? Isaiah, Daniel. Those? You're saying the Book of Revelation is real but anyone since John is a fraud?"

"Isaiah has a book and Daniel has a book and there's a Book of

Revelation but there's not a Book of Nostradamus. Not in my Bible."

"Yeah, next you'll say that the only real Bible is the one King James commissioned. The modern versions aren't the true word of God." The perplexed expression on her mother's face told her not to bother pursuing that line of reasoning. Madison scrubbed harder at the plate and ignored the next one in the stack. "What about reincarnation, Mama? Do you believe in that?"

"Absolutely not. We live out our time on this earth doing good works in His name and if we accept Christ as our savior, we go to Heaven. If we don't, we go to hell. And that's that."

"Do you ever think Heaven might get boring?"

Mama's eyes widened at the sacrilege. She slipped another plate into the stack. "Heaven will be filled with joy. You know that."

At the risk of heresy, Madison continued, feeling the ice thin under her feet. "But there's only so much harp-playing and streets-of-gold-walking we can do."

"You're not getting mixed up in the occult, are you?"

"No. Nothing like that." Not...yet. Too close to the edge. Madison quickly doused each plate in a stream of running water and then dried each one.

"You've been thinking a lot about religion lately?" Mama's voice sounded hopeful.

"Um, no. But I have been thinking about spirituality."

"There's a difference?"

"I think so." Madison stacked the dried plates on the counter and waited for her mother to pull the last dirty dish out of the suds.

"Oh, honey. You're mixed up with devil worshippers, aren't you?"

"No, Mama. But I have been thinking a lot about reincarnation lately. I've got these yearnings I have no right to have. And I can't explain them. Unless they're the remnants of something that's happened before this lifetime."

The plate in her mother's soapy hands slipped through and shattered on the floor. Madison dropped to her knees. She picked up pieces as fast as she could. Her mother, more slowly, knelt beside her. Her wrinkled hands trembled as she reached for the jagged edges.

"God gave you to us for a purpose. I prayed and prayed for a daughter. I begged. They said I'd never have a baby, that I was too old. But God looked ahead and knew that you had a purpose in this life. That's why we had to take such good care of you. Be so hard on you. Not let you slide. You have purpose."

"I know. And I'm looking for that purpose now. I've heard—" from Jon's long-winded tales about his mother—"that there's sometimes bleed-through from past incarnations. That when you're a child, you retain some of your talents and glories and likes and dislikes from your previous life. I was wondering if I'd said anything unusual when I was little."

Her mother laughed nervously. "Lorelei, everything you did and said was unusual. Still is. You always were the strangest child. Always so determined. Not quite sure of yourself. But that's not reincarnation. It's—I don't know—my clumsy genes coming through in you." She laughed again. It sounded hollow to Madison's ears.

"Mama, when did you get religion?"

Her mother used the counter's edge as a crutch to pull herself up to her full height again. Her knees creaked as she rose, half the broken plate in her hands. "I suppose I've always had religion. My parents took me to church when I was knee-high to a grasshopper. Not a big conversion experience like some people. Not like I used to ride with Hell's Angels, you know. When God told me I was going to have a daughter and she was going to do great things, it was like I felt the shiver of the Holy Ghost run up and down my spine."

"So you did have a spiritual experience."

"Yes. I think you could call it that."

"Then what makes your spiritual experience any more valid than my spiritual experience? Whether it's conversion or reincarnation or simply contemplating the soul and the mysteries of life? At least we're thinking on it, aren't we?"

Madison took the shards from her mother and dumped them into the open trash bin under the sink.

Agnes Steele wiped her hands on her apron. "Thinking's always gotten you into trouble, Lorelei."

Thinking and not thinking. But she understood her mother's warning. Why question the status quo and risk an answer you can't stand?

"Lorelei," Delilah called from outside in her usual upbeat, singsongy, beautiful little voice.

Madison stood on her tiptoes and peered out the window over the sink. Through the dusty screen, Delilah grinned up at her, made the connection, and Madison smiled back. "Hey, sweet-sweet," Madison chimed. "What are you doing?" No telling how long the kid had been eavesdropping from below the window sill.

"I was throwing out bread for the birds. Come see."

The way Delilah stood there with her fists pressed firmly into her hip bones reminded Madison of herself. The way she expected Madison to drop whatever she was doing and see the world through her eyes dredged up memories of Tim. Would Delilah ever be old enough to be her own person and not a reflection of her someone else?

"Lorelei?"

"Yes?"

"Come see the birds."

"I'm busy with—" Busy with what? The words had tumbled out of her mouth before she had a chance to think. Madison glanced at her mother, who was sopping errant pools of water on the yellowed countertops. All the dishes had been washed and dried. For a change, Madison wasn't busy with anyone else, at least not until she got back to the office tomorrow. "Mama, do you mind?" she asked.

"Go ahead. It's good for you to spend time with your—"

Madison bumped her lips with her index finger. Delilah was listening. The kid heard everything, watched everything, and seldom let adults know exactly how intuitive and smart she was. But Madison knew. She was like a little computer, gathering data on everything that went on around her, processing it, analyzing it. She'll make a hell of a contract negotiator one of these days, Madison thought.

"Be right out," Madison called over the window ledge. She twisted the band of cheap gold on her finger and dried the wet circle underneath as she hurried out the back door and down the steps. Beyond the hay barn, her father cranked the tractor and waved to Jon. A second later the tractor lurched in the direction of the neighboring farm, where Daddy had been helping out Old Man Dugan during his hospital stay for a ruptured disc.

Jon spun on the heels of his boots and strolled through the warm, mid-day sunshine streaming down on the ivy-covered shed at the back yard's perimeter. He wasn't in any particular hurry, and he was whistling a Rod Stewart song she couldn't remember the title of. Why was he always carrying some infernal tune? Maybe she'd get him a CD of Rod Stewart's greatest hits for Christmas. Then again, she really didn't know Jon well enough to know if he owned a CD player. She knew him only well enough to know the scent of his skin, the taste of his mouth, at midnight when stars fell like quick matchheads sputtering out.

"This way, Lorelei." Delilah waited near the flower garden, by the path's edge. She arranged a wreath of ivy on her head like a crown. Then she tapped her sneakered little feet impatiently. So grown up to be so young. Just like her mommy. Madison couldn't remember her ever being playful.

Delilah trotted along ahead of her on the path paved with peanut hulls. She walked tall, proud and defiant. Maybe Delilah had been a warrior in a previous life, too. Maybe her seriousness was bleed through from her last incarnation. Every few feet, she'd take an awkward, giant step over a toppled stalk of Mama's exotic, mail-ordered, Asian lilies that bordered the path. Delilah, like Tim, took special care not to disturb things of beauty unless she was greatly distracted. Any other kid might have stomped right over the flower without noticing. Madison wished to God the kid would laugh more.

Sure, there'd been times in history when children were treated as little adults. Allowing kids to be kids was definitely a twentieth-century idea, and the latter twentieth-century at that. Delilah deserved a chance to play. Now. Now, because the future held so many terrors and hypocrisies and heartbreaks, with every generation shaking its head at the next. Delilah deserved a world full of beautiful things, not the left-overs of previous generations. No one could guarantee the child a bright future. No one but her own mother.

I should be back at work. Today, not tomorrow. Even if it is a Sunday. At least there I stand a chance of finding out who has Project Andromeda.

Madison stepped over a last bank of lilies and into the open field beside the ivy-shrouded shed. The grass cushioned her bare footsteps. Not even her sensible low-heeled shoes could beat the comfort of it.

Tomorrow, she'd report back to work as Austin Wait had dictated and help him catch a spy. In all probability, someone she knew well. Chances were, the disk containing Project Andromeda was gone for good. In most security breaches involving stolen data, the papers were never recovered and in many, many cases, the thief was never caught. Of course, no one had ever breached security on her watch, and for that, she'd see to it hell was paid.

She didn't relish facing the people in her office again. Bad enough to be under OSI suspicion for espionage when all your friends are behind you, but to watch your enemies gloat? Maeve would be back from her TDY trip to Los Angeles and full of her usual obnoxious banter. Raynene would probably direct every inane phone call to Madison's voice mail to annoy her. Mr. Smith would likely be thinking of "less visible" positions to transfer her to, but then he'd realize that a slot in The Lab where she didn't deal with billion-dollar weapon system production programs was certainly less visible and decide not to move her to a different sweatshop. And Sarabeth. Madison shuddered at the memory of Sarabeth in her pearls and perfect shoes at Roxie's funeral. The way Sarabeth had studied Madison's every move, the baby in her arms, Jon at her side.

She didn't like Sarabeth. Madison couldn't help it, and she wouldn't be a hypocrite and hide it.

Two years ago, Sarabeth had complained about one of her dog programs until their favorites-playing supervisor switched the dog with one of Madison's better projects. How could Sarabeth have known Madison and the program manager would get along so well and turn a dog into a plum project? The project evolved after that, with the United Kingdom tossing in funding to become part of the project. Then, of course, Sarabeth had complained about Madison's foreign travel opportunities. As if leaving the U.S. on Monday, arriving at London's Gatwick International Airport on Tuesday, meeting with the Defence Research Agency on Wednesday and flying home on Thursday was a coveted trip! The only sights Madison had seen on those trips were rolling pastures, dingy townships, and a rail-side cemetery—all through the foggy windows on the train from Victoria Station to Farnborough and back. But Sarabeth had complained again, and their supervisor had caved. As always. Soon after, Sarabeth took too long to nit-pick her way through a negotiation, the U.K. pulled their funds, and the project died. Madison refused to pretend she liked the whiny bitch.

If Roxie's murderer was indeed someone close to Madison, at least physically, then Sarabeth with her pristine office next door certainly met the criteria. She was as good a candidate as any for a person who might set up Madison for treason and murder, though Madison couldn't see Sarabeth actually pushing Roxie into a vault and locking the door. Even with her tight Junior League schedule, murder seemed incongruous with Sarabeth's style. And there was always the possibility of messing up her nails.

Sarabeth and all the others with their ears to the rumor mill floor! Didn't they have anything better to do? Like catch the person who'd really stolen the proposal disk? Like stop chattering and speculating and for once try to solve the crime instead of contributing to the vast and inaccurate reporting of it?

Didn't anyone understand how serious the loss of Project Andromeda was? If the wrong people got their hands on the proposal disk, the strides to contain biological warfare would be halted for at least the next two or three years. That proposal contained the best ideas available as of early September. What would come out of the contract's first year deliverables next year and the option year's deliverables the year after would not stop terrorists in the meanwhile and might not afterward, but Project Andromeda would provide a quick remedy and save countless lives, maybe even the whole planet.

If The Cameron Institute's proposal fell into the wrong hands, whether those hands were French, Iraqi, anti-Government militia, or Sleeping Dog terrorists, America would be years behind in the technology race. Whoever had the disk would know which countermeasures the U.S. planned to use against chem and bio warfare. They'd simply make their apocalyptic weapons superior to whatever was in TCI's proposal.

It wasn't that the average Joe-Blow American wasn't interested in chemical and biological warfare. It made great fiction.

Movies played out on the big screen with heroes trying to figure out how to keep a plane full of passengers and a cargo full of nerve agent from crashing into the Nation's capitol.

Television movies glamorized outbreaks of deadly viruses that in reality could turn the human body into anything but glamorous. Or they depicted made-up biological agents that threatened to destroy the entire Eastern seaboard.

Why would aging baby boomers watch weekly TV series about concocted germs and plagues when there are plenty of the real thing in the world? she wondered.

And why would the same men and women forgo plastic surgery to have a shot of botulinum derivative injected into the flesh around their eyes and between their eyebrows and into their upper lips to paralyze the muscles and relax the lines etched by time?

Jesus H. Christ, what a fucked-up world!

"Lorelei?" Delilah tapped her on the arm.

"Wh-what?" Madison blinked. Delilah stood in front of her, her lips puckered up in disappointment. Birds, obviously migrating from North, fluttered on the ground and sought perches on nearby fence posts and trees dead from lightning strikes. Several soared away with scraps of stale bread in the beaks.

"You're not listening to me."

"Oh, sweet-sweet." Madison dropped to her knees and gathered Delilah awkwardly into her arms. "I'm so sorry. I was thinking about work."

The little girl gave a quick flip of her black hair. "You're always thinking about work."

Madison smiled. "Yes. I suppose I am." Against her will, she let Delilah wriggle free of her loose grip. "My job is to make your world safe."

"I'll be fine. I'm always fine."

She might as well have kicked Madison in the stomach. Like mother, like daughter. She'd adopted Madison's motto.

"Did all the birds come here because of you?" Madison asked, doing her damnedest to lighten the conversation and failing.

"Un-huh. Because you're here."

A brown bird—she didn't recognize the species—spiraled down to her feet and plucked up a morsel of bread. It regarded them both as it wrestled with the scrap.

"I don't think so, sweetness. I think they came here because you were generous with your bread on their journey south for the winter."

"Yeah, and I'm teaching them to fly, too."

Madison chuckled. "Sure you are."

"I am! Some of the sparrows can't fly so good yet. Like those over there." She pointed at several brown birds skittering in the grass. The birds must have hatched late in the year from the nests that dotted the rafters of the hay barn because they're weren't quite grown. Fledging time was critical for Delilah's pets because if the young birds didn't learn to fly in a few days' time, the stray cats that chased mice around the barns would claim the sparrows for dinner.

"Want to see me teach one to fly?"

Before Madison could answer, Delilah tiptoed like a cat on the prowl to the sparrows, scooped one up in her hands, and carried it back to Madison. With a whoosh, Delilah tossed the bird into the air like a kid making a free throw from half-court. It flapped its wings, probably in terror, and then plummeted unhurt to the thick grass.

"Not like that, sweet-sweet. Here. Let me show you."

Tenderly, carefully, Madison picked up the bird and nestled it against her chest. Through the soft feathers of its underbelly, its heart pattered like an insistent, leaky faucet. Madison stretched out her left arm, her hand even with her head, and perched the sparrow on her wrist. The stupid little bird cocked its head. She swayed her arm once, and the bird flapped off her wrist and sailed with ample grace to the ground.

"If that weren't a house sparrow on your wrist, L. Madison Steele, I'd swear you were a mighty falconer."

At the sound of Jon's voice, she smiled, then turned to face him. Instead of a teasing smirk on his face, he simply frowned at her as if he'd seen a ghost. "Well, you know how it is," she joked. "One day, sparrows. The next day, falcons."

"Or vice versa," he murmured.

Delilah stooped at her feet, retrieved the bird, and repeated Madison's attempt to teach flight. The bird landed a good four feet in the other direction. With a magnificent smile on her face, Delilah followed the silly bird across the pasture and tried again.

"She's something else," Madison whispered.

"So are you."

He stepped closer to her, and she steeled herself not to move. She'd touched him last night, kissed him. Maybe Austin Wait was right: he was hers for the taking. If she cared to repeat history.

"I liked stargazing with you last night," he said.

She didn't look at him. She kept her eyes trained on Delilah, soaking up the sight of her and memorizing it for another week or two until the next visit. "I should be getting back to the office. If I don't, who knows? There might not be anyone left to gaze at stars."

"We'll figure it out, Madison. I'll help you."

"I have to do it myself."

"You and Special Agent Wait, you mean. Watch it, Madison. He'll throw you to the wolves. He *is* a wolf."

Madison fought down a smile. Jon was jealous, but he was right. Austin Wait had his own agenda, and even if she was walking into trouble by volunteering to help him catch Giselle Villemaire, Owen Plummer, and whoever else was involved in stealing Project Andromeda, she would willingly walk into that trap. This was a battle she would win—had to win—even if it meant her own destruction.

Jon was different. Too much like Tim in some respects. To Austin Wait, she was another "source" on yet another case and he'd gladly sacrifice her if he had to. And why not? He'd already sacrificed his family. Winning at work was the only way he could keep from losing.

Jon, on the other hand, would sacrifice himself to protect her. The past few days had brought home a cold, hard reality to her: Jon was quite possibly the only person at work who genuinely cared about her well-being.

Roxie was dead, and life went on without her. Buyers still worked overtime to get the job finished, defense contractors whose proposals hadn't won the competition still protested to the General Accounting Office, and a group of a dozen COPPER CAP trainees—minus Roxie—still met on Friday mornings in the main procurement building to plan ice cream sundae fund-raisers for the next office Christmas party. Give it a few more months, and no one would notice that Roxie had ever been there.

Roxie had worked almost as many hours of overtime as Madison had, yet it no longer mattered. Then it had been so important that they hurry and get each and every project on contract. Otto had promised to take them both on the kick-off meeting to The Cameron Institute, but now Madison doubted whether he ever meant it. Program managers would say anything, do anything, to pressure a contracting officer into working harder, faster, smarter—as if they weren't already.

In the end, the hard work would be forgotten, exactly as Roxie would be. Just as, once Madison was no longer of any use to save the world for the team, she too would be forgotten. Such was the life of a contracting officer.

"Okay," she conceded. "I'll let you in on what Austin wants me to do. If there's anything you can do, I welcome your help."

Jon beamed at her as if he'd won a major victory. Then he nodded toward Delilah who had once again resorted to tossing sparrows into the air. "Great way to burn calories, chasing after birds."

"New form of aerobics. Maybe we'll franchise it now that I have no one to play tennis with." She sombered. "Roxie and I used to play tennis once or twice a week on our lunch hour, when we didn't work through lunch."

"That often? You always came back to The Facility so refreshed. I couldn't tell you were out there sweating in the heat."

Madison laughed. "Sheesh, Jon! What did you think we did? Went out there and got all sweaty and put our clothes and make-up back on over the sweat?"

He shrugged. "I don't know. I guess I'd never thought of you as sweaty. Not while playing tennis anyway. I mean...never mind."

"Oh, yeah. There's a shower in the basement of Building 11. In the back of the women's bathroom. There's a men's room and shower down the hall. Didn't you know?"

He smiled, lost in what she hoped was a wonderful daydream winding its way through his head. Maybe one day he'd suggest playing tennis with her on her lunch hour and instead, they'd get really sweaty in the back seat of her car down at Camp Robbins near the bayou. She'd go back to the shower and wash the scent of him off her, and no one would know any better. Or maybe he could sneak through the window of the women's bathroom and join her in the shower. Afterwards, he'd quickly towel her off and slip back out the window. Or maybe....

"Madison?" The smile had faded.

"Yeah?"

"What do you wear when you play tennis?"

"Tee shirt. Shorts. None of those pretentious little tennis dresses. I play for the exercise, not the art form. Why?"

"So tell me what you do when you take off your clothes?"

She shot him one of her eat-shit looks. "You're sick," she teased, though she wasn't entirely uncomfortable with the new direction of their conversation.

"No, really." He blushed right on cue. "Bear with me."

"Bear or bare?" Was that on his mind, too?

"You take off your clothes, right?" She nodded. "Then you put on your tennis clothes, right?"

"If I'm bouncing around on the tennis courts instead of tabletops, yeah."

"What do you do then?" He spoke slowly, as if she were either stupid or he wanted her to understand the full impact of his discovery. "What do you do with the access card that was clipped to your jacket?"

"I unclip the card," she said, equally slowly, "and clip it to my T-shirt."

"Oh. That shoots that idea to hell and back."

"I told you, Jon. I never take that card off. I wear it wherever I go. Except for bed, and we've already established that. We don't think anyone broke into my house and stole the card while I was sleeping."

"Yeah, and I'm surprised you don't wear it clipped to you ear while you sleep." He made a disrespectful face, but she ignored it. "Madison?""

"Yeah?"

"You don't wear that access card *in the shower,* do you?"

"Oh my God." She unclipped it from her dirty T-shirt, attached it to her jacket, pulled the curtain, and buried her face in the cool rush of water. Anyone near the showers could swap cards with her, and she would never know it. How could she have been so careless? "I think we've established opportunity."

"Who else knew that you and Roxie were playing tennis twice a week?"

She tried to sort through the fog. "Gavin knew. Sometimes he'd come watch us. Though I guess now he was actually watching Roxie."

"I can't see Lt. Col. Ballard having the balls to crash the women's showers to steal your card. Who else knew? Female, that is."

"Let's see. Beatrice knew. But her idea of exercise is playing cards with her bridge cronies. And Cathy knew, but she works through lunch every day. And Lynette, though she's still out on stress leave. All of them had a need to know, though. They work for me, and if something falls apart on my lunch hour, they need to know how to find me."

"Sheesh. Ever thought of getting a beeper?"

"Then I'd be getting calls every time I walk down the hall to the bathroom. No thanks."

"Who else knew about your tennis dates? Everybody? Except for me?"

"No. Just people who needed to know. Oh, wait a minute. Sarabeth knew."

"Her name keeps popping up a lot."

"Yeah. It does. I've run into her in the locker room on a couple of occasions. She and a couple of friends from her church group meet there every day to do aerobics to the beat of Christian rock."

Jon shook his head. "I keep remembering how she trashed your office, went through all your personal stuff."

"She's a good candidate."

"Anybody else you ran into in the showers? What about your procurement clerks? Raynene and Eileen?"

"No. Never saw them around the showers either...uh-oh." She gasped. It had been weeks, and she'd completely forgotten—

"What? You remember something?"

"Miri knew."

"My roommate Miri?""

"Yeah, unless you know another Miri. Several weeks ago, Roxie and I were headed out the door to the courts when Gavin called me with a problem on the rail gun launcher contract of Cathy's. I had to go back to the office for a conference call, and Roxie was bitching about how it was the second time in a week I'd had to cancel on her, and since Miri was standing right there, she volunteered to take my place on the courts."

Jon shook his head harder. "It can't be Miri."

"Hey, you did ask. Maybe there's a side to Miri we don't know."

He shuddered. "You're telling me I've been living in the same house with a murderess?"

"I'm not telling you anything, Jon. You asked who knew, and I told you. Who knows? Maybe she's got a thing for you, and she's trying to get rid of me because she thinks I'm a threat." Madison meant it as a joke, but Jon didn't laugh.

"Miri's totally drooly-faced over her fiancé. She can't think about anything or talk about hardly anything except for wedding plans."

"She's planning a big wedding, huh?"

"The biggest."

"And she needs money to pay for it, right?"

"Can't be her. She doesn't have her act together well enough to steal a classified project, blame it on you, and cover it up. For heaven's sake, she's got a maturity level of a sixteen-year-old."

Madison skewed her jaw to the right. "Maybe that's what she wants us to think."

"What's with the paranoia?"

"Hey, you asked. You know, you and I have been sort of close this past week. The only other person who's been as close to me is dead now. Maybe we should be concerned about your safety. I suppose I could let you stake out a permanent corner of my sofa. I'll protect you."

He raised one eyebrow as if to question who would protect him from her.

"Oh, crap." Madison folded her arms in front of her.

"What? Did you remember something else?"

She tilted her head toward the gray sedan pulling into her parents' driveway. Jon followed her gaze. "We've got James Bond for company," she muttered. How was she ever going to explain Special Agent Austin Wait to Mama and Daddy? In the past seven years, they hadn't met a single male friend of hers. In less than twenty-four hours, she'd had two contenders for her affections. That was more than her parents could handle. More than she could handle, too.

Her heart skipping a beat, Madison scanned the field and sheds for Delilah. Austin Wait couldn't see her. The man wasn't stupid. Putting puzzles together was his occupation. Jon was young and impressionable enough to be fooled into thinking the little girl was Madison's adopted little sister and nothing more. Austin Wait had been trained to see through lies.

"There's a path behind the shed. It leads to a creek down in the pasture. I want you to take Delilah for a walk."

He glanced over his shoulder at Austin's car and sniffed. "I've got a better idea. You take your sister for a walk, and I'll stay here and debate James Bond."

"You wanted me to ask for your help. I'm asking." She heard a distant knock and knew Austin was hammering away at the front door. Another few minutes and either her parents would let him in or he'd figure out the front door was for insurance salesmen only and come around back. In any case, he was dangerously close to her secrets.

"All right, all right," Jon conceded. "I'll take Delilah for a walk. You're afraid I'll beat him to a pulp."

"Yeah, that's it. I don't want you getting arrested in front of Mama and Daddy."

Delilah tossed her sparrow into the air before Jon could reach her. The much abused bird landed on the shed's tin roof, high above Delilah's head. In frustration, she kicked at the grass.

"Delilah? I want you to take Jon down to the creek. *Now.*"

"But my bird—"

"He'll come down when he's ready. Probably needs to rest."

"But he'll fall. Make him come down."

"You take Jon to the creek. I'll take care of the bird."

Reluctant but satisfied, Delilah slipped her hand into Jon's and tugged him down the path. "You're not helping my bird," she called over her shoulder.

Madison felt like growling but decided to save that for Austin. He'd tracked her to Georgia. Not good. She hadn't told him where she was going. Oops. She winced. Maybe that's why he'd shown up with the angry gait. She'd promised not to leave town, yet she'd taken off without a word. Austin was probably plenty pissed off at her. She knew what he'd say: how was she going to help him catch a spy when she disappeared without a moment's notice?

She shuffled through the thick grass toward the shed and envied the bird for being able to fly away, or at least flutter out of sight. Reaching for the sparrow, she stood on her tiptoes, contemplating her strategy for keeping Austin from either dragging her back to Florida or cutting her out of his plan of action.

The skin on the back of her neck prickled, the hair standing straight out as if lightning had struck her. Her stomach churned. She let the bird remain on its precarious perch and settled back onto her heels. She drew in a shallow breath and then spun around, fists clenched.

Owen Plummer stared back at her with soulless eyes. He couldn't have been any more than five feet away from her, and he looked as caught off guard as she was, as if he hadn't expected to find her there.

Unable to breathe, she studied him—the sandy hair, the angular face, the strange cut of suit, the long-barreled gun tucked neatly into his belt. Something inside her twisted, convulsed, folded in on itself. She fought back the wave of nausea that seared through her veins and demanded she flee for her life. Right down to her cells, she knew his presence wasn't natural. Nothing mattered but getting away from him.

He must have been the one who killed Roxie. She could feel it in her bones. The man was a murderer. How else could she explain the violent reaction to him? The terror went deeper than death.

She backed away, wondering, hoping her daddy kept the pitchfork beside the shed as he had in her youth. Even if the pitchfork was there, Owen Plummer had the more powerful weapon. One bullet in the brain and that was it. He'd be waiting for Delilah with a second bullet. Jon and Delilah. Then her parents and Austin Wait. She wouldn't let that happen. If she was going down, she was going down with the grandest fight of her life.

Her breath came back in a rush, whistling back and forth over her teeth. She was ready.

Owen Plummer's hand touched his gun, almost protectively, then flew to his mouth. Surprise sparked in his light-colored eyes. His chest heaved uncontrollably. He doubled over and vomited into the grass, all the while slanting a glance of helplessness and confusion at Madison.

"Lorelei!" her mother's voice called from the other side of the shed. "Where are you? There's a nice Government policeman here to see you."

Madison glanced away for a second—a split second—and Owen Plummer was gone as if he'd never been there.

The air seemed to crackle where he'd stood. Nothing proved he was ever there except the flattened grass and the pool of vomit soaking into the ground.

Overhead, the sparrow chirped and flew away.

PART II

THE DAY AT HAND

Not later than thirty days after final approval within the Department of Defense of plans for any experiment or study to be conducted by the Department of Defense, whether directly or under contract, involving the use of human subjects for the testing of chemical or biological agents, the secretary of Defense shall supply the committees on Armed Services of the Senate and House of Representatives with a full accounting of such plans for such experiment or study, and such experiment or study may then be conducted only after the expiration of the thirty-day period beginning on the date such accounting is received by such committees.

—50 USC 1520 (a)

CHAPTER ONE

Monday, 4 October 1999, Eglin Air Force Base, Florida

The woman should have had her own soundtrack. Something that rocked. Maybe ZZ Top.

She wore a fire-engine red suit Jon hadn't seen much of but it was well-worth remembering with its tailored jacket and short, slender skirt that emphasized her long legs and scarlet shoes. Her new access card with its grainy photo of her hung from her lapel. Madison kept both her shoulders and her jaw squared as she stalked down the hallway at a good 3.5 miles per hour. Though she'd pulled her blond tangles into a severe sweep, tendrils escaped their hold and softened the sternness of her face. This was Madison's poker face, when everything was at risk in a negotiation and her adversaries were left to wonder if she'd heard either their blatant digs or their disturbing sobs.

Jon kept to a discreet distance as he followed her down the hallway. Well, discreet to him. The occasional backward glance made it plain to him Madison was not thrilled with his attempt at being her guardian angel, yet her protests had been weak, more out of habit than rage. When not protecting her, he could spend his spare moments interviewing civil servants about their morale level for Col. Kildee's special project.

On one hand, Madison was her old self again: the take-charge, take-no-prisoners L. Madison Steele she'd been before an abandoned baby had paralyzed her will. On the other hand, for being as tough as she was, she'd been unusually on edge since coming back from Georgia. She'd been stern about getting Delilah and him out of the way while Austin Wait confronted her about why she'd left Florida on such short notice. Sure enough, by the time Jon and Delilah returned from the creek, Wait had planted himself on the hood of her car, fuming, waiting. That was to be expected, but he'd never seen Madison come totally unglued. She'd kissed her little sister good-bye behind the shed and pushed her quietly into the house. While Wait paced outside and Jon paced around the living room, Madison had stood in the kitchen and pleaded with her parents to take a vacation, go somewhere, go anywhere, take Delilah and get away from the farm for a while. Her parents weren't safe, she'd claimed. Delilah wasn't safe.

"God will take care of us," Madison's mother had said. "And He'll send His angel to watch over you, too."

Jon didn't know whether to pity the old woman for her naiveté or envy her for her faith.

Nearly an hour later, Madison had reluctantly crawled behind the wheel of her car and, flanked by Wait's sedan and Jon's motorcycle, headed southwest to Florida. Whatever had terrified her on her parents' farm, she wouldn't say, but he had a feeling it had nothing to do with Austin Wait.

"Hey, Colt!" Figmo waved to him from the door of the mailroom. "Come here a sec."

Torn, Jon watched Madison walk down the long corridor alone. The engineers in the hall stared down at their feet rather than say hello to her. Others waited for her to pass their offices, then came out and exchanged whispers as she kept right on walking, her head high, her chin tilted upward as if nothing could hurt her. Jon knew better. The woman cried in her sleep.

"What's up, Figmo?" he clipped out.

"What do you mean? 'What's up, Figmo?' I haven't seen you in days. Where've you been?"

"Out of town."

"Let me know sometime, okay?"

"Who are you? My mother?" Not even Miri quizzed him on his absences, let alone the happy-go-lucky Casanova he shared a roof with.

"Screw you. It's like you're not even living in the house with us any more."

True. In the past week, he'd spent maybe five minutes a day in the house he shared with Miri and Figmo, and that was only to change clothes and water the sickly ficus tree the roommate before him had left behind. Already Jon had a toothbrush at Madison's and a package of disposable razors.

"Look, man, I've got a shot at a great condo overlooking the beach. A real babe lure. The lease is up on our place in a month and Miri's going back to her parent's house in Seattle to get married on Christmas Eve and she's practically living at his place anyway. What do you think? Is life a beach? You gonna move in with me?"

Jon shrugged. For some reason, the perennial beach babes didn't hold the same appeal they had back in the spring.

"Speaking of Miri, have you seen much of her lately?" Christ. Jon couldn't believe he was asking this. Miri was more of a kid sister than a roommate. She couldn't possibly have anything to do with Roxie's murder.

"No, man. Like I said, she's practically living with Ralph already."

"Have you, um, ever heard Miri say anything bad about Madison Steele?"

Figmo grunted. "I've never heard her say anything about anybody except Ralph." He followed Jon's gaze down the hallway. "Are you messing with that?" he asked, jerking his head in Madison's direction. "Man, she'll break your balls."

Jon unintentionally puffed out his chest. "I can handle her."

"I can't stomach her."

"Why not?" he demanded, then shrank back. He was defending her too hard.

"I don't know, Colt. It's like she's always got to be on top. Like she thinks she owns the world or something. And you know what I really hate? The way she refers to us as *her* engineers and *her* program managers and *her* lieutenants. Like we belong to her or something."

At the end of the hall, Madison turned the corner into the contracting suite. She'd never looked colder or more distant or stronger or more alone than she did right now.

"Some of us do belong to her." Without waiting for Figmo's response, Jon trotted down the hall after her. He nearly slid on the orange carpet as he rounded the corner into the reception area. He didn't have a particularly good reason to be there and he couldn't very well say he was there to guard-dog Madison. Maybe he could tell them he needed to interview Sarabeth about her morale level. A benign enough reason, but it wouldn't keep him in the office for the rest of the day.

"Maddie, lass." Old Mac McNeeley drooped his teddy bear arms over Madison's shoulders and hugged. "Oh, Maddie-lass, I have missed you, Darlin'."

"I missed you, too, Mac."

Jon's heart went out to the old man. At least someone gave Madison a warm welcome back to the office. Not like the engineers and scientists in the halls and the other contracting people in her office. Standoffish or worse. Whispering as she walked past. They'd all heard the rumors: Was Madison still a suspect in the security breach? Where did the baby she'd held in her arms at Roxie's funeral come from? Was it true she was thinking of adopting Tim Sandusky's love child by another woman?

Austin Wait—blast him—could have stepped in and made a difference. One word from the OSI and Madison would have been cleared of all suspicion and the rumor mill could grind up some other miserable soul.

But instead, Austin Wait had explained in his two-hour rampage at Madison's house that she was to let the suspicion fester. Let whoever had set her up for espionage and murder see her tottering on the edge and rush forward to shove her to her doom. Over the weekend, Madison's office had been equipped with microphones and miniature cameras. Only a matter of time, Wait had said. Too bad time wasn't on their side.

Jon slithered around the corner and into the file room. If Madison saw him, she'd kick him out of the contracting suite.

"Hey, there, Sweet Cheeks."

A thirtyish woman with trendily styled reddish-brown hair and a wide mouth grinned at him as she shoved a file folder into the rack. He hadn't seen her before. She was probably Maeve, the comedienne Madison disliked, though why was a mystery to Jon. Maeve was friendlier than most of the contracting pukes. Maeve had been TDY to Los Angeles last week, so he didn't have to worry about her being the one who'd set up Madison.

"Baby Doll? You look like you're lost."

He shrugged. "How did you know?"

Hard to believe Maeve worked for Sarabeth, Madison's rival contracting officer. Sarabeth Hubbs dressed like something out of a 1960's sitcom, one of the old black and whites that showed in the late afternoons. Not Maeve. She dressed like a college girl. Even with the tiny lines at the corners of her eyes betraying her closeness in age to Sarabeth, Maeve looked a good ten years younger.

"Is there anything I can help you find? Anyone? Me, perhaps?"

He grinned and shook his head. Jon glanced down at the carpet. In some respects, she was more intimidating than Madison.

"Get with it, Sweet Cheeks. You gotta give me a hint if you expect me to help you."

"I came by to see Sarabeth Hubbs," he told her. If Maeve insisted on leading him to Sarabeth's office, he'd pull the phony excuse of interviewing her for Col. Kildee's project and hope she wasn't still mad at him for making her cry.

"Why didn't you say so? You're here to congratulate her. She's over in Mr. Smith's office, but she'll be back in a few. I guess I'll get stuck with planning her going-away party. You will be there, won't you?"

If Sarabeth was going away, he'd definitely be there. If for no other reason, he'd make sure she was gone. "Count on it."

"Good deal, Baby Doll. Say, honey, are you single?" He nodded once. "Fabulous! You're just about the right age for my little sister. She's going to be down here visiting during Christmas holidays. I think you two would be perfect for each other."

"I don't know about that," he started.

"She's got a cute personality. Oh, don't give me that look! She's got a cute face and bod, too. Just like me but younger."

"I'm not sure I'll be in town." Or if he'd be in Madison's life then.

"Then you clear your calendar because once you've met my kid sister, there's no going back to whoever's got you on a leash." She plucked a second file folder from the shelf and turned to leave. She stopped short at the file room door. "Will you look at that!"

"What?" He peered over her shoulder in time to see Madison's clerk, Eileen, give Madison a quick, tearful hug and a stack of phone messages.

Maeve chortled. "Doesn't that beat all? I never thought she'd show her face here again."

"Who?" He knew the answer.

"Madison Steele. I'm sure you've heard of her."

"A little."

"Stay away from her if you know what's good for you. Did you hear what happened last week? She tried to steal some classified files. They caught her red-handed with the papers in her office. I cannot believe they let her come back to work. You know what else I can't believe? I can't believe she has the nerve to show up here."

Knots tightened in Jon's stomach. Maeve hadn't witnessed last week's events, yet she was perfectly willing to pass off the rumors as first-hand knowledge.

"Conference room!" someone yelled. "Now! Col. Ballard's got an announcement to make!"

"Oops," Maeve said. "Gotta go. Join us if you'd like. Anything else I can do for you?"

"Uh, yeah. I need to borrow a phone." He had no business in the conference room, but he needed an excuse to stick around.

"Sure, Baby Doll. You can use the phone in my cubicle." She pointed down the partition-lined corridor to an opening across from the conference room. She waltzed away from him on mind-boggling high heels.

He waited for Madison and at least another ten people, including Sarabeth, to venture into the conference room before he moved. The mood in the office was animated, a loud steady hum of anticipation. According to Madison, Lt. Col. Ballard seldom called a staff meeting because he might be asked a question that concerned them all and he'd have to answer on the spot and look stupid. Instead, Ballard hid in his office, playing with Excel spreadsheets of lead-times, and coming out only when it suited him. Which was why Madison's co-workers speculated so over a called meeting. Did it have something to do with Madison's return?

He tiptoed into Maeve's work area. Plaques filled three of the walls—worse than Madison's—with trophies on the fourth wall. Amazing that the partitions were strong enough to hold it all.

Maeve poked her head inside the cubicle. "Phone's right there, Sweet Cheeks. Call me if you need anything." She winked as if they shared some scandalous secret and was gone.

Without looking, he reached for the phone and pressed one of the buttons for an outside line. If Maeve or anyone else came in, he'd simply dial time-and-temp, frown a lot, and pretend to be embroiled in conversation.

"Yes, sir, she's back in the office," a woman's voice said when he held the phone to his ear. Beatrice? "You should get on the next flight down here and try negotiating in person. You'll see that Ms. Steele is very reasonable if you'll only give her a chance to explain."

Jon cringed. He'd punched the button for a direct line and ended up in the middle of someone else's business conversation. He covered the mouthpiece quickly. Back in Montana, his father had taught him how to listen in on telephone calls, and this was definitely not it.

"Find everything you need, Sweet Cheeks?" Maeve stood in the doorway again. Jon nodded furiously until she went away.

Jon clicked another line and heard a dial tone. The way Madison talked, conversations like that happened all the time. Always a disgruntled contractor or an upset Senator or some kind of crisis. Nothing was ever simple.

Keeping the phone to his ear, he perched on the corner of Maeve's desk. From there, he could see into the conference room. Madison stood near the doorway with her back to Sarabeth, who alternated smiles and scowls when Madison wasn't looking. Beatrice and Raynene rolled up behind Sarabeth. Raynene squeezed by into the conference room, but Beatrice flung her arms around Madison's neck.

"It's so good to have you back. If I'd known you were coming in today, I would have brought in chocolate cake for you. I've got this good recipe that's been in the family for years. I always thought if I had a daughter, I'd pass it down to her. If you like it, I could—"

"Everyone, quiet down." Jon couldn't see Lt. Col. Ballard, but he could hear him banging his fist on the table for attention. "I've got an announcement to make."

Jon held his breath. Maybe Austin Wait had told Gavin Ballard the truth, that Madison didn't have anything to do with the stolen Andromeda disk. Maybe this meeting was the first step in clearing Madison's name.

"Is everyone here?" Ballard asked. "Good. I have some good news today. For a change. As you may know, one of the weapons systems program offices has been looking for a supervisory contract specialist to take on a new project. Someone with a proven record of pulling the team together and getting the job done in a crunch."

Jon's heart leapt. What better way to describe L. Madison Steele?

"You all know that Project Andromeda could not have been awarded without her. We'll be very sad to see her go but happy for her. This new job is a promotion and a great career move for a contracting officer."

A smile crept across Madison's face. She'd waited so long for the rewards for her hard work.

"Everyone, please congratulate the newest GS-13 on Eglin Air Force Base: Sarabeth Hubbs."

Jon gasped. It had to be a joke. His gaze darted to Madison. She didn't flinch, but her jaw tightened almost imperceptibly. Madison kept the smile, though it wasn't quite as natural as it had been a moment before, and was the first to extend a hand of congratulations to Sarabeth. Then, with more grace than he would have thought possible, Madison headed back to her office, the telephone messages clutched in her left fist.

He couldn't hang around Maeve's office forever, pretending to be on the phone. And Sarabeth, the last thing he wanted to do was interview her about her morale level, which was a hell of a lot higher than Madison's at the moment.

The conference room thrummed with congratulations and acknowledgments of how fast and how well Sarabeth had finished the Project Andromeda source selection. It wasn't fair. Then again, what in life really was?

Jon sucked in his stomach and headed out of Maeve's office to console Madison. He hadn't expected the line of people outside her office. And none of them there to offer their heart-felt sympathy.

He stopped at the bookcases outside Madison's office and pulled down a notebook from the shelf. He pretended to read from one of the contracting office's 72,000 regulations. At least there, he could hear what was going in on inside Madison's office and keep an eye on her without her knowing it.

Cathy was first in line, tapping an impatient toe, and reminding Madison her sole source document was nearly a week past due and still needed Madison's signature. Raynene, behind Cathy, waved a suspense from the review committee. Beatrice claimed third place, with a stack of folders in her arms. The next two in the line-up were a captain and a lieutenant, engineers from the airframe division. Jon had a sneaky feeling most of Madison's Mondays started out this way.

"Pssst. Who's in there now?" he asked Cathy.

She rolled her eyes and mouthed, "Maeve."

Jon maneuvered next to Cathy so he could see into Madison's office. No one had bothered to clean up the mess from last week. Madison nodded and seemed to listen to Maeve, but her gaze drifted to the kicked-over stacks of paper and the invaded privacy. To anyone else, Madison would have looked stony solid, but to Jon's trained eye, the condition of her office had left her shaken.

"Fantastic TDY, absolutely fantastic," Maeve was saying. "Gavin's going to talk to Mr. Smith about me studying for my warrant so I can be a contracting officer by Christmas. It's absolutely unbelievable how much power I've got already. Once I get my warrant, I'll be invincible."

Madison smiled unsteadily. "If that's what makes you happy, go for it."

"LaDonna and I were talking on the plane all the way back from L.A. She's really cool. First female deputy director this Lab has had, and she thinks I walk on water." Maeve laughed broadly, showing her fillings. "She wants me to work on this really hot new project once I get my warrant. Two hundred million bucks and the most important weapons program this place has ever seen!"

"That's wonderful for you," Madison agreed. Her words lacked heart.

"Madison? Have you been sick?"

"No."

"Oh. Well, you must not have been getting much sleep lately. Your eyes look really tired."

"They do?"

"Hey, great suit!" Maeve reached forward and tugged on Madison's upper sleeve. "Did you get that at the thrift shop?"

"I don't remember. I've had it a while. Does it matter?"

"Not to me. I thought I recognized it. Fall of '94 collection?"

Enough of this. Enough of Maeve. Any other day and Madison might have thrown Maeve out on her ear, but the adventure in Georgia had left her bruised. If Maeve kept up the subtle barrage, Madison was going to need serious counseling.

Counseling. That was it!

Jon stalked into Jarvis Barton's empty office and dialed Madison's intercom. "Barton's office," he said the second she answered. "Right now."

Less than a minute later, Madison closed Barton's door behind her and slumped against the wall. "How am I ever supposed to get out of my office with that line out there? Sheesh. Tell me again why I love my job so much."

"Madison, I was thinking. My mother has a way of helping people figure things out."

"You mean the psychic stuff?"

"Beyond that."

"Tarot cards?"

"Beyond that, too. She has a way of asking questions so people figure the answers out themselves. "I think we should call her."

Madison bit into her lip, then nodded. "I hadn't thought of that. That's a great idea. We call your mom and let her use her psychic abilities to tell us who stole Project Andromeda and where it is."

"That's not exactly what I had in mind. I told you, I don't believe in psychic mumbo-jumbo."

"Nothing else has worked. Why not try it? We don't have any other clues, and Austin Wait probably hasn't tried that yet."

Jon sighed, pulled out his long-distance calling card, and dialed his mother's home number. It was still early in California, not even 7:00 yet, but his mother answered on the first ring. "Hi, Jonathan," she said. "I've been expecting you."

Argh! He hated it when she did that. "Mom, hold on. I'm going to put you on the speaker phone. There's someone I want you to meet." He pushed the speaker phone button as Madison scurried into the chair opposite him.

"Hi, Mrs. Colter. My name is Madison Steele—"

"The Falconer, yes. Lorelei. The High Priestess of the Remnants of Humanity. I'm honored."

Flustered, Madison shook her head. Vintage Lydia Colter, but not quite what Madison had expected.

"Hi, Mom," Jon chimed in. "I told Madison that this was ridiculous, but maybe there's a snowball's chance you can answer a couple of questions for her."

"I'm at your service, Ms. Steele." As usual, his mother was cool, calm, and collected. She was like Madison in that respect. Very little could rattle her. "I've been thinking often of you. You must never doubt the sacrifices you have made. Or the ones you will make. I know you have doubts. I can feel them. Your past will catch up with you, but don't fear it. Embrace it. Your future depends on your past."

Madison swallowed. Already Jon's mother had thrown her off kilter.

"Mom. We're not calling so you can give Madison a reading."

"No? But she needs guidance."

L. Madison Steele needing guidance? Now there was a first!

"What we'd like know," Madison interjected in her old-self way, taking charge of the conversation, "is if maybe you can point us in a direction we haven't thought about. Jon's filled you in on what's been going on here with the security breach and the death of one of my trainees?"

"What he hasn't told me, I've sensed. You have an enemy. A very ancient enemy. You fought him long ago."

"Him? It's a man?"

"In a previous life, he was a man. In this lifetime, I don't know. The Universe has not chosen to reveal that to me. You were the young Turk.

You treated him like a beloved older brother, and you trusted him until he betrayed you. You fought him and won and will again this time though he has cost you an innocence you will never regain."

"Doesn't sound like Miri at all," Jon whispered.

Madison nodded her agreement. "Who is he? Someone I work with?"

"Someone close to you. And close at hand. This betrayal will offend you greatly because in this lifetime, as in the last, you did not know he was your enemy. Though you should have."

Somehow Jon couldn't see Madison feeling personally betrayed if Miri had done her wrong. They simply weren't that close.

"Come on, Mom. How about a name? Show off a little for my friend, will you?" He bit back the words as soon as he'd said them. Somehow the subject of psychic abilities always gave him a case of the smart-mouths.

"It doesn't work that way, Jonathon. I can only tell what is told to me. I don't know the betrayer in this lifetime. I've only glimpsed what he was in the past."

"If I give you a name, can you tell Madison if that's the person?"

"Perhaps. It's not always so clear. The Universe does not reveal its secrets until the time is right."

"Gavin Ballard," Madison offered. "He's my boss. I'm always trying to fix what he breaks. I think he thinks I'm trying to overthrow his rule."

Lydia Colter laughed. "Gavin Ballard has never been your ruler. He's terrified of your will and envious of your strength and does not know how to handle the task assigned him. That's why he overburdens you. Not because he hates you, but because he knows the work will be done if he delegates—no, abdicates—his responsibility to you."

Madison's jaw dropped. Okay, so she recognized, too, that Lydia Colter had pegged Ol' Gavin.

"Sarabeth Hubbs?" A natural guess for Madison. Sarabeth had a history of taking credit for Madison's work, and with Sarabeth's snatching a long awaited promotion out of Madison's hands, an obvious guess.

"Contrary to what you believe," Jon's mother continued, "Sarabeth does not lie awake at night dreaming up new ways to torment you. You're selfish to think her life revolves around making you unhappy. You may see her as an enemy, but she's not a malicious one, and if she hurts you, it's according to her own ethical code. You know in your heart that she would never jeopardize the security of her country or take the life of another, even if she disapproved of the victim's morals."

Madison nodded again, this time sheepishly.

"Giselle Villemaire," Jon spat out.

"An enemy who will become an ally."

"Whew! You missed one, Mom."

"Owen Plummer," Madison said, and even the name carried a weight of silence.

"Oh...ooh!"

"Mom?" Jon leaned into the speaker phone's mike. "Mom? Are you all right?"

"I had a glimpse of something disturbing. Like fire and brimstone." The phone line crackled and quieted.

Madison broke the silence. "You mean the man who's been following me, right? Or do you mean the real Owen Plummer? The real Dr. Plummer died in some kind of explosion back in the early 60's. That would explain the fire and brimstone."

"They're one and the same. He has so much power at his fingertips. Like an archangel. I sense a...a dichotomy within this Owen Plummer. He's walked the far future, wracked with guilt for what he's done and determined to make amends. He's walked another future, not too distant, in a time of celebration and transformation. A new age of enlightenment. I see him marveling at a great leader."

"Who?"

"The greatest leader of this century, maybe of all time. One who will begin to bring together the people of this country in the year 2000. He'll unite the planet in a golden age of knowledge and peace and spirit in the year 2008 and four years later, the world as we know it will be transformed into a new dimension, a new dawn of time for our race. He'll be the youngest President ever elected and by an overwhelming majority. He'll launch a new millennium. He'll fulfill the prophecies of hope."

"Who will?" Jon interrupted. As usual, his mother wasn't making much sense. "Owen Plummer? Owen Plummer's going to be President?"

"No. Owen Plummer sees it. *Has* seen it."

Madison twirled one long curl around her forefinger until she pulled her hair taut. "Then Owen Plummer's from the future. Hypothetically."

"And the past. And the present. I keep seeing the words *jump gate* and *multiverse theory."*

"Mom!" Jon wailed. "You're talking about time travel. Do you realize how ridiculous this is?"

"I know only what is revealed to me, Jonathan. We can't change our past, but we can choose from many possible futures."

"I've been 'read into' programs related to quantum physics," Madison acknowledged. "Austin said Plummer's file said he was working on a special project. Enoch's Gate. It would make sense. Hypothetically." Madison cut her gaze toward Jon. "The way he just...just vanished at the farm."

Jon stiffened. "Plummer was at the farm? And you didn't say anything?" That was it. The reason she'd pleaded with her parents to leave for a while and take Delilah with them. Owen Plummer had threatened her somehow. And, because she always had to handle everything herself, she hadn't told anyone.

"He came up behind me and I looked away for half a second, and he was gone. He must have come through time to kill me and went back when he realized Austin was nearby. He was just gone. I can't think of any other scientific explanation short of UFO's or divine intervention."

Jon jabbed at the mute button on the phone. "So much for scientific. Madison, do you know what you're saying? If Security hears you talking like that, they'll pull your clearance and you'll end up answering the phone for Base Transportation for the next two years."

She waved him away from the speaker phone and punched off the mute button. "Mrs. Colter, you said we were going to have an age of enlightenment? No doomsday? No bearded stars falling to the earth?"

"Actually, the prophecies of the future tend to go in one of two directions. One is an age of enlightenment and harmony. The other is the end of the world as we know it. The planet shifts on its axis and all is chaos."

Jon grunted. "Sounds like a 50-50 shot either way."

"Mrs. Colter, is there any way you can tell for real if Owen Plummer is some sort of time traveler?"

Jon rolled his eyes at her. She needed more sleep. That was it. "Come on, Madison. Stop fooling around. How can a logical woman like you believe—"

"—That he's come from a dark future to save our present? To give us that future of enlightenment?"

"If he has, it isn't working," Jon said. "Do you see any bright political leaders anywhere? Un-huh. They're all cheaters and embezzlers and out-of-touch old men and, well, standard politician fare. We have no honorable leaders these days. No role models."

"Am I right?" Madison spoke into the microphone. "Owen Plummer is a time traveler from the future?"

"He has an interest in you and your daughter. And not necessarily a benevolent interest."

"Madison doesn't have a daughter, Mom." Jon frowned at Madison. The color had drained from her cheeks.

"You can't change the past. It's scientifically proven. Be careful," Lydia warned. "This man is not what he seems. He's interested in his future, not yours. He'll only use you."

"Yeah, so don't all men?" she murmured.

CHAPTER TWO

Thank God, Cashwell hadn't brought the baby.

The kid was too much like Delilah as a baby, and Madison couldn't stand that right now. She had to be strong, invincible. One look at Bronwyn Cashwell's little face and Madison's resolve would crumble. She absolutely refused to be anything less than stone in front of the piercing stares that followed her down the hall.

Sheridan Cashwell stood awkwardly in the doorway of her office, a white, #10 envelope twisting in his grip. He smiled at her, a little nervous, a little off his turf. In his gray slacks, white button-down, and red tie, he could've been any one of her civilian program managers. Except for the baby spit-up on his shirt pocket.

"Miss Steele?" He took a baby step forward as if entering her disaster area of an office posed a danger to life and limb. Maybe it did. "Could I have five minutes of your time?"

"How did you get in here?" she demanded, watching his expression change with the tone of her voice. He had no business in the contracting suite. None. "No one's allowed in here without a Government escort." Which meant, really, no one who didn't work for the Government was allowed.

"Mr. Terranova walked me in. Did I do something wrong?"

Probably not. Theoretically, he could have overheard a sensitive conversation between contracting officers or spotted a rival contractor's cost data on Madison's desk. Or he could've been a spy interested in Project Andromeda.

"You didn't do anything wrong, but I'll have a talk with Lt. Terranova. Let's get you to a public area before Security finds you in here."

Madison popped up out of her chair, squeezed his elbow, and led him down the corridor. "Sorry 'bout that," she clipped out with a forced smile. "What can I do for you?" She gestured toward a straight chair in the reception area. Beatrice slid between them, excusing herself, and headed for the water fountain. The reception area wasn't exactly private, but it was the best she could do on short notice.

"You're very busy. I can come back at a better time."

"There's never a better time. And I'm always this busy. Usually busier."

Damn. She sounded like such a bitch.

He frowned. "You're so...I don't know. You're so different from the way you were last Saturday. I was hoping we could get together but...."

She knew. She wasn't the sweet substitute mommy who'd loved his daughter as much or more than he did. L. Madison Steele was back in tough-as-nails format with none of the softness or tenderness Sheridan Cashwell had wanted to get to know better. A little guilty for the change in her demeanor but glad she'd squelched Cashwell's interest in her, she let her forced smile waver into a real one.

"Mr. Cashwell." Madison laid a gentle hand on his wrist. Best if she never saw him again. Or his daughter. She didn't need to be reminded of the child she'd held and protected and almost let herself fall in love with. She had a child of her own to worry about, to protect. "While I was baby-sitting your child, no one was doing my work here at the office. As you could probably tell if you were blind in one eye and couldn't see out the other. I've got as ton of work to do, so if we could make this quick, please?"

"Yeah. Okay. I, uh, know the cops in Tallahassee arrested your sister-in-law. She says somebody else gave her the baby to take care of and she didn't know the baby had been kidnapped. She's willing to take a lie detector test."

"My sister-in-law is a pathological liar. She lives in a dream world and talks herself into believing her fantasies are the truth. I have no doubt she'd pass a polygraph without blinking."

"Oh. I guess I was kind of hoping she didn't know and that she was just a mixed-up kid in the wrong place at the wrong time."

"She is a mixed-up kid. And because of what she's done in the past, I'm afraid she's all alone now." Madison fought down a pang of guilt. Given the way Jolene's lies had ruined Toby's medical career and Mama and Daddy's dreams for their remaining child, Madison couldn't summon as much sympathy for the girl as she would have liked. Madison had hoped she was a better person than that, but she wasn't.

"Once again, Miss Steele, thank you for everything you've done for me. For Bronwyn and me. I can appreciate how busy you are here, and I'll try not to involve you any more than necessary in the court proceedings."

"Thank you. I appreciate that." According to Austin, Madison could have been charged as an accomplice to kidnapping, but given that Madison had done her best to rectify Jolene's wrongs and had asked Austin for help, the charge would have been a waste of tax dollars. "If you need me to testify or give a deposition, I'll do whatever's required."

Part of her wanted to see Jolene rot in jail for the hell she'd put everyone else through, but part of her—a little part—wanted to wrap the stupid girl in a warm blanket and extract promises from the prosecutor that Jolene would get the help she needed. Even for people who hurt her, the protector in Madison's soul always emerged.

But who would protect Madison? What would Mama and Daddy think, or Toby, once they found out she was the one who had turned in Jolene? And what would it matter? If it was right, Madison had to do it. No matter the cost.

"Thank you," Sheridan Cashwell whispered. "Do you have children?"

Stunned, Madison stared back at him. An innocent question, yes, but laced with the power to conjure up old demons. "I never married," she said, hoping he was old-fashioned enough to make an old-fashioned assumption.

"Then you can never understand how grateful my family and I are that you returned Bronwyn to us." His eyes swam with meaning, his cheeks red and flushed. "You can't possibly know how much she means to us."

Madison swallowed hard. "Can't possibly...."

"I want you to have this." He tucked the envelope between her fingers. She turned it over in her hands. "It's a check for ten grand. The reward money my parents offered."

She dropped the envelope. Hands shaking, she retrieved it and thrust it back at Cashwell. "I can't accept this."

"Yes, you can. Please. You deserve it."

"No. I won't profit from Jolene's deeds. I didn't turn her in for the reward money. I did it because it was the right thing to do."

"Then take it as payment for your time away from work and for all the formula and diapers you bought."

"It's too much."

"It's not enough." He held up his palms as a shield against the envelope. "Take it. Give it to charity if you want, but isn't there something you could use it for?"

Delilah. Ten-K would make a nice addition to Delilah's college fund. Madison closed her eyes to block out the glimpses that played across her vision: Delilah tossing sparrows into the air, Delilah wearing a wreath of ivy and no shoes, Delilah flinging herself into Madison's outstretched arms. Even now, Madison could remember Delilah's scent, the warmth of her tiny body, the spark of curiosity in her Sandusky-blue eyes. Any advantage Madison could give her was worth the price.

"At least think about it," Cashwell urged.

Ten-K would pay off Mama and Daddy's medical bills. The rigors of age brought with it bills for doctor's visits, drugs, and the occasional hospital stay, only part of which Medicare covered. Ten-K could make life easier for her parents. Ten-K could help make up for having to run after a small child when they could barely get up and down to change the TV channel to the nightly news.

And 10K might pay a bodyguard to watch over the farm until Madison could figure out a way of keeping a time-traveler elsewhere and elsewhen.

"All right. I'll think about it." Maybe hold on to the check for a few days.

"Good. Good. Thank you. I'll find my way out—"

The Gutless Wonder barged between them. "Madison, I need to see you."

"You see me," she tossed back. "I have to escort Mr. Cashwell out of the building. Give me five minutes."

Gavin slanted an annoyed glance at Cashwell, then pivoted to lean into Madison's face. "Let him find his own way out. In your office—now."

"Security says—"

Gavin motioned to Beatrice, who was still slurping water from the fountain. "Bea, walk this guy out." Before Madison could do much more than shrug her good-bye to Cashwell and leave him befuddled in the middle of the hall, Gavin latched onto Madison's upper arm and steered her back to her office.

Madison started to protest. Austin Wait had rigged her office with cameras and microphones and told her to stay away from her desk as much as possible. She'd barely been out of the office at all since lunch. Give her enemies a chance to set her up again, he'd said. Had Gavin forgotten? Had Austin neglected to tell her boss that her office was under surveillance? Not that she had anything to hide, but she didn't particularly relish having one of Gavin's bitch-fests on tape.

Collapsing into her chair, Madison tore open the envelope. Ten-k. Yes. A cashier's check. She balanced the check on her keyboard, then crumpled the envelope and flung it at her trash can while Gavin paced in a tight circle and reached to close her door.

He banged his fist against the wall. "God Almighty! Why don't you have a door?"

"Because you won't stand up to Mr. Smith and—"

"How can you carry on business without a door? And look at this place!" He gestured wildly at the file folders and stacks of paper knee-deep on the floor. It had been a mess before Sarabeth and her other nosy co-workers had torn it apart, but at least it had been an organized mess. "I want this place cleaned up. It's a pig sty. Right now!"

"Before or after I finish looking at Cathy's acquisition plan and answer that congressional inquiry to Mayer-Frick?"

He hadn't heard a word she'd said. Not that it was uncommon for Gavin to rant over nothing, but she'd never seen him quite so red-faced. Or with bloodshot eyes. Dark circles. Good grief! The man was falling apart in front of her.

"We've got a situation."

Oh, God. What now?

"Mayer-Frick and Associates are on their way up," he continued. He twirled in a small circle, hands deep in his pockets. "They want to talk about Andromeda. They were one of the bidders, and they're mad as heck they didn't win. What are we going to do? They'll be here in thirty minutes or less."

Madison shrugged. Not her problem. Not this time. She tracked down the mouse to her computer and clicked on her electronic in-box. Might as well read her e-mail while Gavin prattled on. "So? Send Sarabeth to diffuse them. You gave Project Andromeda to Sarabeth, she awarded it, she got credit for all the work I did on it. Let her handle debriefing the unhappy contractors who got their butts beat by TCI."

And good luck to her, Madison thought with a smirk. Mayer-Frick and Associates was one of those occasional three-man businesses without a technological clue but plenty of ego. Dr. Frick had based his company's proprietary proposal on flooding bio-contaminated areas with gallons and gallons of antibiotics. Totally impractical, but the man held some minor patent related to aerosol dispensers, so he claimed his was the only company in the world that could answer the call of Project Andromeda, particularly if the U.S. paid him a whopping $200 million for his questionably brilliant idea. That was almost $140 million more than Congress had appropriated for the project. Mayer-Frick and Associates was the same firm that had complained to their congressman on one of Cathy's projects—the inquiry that was already a week late. Dr. Frick would not be a happy camper.

"Sarabeth can't do the debriefs."

"Why not?" Too distasteful for her? "If Project Andromeda's hers, then it's hers. Don't give me the shit work to do while she gets all the glory."

Gavin sank into the chair opposite Madison. "Sarabeth can't do the debriefing because she's been promoted."

"Yeah, I heard. How wonderful that she could get my project awarded in record time."

"Now Madison, don't be like that. Mr. Smith pulled her out of here an hour ago. I expected her to stay the obligatory two weeks or at least until the end of the pay period, but they want her now. As of noon, she's working in her new office, and Mr. Smith's not going to let us keep her just to tell a bunch of losers where they screwed up in their proposals. Besides, you know more about Project Andromeda than Sarabeth. You're the best person to handle this."

Madison abandoned her e-mail and shot him her best eat-shit look. "Maybe I was the best person for the promotion, too." Somewhere in the clutter of her office lay the cert from personnel that said she was on the short list of contenders for a GS-13 supervisory contracting specialist position and that she might be hired without an interview. Instead, Sarabeth had been chosen, reportedly because of her ability to award Project Andromeda in the face of an investigation and all hell breaking loose.

"Damn it, Madison! Don't argue with me. I'm your division chief and goddamn it, you'll respect me as such."

Madison blinked and let her silence speak for her. She'd given him respect until the first time he'd thrown her into the lion's den and looked the other way. If Lt. Col. Ballard weren't such a wimp, she'd have somebody to fight her battles for her. Or at least not to disarm her every chance he got.

"Mayer-Frick and Associates will be here in a few minutes, and you will handle it. Got that?"

"Yes, sir. Anything you say, sir." She saluted just to piss him off.

He started out her office and spun around. “And another thing.”

“Yes?” She drummed her fingers against a clean spot on her desk.

“With Sarabeth being snatched out of our office, we’ll be down one contracting officer for at least a couple of months while we interview for a replacement. Possibly Maeve, but I don’t think we can get her a warrant before January. I know you had use-or-lose leave scheduled, but we can’t afford for you to be out of the office. Besides, you don’t have a family. I’m canceling all of your leave through the end of December.”

She stopped drumming. Vacation time she’d planned to spend with Delilah and her parents at Thanksgiving and most of December. Delilah would never understand. Madison had promised her Disneyworld during Christmas holidays. Just the two of them. A sisterly event since it couldn’t be anything else.

“You can’t cancel my leave.” Her throat hurt.

“No choice. You should’ve scheduled leave earlier in the year instead of waiting until the last possible minute.”

“Gavin, I couldn’t. I was busy with the railgun launcher and the smart-bomb and then Andromeda. And you wouldn’t approve leave until they were all done.”

“Go ahead and be selfish.”

“Selfish! Gavin, I’ve got enough leave saved and enough under-the-table comp time due me that I shouldn’t be in the office for the next year, and you’re going to deny me a few extra days at Christmas to spend time with my aging parents and my little—” she bit her tongue—”sister? And you call *me* selfish?”

“At least you’ve got holidays to look forward to.” He hid his face in his palms. Slowly, his shoulders began to shake as he slumped onto the chair. The red in his face deepened. He sucked in a snort-like breath.

Great. She hated it when men cried in front of her.

Gavin raked his palms over his face. His lips peeled back in a blubbering squall. “It’s all my fault. Jesus, God, Madison. It’s all my fault.”

Had she heard him right? Madison leaned across to him and patted his knee as she might a scared little boy. In the year she’d worked for Gavin, she’d never heard him take responsibility for anything that went astray. First time for everything, she supposed. “What’s all your fault?”

“Roxie.” A bubble formed on his lips and burst.

Roxie. Who could forget the way Gavin had stared at her casket? The gaunt pull at his features? The torment in his eyes? The Gutless Wonder didn’t usually show concern for his troops, and he’d never—at least not publicly—shown any positive interest in Madison’s prize trainee or her work. Could Jon be right? Could Roxie really have been in love with the slimeball?

“Oh, Jesus. Oh Jesus, God, Madison. I could’ve saved her. And I didn’t.”

Madison groaned. If ever she needed a door to her office, it was now.

"Shhh." She rubbed his shoulder. Why did people always have to turn to her for strength? She missed Roxie, too. She missed a lot of things.

"Oh, Jesus, God." Gavin fell forward on one knee, clumsily circling Madison's waist with his beefy arms and burying his slobbering face between her breasts.

"Uh, Gavin?" Hell, what could she say? The man was hurting. She of all people knew what it was like to lose a lover. With a sigh, she stiffly embraced The Gutless Wonder and patted his back as she had Sheridan Cashwell's baby. "Shhh. You didn't kill Roxie. It's not your fault."

"It is. Oh Jesus, it is. I was supposed to meet her at The Facility at 9:30." He didn't say why. He didn't have to. Jon was right. "Oh, God, Madison. I sat in my car and waited and waited, and she didn't come out. Her car was there and the lights were on in The Facility, and she didn't come out."

"Shhh." Madison rocked him against her and stroked the wispy remnant of hair on the back of his head. "Why didn't you go in?"

"I couldn't," he blubbered into her chest. "Eugene Foley's an old gossip. You know that. He would've seen my access card on the computer printout for The Facility and would've wondered what I was doing there with Roxie at ten at night. So I sat in my car and waited."

Mac stumbled into the doorway, and Madison gave him a subtle jerk of her head to go away. Mac registered the scene: their boss on his knees between Madison's legs, her skirt awkwardly shoved up to her thighs, and Madison whispering comforting noises to a man whose comments generally elicited a snarl from her. The fact that Gavin was sobbing rather loudly evoked an impression of compassion rather than passion. Mac, good soul that he was, turned his back to them and blocked the doorway, shooing away everyone else.

"The whole time I was sitting there, Roxie was locked in that safe. She w-was alive. Austin Wait s-said her fists w-were bloody from beating on the vault door. If I'd gone inside, if I'd just gone inside, I might have heard her. She'd be alive t-today."

And if someone hadn't glued Madison inside her office, she might have gone straight to The Facility, against orders, and kept Roxie from being shoved into that small walk-in vault with the missing oxygen tank and a pitifully few hours' worth of fresh air. Roxie had died knowing her killer, died in a dark, upright casket of air-tight metal. If Madison had defied orders then, as she so often did, she might have saved Roxie.

"Shhh," she whispered to Gavin. "You couldn't have known."

He snorted through his tears. "I knew something was wrong. I should've called Security. I should've done something."

Why? He'd never "done anything" for as long as Madison had known him. He was washed-out pilot who hated desk work but had nowhere else to spend his time "productively" until he retired. Hence, he'd been sent to whip Contracting into shape. He'd either done a super job of using his slick rhetoric to convince someone he was the man for the job, or someone knew how inept he was at paperwork and had set him up. Poor fool.

"Gavin," Madison said gently, "how long did you wait for Roxie?"

"One in the morning."

Madison let out a hard breath as if she'd been kicked in the stomach.

"Roxie was inside d-dying while I was sitting in my car pissed off at h-having to wait."

That was it. The torment, the guilt. So Gavin Ballard was the secret lover Roxie had been meeting since her divorce and maybe before. Gavin Ballard, who couldn't risk the minuscule chance he had at a promotion to colonel, couldn't risk his marriage to a woman who demanded he have dinner with their three kids every night, even if he said he had to go back to work later. Back to meet Roxie.

So Roxie Daniels had been the reason Gavin peered over Madison's shoulder so often. It wasn't Madison's work he was checking up on; it was her tall, dewy-eyed COPPER CAP. Roxie had known, according to Jon, whoever had used Madison's card to access The Facility and steal a classified proposal but to save Madison, Roxie would have exposed her lover. Her reward? Slowly suffocating to death, screaming Gavin's name and beating her fists to bloody pulps while The Gutless Wonder cracked his knuckles and fretted in his car.

"Gavin? Don't you think you might want to talk to Austin Wait about this?"

"Huh?" He stretched back on his heels and backhanded the snot from his nose. "Why would I want to do that?"

Other than the fact that he'd babbled about his affair in the presence of OSI surveillance equipment? Adultery was still a court-martialable offense and groveling at Madison's feet probably qualified as conduct unbecoming an officer. "Talk to Austin, okay? You might be able to tell him something useful."

"I don't know anything useful. If I did, I would've said something already."

"Maybe you know more than you realize. Talk to Austin. Please?"

"I'll think about it."

"Before he talks to you." She drew out the words in a warning he couldn't miss.

Gavin dragged himself to his feet. "Yeah, okay."

God, he looked awful, all red-faced and bleary-eyed. But he had to live with what he'd done.

Or hadn't done.

"Yeah. You, um...." He cleared his throat as if he'd forgotten the past few minutes on the floor in her arms. "You get out there to the conference room and handle Mayer-Frick. And I don't want to hear any more whining."

"No, sir. No more whining."

She watched him squeeze past Mac, then plucked a Kleenex from her desk drawer and wiped the trail of snot from the lapel of her good red suit and the corner of her access card. She tossed the tissue at the grimy circular excuse for a metal trash can, missed, and then headed for the conference room.

If she hadn't been thinking about Roxie, she would have paid more attention. She should have grabbed Mayer-Frick's file or at least a copy of the evaluation of the technical proposal so she'd be able to tell them what they'd done wrong in their bid for Andromeda, but honestly she didn't know where the file was. Very likely still locked in a file cabinet in The Facility. The proposal wasn't classified. Hadn't been that much to it, which was a sure-fire indicator of how off-base Mayer-Frick's proposal had been. Without a file in hand, she'd be forced to talk off the cuff to the miserable little man who needed all the help she could give him.

Normally she loved working with ultra small businesses. The "Mom and Pop shops" as she called them, the ones terrified of the Federal Government's red tape and willing to offer up their first-born sons out of gratitude if she would lead them through the process of doing business with Uncle Sam. She wouldn't dare admit it to anyone else in the acquisition field, but she got a real kick out of holding their hands.

Mayer-Frick and Associates didn't want hand-holding. They had wanted their hand *out,* and they wanted the Department of Defense to fill it with cold hard cash. They'd learned that expectation from middle-of-the-night, "Get your free Government money" info-mercials and from Congressman buddies who didn't think conflict of interest rules applied to them. Anytime Dr. Frick didn't like the official answer and couldn't get some poor slob in Contracting to bend under gentle pressure, he took his fight to his Congressman's office staff, who promptly—and usually without reading or understanding the allegations—filed an inquiry into the Contracting Officer's decision and tied up Government personnel for weeks at a time, doing nothing but answering the mail with an extremely enhanced and well-reviewed version of the answer Dr. Frick had already been given. In the past year, Madison alone had successfully fended off six Congressional inquiries from Dr. Frick's stooges in Washington.

Madison stalked toward the conference room, down the corridor lined with odd-colored partitions. She kept her head down as she walked, noting the toes of her red shoes preceding her, clashing with the orange carpet. She had about five seconds to pull together in her head what she was going to tell Dr. Frick. Too bad she couldn't remember enough about their proposal to give them a decent debriefing on the spot. Besides, she'd want to refer to charts and pull actual paragraphs out of the source selection documentation to give him a useful explanation. One that would stand up in court if it came down to it. She really hated being misquoted.

The hardest part would be finding something good to say about their proposal, other than the dubious asset of readable type and wide margins. No, not even that. Even the page format had been eye-straining. Utterly nothing redeemable about their submission. Somehow she had to find something to say that they could use to improve their next proposal although, if Dr. Frick held to true form, he wouldn't believe he could do anything to improve. And people who refused to improve were destined to fail.

She poked her head inside the door of the conference room. Dr. Frick, who looked like a nerdy John Wayne, stood alone on the other side of the room, not even a briefcase in his hand. With a heavy sigh, she closed the door behind her and walked inside.

"Dr. Frick," she said with the softness of a physician announcing the death of a loved one, "I'm L. Madison Steele. What can I do for you?"

"I know all about you."

Her heart caught in her throat. "Excuse me?"

"I got an anonymous call this morning and got on the next plane down here. I knew you were in bed with TCI. That phone call this morning verified what I knew all along: doing business with you was a waste of my money."

"What?"

"You heard me. I spent fifty grand of my own money writing a proposal you never gave a chance." A muscle twitched under his left eye. "Dr. Frickenfrack," Roxie had called him.

Roxie. Her shy trainee with the skewed sense of humor. Roxie, who'd been by her side for months. Roxie, who'd screamed for help until all the oxygen in the vault had thinned to nothing. Madison hadn't been there to save her. Why did Gavin have to unload his guilt on Madison? She'd never get that awful picture of Roxie out of her head.

"I assure you, Dr. Frick, TCI won the Project Andromeda contract on the basis of a fair and impartial evaluation. It had nothing to do with personal preference for their company or a dislike of yours. We were looking for the best technical approach for the money we had." Madison steadied her breath and crossed the room to meet the man. She looked down at his hand in time to see it form a fist.

And then, from the dusty, orange carpet, she stared up at the stained ceiling tiles.

***

"Madison? Answer me. Are you all right?"

Jon's voice lured her back through the haze. She was still on the floor, propped on her elbows. Her jaw ached with a vengeance.

"Wh-what happened?"

"I don't know. I was going to ask you that." Jon knelt beside her. He had that persistent worried look on his face, like he'd been frowning for so long he'd forgotten how to do anything else. "I was coming by to check on you, and the conference room door was open and you were on the floor. Did you faint?"

She almost laughed. "I don't faint." She nursed her jaw in one hand. "Ah, that's right. Dr. Frick." She jerked her head up. "Son of a bitch punched me!"

"What! Where is he now?" Already Jon was clenching his fists and heading for the door.

"Don't," she called after him. "It won't do any good. He's a disgruntled contractor. He doesn't trust anybody in the Government, but he's more than willing to claim what he thinks is his share of the Defense budget."

"He cannot waltz in here and attack you. I'm calling Security. How'd he get in here anyway?"

"He's got an access card. Otto gave him one so he could come in and talk to Col. Kildee anytime he wants."

"We'll tell Security to revoke his access. At least until you can file charges."

"I'm not filing charges." She shrugged. "No use in doing that. He's offended because his proposal didn't win the Project Andromeda contract and it only costs him the price of a stamp to protest and if he does, I'll be buried in paperwork twenty-four hours a day, seven days a week for the next two weeks." Maybe if he filed a protest, then she'd file charges, but why give him incentive to make her life hell?

"You should at least go to the Base hospital and get your jaw looked at. It's as red as a beet. Doesn't this qualify as an on-the-job injury?"

She grinned. It hurt her jaw. "Leave it alone, will you? I've got too much work to do."

"You're backing down? He must have hit you harder than I thought. I've never known you to back away from a fight."

"Yeah, well, I like to save my bullets." He helped her to her feet, whether she wanted him to or not. She brushed the carpet fuzz off her good red suit.

"I wish I'd been here earlier," Jon said. "I would have stopped that sleaze ball."

"Oh, stop pouting. I don't want you looking over my shoulder every minute of the day." Bad enough he spent his days and nights studying her with unabashed longing. She was perfectly capable of taking care of herself. She didn't need Jon, didn't need Austin Wait, didn't need a guardian angel.

"Sorry. You weren't in your office, and I got worried. I thought Beatrice was going to call Security on me for not being escorted in."

"Beatrice wouldn't do that. She knows you're a friend of mine."

"I don't know. She was spastic when I walked in on her in your office."

"Beatrice was in my office?"

"Yeah. Sitting at your desk."

The only times Beatrice ever sat in Madison's chair, something awful had happened. Usually it meant Beatrice was fretting about her retirement and being left in the technological dust by the advances of the Computer Age. Beatrice had always thought of a state-of-the-art computer system as a gigantic paperweight.

"Where is she now? I'd better check on her." Maybe she was upset about Roxie. "Was she crying?"

"When I walked in, she tore out of your office. And no, she wasn't crying. I don't think she likes me. The only thing she ever calls me is 'lieutenant,' and I know she knows my name."

"Don't take it personally. She calls every officer by his rank. I think she's seen so many lieutenants and captains and colonels come and go in the past few decades that she can't remember anybody's name. She doesn't mean anything by it. Now go find somebody else to hover over. I've had my daily quota."

Good grief. This hovering of Jon's was sure to ruin her reputation for toughness and risk his career. The rumor mill may have chosen murder and intrigue for its latest Steele grinding, but no doubt it still recalled the hot night when she had sprawled across her desk for Tim's pleasure. Jon did not need to be seen in her office too many times in one day.

Without looking back, she walked away from him, back down the orange carpeted corridor and into her doorless office. She stopped short, surprised to find Eileen and Cathy standing at her desk, looking hurt and confused.

Tentatively, Cathy met her gaze. Eileen stared at the floor. Both held their breath with the same reverence they'd given Roxie at her funeral.

Cathy wet her lips. Her hand trembled. In her quivering grip, Cathy held the cashier's check for ten thousand dollars.

CHAPTER THREE

Tuesday, 5 October 1999, Eglin Air Force Base, Florida

Something strange was happening. Jon couldn't remember ever seeing people line up on the crosswalk outside Building 13. Mostly they were military in blue uniforms, a few in camouflage battle dress uniforms known as BDU's, but from his position at the traffic light, he couldn't tell who they were.

Maybe a fire drill, he guessed as he waited for the light to turn green. But where was big yellow fire truck and the men in tinfoil-like clothes? Maybe a bomb threat, but the building would have been cleared out and people standing on the far side of the parking lot rather than on the crosswalk next to the front doors.

The light turned green. He followed Madison's car into the parking lot and circled the lot twice on his motorcycle while she parked and headed for the crosswalk. He needed to give her enough time to enter the building alone. If he followed too closely, someone would notice. And everyone would talk. Madison had asked that he give her a head start and he'd agreed. Given that she'd let him spend another night on her sofa, for "protection," he'd do whatever she wanted, no questions asked. He supposed Plummer's unexpected presence at the farm had been enough to spook her into needing company, so some good had come of it.

He parked his bike and climbed off, pausing to pry off his helmet and chain it to the bike. Another dozen people had gathered on the crosswalk, many civilian. Madison climbed the stairs in her dark navy suit. Even if he hadn't recognized her clothes, he would have known the sway of her walk. He was a veteran watcher.

To his surprise, the crowd parted for her. Jon tugged at the collar of his BDU's. It was only a few minutes after seven in the morning but the air seemed too hot and stale. Something was very wrong. He set off in a dead run for the crosswalk.

Jon elbowed his way through the crowd. They'd opened their ranks for Madison to pass through and closed behind her.

Miri and Figmo made room for him. "Hey, Colt," Figmo said. "Just in time to see Miss Perfect get her comeuppance." His eyes danced with pettiness.

Jon shoved past Beatrice and Sarabeth, sidestepped Otto, and almost fell into the clearing around Madison. She stood a few yards away from the glass doors, but people thickened in front of the doors and she couldn't get through. They all seemed to be watching as if they were making a dodge ball circle and Madison was the only one left to aim for. Eileen and Cathy waited closest to the door, both of them looking devastated. Eileen raised a handkerchief to her swollen eyes. She looked as if she'd cried all night. Eugene Krueger stood beside them, mopping his forehead and shaking his head with disapproval. Old Mac leaned on the railing for strength. He looked as if he'd lost his last friend.

Madison stopped and slowly turned around. She twisted a ringlet in her hair. "What's going on here?"

Jon gave a little shrug and started to step into the circle with her. He could break through the crowd. He could escort her into the building. Figmo jerked him backward.

"I wouldn't," Figmo whispered. "Not if you want to make captain."

The glass doors behind Cathy and Eileen opened, and three men walked through. Jon didn't recognize the first man, but the access card clipped to his crisp white shirt indicated he was from Security. The second man was Mr. Smith, the head of the entire contracting organization. The last of the trio was full-bird Colonel Zed Kildee, the director of The Lab. Whereas Smith was tall, lean and fiftyish with a full head of white hair, Kildee was average height, early forties, with a little more blond hair than Gavin Ballard's red, and glasses that rested on the rim of his nose. Kildee was almost too heavy for his blue uniform. Rumor had it, the only thing that would keep Kildee from making general was a diet that rivaled a teenager's. He was universally well-liked by the engineers in The Lab because he often met up with many of them at the O-Club after work to share a joke, a slap on the back, and a slice of pizza.

Kildee frowned at the crowd on the crosswalk. "Where is she?" he asked in an aside to Smith. He didn't wait for the head of contracting to answer. "Which one of you is Madison Steele?" He glared at the civilians closest to him. They seemed to back up.

Madison took a single step forward. "I'm Madison Steele."

Kildee looked her up and down and then turned back to Smith. "Who is this person?"

"I'm one of your contracting officers," Madison began. "Don't you remember me, sir? You gave me an award last month for my work on the smart-bomb program."

Kildee shook his head with undisguised disgust. Madison rubbed at the blue spot on her jaw. She was out there all alone, but Jon knew better than to interrupt a colonel.

"I want her out of here," Kildee growled at Smith. "In five minutes, if possible."

"Wh-what's going on?" Madison asked for the second time.

"I might ask you the same," Kildee lashed back. "Over 450 days without a security breach, and you ruin it. And now this."

"Sir, I didn't ruin your record, and I don't know what you're talking about."

The weasel from Security stepped forward and plucked the one-day-old access card from Madison's jacket. "Col. Kildee has ordered us to set up a special security file on you."

"No," Jon breathed. Austin Wait could have kept this from happening. All he had to do was step forward and say Madison had been cleared of the breach and this would all go away.

"Why?" Madison wailed. "I don't understand." She reeled on Mr. Smith, the only one there in her chain of command. "Why?"

Smith kept his poker face. "It appears you've been taking kick-backs for the information on Project Andromeda."

"Why would you think that?"

"Two eyewitness accounts of a suspicious check made out to you for ten thousand dollars. A week after Project Andromeda was stolen."

Sheridan Cashwell's check. She'd told Jon all about it last night over spaghetti. Reluctantly, Madison had deposited to her account on her way home.

Jon glanced at Eileen and Cathy. Cathy looked away. Eileen sniffled and wiped her eyes. Madison often said they were as honest as employees came.

Madison anchored her hands on her hips. "That check has absolutely nothing to do with Project Andromeda. There's a perfectly logical explanation for it." She glanced over her shoulder at the dozens of pairs of eyes. "An explanation that happens to be nobody's business. If we could step inside for a minute, sir, I'm sure I can make it clear to you what's really happened."

"That won't be necessary," the Security weasel said. "We've pulled your clearance and we'll have you under surveillance for the next forty-five days while we review your files."

"But I have to be in the office for the next few days."

"Oh? Something else you want to tell us?"

"No," she sputtered. "I've got work to do. I've got to be in the office."

"Not any more you don't."

"Sir?" She ignored the Security weasel and turned back to the colonel. "If you'd let me explain—in private—"

"Isn't it great?" Figmo whispered in Jon's ear. "The secretary in Security spilled the beans."

Jon wrenched free of Figmo. He was a worse gossip than Maeve. No wonder everyone had turned out to see the show. They all knew before Madison did that public humiliation would meet her at the front door this morning.

Col. Kildee didn't seem to notice their audience. "Mr. Smith has decided to reassign you," he said. "At least temporarily while we review your security file. You'll report to the contract admin office over in the main procurement building."

"Admin?" she asked incredulously.

"I'm sure you can handle it until we make permanent plans. You won't have to learn any new skills. It's only a matter of pulling file folders and putting them back all day long."

Pulling files? Of course they wouldn't send her home on administrative leave. If she were guilty, that would be like giving her a free vacation. So instead, they'd assign her to some benign place where she could still be useful to the taxpayer and still earn her GS-12 salary. The contract admin office was considered a dungeon, even by the low standards of fellow procurement personnel.

"I am a contracting officer," she reiterated through tight jaws. "I have special skills that are very hard for my organization to come by. And you're going to send me over to pull files all day? A trained monkey could do that."

"A trained monkey or a contracting officer without a security clearance."

He was right. Without her clearance, she couldn't sign contracts on behalf of Uncle Sam, couldn't review files for her buyers, and couldn't sit in on meetings. Come to think of it, a trained monkey had more latitude than she did.

Madison's face reddened with fury. "Tell you what, Mr. Smith. I've got plenty of comp time. Why don't I take the next forty-five days as comp time, and I'll spend some long overdue time with my family."

Hanging around the farm to keep Plummer away, no doubt.

"I don't know anything about any comp time," Smith said.

"Gavin has a record of my comp time." She cast a tentative glance around the crosswalk. Everyone seemed to be present except Gavin Ballard.

"Like I said, I don't know anything about any comp time."

"Fine. I have plenty of sick leave, and right now, I'm feeling sick to my stomach." She whirled on the ball of one foot and pushed through the crowd.

Damn them. Damn them all for doubting her.

"She's not on top any more," Figmo said with a laugh.

Jon shoved him aside and followed Madison. People closed in around him, their chatter deafening as they exchanged their eyewitness accounts from different angles on the crosswalk. Jon reached the steps and scanned the parking lot for Madison. Beatrice hurried down the steps ahead of him. Madison was already at her car door.

"Madison! Wait up!" He shoved past Beatrice and ran as fast as he could.

***

Madison sat on the hood of her car and stared out at the blue bayou. At this early hour, Camp Robbins was deserted, with nary a camper, picnicker, or swimmer in sight. Nothing but calm breezes and still water to counter the morning's disaster.

"Look, Madison," Jon said, leaning on the hood and gazing up at her, "we'll get you cleared. Things will get better."

"How can they? I would rather be fired than relegated to a position where I can't do anybody any good. Not that there's anything wrong per se with filing paper for a living, but it's not what I've trained to do. I should be out there negotiating. Handling business, not stuck in administrative hell."

"It's only for a little while. Once Security's had a chance to talk with Sheridan Cashwell, they'll understand where the money came from."

"But I don't want anybody to understand where the money came from. I don't want the publicity that comes with it." Madison shifted on the hood, drawing her legs up under her.

"You got your clearance yanked for unexplained affluence. So explain it."

"I don't want anyone to know what that money was for. If people know about it, it'll be like I profited from someone else's ill fortune. Anyway, it's nobody's business."

"Look, you've got the power in your hands to clear this up. All you have to do is go to Security, explain it to them, you get your clearance back, you get your job back. You fight for everybody else. Why don't you fight for yourself? Otherwise, you could be filing papers for up to two years."

She sighed. "All right. I'd rather be at work than at home."

"On the other hand, you might want to wait a few weeks before you do that. That way you can use up some of that use-or-lose leave and take a well-earned vacation. And—"he grinned—"someone else can handle the Project Andromeda debriefs."

A smile tugged at her lips. The first in a long time. "Don't tempt me."

"Joke's on them. See? You don't have to fight all the time." Lord knew, she even fought herself.

"I don't know any other way to live but to fight uphill battles. Your mother must be right: I was warrior in a past life. Seems I'm always fighting and—"she paused as if she had to admit something to herself. "I think maybe I'm not happy unless I'm fighting. I have to be in the middle of the fray. It's not enough for me to be in hot water. It has to be boiling."

"The world needs revolutionaries." *So does the Universe* echoed in the back of his mind.

"I was raised to believe that once I found religion, I'd found contentment. But I haven't. I wonder if I ever will. Jon, if I find contentment, I'll be bored, miserable. I need the passion of the fight, even of the struggle, to stay happy." She laughed. "Am I strange?"

"Yeah, but it's a good kind of strange. Maybe we can both take off for a couple of weeks and spend a little time playing as hard as we work. The beach is beautiful this time of year. Emerald water, white sand."

Her eyes took on that dreamy, faraway look. "I live ten miles from the beach, and I haven't sunk my toes in the water in over a year. Maybe it's time."

He'd meant it as an invitation to spend a holiday with him, not alone. Carefully, he tried again. "Let's take a break from this whole Project Andromeda mess. Biological warfare was around long before you were born and it'll be around long after you're gone. Let the OSI handle it for a change. Besides, it won't kill you if you're away from the job for a couple of weeks. Your life's full enough."

She paused, lost in the lure of something faraway. "I used to think that my life was too full until I lost a few of the things that made my life so full. Maybe it was God's way, or the Universe's way, of making room for other things. All I know is that the emptiness hurt to the core so I filled up the holes as fast as I could, mostly with work. Not with friends. Not with family. Not with anything that really matters, except work. And work's always mattered because nobody knows my projects like I do. I'm the only corporate memory left on those projects. Do you have any idea how much time it would take to bring someone else up to speed on my programs? Nobody can work those programs as well as I can. But sometimes I wonder if I've filled up my life with the wrong things. I've read every book ever published on time management, and I've done my best to make every moment of my life productive. And for what? I'm all by myself. It's all a blur from one negotiation to the next. One fraud investigation to the next. Regulations piled on top of regulations. And all I can think of is, what was Delilah like when she was little? I can't remember ever holding her in my arms, but I did. I know I did. Until I held Sheridan Cashwell's baby in my arms, I'd forgotten what Delilah looked like as a baby." Her voice cracked. "Or what it felt like to hold her in my arms. All this time I've been on the fast track, and I've been careening past my own life."

She sounded as if she might cry loud, heaving, heart-wrenching sobs, but Jon knew better. Tears were something never to be shed by L. Madison Steele—only by the human twin who slept in her bed.

"You're not alone now."

"I'm more alone now than I've ever been in my life."

"I think you like being alone," he grated out. He was tired of her blindness. He stopped hiding the harshness in his voice. "I have been by your side for months now. I've been there for you. It's not that you fail to realize that. You fail to recognize it. You like wallowing in your abandonment. Because it makes you colder and it makes you stronger, you think. It makes it easier to be hard."

"You don't understand."

"Try me."

"You don't understand what it's like to give up everything you love out of duty. I have to be the pillar of strength because if I crumble, then everything else does."

"There's that goddamned god complex of yours again! You cannot save the world if you cannot take care of yourself. You're so busy protecting everybody and everything around you that you've forgotten to nurture you."

Several minutes passed in silence. What if he made her angry and she shut him out, too? Jon wanted to regret the way he'd spoken to her, but he couldn't. Someone had to force her to wake up.

"Will you...will you help me remember how?"

He softened. "In a heartbeat. Let yourself lose control."

"There was a time, years ago, when I let go. I'm still paying for it."

That guy. The lieutenant. Tim. "Sometimes you have to take a risk." *Take a risk with me,* he willed her.

"I know all about risk. The first time I ever did anything risky, I nearly ruined my career. I was a buyer over in one of the missile systems program offices. I saw some things going on that I shouldn't have. They weren't exactly illegal, but sometimes you have to ask yourself not whether it's legal but whether it's right or wrong. Well, this was wrong. I tried to do something about it, but I couldn't get my contracting officer to take a stand. So, when she went out on sick leave, I stepped up and took over and I took care of the job and I knew the risks. There were generals and Congressmen and staffers who all wanted the same thing, but it was wrong. Nobody else would stop it but me. And they crucified me for it. I knew they would. But they kicked me where it hurt the worst—in my heart. And then when Beatrice came back to work...."

"Hold it. What's Beatrice got to do with this?"

"She was my contracting officer."

"Whoa. Whoa, whoa, whoa, whoa. You're her contracting officer. She works for you."

"Right. Now she does. But back then, I was a trainee working for her."

"That explains it then."

"Explains what?"

Jon perched on the hood beside Madison. "Why she's always badmouthing you."

"Beatrice? Why would you think that?"

"Because I've heard her with my own ears, that's why."

"Beatrice gripes about a lot of things, but I'm not one of them. She's told me more than once how glad she is to be ending her long career under me."

He'd heard almost the same words from Mac. Mac could have retired years ago, but when he spoke of Madison, Jon could see in his eyes the truth behind his decision to stay with the job. The old teddy bear was in love with her. But when Beatrice spoke of her contracting officer, the older woman often complained that she'd been working for the Government when Madison had been little more than a twinkle in her father's eye. To be so astute in professional negotiations, Madison was a poor judge of character in her personal dealings.

"Madison? Trust me when I say this: Beatrice does not talk to you to your face the way she talks behind your back. She resents the hell out of your youth, and if you stepped on her turf and took over her job while she was out sick, I think she resents a lot more than a three-decade difference in your ages."

"You have an enemy. A very ancient enemy. You fought him long ago."

"Beatrice?" Madison looked stunned, stung.

"Why not Beatrice?"

"She's been a loyal Federal employee for thirty years."

"Loyal to what? She plays bridge with Otto's secretary. I've heard her whining outside my office. The only things that motivate her are building her dream house and going on as many TDY trips as humanly possible."

"Beatrice does like her business trips," Madison conceded. "After being in Civil Service as long as she has, she has tons of annual and sick leave so she usually tries to combine business with vacation." Madison frowned. "Of course, that translates to her being out of the office an awful lot. The rest of the time she's off and not flitting all over Europe or Washington, she's checking up on the contractors building her dream house. They've been working on that monstrosity for at least two or three years."

"Why doesn't she go ahead and retire?"

"She can't. Her house contractor suggested too many times how easy it would be to add a wall here and there and have another room in the house. Sounded like a good idea at the time. With all the changes to the blueprints, the Harpers have underestimated building costs by at least a third. Beatrice was really hoping she'd get the $25 thousand bonus for retiring early, but Mr. Smith said we're so undermanned, he can't justify paying her to leave and then have us down by one more man."

"She was counting on the retirement bonus?"

"Yeah. She's got huge house bills."

Jon's pulse quickened. "Okay. I think we've established motive. The financial need and the personal satisfaction of pinning an espionage charge on you."

"Lots of people in my office would take great personal satisfaction in pinning something on me. And lots of people in my office have a financial problem. That doesn't mean Beatrice has a vendetta against me."

"She knew you and Roxie played tennis twice a week."

"So did other people. We've been through that already. Beatrice never came over to the gym." The expression on her face soured. "Except...."

"She did, didn't she?"

Madison scrunched up her face when she didn't want to admit something. "Okay, yes. She did. Once."

"Once was enough. When?"

"A month ago maybe. She had an emergency on one of her contracts. She followed me off the courts, into the locker room to get my signature."

"Must have been pretty important." He had a feeling about this. A "feeling."

"Not especially. One of Beatrice's contractors needed confirmation on some direction I'd already given them. Beatrice could have pulled it from the computer, but she's of that old school. She doesn't see the need in learning computers when she's about to retire."

"Looked like she'd learned them pretty well when she was in your office yesterday."

"You didn't tell me she was trying to use my computer."

"Not trying. Using. She'd started to send an e-mail message. When I came in, she logged off real quick."

"Maybe she was experimenting while I was with Dr. Frick."

"Who?"

"Dr. Frick. The guy who punched me."

"Because you awarded Project Andromeda to TCI instead of them." Someone had been on the phone when he'd stalled in Maeve's office. Right after Madison showed up and before Lt. Col. Ballard announced Sarabeth's promotion. "I think Beatrice is the one who called Dr. Frick."

Madison's cheeks grew redder by the second. "She's got some questions to answer." Hurt and fury rang in her voice. "Come on. We're going back to my office."

"We can't go back to your office. You've been barred from the building."

"We'll use your card to get in."

"Besides, Beatrice isn't there. She left right behind you. And that wasn't a look of concern on her face."

"Come on. Let's go." Madison jumped down from the hood and opened the car door before Jon could scramble after her.

"Go where?"

"To Beatrice's dream house."

CHAPTER FOUR

She'd heard enough to howl. She'd known Beatrice longer than she'd known almost anyone else at Eglin. And Beatrice knew more about her than anyone else. Including Jon. Including Tim Sandusky.

Beatrice had come back from emergency medical leave only days after Madison had been caught red-faced with Tim. Without her lieutenant, she'd had no one else to turn to, and Beatrice had been there with open arms and open ears. Beatrice hadn't seemed mad at all that

Madison had tried to make changes in her absence, even when Beatrice later had her contracting officer's warrant revoked. If Beatrice resented Madison's private fight for justice, it never showed, but surely Beatrice had had a good laugh at Madison's ill-fated rendezvous with Lt. Tim Sandusky and their surprised guests.

"Oh, God."

"You okay?" Jon asked from beside her.

She looked up from the steering wheel. "Fine. I'm always fine."

Not only did Beatrice know the truth about Tim, but she had an honest inkling about the baby. In a moment of weakness, Madison had sobbed into Beatrice's shoulder and admitted her fear that there was minuscule possibility that she might be suffering from morning sickness and Tim had been gone less than six weeks.

Madison's hands shook. She couldn't fathom the betrayal. Being the gossip she was, if word about the baby had not gotten out to everyone at Eglin, then Beatrice must have saved the secret for herself. Beatrice could easily, for amusement or revenge, have arranged Jolene's child-napping to thrust a second newborn into Madison's life and decimate Madison's soul. Only Beatrice would know how much that would hurt.

"I don't suppose I should take it so personally," Madison grated out. "I'm not the only one she betrayed. She betrayed her country. And for what?"

"For that." Jon pointed across the street at Beatrice's dream house, mostly finished but lacking shrubbery in the front yard and trim-out touches. A Tudor monstrosity. It looked as if construction company had left it as it was. Almost as if they'd run out of money and walked off the job. A house of that size and in this neighborhood, Beatrice must certainly have sunk all her retirement savings into the pricey lot and floor plan. She'd mentioned once to Madison that she wanted a house big enough for her son to move his family into if he ever married. During her trainee days, Madison had suffered through one blind date with Charlie Harper, who was one month older than Madison. She couldn't stomach his negativity and she'd had to phrase the rejection delicately to keep from hurting Beatrice's feelings. Rejecting Beatrice's son was probably strike three.

Madison lapsed into a bitter silence. Jon stared straight ahead at the three-story house and started humming "Young Turks." Wearily, Madison reached for the cell phone Austin had insisted she carry.

Austin's extension rang four times before his voice mail kicked in. Madison hung up and redialed the primary number for OSI headquarters.

"I'm sorry. Agent Wait is not available right now," the receptionist told her.

"He's got to be available. He carries that damned walkie-talkie everywhere he goes. Is he in a meeting? Is he there?"

"Yes, ma'am. He is in a meeting, and he is not available."

"Then interrupt him. This is L. Madison Steele. I need to talk to him right now. It's about Project Andromeda."

"Please hold."

Madison motioned for Jon to lean in close to hear the other side of the conversation. This time, she wanted Jon to be a partner in asking for help. She inhaled his scent and held her breath. His cologne reminded her of rolling in tall grass.

"Ms. Steele." Austin's voice rang across the line. Good to know he wasn't "available" but he was available for her. "We were just talking about you."

"We?"

"Yes. Lt. Col. Gavin Ballard and I. He called me at o-dark thirty this morning and wanted to talk. Seems your division chief had a rather sleepless night. One of many. Had a few things to get off his chest. Just as well, too, considering that scene he made in your office yesterday. You were right: I would have talked to him if he hadn't come to me."

"Never mind all that," she said. "I know who did it. I know who stole Project Andromeda and killed Roxie."

"Beatrice Harper."

"You got her on film at Madison's computer?" Jon asked.

"No, wonder boy. You scared her away before she did anything."

Madison groaned. Then how did you know?"

"Ballard told us. Roxanne Daniels was waiting outside The Facility to meet Ballard the night of the breach. She saw Harper go inside after you left and told Ballard."

Shit. He knew. All this time, he'd known. Weasel. Gutless weasel.

"I don't believe this. That weasel sat in my office the night of Roxie's death and talked about the break-in and how I was a prime suspect and the whole time, he knew Beatrice had had unauthorized access to The Facility." And he'd been too gutless to risk the rumors. And for his lack of spine, he'd lost the one woman who adored him. "Did he give Beatrice the combination to the cipher-lock and safe, too?"

"Indirectly. One of Roxanne's last discussions with Ballard was why he'd sent Beatrice Harper to get the combinations from Roxanne. He hadn't. Harper was counting on the lack of communication and Ballard's need to keep his relationship with Roxanne quiet."

Jon grabbed the cell phone and pulled it and Madison closer to his ear. "So you're going to clear Madison's name now, right?"

"In time. We have to verify Harper's the one, and I need to keep you in place for that."

"But Col. Kildee pulled a security file on Madison this morning and relieved her of her contracting duties. Didn't you know?"

Austin swore. "I do wish they'd coordinate things like that with me. Madison, you're critical to this investigation. I need you in the office." He sighed. "But that's secondary. I'm on my way to the contracting office to interview Harper and if all goes well, I may have to mirandize her."

"She's not there," Jon interjected.

"Oh? Where is she?"

Beatrice traipsed out of the house and to her car. She didn't look up or she might have recognized Madison's clunker. "About fifty feet in front of us."

Austin hesitated. Silence crackled over the phone. "And where are you?"

"In an ally across the street from her house."

He cursed again. "Okay, both of you go back to Madison's house and wait. I'm sure you'll find some way to entertain yourselves. I'll send somebody to Harper's right now."

"Won't do you any good," Jon said. "She's leaving. She's getting in her car now, and she's got a paper bag full of groceries with her."

"Why is she carrying groceries *out* of her house?" Madison wondered aloud. Beatrice walked spritely for a change. Nothing like the woman who complained daily of her many medical problems.

Austin agreed. "This is it. Harper's been waiting all this time to get you out of the way to make the drop. She's headed to meet Villemaire and Plummer. Or whoever the hell he is."

"Don't worry. We're on her." Madison cranked the car and veered into the road after Beatrice.

"No!" Austin shouted back over the phone. "You're not on her! You get back to your house and wait. This is dangerous. You've done your part—it's my job now."

"I can catch her. I know I can. We don't have time to wait on you to get here."

"Madison, don't."

"I'm on her. I'm on her!"

"No, you're not. Go home. *Go home.* Colter, make sure she goes home. I don't want her in the line of fire."

"I'm on her." She punched off the cell phone, squared her jaw, and stamped the accelerator.

***

Fifteen minutes later, Madison veered right at the entrance to the resort community of Bluewater Bay. She'd managed to keep at least two vehicles between her and Beatrice's car up until traffic had thinned unexpectedly.

Plenty of military and civil servants from Eglin lived in Bluewater. Otto, as she recalled, had bragged about his half million dollar mansion in a gated subdivision with its own security patrol. She wouldn't have been the least bit surprised to learn Beatrice was headed for Otto's house to make her drop, but with a guard gate blocking the entrance, how would they ever get inside?

Madison followed Beatrice's car around the curve of the lake and up to a four-way stop. Instead of closing in on Beatrice's bumper, she gestured for an errant golf cart driver to cross in front of her on his way to the marsh course. She didn't want to get too close. Lord knew, Madison didn't need any temptation to run the traitor down and back over her body a couple of times.

"Do you think she's trying to lose us?" Jon asked.

"I don't think she knows we're here. As far as she's concerned, I'm still being humiliated in front of everyone I know." Her voice cracked.

Up ahead, Beatrice's car made a left turn. Madison paused a few seconds at the stop sign to give Beatrice plenty of time not to detect her. While they waited, Madison's old clunker stalled out. She swore at it, cranked it again, and lurched to a start.

"Want me to call for back-up?" Jon reached for the cell phone.

Madison slapped his hand. "You're my back-up. Why did you think I let you come along?" She'd never admit it, but she couldn't imagine doing this alone.

Beatrice's car disappeared into the brick and cement parking lot near a batch of upscale condos reputed to boast 18-carat gold faucets and crystal chandeliers in the bathrooms.

"Austin Wait will want to know where we are," he reminded her as they bumped into the parking lot.

"Why? So he can take credit? Forget it." Austin might do something stupid. Like fail. If Plummer got away, he might skip over in time to the family farm and destroy what little was left of her family.

"I like Wait a whole lot less than you do, but I think we should call him. You don't know where Beatrice is going. If this is the drop, she could be meeting that Giselle woman or Owen Plummer or God knows who else. We don't know what we're rushing into."

Ah, Jon. Why did he have to pick now to be cautious? Where had all the brashness of his youth gone?

"You know what they say about fools rushing in where angels fear to tread."

"What if they're armed?" He reached for the phone again, and again Madison slapped back his hand.

"You don't know what you're walking into," he pleaded. "At least the OSI has guns. What do you have?"

"My bare hands if that's what it takes. And a thirst for justice. And Willpower. I have Willpower."

If she knew she could wrap her fingers around Beatrice's neck and squeeze the betrayal out of her and get away with it, she would. She'd trusted Beatrice for almost ten years. The older woman had been a substitute mother to her in lieu of her own. Madison had listened for hours to Beatrice's family woes and on occasion, Madison had opened up and told a few of her own problems with Daddy and his lack of faith in her. Unfortunately, the secrets had gone deeper.

Beatrice had lied about everything. She'd even called Dr. Frick and cooked up some lie that had brought the annoying little man barreling into the office and distracting her while Beatrice set her up yet again.

Now she wondered if Jolene had told the truth. Maybe Beatrice was the mysterious woman who'd called and begged Jolene to come for a visit. What if Beatrice was the one who'd set up Jolene with Cashwell baby? Madison had been inclined to trust the woman she'd worked with for years and take as lies every word that Toby's stupid, foul-mouthed, juvenile-delinquent of a wife spewed out of her mouth.

Madison had fallen into her own trap. She'd taken appearances as truth. Madison was no better than the rest of her gullible co-workers.

"Jon, you stay here. I'm going in."

He stretched in his seat to see Beatrice hurry out of her car and head for the next to last condo, clopping along in her brown loafers with her grocery bag in one arm and her brown cowhide purse dangling from the other. "I'm going with you."

She laid the keys on the edge of the seat for him. "No, you're not. I'm not going to be responsible for your death, too."

"It's Roxie, isn't it? You're not responsible for what happened to her. Beatrice is. That woman there—" He pointed. "She's the one at fault. Not you."

"But I should have stopped her. You said once that I'm a poor judge of character when it comes to personal issues. I think maybe you're right. If I'd only seen what was right in front of my face all these years instead of blindly trusting the one person I never should have trusted, this whole mess with Project Andromeda never would have happened. My reputation would still be in tact, Beatrice wouldn't have the Andromeda disk, and Roxie wouldn't be dead. Everything that's happened, I could have prevented it."

"You and your god complex. Next you'll choose to lose your own life to save the people who wanted to crucify you a few hours ago."

She unbuckled her seat belt and leaned across the firmness of his knee to unlatch the glove compartment. She retrieved a small, pearl-handled revolver. "I have no intention of losing my life."

"You have a gun?" Jon asked incredulously.

"Mama said God would send His angel to watch over me. Daddy's a bit more practical."

"You have a license for that thing?

"No, but Daddy does. Hey, don't look so shocked."

"Do you know how to use that thing?"

"What do you think?" She tucked the revolver into the waistband of her skirt. "Around seven years ago, I lived with my parents for a year while I was on Long-Term Full-Time leave to get my master's degree. I had to drive forty-five minutes every night to Dothan, Alabama, for classes and forty-five minutes back. Daddy didn't want me on the road alone so he insisted I carry some protection in case I ran into trouble. Daddy wasn't very happy with me back then. Said I didn't have any willpower. So that's what he called this. 'Willpower.'"

She unlocked the car door and climbed out.

CHAPTER FIVE

Jon stared after her. She was gone.

In a matter of seconds, she'd marched off to take charge and make the world safe again. With a bizarre clarity, he knew that it would take even less time for her to die. He could feel her in a distant past flinging herself between a sharpened, stone axe and his heart. With a cold shudder, he shook off the sensation.

One thing was for sure: The Falconer wasn't going to fight this battle without him.

He started to reach for the cell phone to call Austin Wait. No time. The split second it took to call for backup might mean life or death for Madison.

Leaving his military hat on top of the keys on the seat, Jon tumbled out the car door and ran after her. He reached the oak and brass door to Villa #19 as Madison reached for the handle. He seized her wrist. She gasped in surprise. Did she really think he wouldn't follow her?

He leveled his sternest gaze at her and hoped to God she respected him enough to listen for a change. "You can't go marching in there."

"I wasn't marching anywhere."

"Oh? You were going to knock on the door? I'm sure they'd invite us in."

"Well, no. Bust the door down?"

If he knew for certain she wouldn't beat the hell out of him, he'd throw her over his shoulder, carry her back to the car, and call Wait.

Please, God, he prayed, *let the OSI already have Giselle Villemaire's condo staked out.* For once, he'd be thrilled to find Austin Wait hiding in the shrubbery.

"Don't look at me like that. I wasn't going to break down the door." Though from the tenseness of her fist, she'd been serious.

"No? Then what? Crawl through a window?"

Devilment caught the corner of her mouth and yanked upward. "Perfect," he thought he heard her say. Whatever else she might have said was lost to the tinkling of wind chimes in the breezeway between Villa #19 and Villa #20 as she bolted around the corner.

"Wait!" he whispered as loud as he dared. "Madison!"

By the time he rounded the corner, she was already pacing back toward him. The windows on the side of the pricey condo were six feet off the ground and too narrow for even a toddler to squeeze through. Probably a death sentence for anyone trapped inside in a fire. He'd read about these "villas." The lesser reasons for their extravagant price included the designer features, the internationally acclaimed golf course a pebble's throw away, and the sugar-white, private beach within a ten minute walk. The main reason for the fancy price tag was the combination of imported European stones and architecture designed to withstand a Category Five hurricane long after the golf course, beach, and most of Florida had been blasted away. A house that could keep out 170 m.p.h. winds could surely keep out L. Madison Steele. Well, maybe.

"Come on," she urged. "There's got to be another way inside."

He shook his head and followed her through the breezeway toward the rear of the condo. Why hadn't she simply called the OSI and let them handle this? He had a "bad feeling," as his mom used to say, and if he'd inherited her knack for fortune-telling, he'd slit his own throat.

Madison stopped short at the corner and peered around a huge, white-blossomed oleander. Jon spooned against her, his hand on her waist to hold her back. Her body vibrated with anticipation as if she were prepared for the battle of her life. Almost automatically, her hand brushed against the revolver to verify its presence. Jon followed her gaze upward to the second floor of the condo and the sound of women's voices too soft to be understood.

The morning sun glinted against a magnificent stained glass window of what, on the less impressive sunny side, appeared to be mountains and waterfalls. Beside the window, French doors opened wide onto a half circle balcony overlooking a lush rose garden and the biggest bougainvillea Jon had ever seen.

Seduced, Madison nodded toward the balcony. "That's our way in."

"Yeah, right." He gestured at the bougainvillea with its purplish-pink blooms and thorns like razor wire. The occupants of the condo could leave their balcony door open any time they wanted. The plant was a better security system than any siren. "We'll be cut to pieces."

"Then don't drop me."

Jon swallowed a few choice swear words. When Madison got an idea in her head, little or nothing could stop her.

"Maybe we should have knocked on the front door after all."

"Be quiet and help me up." She skinnied the dark blue skirt up her thighs. Thankfully, this skirt was a little fuller than what she usually wore.

Avoiding the lower branches of bougainvillea, he knelt on one knee and cupped his hand for her foot, but instead she swung one leg over his back and prodded him to his feet. So much for being a gentleman.

Madison gripped the lower rungs of the balcony railing and pulled herself up without snagging her ankles on the thorns. She accidentally nudged Jon's ear with the heel of her shoes as she pushed off him. She straddled the balcony and tumbled over onto her tiptoes.

She froze for a second, listening to see if she'd been caught, then turned back to Jon. "Stay there in case I need you," she whispered down to him.

"Like hell." He wasn't sending her in alone while he milled around the garden in his BDU's and smelled the roses. He didn't need her protection.

Stepping carefully around the thorns and blooms, he chose the footsteps most likely to succeed and swiped at the balcony rungs. He hung on almost too long before catching his breath and hoisting himself up. He landed with a soft thud that probably deserved the glare Madison shot him. He crouched behind her, feeling foolishness and adrenaline pumping through his veins.

Madison raised her hand for quiet and leaned into the open doorway, straining to hear the feminine voices inside. With a quick gesture for him to stay put, she tiptoed into the empty bedroom. Jon followed.

The architect had probably considered the bedroom suite the epitome of the luxurious condo. No wonder the resort's marketeers had dubbed them "villas." The elevated master bedroom overlooked a marble foyer and white sunken tub. The entire condo had been decorated in shades of white—white carpet, white walls, white furniture, white curtains. The furniture equaled anything he'd ever seen in a European museum, but the most splendid item and the only color in the deceptively small condo was the stained glass window that claimed most of the rear wall. The morning sun gleamed in every twist of glass, illuminating majestic mountains and verdant valleys, gardens of ivy and holly, and a shimmering pair of unicorns at play. Okay, so spies had taste.

He bumped into Madison from behind and silently cursed himself for paying more attention to the beauty of his surroundings than the danger of them. Madison grabbed the sleeve of his camouflage uniform and hauled him closer to the smudgeless wall that rose chest-high and sported a row of large, plastic ferns perfect for peeking between. On the other side of a smooth white sculpture of a jackal-headed woman, Beatrice lounged on a damask sofa, reveling in her own importance. Opposite her, in an elegant chair, a slender woman with the features of a super model drew hard on a cigarette and then exhaled in a steady, controlled stream. Dressed in black, she stood out against the background of stark white.

Giselle Villemaire. One of the top information brokers on the planet. And possibly one of the Sleeping Dogs.

"Enough of formalities," Giselle said in a heavy French accent. "I have an aeroplane to catch."

Beatrice looked dumbfounded. "I thought you said we could be friends."

"We could be, but we are not. I prefer that we keep our relationship to business."

"Then you're not interested in meeting my son? You'd make such a cute couple."

"You have only one thing I want. I have waited long enough."

"I couldn't bring it to you any sooner. I would have blown my cover. The people at work think I'm a stupid old woman."

"You do not have a cover." Giselle aimed a steady stream of smoke between Beatrice's eyes. Beatrice coughed and leaned backward. A smile twitched at Giselle's lips. "I have no more time for chit-chat. Now give me the disk."

Jon held his breath. If only he'd taken the time to call the OSI, Austin Wait could have been busting down the door about now. Beatrice would have been caught red-handed along with the notorious Giselle Villemaire. Too bad Owen Plummer wasn't there to get caught in the web, too.

Beatrice bent over the side of the sofa and retrieved the bag of groceries. "I did what you said," Beatrice rambled as she extracted a double-roll package of toilet tissue from the sack and set it down on the coffee table between them. "I made it look like I was delivering groceries to you, so I wouldn't arouse suspicion." She plucked out a loaf of bread, a six-pack of Diet Pepsi, and a small carton of Fruit Loops.

Giselle picked up the box of cereal from the table and frowned at it. "What? No gourmet treats?" Her voice dripped with acid. She opened the top of the box and fished inside the space between the wax paper bag of Fruit Loops and the outer cardboard box and withdrew a shiny compact disk. Squashing out her cigarette, she stood and then walked away.

"Where are you going?" Beatrice demanded. "Where's my hundred thousand dollars?"

"All in good time. You expect me to pay for merchandise I have not seen?" Giselle lingered in front of a narrow white cabinet, opened the doors to expose a large-screen monitor and a towering CPU, and then pressed the disk into the computer's CD drive.

Madison flinched and reached for her revolver. On the other side of the jackal-headed woman, Giselle Villemaire held in her hands classified information Madison had vowed to protect.

"Unfortunately, I have an aeroplane to catch and not enough time to peruse your information at my leisure." She typed in a quick command for a directory check and a long list of text and graphic files spilled across the computer screen. Giselle nodded and ripped the disk out of its drive. "All there. Our business is concluded. For now."

"My money?"

"Ah, yes. Your money." She opened a well-disguised broom closet and dragged out a small aluminum bucket and a rag mop. She tilted the bucket enough to let Beatrice see the packages of money deep inside, then jammed the mop down on top of it with a malicious fervor. "You would not want to arouse suspicions, eh?"

Beatrice didn't catch the insult. She rose and picked up the bucket and mop. "Good idea."

"Maybe we can do business again in the future."

"Oh, I doubt that. With this little windfall, I'll be retiring soon." Beatrice held out her hand to seal the deal. "Thank you anyway."

Giselle scowled at the outstretched hand but shook it. "Then you will not much longer be of any use to me."

"You think I could make more money at this? I don't have to retire yet, you know."

"I advise you to stay on for another year or two. Perhaps you should volunteer for projects dealing with high power microwaves or electromagnetic pulsing. I could make it worth your while. I will be in contact." Giselle yanked a can of Diet Pepsi from the table and popped it open. She took a long sip of the warm drink before setting it down too hard on the coffee table. "Please," she said, "show yourself the door."

Giselle lit a second cigarette from a small, bejeweled lighter, drew hard on the long, white cylinder, and exhaled another slow, controlled stream of smoke. She was taller than Madison by maybe three inches and thinner. The ebony unitard stretched uncomfortably close to all visible curves, the invisible ones hidden by thigh-high black boots, a wide black belt, a black leather jacket, and a mane of black hair that would have made a Cosmo cover girl jealous. Jon sighed. She had the kind of body that would have elicited a response from any twenty-three year old male, whether he liked it or not.

As soon as she angled the cigarette precariously on edge of a white ceramic ash tray, Giselle tucked the disk into a small black purse, slipped its long strap over her shoulder, and took another sip of Diet Pepsi. Onyx rings on nearly every finger, she wiped the dampness from her open lips with her middle finger and let her small hand slide down her neck and through the valley between her breasts.

Any guy would get a hard-on watching that, Jon told himself. Any guy.

Then Giselle's hand slipped down to her waist, to the wide belt, to the 9mm Beretta snug against her hip bone.

"I love the cologne your friend's wearing. You can come out now, L. Madison Steele."

CHAPTER SIX

Think fast, Madison told herself.

Beside her, Jon slowly raised his hands and stepped out from behind the plastic ferns. Madison followed suit, raising hers to half-mast. Any more and she might have revealed the pearl-handled revolver tucked into the waistband of her skirt. She was glad now that she hadn't divulged her little "willpower" earlier. As long as she and Jon weren't much of a threat, they stood a chance of getting out of the condo alive. One wrong move and Giselle Villemaire would splinter Jon's skull. She'd take the blow herself before she let that happen.

Madison cleared her throat. "Why didn't you kill her?" she grated out in her toughest negotiation voice. She hoped her skirt was long enough to hide her shaking knees.

Giselle frowned and lowered the gun half a notch.

Good. Madison had caught her off-guard.

"Kill whom?"

"That idiot who ran out the front door. Who do you think?"

Deeper frown lines creased Giselle's perfect face. Then a peal of laughter burst from her throat. "You break into my home and suggest I kill a guest who was invited into my home?"

An enemy who would become an ally, Jon's mother had said. Madison desperately hoped that the Universe hadn't withheld any secrets from Lydia Colter. Madison should have asked Lydia her percentage of correct psychic revelations.

"Beatrice Harper's of no use to you," Madison pointed out, laying out her argument with the precision of any missile negotiation. "You heard what she said. She's retiring. For all intents and purposes, she's already RIP—retired in place. They're not going to assign her any of the special projects that would be useful to you, even if she volunteered. Me? I can have any project I want. High power microwaves, EMPs, exo-atmospheric manipulation, biological warheads. If you looked into my record at all, you know I'm telling you the truth."

This was like a job interview. She had to sell herself, except this time it was to stay alive.

"I know who you are, Lorelei Madison Steele," Giselle said with a thick accent. "And I have reviewed your dossier."

Madison swallowed hard. She had a dossier? An FBI file to be sure, but what exactly did international spies really know about her past? Anything about Tim? Delilah?

"You were my preferred choice for information," Giselle continued. "Somehow I did not think you would be interested."

"I'm not good enough for you or something?"

Giselle laughed and motioned to the white sofa and matching love seat. "Please. Seat yourself."

Cautious but curious. Good, Madison thought.

"So," Madison said, settling herself down onto the sofa beside Jon and tugging her jacket neatly into place over the pearl-handled revolver, "why didn't you pick me? My feelings are hurt."

"As I said, I did not think you would be interested."

"In making a little extra cash on the side? It should be obvious the Government doesn't pay me enough for my skills. I'm very good at what I do."

Giselle nodded with a certain kinship. Madison almost liked the woman. Maybe even respected her. As with any negotiation, it was important to establish a common bond. Very little could be won in a hostile discussion.

"I, too, excel at my work. I am an information broker. A legal occupation, yes? I interview persons. Scientists, engineers, Congressional staffers, White House aides. *Contracting officers*." Giselle raised an eyebrow for emphasis. "I am also a very thorough researcher. I was searching for a source who would be a little more enthusiastic."

"I can give you enthusiastic. For the right consultant's fee, I think a relationship between us might be mutually beneficial.

Giselle tapped her perfect chin with the barrel of the gun. "You do not seem the consultant type."

"And what type do you think I am?" Madison tried to sound offended.

Giselle leveled her gaze at Madison but didn't blink. The woman was good. "I think you are the martyr type."

Jon grunted. For a second, Madison thought he would laugh. Then he shook his head, and Giselle grinned, thinking she was right on target with her assessment. Jon nabbed one of the Diet Pepsi's from the coffee table and idly traced the rim of the can as if he'd forgotten the woman was armed and dangerous.

Typical engineer, Madison admitted with a dull throb in her head. Always agreeing with their opponent when they should be quiet.

Before Madison could protest the assinine "martyr" comment, Giselle casually aimed her gun again at Madison. "I also think Monsieur Wait sent you here. I think you come here to entrap me out of some odd sense of duty. I think you are wired under that quaint ensemble. This place, it is equipped with electronic interference to prevent monitoring of my calls. Too bad for you." She stood, keeping the gun angled at Madison's chest. "I think you try to catch me even if you know I am to blow your head off your shoulders." She smiled. "And I will."

A single drop of sweat trickled down between Madison's breasts, well hidden behind the jacket lapels. Leaning against the overstuffed sofa arm, she tried to look bored. She was pretty sure she'd been in tougher situations but right now she couldn't remember any. "I'm not wired. And if you were a better researcher, you'd know I have no love for the OSI, particularly after what they put me through last week. Frankly, I'm kinda pissed off at the way I've been treated."

Giselle tossed her head back. Her hair settled on her shoulders like a dark cloud. "That old fool was to bring me the disk. That is all. Setting you up was not part of our deal. She was—how do you say?—freelancing."

"Say it any way you want. She led me right to you."

"What? What are you saying?"

"No one else could find you. Beatrice was useful for that if little else. What can I tell you? I'm tired of working so hard. I don't want to bang my head against the wall for the Department of Defense for another twenty-five or thirty years so I can go home and eat Beanie Weenies on my pension. I'd like to retire early. Very early. Find some little mountain cabin to wile away my time in bed with my lieutenant while I'm still young enough to enjoy him."

Jon shot her a shocked glance. Later, she'd apologize and remind that she'd say anything to keep the two of them alive as long as they had a gun pointed at them.

Giselle gave Jon a quick once-over and curt nod of approval. Jealousy twitched in Madison's gut, but the urge to survive was stronger.

Madison cleared her throat to wrench Giselle's attention away from Jon. "Amazing. As ignorant as Beatrice Harper is, she's stumbled onto a good thing with you. I know a hell of a lot more than she does. I want my piece of the pie."

She forced herself not to stare at the gun barrel inches from her chin. Like any good negotiator, she aimed her own unwavering gaze into her opponent's. Even if Giselle squeezed the trigger, Madison wouldn't flinch. She prayed that Jon was as strong, though if she looked to see, she'd lose this precarious game.

"You are very convincing," Giselle conceded, "but I prefer to work with weaklings. There is a plethora of civil servants, soldiers, Senators who are happy to talk with me for a fee or a kiss on the mouth. I can learn all I need to learn about United States top secret technology from them. I am sorry, L. Madison Steele, but you are not worth the risk."

"Not even," Madison said quickly, grasping, "not even for information on time travel?"

Giselle's jaw dropped. She held the gun steady. "You have information on Enoch's Gate?"

A tiny red dot formed in the middle of her forehead. The dot grew larger, a circle of bright red light. Madison felt the presence before she saw it. Madison jerked her head forward to see who had slithered into the room, but Jon turned on the sofa beside her, blocking her view. He dropped the soda can onto the table with a thud and raised his palms. Drat. He was protecting her again.

Giselle pulled the gun up hard in front of her, aiming at the front door, at whoever stood there posing more of a threat than a contracting officer and her young lieutenant.

Madison calculated the distance from where her hand rested on her knee to the pearl-handled revolver in her waistband. Could she get it out in time to fire off a round of shots while Giselle was distracted?

The black-haired beauty swung the gun around at Madison again, squelching that idea. "One more step," she warned her newest rival, "and I will kill her. Both of them."

A tall shadow extended toward the door. Jon's protective posture blocked Madison's view. Austin Wait. She hoped to God it was Austin Wait and not Owen Plummer.

He stepped into view. Definitely not Austin Wait. Tall, lean, and white-blond. Fortyish. She might have expected Owen Plummer, but this man was far colder. The kind of soul-less eyes she would remember if she'd ever seen them before. Like an Aryan god who had destroyed his people. Beatrice must have let him in.

Giselle swung the gun back at the man. Madison was glad she hadn't plucked her own piddly little pea-shooter from her waistband. Between the gun in Giselle's fist and the massive firepower in the man's grip, she was definitely outgunned. He wore a white Polo shirt, casual blue slacks, running shoes, and a lightweight windbreaker. He looked like any other upscale Florida tourist in early autumn after the college kids had gone home, but instead of a camera around his neck, he carried a mean-looking gun.

Giselle clenched her jaw and skewed it to the left. She twisted it to the right. Maybe she wasn't such a good negotiator when the guns were on her and her powerbase was fast dissipating.

"I am not surprised," Giselle spat out. "You would kill your own."

Kill your own? Did Giselle mean Madison and Jon? The gunman wasn't an OSI agent she'd ever seen before, and Austin Wait had insisted he didn't work with a partner. Ah, well. If she and Jon were meant to die here, she might as well stir up a little trouble.

"Oh, he's not with us," Madison said with a hint cheeriness.

Giselle held the gun steady on the man and turned only her eyes toward Madison. "You lie. He is Government. As I say, I am an excellent researcher."

"The disk." The blond opened one palm. He didn't wear any rings on his overly large hand. Nothing to identify him. Not even a hint of an accent in his voice.

Madison held her breath. If the man wasn't with Giselle, and he wasn't with the OSI, then who? FBI? CIA? If he was with the U.S. Government, they were safe. A U.S. agent wouldn't kill them. They'd be taken somewhere later for a debriefing of this incident and threatened within an inch of their lives if they ever breathed a word of something this classified, but they'd survive. Any second now, agents would probably burst through the door, overtake Giselle, confiscate the Project Andromeda disk in her shoulder purse, and life would be back to the ho-hum of pushing paper and arguing with power-hungry Congressmen.

She let out a long, slow breath. They'd be okay, they'd be okay, they'd be okay.

"The disk," the man said again. "I paid for it. I want it now."

The small leather purse swung from the thin strap over Giselle's shoulder. Out of the corner of her eye, Madison glimpsed movement. Slowly, carefully, Jon lowered his palms, picked up the can of Diet Pepsi, and nervously let it twist from side to side in his hand. So much for being outgunned. It looked as if Jon planned to bean Giselle in the forehead with a can of Diet Pepsi.

"The disk, I said! You double-crossing bitch. Where is it?"

The telephone shrilled from a columnar pedestal between Giselle and her elegant bedroom. "If I do not answer that," she said with a smug smile, "my contact will be waiting outside to pick you off as you leave."

With the barrel of his gun, the man gestured toward the telephone. "Then answer it. Fuck up and you're dead." He jerked his head in the direction of Madison and Jon. "So are your friends here."

Friends? Okay, that was taking the charade a bit too far.

Giselle inched sideways and picked up the portable phone on the fifth ring. "Allo?" she said to her contact on the phone. Probably Owen Plummer. He was the only member of the wedding missing. Giselle frowned. She pressed the receiver to her ear with one hand and sported the gun in her other hand. Then she held the phone away from her jaw and frowned into the ear piece. She thrust it outward at the blond. "For you."

The man actually took a step backward. He didn't take the phone from her. "For me!"

The phone call had them both off kilter. Madison had a bad feeling the man was no more their friend than he was Giselle's.

Giselle thrust the phone at him again. Probably a trick. "You are Colter, non?"

Madison sucked in her breath. Beside her, Jon startled. "I'm Colter," he said, struggling to his feet. He'd been sitting with his left arm shading the embroidered name on his uniform. Hands shaking, he shuffled the Diet Pepsi can from hand to hand. Madison fought the urge to take his larger hands in hers and steady them. "But nobody knows I'm here," he added.

Argh! Madison could have kicked him. As long as Giselle and the blond thought Madison and Jon might have some back-up waiting outside, maybe they stood a chance.

"Oh, yes they do, darling," Madison lied through her teeth. Okay, so she was setting herself up to be taken hostage, but the longer she could keep her and Jon alive, the better their chances of escaping and getting Project Andromeda back. "I called Austin Wait on my cell phone when we hit the parking lot."

Giselle uttered a curse in French, the gunman in English. Both waved their guns at each other.

Slowly, Giselle shifted the phone to her ear, her eyes growing wider, wider, as she listened. She took a step backward toward the incline to her bed. Then she glared into the phone. "No one knows about that!" she screeched. "Is this some kind of trick?" She looked from Madison to Jon, then at the gunman. "Nobody knows about that! No—" She stopped, listened again. She frowned at Madison. "I-I understand."

"Enough of this! Hand over the disk or I'll take it off your body. What's left of it."

Giselle Villemaire was as white as everything else in the condo. Something had the girl spooked and that something was worse than the probability of having her blood stain her thick, ivory carpet.

With her thumb, she punched a button on the handset and laid it back in its cradle. The gun still aimed and shaking even worse in one hand, she slid her shoulder bag down her other arm until she clutched it in her other hand.

"Lorelei!" she shrieked. "Catch!"

In a wild gesture, she flung the leather purse at Madison, the gun at the blond. The man ducked instinctively.

Madison was on her feet. She caught the purse, clutched it to her chest.

Giselle dove over her bed. She struck the stained-glass window with a crackle. Sunlight burst through. She fell through the wall of glass, shards of color jangling to the floor. The gun landed closer to the blond than to Jon. The gunman recovered his balance in time to fire at Giselle, but she had already hurled herself through the window. With the barrage of shattered glass raining down on the bedroom, he couldn't have gotten a good shot at her anyway.

Then he swung the gun toward Madison.

She was going to die. She was going to die in a room devoid of color. A room with plastic ferns. She was going to feel the burn of metal tearing through muscle and bone.

She was going to leave this world with Delilah in capable hands, Tim in the hands of another woman, and the rest of the world in the grip of terrorists who would wield biological weapons as if sprinkling sugar over cookies.

If she couldn't save herself, if she couldn't save the world, maybe she could save Jon.

Before she could shove him out of the way, her lieutenant sprang forward. He popped the top of the soda can with his thumb. Carbonated cola spewed from the can and caught the blond hard in the face. Instinctively, the man dropped the gun and clawed at his eyes.

"Let's go!" Jon yelped.

CHAPTER SEVEN

"Let's go!"

Jon grabbed Madison's wrist and tugged. She stumbled along after him. Her eyes wild with the fierceness of a mother grizzly, she clutched Giselle's purse and the disk inside tight against her chest. Jon pulled harder. He'd get her out of there if he had to die trying.

The man wiped furiously at his eyes and patted the soda-stained carpet for his gun. They had to hurry.

"Faster!" Jon pulled harder, and Madison in her skinny skirt and low heels tried to catch up with his long legs. When they reached the white marble foyer, they both skidded.

Without looking over his shoulder, he yanked open the front door and lurched across the welcome mat. He nearly tripped over a pair of loafered feet. He froze. Madison bumped into him from behind. A sinking feeling kicking at his gut, he followed the line from ankles to veiny calf to knee to—

Ugh. Beatrice. He recognized the clothes, though he couldn't be certain the rest of the heap was the woman who had minutes earlier sold out her country for a couple of extra bedrooms and a sky-light. The spongy stuff above the neck didn't look human, though the nearby bucket spilling packets of paper money soaked in crimson didn't leave any doubt that Beatrice had merrily waltzed out of Giselle's villa and come face to face with one of the occupational hazards of spying. Either Beatrice had known him and let him in or her killer had been waiting for the door to open so he could silently gain access. He'd retired her quietly and dumped her between the Russian tea olive and the oleander. In any case, she wasn't of any use to them any longer, and she'd probably had a split second to realize that before she departed Earth for hell.

Jon grunted. What a fitting end for someone who would frame Madison for treason and lock poor Roxie in a narrow vault to suffocate slowly.

Behind him, Madison gasped. He could have kicked himself. Even though the woman had betrayed her, Madison would somehow find a way to take responsibility for it. She didn't need to see Beatrice's fate up close and personal so she could berate herself later. If nothing else, the woman did look too much like Madison's mother, and that alone would have been disturbing.

"Hurry," Jon urged. He slipped his arm around Madison's waist and helped her across the blood-slick steps. They left red footprints on the cobblestone path. He caught a glimpse of Madison's pale cheeks as they ran for her car.

"What about Giselle?" she asked between breaths.

"Long gone, probably." He grabbed the handle to the car door and thanked his lucky stars he hadn't locked it. Maybe the gunman hadn't noticed their car or the keys on the seat under his hat.

Somewhere behind them, on the other side of the copse of scraggly trees and shrubs, a door slammed.

"I'll drive," Madison announced, scrambling to his side.

"Not this time." His dad had made sure Jon learned evasive driving that last summer at the paramilitary training camp. He opened the door and shoved Madison hard into the passenger seat. If he gave her an inch to argue, he'd lose. They both would. By now, the gunman had certainly wiped the sticky, sugary soda from his eyes and started after them with a vengeance stronger than Beatrice had seen. Jon jammed the key into the ignition, cranked it on the third try, and then squealed out of the parking lot.

Madison buckled her seatbelt and leaned back against the headrest with a sigh. "We got it back," she whispered, patting the shoulder purse. "We got Andromeda back."

That was it. Not we-made-it! or thanks-for-saving-my-butt-Jon-I-love-you-let-me-show-you-how-much. Her relief lay not in her safety but in her responsibility to rescue the project and save the world.

He nodded and picked up the cell phone, careful not to lose control of the car while he felt his way through the phone number without looking at the keypad. Traffic was heavier now, a product of Eglin Air Force Base employees heading into the surrounding small towns for lunch in the middle of the work day.

"Special Agent Wait," Jon told the receptionist who answered the phone. "Tell him it's Lt. Jonathan Colter."

"Colter!" Wait blasted a few seconds later. "Where the hell have you been?"

"Oh, we're fine. Thanks for asking."

"Don't be a smart-ass. Is Madison Steele with you?"

"Yeah. So's the disk. That's what you're really interested in, aren't you?" A man with an agenda of his own: get the bad guys even if you have to kill the good guys to do it.

"Did you see anything of Plummer or Villemaire?"

"Plummer was a no-show. Villemaire took a dive out the window. Harper's dead. You'll want to send somebody out to Giselle's temporary headquarters. Villa number nineteen at Bluewater." Jon glanced in the rearview mirror. "And we're being followed."

Madison twisted in her seat, then fell back against the headrest in weariness.

"Where are you?" Wait demanded.

"Just leaving Bluewater Bay. He's in a green Explorer. Maybe six cars back."

Wait muffled the phone and barked orders. When he returned to the phone, he said, "Done. Can you identify the man following you?"

"If you mean give you a name, I can't. If you want a description, sure. Taller than me. I'd say six-three or more. White-blond hair. Light eyes."

"You sure he's not Owen Plummer?"

"Positive. Plummer's younger. Giselle had sold the disk to this guy. A double-crosser, he called her." Jon eyed the rear view mirror, then the road. "Giselle insisted he was one of us. With the Government, I mean."

Wait didn't answer.

"You there?"

Wait cleared his throat. "I'll check it out. Where is he now?"

"About five cars behind us. We're headed over the Rocky Bayou bridge. We'll be hitting a four-lane in less than a mile. It'll be easy for him to catch up to us."

"Then make it hard for him. I'm sending help, but you've got to get to the Base."

"Great," Jon muttered. "That's maybe ten miles."

"Get through the guard gate," Wait instructed. "I'll notify them you're coming. He won't be able to get through. Go to my office and wait for me."

Jon ended the call and laid the flip-phone on the seat between Madison and him. He tried to reassure her with a smile. "No sweat." Then he glanced in the mirror. The gunman had passed a car on the narrow, two-lane bridge. Only four cars behind.

Madison stared straight ahead. Her hands shook.

"Don't be scared. I can out-drive anything." Jon patted her quickly on the knee. If they made it through this, he'd screw up his courage and tell her how he felt. After he'd hugged her for a long time and memorized how her skin felt under his touch.

"I'm not scared. I'm boiling mad."

"That's healthy. You should be mad. Beatrice sold you out. She sold us all out."

They shot off the bridge. Jon pressed the accelerator all the way to the floor. They had to get far enough ahead of the green vehicle that the gunman wouldn't catch up to them at the next red light.

"I'm not mad at Beatrice. I'm mad at myself. All the signs were there and I missed them all. Jon, I can look at a spreadsheet in a contractor's proposal and spot a two-cent error, but one of my buyers tries to frame me for murder and kills another buyer and I miss it? What's wrong with me?"

He took a chance and squeezed her knee, then changed lanes. "The people who work for you are considered the dregs of the Federal employee population, aren't they? Didn't you tell me you get the problem children?"

"Yeah, more or less. Beatrice learned a long time ago to 'pace' herself so she could turn out the bare minimum of supposedly fully satisfactory work and file a grievance if her evaluations dropped below a 'fully sat.' Mac could have retired years ago. I don't know why he keeps hanging on."

Jon smiled to himself and swerved around a small truck. He knew why Mac hung around. The old man adored Madison. Seeing her every day gave him something to live for.

"I got Cathy only because the idiot division chief we had before Gavin thought she'd be worthless because she's black. And Lynette's doctors say contracting work is too stressful for her to handle and that we shouldn't make her carry a workload. And Roxie—" Madison expelled a ragged sigh. "Everybody figured she left her husband for another man, but nobody knew it was Gavin. With a reputation like hers, it didn't matter how good her work was."

"You told me why they're not supposed to be good employees, but I've heard you talk about them in front of other people, even in front of me. You're ready to pummel anyone who says a word against your buyers. I've seen you jump all over Otto Trollinger for griping at Roxie, and everybody knows nobody argues with the Troll. Plus, you've snapped at me a couple of times for pointing out Beatrice's suck-up skills."

She hiked her chin. "They may not all be great employees, but they're mine."

Jon roared through the traffic light as it turned red. He checked the mirror. The Explorer was three cars behind in the other lane.

"You see their faults every day of work, Madison, and you may be able to admit those faults to yourself, but you'll never admit them to anyone else. You have to protect your people, even the ones who stab you in the back."

She nodded slowly, letting his words sink in. "Still, to see Beatrice like that. Discarded. No human being deserves that."

"She did the same to Roxie. She tried to do the same to you, but in a different way."

"I suppose I have to face it: she killed Roxie on purpose. Maybe I can see how somebody would sell secrets for money. They might not see the effects of their deeds in their lifetime. Easy to put it in the past and forget about it. But to murder someone?"

"She had to make sure Roxie kept her mouth shut."

"Roxie had her own secrets. She would have kept quiet. She wouldn't have exposed Gavin, not even for the sake of national security. She loved him too much."

"It was a risk Beatrice couldn't take. And speaking of risks, I think we lost our friend in the Explorer."

"Good." Madison sighed again, but this time she seemed to relax.

"Now the million dollar question, Madison: who's the guy in the Explorer?"

"I don't know. I thought at first he was OSI."

"Crossed my mind, too, but those guys usually wear three-piece suits and are on our side."

"We know he was one of the guys Giselle double-crossed. Austin Wait said she was selling Project Andromeda information to more than one group. I guess our tailgater found out and didn't like it."

Jon slowed to the normal 45 m.p.h. flow of traffic. No use in getting pulled over by the local cops. Their tailgating gunman could quickly spot them if he had a revolving blue light pointing the way.

"Who do you think was on the phone with Giselle?" Madison asked. "Nobody knew you and I were there. Couldn't have been Beatrice. She was already dead."

"Plummer?"

Instead of answering, Madison unsnapped Giselle's purse and dumped the contents on the seat between them. Lipstick and eyeliner rolled onto the floor. Madison rummaged through the papers.

"What did you find?" he asked as he braked for a red-light.

"Project Andromeda disk," she announced triumphantly even though they both knew it was there. "Credit cards. Passport. A keyring with a BMW key and what looks like three house keys. One's marked 'Villa #19.' One's for the Metropole hotel. The third one's for a chateau. Probably as much of a chateau as that villa back there. Ooh, and look: a one-way plane ticket to Quebec City, Quebec." She jerked her head up. "Leaving the local airport in twenty minutes."

So Giselle had told the truth about having a flight to catch. "Anything else?"

"A Post-It note. Something in French."

"Do you know any French?"

"I took a few years in high school. The writing's bad. Hmmm, to be as pretty as she is, Giselle has terrible penmanship. Maybe there is justice after all. It looks like some kind of place. The Rude Treasure? There's a date." She squinted at the slip of paper. "It's tomorrow. Noon, I think. Though it could be evening."

"A name. Is there a name?"

"No, that's it." She peered into the empty purse. Then she gathered its contents and shoved them into her own overstuffed purse.

The light turned green. Jon glanced in the rear-view mirror. "Oh, shit."

"What?"

"The Explorer's two cars behind us and we're still a good three or four miles from the Base." He held his breath and veered right, ignoring the screech of brakes and honking horns as he crossed from the inside lane to the center lane and then into the lane turning right onto a four-lane highway to Ft. Walton Beach.

"Where are we going? This road takes us farther from the Base."

"The other road takes us closer to the Explorer. Don't worry. We'll get on Base through the north gate instead of the east gate. The Explorer will have to go another block or two to turn around. That should buy us some time."

Jon gunned the engine going up the hill, but the old car sputtered and shook. Once they topped the hill, they began to pick up precious speed.

"We don't know that Giselle is going to Quebec to meet Plummer," Madison said thoughtfully. "Maybe they're not partners. We assumed they were."

"Maybe our tailgater is Plummer's partner."

"Or maybe Plummer doesn't have a partner. Maybe he's buying information. Maybe he was double-crossed, too."

"Once we turn everything over to Austin Wait, we'll never know unless it shows up in the newspaper somewhere. And if it does, you know damned well Wait will take all the glory. You know what they say about rewarding the non-participants and blaming the—uh-oh." The Explorer was only a distant speck, but closing fast. "We've got a problem."

Madison twisted in her seat to look behind them. "Come on. Faster."

"This thing won't go any faster." He studied the speedometer and the gauges around it. "Geez, woman. Don't you know to keep a full tank in case of emergencies? We've got an eighth of a tank left."

"Sorry. I haven't filled it up since we got back from Georgia."

"We've got to get on Base. The guy in the Explorer has a gun. He won't be able to get on Base with it unless he runs the gate and that'll attract a lot of attention fast. Austin Wait will have field day."

"No."

"What do you mean, 'No'? I'd like to not get shot if you don't mind." Or see Madison shot. How hard would it be for the guy in the Explorer to pull alongside Madison's old clunker and shoot her through the window?

Madison's face took on a hard kind of serenity. "The airport. It's coming up on your left in another mile or two."

"You're right!" He slapped his palms against the steering wheel. Relief washed over him. "It's got everything we need to keep him away from us while we get help. Security guards, metal detectors, a security checkpoint—"

"Airplanes."

"What?"

"Airplanes. More specifically, flights to Quebec City, via Memphis and Boston."

"Quebec! What would we want to go there for?" The green dot grew exponentially by the second. He couldn't get on an airplane. Not in his BDU's. That was "base only" attire, and Col. Kildee would have his ass for breaking the rules.

"A negotiation ceases to be a negotiation when one party loses its power base. As long as we've got the disk, we're in control."

"Madison, I don't know if you've noticed or not, but we're being followed by a man who has killed once in the past hour and would have killed another three times if he could have. I don't feel much in control at the moment."

She ignored him. "We've got the disk. He doesn't. The negotiation isn't over. There's only one way to find out if Owen Plummer is Giselle Villemaire's partner, and that's to go to Quebec. I'm not going to let Austin Wait get all the glory when I've given up so much."

"That's not it and you know it. I know you, Madison. Better than you think. It's not the glory that concerns you. You blame yourself for everything that's happened, and the only way you think you can make things right is to fix the problem yourself. I don't want to die because of your misguided sense of responsibility."

"Who said you were invited to come along?"

Arguing with Madison Steele was useless when she was this determined. He didn't agree with her, but he wouldn't let her go alone.

Somebody had to watch out for her.

CHAPTER EIGHT

Madison slipped the cell phone back into its cradle as they careened across the busy highway. She flinched and squeezed her eyes shut. A second later, she wondered how they'd managed to cross the road in front of the airport without being struck by an oncoming car. She hadn't known her old clunker could balance on its left wheels.

"Okay," she said, hoarse. "We've got tickets on the next flight out—provided we can get there in the next few milliseconds."

"Got it covered," Jon muttered, rounding the curve too fast.

Madison tucked her credit card back into her purse and held on tight to her drivers' license and Government I.D. She'd have to present them at the ticket counter and she couldn't waste precious time digging through her purse. Any delays might get them killed and then she'd never learn who Owen Plummer was and why he'd been stalking her since the night of Roxie's murder.

The answers lay in Quebec. She felt it in her gut as surely as she felt anything when sitting through a grueling negotiation. She had to get to Owen Plummer before he got to her little girl.

Wearily, she slipped the pearl-handled revolver out of her waistband and hid it in the springs under the seat. She hated to leave it behind, but she had no choice. She'd never get it through airport security, either here or Memphis or Boston. But that was good because their tailgater wouldn't get through either.

"We'll have to leave the car here." Jon braked hard in the loading zone, killed the engine, and pocketed the car keys. He grabbed his blue slip of a hat from the seat. A good soldier was never without his cover.

Madison shrugged. "Might as well leave the car where it is. It's not worth as much as the towing bill." Certainly not worth dying over to look for a legal parking spot.

Before Jon could slam the driver's door, Madison was on the curb and running for the sliding glass doors of the airport's main entrance. She tossed a single glance over her shoulder. The green Explorer was still on the highway, but slowing to turn into the airport parking lot.

Out of breath, they both flung their IDs down at the ticket counter. The uniformed man on the other side of the chest-high bar seemed to take his time printing off their tickets and stapling their boarding passes into the folded packet that advertised their airline's responsibilities and denials. He reminded her of Mac with his friendly but ultra-slow movements, and couldn't have been any younger than Mac.

Like an owl, Madison looked one way and then another. The Explorer had turned into the parking lot. Why had she let Jon talk her into letting him go with her?

"Could you hurry up?" Jon croaked. "Please?"

"Almost done. You kids have a minute or two left. They just now issued the final boarding call. You kids got any bags to check?"

"No," Madison said quickly. "One carry-on. My purse."

"Sure are traveling light," he drawled. "You two running off to get married or sumpin'? I can always tell when two young people are in love."

"We've got to get on that plane. Now. Could you work a little faster, please?"

Damn! Was she the only one who could get anything done fast? She was of a good mind to hop over that counter and finish the job for him.

"Hold your horses. I'm almost done." Every word seemed to take an hour an enunciate. "Jes' need to ask you two a few questions. Now, did anybody give you anything to carry for them—"

"No! No, no, no! Nobody gave us anything to carry for them, we packed our bags ourselves, they haven't been out of our sights, we're not carrying any concealed weapons or drugs. Can we go now?"

Jon laid a firm hand on her trembling wrist. People had started to stare. The ticket agent, instead of hurrying, froze and gawked at her. She'd lost control. She'd actually lost control.

"We're a very big hurry," Jon told him gently. "We really need this little getaway."

The ticket agent mumbled something under his breath that was probably best if Madison didn't understand it and handed them back their ID cards and the ticket packets. She shot a worried glance at the airport entrance. The gunman hesitated on the sidewalk long enough to activate the sensor that slid open the heavy glass doors.

Madison made it to the security checkpoint a few steps ahead of Jon, shoved her purse onto the belt of the X-ray machine, and ran to the other side to wait for her purse to come out.

The metal detector beeped loudly behind her. She spun, expecting to find the gunman with his laser sites trained on her. Jon stood in the archway, surprised and frowning. Then he dug out his keys, her keys, and a handful of change and slapped them down on a tray for the security technician. When he went through a second time, the alarms didn't go off.

"Going to Memphis?" A perky female ticket-taker called from the gate to their plane. "Better hurry. We're closing the doors now."

For the first time ever, Madison thanked God for the smallness of the airport. She handed over their tickets to the woman and stared one more time over her shoulder. The gunman broke into a run for the ticket counter.

"Come on." Jon pressed the small of her back to urge her onward. "Even if he manages to get on this flight, he won't be armed. That's something, isn't it?"

"Yeah. Something."

Purse close to her heart, she ran down the jetway ahead of Jon and then ducked through the door of the small jet. Breathing too heavily to hear anything around her, she made her way down the aisle. She assessed each face on each row. Giselle's seat had been number 3a, but it was empty. Giselle hadn't made it. Maybe the gunman's bullets had been accurate amid the hailstorm of stained glass.

Jon found his seat, a center seat on the seventh row, and slid in between a nerdy-looking guy with a pocketful of pens—either an engineer or a price analyst—and a colonel with a bit of distinguished gray at the temples.

"Would you like to swap seats so you two can sit together?" the colonel asked Madison. He frowned at Jon's uniform but said nothing.

She glimpsed a gnarled but familiar face several seats away. LaDonna Levine. The senior female engineer in the Lab. Rumor had it she'd once been fun to work with, but her personality had shifted to bitter after a bout with Bell's Palsy had left her with only an 80% recovery and a drooping right side of her face that had ruined her social life.

Last week, she'd been TDY to Los Angeles with Maeve, the Mouth of the South. They'd had fun shopping and—no doubt—gossiping. Madison might have known somebody from work would be leaving on the same flight.

"No thanks," Madison told the colonel as casually as she might have if she'd never seen Jon before.

She found her own seat in the twelfth row and settled into it, buckling her seat belt and hiding her face behind one palm for privacy. She watched the aisle ahead of her, willing it to stay empty of tall, blond murderers. The flight attendants finally closed the door. The ticket agent must have been as slow for gunmen as he'd been for Jon and her.

Madison closed her eyes and leaned back. Safe. Safe for now. She opened her eyes and smiled.

Jon turned in his seat. Their gazes locked, but Madison looked away first. It was a negotiation she couldn't handle. Probably for the best that they hadn't found seats together. She needed time to think.

She was in over her head, but she couldn't admit it to anybody. Poor Jon loped along beside her, trusting, hopeless. He really thought she knew what she was doing.

For seven years, she'd made it a point not to get emotionally involved with men. The occasional long distance lover who kept her entertained on TDYs made her feel wanted and beautiful, and she traveled often enough to keep her need for sex discreetly placated. Lack of an obvious social life helped keep the rumors at work in check and contributed to the common belief that, after Tim Sandusky, she was coldhearted and untouchable.

She was neither.

Jon Colter had somehow seeped through the walls she'd erected around herself. It wasn't just physical. He had a wonderful body, best she could tell under that boring, jungle-print uniform, and smelled of passion. If she'd met him on a TDY and knew she wouldn't have to work with him, she might have seduced him already. Given that they were both single, she could theoretically have pursued him at home. But people would have talked. She couldn't do that to Jon.

So she kept her hands—and her heart—to herself.

Did they really look like two kids in love? Was she that transparent? Of course, Jon looked like a kid in love. He *was* a kid. And twenty-three-year-old boys thought about sex all the time. It didn't mean he thought about her.

Still, the ticket agent had thought there was something between them. So had the colonel in the aisle seat. So had she the night they'd watched the stars fall and he'd given her clear title to Rigel.

She twirled the gold band on her left hand. She couldn't let herself fall in love. She had Tim to think of. He'd come back one day. He'd find her again, and she'd tell him all about their daughter and how Delilah had his same dark features and sense of light. About how she sometimes listened for hours to adults talk and never said a word but you could tell, you could tell, that she was taking in every syllable and analyzing it. The way Tim used to do.

Maybe Madison was living in the past. Maybe her past *was* catching up with her. Tim had been gone for seven years. Over 2,500 days. And nights.

Sometimes, she thought he was dead. He must be dead or else he would have kept his promise and come back to her. Then again, if he were dead, she would have felt it. How could anyone occupy the most secret, most sacred chambers of her heart and die and her not feel it? No, Tim was still alive, and as long as he was out there—somewhere—she couldn't give up hope.

Tim had been about first times. The first time she'd really fallen in love. The first time she'd seen Arizona and the Grand Canyon at sunset with a bottle of burgundy between them and no glasses. The first time she'd eaten Greek food. The first man to fall in love with her hair and beg her to keep it long for him forever. The first time she'd slept on the beach and made love at sunrise. The first time a man had ever driven her around on her lunch hour and listened to her rant about fraud and justice and Beatrice's slack enforcement of contracts until finally he'd stopped listening and slammed on brakes and interrupted to say, "I just realized I love you." Every day, every conversation, every kiss had been a new experience for her. Everything with Tim had been a first time.

She'd always thought a first time meant it would happen again, but it didn't. There was a first time for everything, and a last time. All those first times with Tim had been last times, too.

She'd seen life as stretching out before her with infinite possibilities. She never worried about how many more times she'd see Tim because she hadn't realized life gives only a finite number of experiences. Her soul might be immortal, but not this lifetime.

Beatrice had probably thought that at her age, she had several hundred more times to greet the morning sun through her skylight. Roxie had probably thought she'd marry one more time. She'd probably thought she'd sneak out to meet Gavin at night maybe another ten times before he confessed to his wife and went home with Roxie for good. For both of them, the number of times had run out.

The clock could end as quickly for Madison or for Jon. Whether it was Owen Plummer or the blond gunman or Jon's bad driving or terrorist groups with access to all sorts of nasty germs. The soul's intervals on Earth were fleeting, and if one day in a far-off future, a hypnotherapist took her into a past life regression to her lifetime as L. Madison Steele, she hoped the interpretation would be positive. Maybe she'd been a woman of great responsibility and she hadn't let her people down and that she'd been productive. She didn't want some future version of herself looking back at a cold and lonely woman who spent her whole life pining for a man who no longer dreamed of her and for a child she'd given away. Epitaphs were often filled with lies, but what was buried in her soul was truth, and at the moment very sad.

L. Madison Steele had never negotiated against death. She held no power base, only concessions.

How many more times would she visit her aging parents? Five? Ten? Twenty?

Or hold her little girl in her arms before she was too big to be held? A hundred?

Or sleep with a man?

Madison propped her chin in her palm and spotted Jon in his seat several rows up. His head bowed, the even cut of his blond hair on the back of his neck made her fingers itch to test its softness. How many times would she have left to brush against his hand by accident or run her fingers through his hair on purpose?

She might have only one time left to fall in love again or to be loved or to make love. Letting those times come and savoring them, that was the best she could hope for.

Because the greatest natural resource is life, too precious to waste on "what-if's" and "what might have been's."

The plane started to roll.

PART III

CASTING OFF DARKNESS

The Secretary of Defense may enter into agreements with the Secretary of Health and Human Services to provide support for vaccination programs of the Secretary of Health and Human Services in the United States through use of the excess peacetime biological weapons defense capability of the Department of Defense.

—50 USC 1524(a)

CHAPTER ONE

Jon stood next to Madison at the cash machine in the Memphis airport. They had twenty minutes to get to the next gate, but it was within sight of their last gate and he was reasonably confident they'd make it with time to spare.

Madison drew a stack of twenties from the slot. Several hundred dollars, it looked like. She retrieved her credit card and paper receipt and jammed everything into her purse. She clutched the purse tight against her chest, the same as she had on the entire flight from the Valparaiso airport.

"I thought it best I go ahead and get cash," she said. "They'll know we've gone to Quebec City, but with enough extra cash, we'll be able to move around discreetly."

"With American money? Not very discreet."

"Oh, crap. Canadian dollars. I forgot." She glanced up and frowned. "You changed."

Jon held the plastic bag containing his uniform away from his body to show off his blue T-shirt and gray sweat pants. He was too self-conscious to twirl for her pleasure. If anyone looked closely enough, they'd see that he still wore the black boots that belonged with his BDU's, and that the T-shirt was a little on the tight side but was long enough to cover up the word Memphis embroidered on the pants pocket. The shirt had an etching of a young Elvis on it, but wrong-side-out, no one could really tell. To complete his almost metamorphosis into the grunge look, he'd washed the mousse out of his hair and dried it under the wall-mounted hand dryers in the john. His bangs drooped gently forward on one side.

"I thought we should both change," he told her. The colonel on the last airplane had chewed his ass for a solid thirty minutes about wearing BDU's on a commercial flight. "The sooner I change clothes, the better. Uniforms make real good targets in foreign airports and I've heard that French Canadians aren't especially friendly to Americans. Besides, if that guy back at Giselle's is looking for us or sends someone after us, it'll be a piece of cake to spot the two of us dressed like we do for work."

Madison checked her watch. "I suppose I need to check out the airport souvenir shop, too, but I don't think I'll have time."

"No need." Jon grinned and held up a plastic bag for her. "I've got your, um, disguise already."

"Disguise?" She hesitated, then took the bag. "I don't know if I like the way you say 'disguise.' You probably bought a string bikini with Elvis' face painted on the crotch."

Laughing, he tried to feign shock. "Me? You think I'd do that? Don't worry. The souvenir shop doesn't carry bikinis." Unfortunately. "Anyway, it'll be too cold for swimwear in Quebec City. Thirty degrees, maybe forty, according to what the guy at the information booth said. We'll wait 'til we get to Boston and pick up a couple of jackets in the airport there. Anyway, I hope you like what I picked out."

She shrugged. "If you picked it out, I'm sure I'll like it."

"Under normal circumstances, I probably wouldn't have chosen that outfit for you." Something more revealing, maybe. A short skirt to showoff her long legs. A cropped T-shirt to show off the trim expanse he imagined underneath. How could she keep a low profile in the clothes he wanted to dress her in? "You know how airports are about clothes: small on selection and big on price."

She nodded and studied him for a bit longer than casual circumstances called for. "I should be getting dressed." She started toward the women's restroom.

"Madison? You might want to do something with your hair, too."

"What's wrong with my hair?" she demanded, spinning to face him. She fingered her long, blonde curls swishing every which way on her shoulders.

"Nothing's wrong with it." Sometimes he dreamed of tangling his fingers in it or having it fall forward like a curtain around his face as her body pressed his into the mattress, but nothing was wrong with it. "Just do something different with it."

"Like what?"

"I don't know. Something. As long as it's not so, um, eye-catching."

With a frown, she disappeared into the restroom, and Jon leaned against the wall to wait. A row of telephones on the opposite wall caught his attention. Someone should know where they were. Just in case. In case they didn't make it to Quebec City. Or in case they did. After all, Madison carried a disk full of classified information. If they both died placating Madison's ego, Project Andromeda would again be lost.

He sighed and strode toward the telephones. Madison would kill him if she knew. She'd take it as betrayal. That he hadn't trusted her enough. That he'd asked for help on her behalf. He'd have to risk her anger. She needed help—his help—whether she wanted it or not.

Jon dialed the toll-free number to Eglin Air Force Base and gave the operator Austin Wait's number.

"Where the hell is Project Andromeda?" Wait screamed into the phone when he finally answered.

Damn him, Jon thought. Didn't the man care anything about the woman he'd pushed into becoming spy bait? Did he care about anything beyond solving a case and carving another notch in his abominable walkie-talkie?

"Project Andromeda is safe. Madison has it."

"Where's Madison?"

"She's in the bathroom. I wouldn't be making this call to you if she weren't."

"Oh." That stopped him. "Where are you? I had a whole team waiting at the East Gate for you."

"We're in, um, Memphis."

"You're *where?"*

"Slight change of plans."

"Memphis is a ten-hour drive from here. That's not slight."

"But it takes a lot less time to fly here."

"That disk should be here. Where it'll be safe."

Jon didn't really want to get into Madison's explanation of power bases. Besides, he couldn't explain it nearly as well. Even when he thought about it, it didn't make much sense to him. "Madison's got it in her mind that this whole mess is her fault and that she's the one who's got to find out who's behind it all. I guess it's her way of making retribution for not being able to read Beatrice Harper's mind."

"You tell Madison—"

"Forget it. Trust me, forget it. When Madison Steele gets something in her head, there's nothing anyone can do to stop her. Nobody can talk her out of anything."

"You could. She's got a soft spot for you, Colter. She'd listen to you."

"No, not even me." He gulped. "Especially not me. I'm only her lieutenant. Look, Wait, I'm concerned, okay? She doesn't know I'm calling you. If she did, she'd take off on her own."

"This is dangerous. Stupid. You tell her—"

"Forget it. I told you, I can't tell her anything. You know how stubborn she is. She's got it in her head she has to follow this lead, and no matter how dangerous it might be, I can't let her go alone."

"All right," Wait conceded. Even though Jon couldn't see the man, he knew the OSI agent was grinding his teeth. "Why Memphis of all places?"

"Not Memphis. Quebec City. Giselle had a plane ticket for there. Madison figured we'd follow her trail to Owen Plummer."

"Giselle's not going anywhere. We picked her up near the villa. Two broken arms and a twisted ankle. Got to give the girl credit. She managed to get half a mile away by the time we got there. We've got her in custody now."

And taking full credit for her capture, too.

"What about the guy who's following us? We lost him at the airport."

"Hmmm. We haven't gotten very far with that one. While the rest of us have been up to our asses in alligators, Giselle held a little auction for the Andromeda disk. Three bidders."

"Was Owen Plummer one?"

"Not by name, but we've narrowed it down to groups. One's a nationwide militia network. The second one's an Arabic faction. The one we're most worried about is the Sleeping Dogs."

Jon whistled softly and hoped his father's militia group didn't have anything to do with this. "The guy at Giselle's didn't look Arabic."

"Don't be stupid. They don't have to look Arabic. He's probably a hired assassin. Blond hair, light eyes. You'd never suspect him of being affiliated with Middle Eastern terrorists."

"Plummer has light hair and eyes, too. You wouldn't suspect him, either. So is he connected to one of the groups or to Giselle?"

"Unknown," Austin interrupted, "but I think what happened at the villa was probably between Giselle and the guy who's following you. See, Giselle had decided this would be her last deal before she retired to a less stressful life and a plastic surgeon. She had all three groups bid silently and told each they'd won Andromeda. They've already wired her account. One of them's already figured out the double-cross and showed up to collect the disk in person. You and Madison were in the wrong place at the wrong time."

"Christ. Story of my life. Giselle insisted he was Government."

"To me, too. If he is, it's—" the line crackled with static—"covert."

Wasn't everything? Covert was one step away from what he'd been warned about all his life. The last time Jon had spoken to his father, it had been inside a militia bunker in Montana where Elisha Colter had ranted about the IRS, UFO's, mind control, and—in every other breath—the Secret Government. His father had insisted the New World Order was already well underway, thanks to the U.N., which had as its true agenda the disarmament of every man, woman, and child in America and control of the world economy. Jon had walked out with a few well-chosen, acidic words about paranoia and the dangers of smoking too much dope back in the 70's.

"Uh, you still there, Special Agent Wait?"

"Find a way to keep Madison Steele from getting on that next flight, will you?"

"I'll try. By the way, Madison's illegally parked at the airport. Could you...?"

"Yeah, yeah. I'll have her car towed for her." If it was convenient for him and he could earn brownie points with his higher authorities, Jon was sure Austin Wait would take care of everything. Jon somehow doubted Wait would care what happened to them as long as he got his fucking disk back.

"And technically, I'm AWOL. Could you...?"

"Yeah, kid. Whatever. You get Madison and that disk back here where they belong. Got that?"

Yeah, he had it. They were on their own. They would probably get home to find her car stolen and Otto Trollinger screaming about a certain know-nothing lieutenant. So much for making sure someone knew where they were in case Madison's quest for justice ended badly.

"Yeah," Jon said. "Got it."

He dropped the receiver back into its cradle. Damn OSI. They were so good at gathering information and so tight-lipped about giving any out. They could neither confirm nor deny anything, and you never knew if it was a cover-up or not. It was enough to make anybody paranoid.

He pivoted and almost bumped into Madison.

"Who were you talking to?" she asked.

He gave her a quick once-over. The baggy, gray sweat pants fit like a glove, exposing a little too much of her ankles and totally inappropriate business shoes. The white T-shirt with Delta Blues etched across the chest hung loosely from her shoulders. Her unwieldy blonde tresses lay at her shoulder, bound in a thick braid. She'd stuffed their spare clothes and her purse into the oversized canvas bag he'd bought at the souvenir shop.

"You look, um...."

"Inconspicuous?" she guessed.

Ravishing, he thought.

"What were you thinking, Jon? The pants are a size small and the T-shirt's a large."

Heat crept through his cheeks. Somehow he'd imagined her top as a large and her hips as a small. "I forgot to check the sizes before I bought them."

"Who were you talking to just now? You looked distressed."

"Er, I talked to the information desk." That much was true, though he'd stopped to ask questions before stopping by the souvenir shop. "When we get to Boston, we'll have to go through customs and immigration to get onto our flight to Quebec. You may have a problem."

"What kind of problem?"

"You've got Giselle's passport, but I don't think you'll be able to pass yourself off as her. Other than a passport, you need to have a birth certificate with you or some other type of proof of U.S. citizenship, like a voter's registration and valid driver's license which I've got but you don't."

"I've got a voter's card."

"On you?" Certainly couldn't have been in the pocket of her tight sweat pants.

"In my purse. Are you surprised or something? Hey, just because my office is a mess and my life is a mess, it doesn't mean I'm not organized."

She knew where everything was, except for the man she belonged with. Usually he was beside her, behind her all the way, but at the moment he was right there in front of her. If only she'd open her eyes and see him for who he was.

"Look," she said, "things could get messy in Quebec. That guy back at Giselle's, it'll be easy for him to find out we've made it as far as Memphis. He knows which airline we left on, but he won't know we've gone to Quebec. As soon as we get on that plane to Boston, we'll have lost him. Then, I'm going after Owen Plummer."

"You sure you want to do this?"

"Visit a foreign country in pants tight enough to get me arrested? Yeah, I'm sure. I told you. I have no choice. If you want to stay behind, I'll understand."

He checked his watch. "We should go. They're boarding our flight to Boston."

CHAPTER TWO

"Where is he?" Madison grumbled under her breath as she pulled her new flannel jacket closer. If Jon had opted to bow out of her quest, that was fine. Safer. He'd insisted on going with her, though she could tell by the worry in his eyes that he thought she was insane to go after Plummer.

But she had to. If Plummer could materialize out of thin air on the family farm and vanish at will, he could put a gun to Mama's head while she gathered strawberries in her garden, pick Daddy off as he crawled down from the tractor, and Delilah.... *Oh, God.*

She couldn't let anyone hurt Delilah. Delilah had been only three days old when her billirubins test for jaundice had come back botched and Dr. Barrett had asked her to bring the baby back in for a re-test. The doctor had asked her to hold Delilah tight while he drew blood from her tiny heel. Delilah had screamed at the needle prick, and Madison had burst into tears. If Daddy hadn't been there with a firm hand on her shoulder, Madison surely would have punched old Dr. Barrett for causing Delilah any pain at all, even though the good doctor had falsified Delilah's birth certificate to hide the truth from prying eyes.

And the first time a little brat in the church nursery—Raymond, she thought his name was—had bitten Delilah and left teeth marks on her arm, Madison had stormed the church to find the little sadist. Only Mama's reminder that the culprit was a two-year-old child kept Madison from what she would have considered justifiable homicide.

No wonder Delilah had gotten into trouble on her first day of school. Madison had taught her to defend herself, so when a third-grade boy had yanked her long black hair, Delilah did her mommy proud and kicked the kid in the nuts. Sure, Madison had caught hell from her parents for teaching her to fight back rather than turn the other cheek, but Madison couldn't be there all the time to protect Delilah.

God. Oh, God. How could she protect her little girl at all from a man like Owen Plummer? She had to track him down, put an end to the threat. Even if she had to...kill him.

"Come on, Jon."

Where was he? She'd instructed her lieutenant to keep his distance, but this was carrying it a bit too far. They had purposely kept their distance on the flight from Memphis to Logan International Airport. Then they'd checked into immigration separately and gotten through with minimal hassle. Keeping their distance had been harder on the tiny airplane from Boston to the teensy-weensy Quebec City International Airport in the suburb of Sainte-Foy. Of the maybe twenty people on the bumpy flight, Jon had been seated across the aisle from her. He'd kept his arms crossed most of the time, dozing here and there whenever he could. Madison, on the other hand, dared not close her eyes. As long as she carried classified information, she couldn't risk sleep.

So here she was—near midnight in an almost deserted airport in a foreign country—exhausted, hungry, and wishing Jon would put his arms around her and kiss her again like he had that night when they'd watched stars fall, like he had that day in her house when she'd turned to Austin Wait for help instead of to him. This time she'd have an excuse to be weak. She was too tired to struggle and too desperate to feel something again.

Yawning, she blinked back a waking dream. She sat in some ancient desert, staring up at the stars of Orion and dictating her diaries to a scribe at her feet. Fevered, she'd come to the end of her time. She had everything she'd worked for, yet she still longed for that one special love. Or at least for immortality, which might give a driven person like her the opportunity to learn to love. She was too late. She'd chosen greatness over all the other things she could have been. She could have had so much besides greatness. She could have had someone to love her back.

"Where is he?"

Madison pulled the jacket tighter and shook off a chill. She'd come through the short line at customs ahead of Jon, stopped by the cash machine to get some Canadian money, learned that her credit card wasn't any good at the Canadian ATM, and rented the Quebecois version of the little red wagon. Enough time had lapsed for Jon to have run a few laps around the airport. All the other passengers from Boston had been met by friends or relatives or had picked up keys to rental cars at the handful of one-person rental desks near the open area where she stood impatiently. The two or three people milling around appeared to be airport employees. Nobody looked suspicious. This was just another rural airport, not even as large as the airport back in Valparaiso.

Jon rounded the corner and headed toward her at a dead run. The corners of his mouth curved downward in agitation, but he still looked adorable. She smiled to herself. She was so good at taking whatever she wanted, yet the things that would make her happy, she denied herself. Somewhere along the way, "not now" and "not yet" had turned into "not ever." She deserved to be happy, didn't she? Just one more time. Didn't she?

"What took you so long?" *I was starting to worry,* she added silently.

"At least you had a bag of something with you. There I was, last in line, with no reasonable explanation of what I'm doing in Quebec."

"Yeah, I hate it when that happens."

"Don't leave me behind again." A demand, not a request. "I speak German, Spanish, and a smattering of Middle Eastern languages, but when it comes to French, I'm lost. So don't take off like that on me again. You're our guide here, remember?"

"I won't leave you." *Unless I have to.*

The woman at customs had greeted Madison in French to which Madison had responded with a half-cheery, half-weary "Hello." At that, the woman had immediately switched to English. Madison had answered in English that no, she wasn't in Quebec on business or pleasure but for a funeral—which she hoped wasn't true--and that unfortunately her luggage had been delayed. Jon had opted for either the pleasure response, in which case he couldn't explain his itinerary, or the business response, in which case he knew nothing about the Canadian Commercial Corporation or doing business in Quebec. No wonder Jon had been stuck behind for so long. He was probably the most suspicious character to enter the tiny airport all year.

Madison held up a key and dangled it in front of him. "Smile, okay? I got us a car."

"Good. For how long?"

"A week."

"A week!"

“I figured it might take a little time to track down Plummer.” Maybe a long while since she didn’t really know where to start.

“Yeah, but a week? I hadn’t planned to be gone that long. I haven’t signed for leave, and Otto will raise hell. I’ll be AWOL. And you could lose your job.”

“I’ll lose a lot more if I don’t find Owen Plummer.” Her parents. Delilah.

Madison blinked back a glimpse of a nightmare. Something to do with Owen Plummer, though she didn’t know what. Somewhere, sometime, it was chillier. She stood in a cemetery. She’d been there before. Her grandparents were buried there. Both sets. And her great-grandparents. She looked down at three mounds of flowers, one mound smaller than the other two. Red, Georgia clay peeked through where the sprays of carnations and roses didn’t quite cover the graves. As quickly as it came, the vision went.

“You okay?”

Madison blinked at Jon. “I should put you on the rental agreement so you can drive, too.”

“You know I’ll be glad to drive but I’m not sure they’ll let me.”

“Why not?”

He winced. “I’m not twenty-five yet.

She’d forgotten. Jon Colter wasn’t the man of her dreams, just the boy of her dreams.

“Did you get directions to that treasure place?”

No, she’d forgotten that, too. She was tired, so tired. She desperately needed coffee to keep her awake. She wanted to sleep, but as long as she carried the classified disk, she couldn’t afford the luxury of a nap.

Madison stumbled back to the rental counter and gestured to the clerk she’d talked with earlier. “Excuse me, but could you give me directions to this address?” She dug the paper with the bad handwriting out of her purse.

The woman read the note and nodded, then in Giselle’ s accent, said, “Ah oui, Madame.” She pulled one of her company’ s standard city maps from underneath the counter. With an oversized marker, she traced the route and ended it with an X. “Rue du Tre’sor is here, not far from the Chateau Frontenac.”

“Chateau?” Madison held out Giselle’s keys. BMW key, Villa #19 key, Metropole #1602, and the last one, the key with the words *Chateau #402* etched in brass and a silhouette of a steep-roofed building. “This chateau?”

The clerk nodded. If Giselle had a place to stay here, they might find Owen Plummer lurking inside. She could have Jon on his way home by morning. As for her, if she had to kill a man, she wouldn’t be going back.

Madison glanced at the map. “How do I find this chateau place?”

The clerk sniffed politely. “Go to the end of the street. You will see it or you will take a swim in the St. Laurence River, no?”

CHAPTER THREE

Wednesday, 6 October 1999, Quebec City , Quebec, wee hours

In awe, Madison stared skyward. Jon followed her gaze.

The etching on the key didn’t do the Chateau Frontenac justice. It was wasn’t a mere chateau; it was a castle. The green copper roof gleamed against the night. The blend of brown brick and gray concrete on its turreted towers betrayed its age. Only the red maple leaf flag flying overhead gave any indication the castle was under British rather than French rule.

“It looks like one of Delilah’s wooden block castles,” she murmured.

“Madison?” Jon peered upward through the windshield. “We’re sitting in the middle of the street. Shouldn’t you close your mouth and get out of the road before we get run over?”

She shook herself out of her glassy-eyed gaze and drove through the chateau’s gate and into the parking area. Doubtful they’d be rear-ended. Hardly any traffic crowded the cobbled street, but the first snow flurries of the evening played havoc with the windshield wipers and Madison looked as if she might fall asleep any second.

The parking area resembled a courtyard. Madison steered their small car into a tight spot. Probably reserved for valet parking. She killed the lights, killed the engine, then sat stock still, gripping the steering wheel and staring dead ahead.

“Now what?” Jon asked.

She held up the Chateau key. “Now we see what’s behind door number 402.”

“You really think Owen Plummer’s going to be there? We don’t even know for sure that Giselle and Owen Plummer have anything in common, much less if they’re sharing a suite.”

“They have something called Enoch’s Gate in common. That tells me there’s a connection.”

“Why don’t you ask the front desk if they’ve seen Plummer?”

She acted as if she hadn’t heard him. “I’m going up.”

“Madison.”

She unlatched the door but stopped. “Yes?”

What was she going to do when she found Plummer? The man was dangerous, and Madison no longer had Willpower with her, as if it stood a chance against the weapons they'd seen earlier. Jon had an uneasy feeling about all this, an almost paralyzing sense in dread in his gut. He wanted to shake some sense into her, tell her to take the disk back to Eglin where it would be safe. He wanted to capture her in his arms and hold her against him, away from the harm's way she was so eager to jump into. He wanted her to care enough for him to be convinced, either by his words or his kisses, to go home. But he couldn't stop her. If only he could banish the awful feeling he'd wasted all those days and nights of longing for her, that he should have thrown caution to the wind and acted on what enticed him.

"Jon? Did you want something?"

You. I want you. "No. Nothing."

"I won't be long." She looked so forlorn. "If I don't come back...."

"You'll come back. I'll make sure of it."

He exited the car before she did, then ran around to the other side to meet her. The night air had turned chillier during the forty-minute drive from the airport in Sainte-Foy. He slipped a guiding arm around her waist, even though she was the one who led him into the vast building and up the stairs. He stayed close behind her. The snow in her hair melted in the warmer air and left droplets amid the curls and long braid. Her eyes took on a sadness that tore at him. He couldn't save her, couldn't protect her.

They passed a maid near the stairwell on the fourth floor. If Giselle kept a suite here, the staff would know anyone as flamboyant as the woman in black. And they'd likely report anyone breaking into her room.

"Madison, you know French. Why don't you ask that maid if she's seen Owen Plummer?" He hadn't told Madison about his conversation with Wait or that Giselle was in custody. "Ask her if she's seen Giselle," Jon quickly added.

Madison ignored him and marched down the hall towards Room 402. The maid moved quietly in the opposite direction and disappeared around a corner.

"Why won't you ask anybody for help?" Jon whispered as he caught up with Madison.

"I don't need their help."

"Yes, you do. We do. Somebody at the front desk or one of the maids could probably tell us if anyone's staying in Room 402 right now. All you have to do is ask."

"No." Case closed. You couldn't argue with Madison once she'd made up her mind. She paused at the door to Giselle's suite. No light filtered under or around the entrance, and no sounds emanated from inside. She tangled her braid around her wrist and twisted.

"No one's here," Madison concluded and aimed the key at the doorknob.

"Yeah, or they're asleep."

She froze, considered his words, and shook her head. "Then we'll have to be very quiet."

"No!" he squawked, grabbing her hand. It was cold in his. Small. Delicate. Powerful. "I can't let you barge in there and get yourself killed. If you won't think of yourself, think of Project Andromeda. You've still got the disk."

Slowly, she nodded. "I'll give you the disk. You wait in the car, and if I'm not back in twenty minutes—"

"If it came down to it, Jonathan, you should lay down your life to keep her safe."

"That's not what I meant. I'll go in. I'll see if Plummer's here."

"It is not your place," Madison stated with her usual I-dare-you-to-contradict-me authority. "Not your responsibility."

Christ, he was fed up with her stubbornness! "And it's your responsibility?"

Rage and something that looked like fear sparked in her eyes. "Yes."

"You know, if you'd ask somebody if anybody's in Room 402, that could save us a lot of trouble. Why do you have to be so damned independent? You fight against Fate to give yourself all kinds of great opportunities and then you deny them to yourself. You take on a woman and a man with guns without blinking an eye, but you can't ask one simple question that could mean the difference between life and death."

"I can't ask for help." Breaking free of his grip, she clutched the key in her right hand. Her jaw quivered with failure. "I can't remember how."

Of course not. He sighed. *Of course not*. The last time she'd asked for help, she'd been a trainee determined to catch an unscrupulous engineer in her contracting officer's absence, and instead she'd been crucified for her efforts. No wonder she had such a hard time asking for help. A little negative reinforcement went a long way, even for L. Madison Steele.

"Next hotel employee we see, you grab and say, 'Excuse me, but the woman in Room 402 dropped her passport, and would you knock on her door and give it to her please.' Okay? Except you say it in French."

"That's the problem," she wailed. "I can't remember how to say all that!"

"What do you mean, you can't remember? You told me you speak French."

"I do. Well, I did. I was the top student in my high school French classes, but I can't remember a thing other than 'Bonjour' and 'Comment-allez vous?' I was listening to the people in the airport. They all talk too fast and with an accent, and the words run together. It's not like French 101 where the teacher says each word slowly and distinctly. All those verbs I conjugated for nothing! And even if I could remember the vocabulary, I'm not sure I could make myself understood." She shook her head in defeat. "An American with a Deep South accent stuck in a country where practically everybody speaks French and no English at all."

Jon sighed and patted her back. He wasn't a worthless tag-a-long. He'd make her glad he'd insisted on accompanying her to Quebec. "Okay. Okay, you wait down the hall and keep an eye on Room 402. If anybody comes out, you haul ass back to the car, okay?"

"Where are you going?"

"To empty the building." In a moment of courage, he bussed her cheek and fled down the darkened hall.

CHAPTER FOUR

Ten minutes passed while Madison paced the hall. The isolation that had seeped into her blood in the airport was back, stronger than before. For so long, she'd thought of herself as alone, but in recent months, Jon's ever-present eagerness had taken the edge off her pain. In the past week, she'd gone from refusing to be alone with him to not being able to imagine life without him at her side.

If he came back. No, *when* he came back, she wouldn't let him out of her sight again. He hadn't seemed so young during those long hours in The Facility. He'd been able to talk intelligently about technical aspects of the source selection, which was probably why Otto had taken him in as his protégé so young and fresh out of basic training. Jon hadn't engaged in idle boasting and silly chit-chat like Figmo and Miri and so many other young lieutenants. Jon was a quick thinker, even if he was a little too impulsive. If he hadn't spewed his soft drink into the blond gunman's eyes, both Jon and she would be dead by now, the Project Andromeda disk would be compromised, and Delilah would grow up without her.

Yet tonight, she'd looked into his face and seen worry amidst the fearlessness of youth. She hadn't realized how young he was. How unspoiled. After tomorrow, after she'd put an end to the threat of Owen Plummer, Lt. Jon Colter would never be the same again. He would witness the lengths she'd go to to save her child, and for that, he would surely lose his innocence.

A siren blasted in the hallway. Startled, Madison flattened her body against the wall before she realized it was a fire alarm. She smiled to herself. Jon. Bless him, he'd found a way to get Giselle and Plummer out of Room 402. She hovered in the shadows while she watched hotel guests hurry into the halls, tugging on fur coats over flannel nightgowns and hastily zipped pants, grumbling in French as they trotted toward the stairwell.

The door to Room 402 did not open. The last of the fourth floor guests passed Madison on their way to the stairwell. Jon fought his way against their tide and emerged a few feet in front of her. He grinned broadly.

"What did you do?" she yelled, grinning back.

He shrugged. "I wouldn't be much an engineer if I couldn't tamper with a simple fire alarm." He took the key from her and opened the door to Giselle's suite. He motioned for Madison to stay put, turned on the lights, and a few minutes later reappeared to draw her inside.

"I checked everywhere," he said. "Nobody's here. Let's look around and see what an information broker keeps stashed in her closets."

Madison locked the door and the deadbolt, then leaned against the wall. The fire alarm still blasted outside, and Jon still grasped her upper arm. He studied her lips for too long. She knew he would kiss her if he let his gaze meet hers. She knew she would let him.

"We, um, we should hurry," she said as the siren faded. Her words came out too loudly. The alarm still echoed in her ears.

Giselle had taste, Madison decided. Room 402 wasn't anything like Villa #19 a continent away in Florida. Instead of crisp white on white on white, the chateau suite flourished in antiques that could have made a museum proud, rich tapestries and fabrics, and a hint of Old World luxury. The wall over the desk bore a magnificent collection of ancient daggers, including one Madison couldn't take her gaze off. She'd seen it before, possibly in an archeology magazine. Possibly in her dreams. A sickle.

While Jon scrutinized the narrow space under the king-sized bed for anything useful, Madison checked out a state of the art computer system hidden inside an elegant armoire. Giselle had left nothing to chance. The hard drive was clean except for basic software—all of which was legally licensed to G. Villemaire. An unplugged zip drive lay on the shelf beside an ultra-fast modem, evidence that Giselle had probably removed her more sensitive files before jetting off to steal Project Andromeda.

"Anything yet?" Jon asked as he groped around the fireplace opening.

"Not yet." She checked the word processing program for recently used files and found references to files on missing disks: *weather.doc, time.doc, dogs.doc,* and *bwpa.doc.* The first two sounded more like utilities. If Giselle needed to know the time and temp, she could probably call a local number or check the Internet. As for *dogs.doc,* that could mean anything. Maybe she preferred dogs over cats. If so, why not use the French word for dogs? *Chien*, Madison vaguely remembered, glad something of her French classes was coming back to her, however useless. Or maybe Giselle meant dogs in the sense of problems. Again, why not in French? Surely there was a derogatory French word for problems. If most of the population of Quebec spoke only French, perhaps using English as a foreign language was safer for Giselle.

The last missing file, *bwpa.doc.,* sent a shiver down Madison's spine. In certain circles, *BW* stood for biological warfare and *PA* could easily represent Project Andromeda.

Or it could mean nothing at all. Without the missing disks, she'd never know.

"Nothing," she said. "Everything's been sanitized."

"Same here. You're disappointed."

"I was hoping to find something we could use. Something that would lead us to Plummer." She closed the armoire. "We should go. We'll need to find a place to stay tonight. We've got a long day ahead of us tomorrow."

He cast a subtle glance at the bed. "We could stay here tonight."

"Are you crazy?"

"Not at all. Who would look for us here? In the arms of the enemy?"

"Bad idea, Colter. Remember Giselle? What if she walks in here and finds us? She was going to kill us or have you forgotten? You expect me to fall asleep when that kind of risk is out there?"

"Giselle's not here."

"Not yet. But she will be."

"No, she won't." He started to say something else but bit off the words.

"You can't be sure of that. And I won't take that kind of risk with you." He was still her responsibility. He certainly wouldn't be chasing spies on his own.

"I'm sure. Earlier, I, uh...." He turned away from her, as if afraid to look her in the eyes. "I've got this feeling."

"Feeling," she repeated.

"Yeah. Don't ask me how I know, but Giselle's been captured. She's not coming to Quebec. At least, not tonight."

Why was he acting so strangely? "You mean you have a feeling like your mother has feelings?"

"My mom says we're all a little bit psychic."

He hadn't answered her question, but he felt so sure of himself. He was hiding something, and it didn't take a psychic to see that.

"Okay," she said tentatively, dropping her bag onto the divan and shedding her jacket. She shouldn't sleep with classified on her person, but she was dead on her feet. If she didn't nap, she'd never make it through tomorrow. "We'll stay tonight. Then tomorrow morning, I'll go down to rue du Tre'sor to find Owen Plummer."

"You mean, 'we'."

"I mean, 'I'."

"I'm not going to let you face Owen Plummer alone. If he's here at all. I'm not so sure he and Giselle are partners."

"I am. When I mentioned time travel at Giselle's villa, she asked what I knew about Enoch's Gate. And Austin Wait said that Owen Plummer worked on Enoch's Gate under President Kennedy. I don't know what it is, but there's a connection. I can't explain why I feel so strongly about it, but I have to do this."

"So there's a connection. It doesn't prove anything."

"It proves I have to find Owen Plummer. If he can show up out of the blue at my parents' farm, what's to keep him from killing everybody I love? If there really is such a thing as time travel, maybe Plummer's found it. He sure didn't look like a man in his seventies."

"Hmmm. You named Project Andromeda after a Michael Crichton book, right? *The Andromeda Strain.* Why?"

"Great book. I read it in high school. Don't remember much about it except how much I enjoyed it and that there was an otherworldly virus or something that turned people into white powder. Otto was calling the program something boring like 'Advanced Defeat of Chemical and Biological Agents', and I interrupted his briefing to suggest we call it 'Project Andromeda'. Pissed him off, but the name stuck. Which pissed him off more. Why?"

"Because if there's a project out there called 'Enoch's Gate', why is it called that?"

"Check that night stand drawer," she ordered, yanking open the drawer nearest her. "Enoch was a great man of the Bible. I don't know if Gideons leave Bibles in Quebec or even if Giselle would let it stay if they did."

"Nothing in here but, er, panties." Jon blushed and shut the drawer on a rainbow of colorful silk.

Madison closed the other drawer. Only a bottle of aspirin, and Giselle didn't seem like the kind of woman who'd ever have a headache in a bedroom such as this one. "I grew up going to Bible study two or three times a week. The only thing I remember about Enoch was the way he died. Or rather, didn't die. Two men in the Bible didn't die—Elijah and Enoch. God took them up into the heavens. He sent a chariot of fire for Elijah. And Enoch, He just took."

But Jon wasn't listening. He wet his lips and frowned at the drawer of lingerie.

She perched on the corner of the bed. He sat on the opposite corner, as far away as he could get and still touch the bed. Not only were they in the same room alone, but they shared the same piece of furniture. A bed. A luxurious, oversized bed meant to make love in, not sit upon. The kind of bed that would be draped in satin sheets they could slip-slide away on. Her nerve endings flamed at the prospect of Jon's closeness. Judging by the bob of his Adam's apple, he was horny, too.

"We should get some sleep," she said. Though there was no way she could sleep and have Jon lying nearby in the same room. She had wasted too much time. She'd never let another night go to waste without Jon Colter.

"Yeah, we should get some sleep." He swallowed hard. Neither of them moved.

Madison started to say something but couldn't think of anything relevant. She was older, more experienced. She should be the one to make the first move. She'd done it before with other men on TDYs to remote places. Just sex. That's all it was. Wild animal passion. Nothing more, nothing less. No regrets. No awkward moments in the morning after.

With Jon, she had a special friendship. One she hadn't realized until now. She didn't want to ruin everything by sleeping with him. Like it or not, sex changed the way people related to one another, and she couldn't risk any disappointments. He'd become clingy or possessive. She'd become distant. In either case, things would never be the same.

She reached for the hem of the bedspread to smooth it down. Jon caught her hand and held it.

"Oh, God," she breathed. Desire drugged her. These were dangerous days if she couldn't shake off her yearning and turn her back on him. It would be so easy to pull him to her, throw one leg over his slender hips, plant kisses along his neck while she rubbed against him until he begged her to stop.

Instead, she jerked her hand out of his and pressed it to her chest. "Are you hungry?" she asked brightly.

CHAPTER FIVE

L. Madison Steele wasn't good at something.

Jon laid his fork and steak knife across his plate and leaned back in his chair to watch her. The idea intrigued him.

He'd thought of her as being an expert at everything she tried and probably at everything she hadn't tried. But she wasn't. If she wasn't good at something, she simply didn't do it. Like speaking French. She wasn't comfortable with her skill level, so she refused to ask for help or even attempt to ask.

It had been he, Jon, who didn't speak a word of French but had asked for help. They'd arrived in Quebec City too late to eat, too late for room service, and too late for the restaurant downstairs. Against Madison's protests, he'd gone down to the kitchen, mentioned Giselle Villemaire's name about a hundred times, and shocked the kitchen staff into action. Apparently, here at the Chateau, Giselle got whatever Giselle wanted. Apparently, too, they'd decided Jon was Giselle's American plaything for the evening and she'd sent him down to fetch dinner as a source of amusement to the staff. A pretty girl folding napkins into accordions had snickered at him. He'd pretended not to feel cheap.

Here, in the privacy of Giselle's room, with Madison on the opposite side of a linen-draped, antique table, he felt more ignored than cheap. Madison toyed absently with her food, then set down her fork and sipped from her glass of caribou, a sweet red wine with a kick of whiskey. No longer did she study him with eyes of weary want as she had before she'd suddenly claimed hunger and dialed room service to no avail. He'd been talking for the past fifteen minutes, but she hadn't heard a word.

"How's the drink? Good?"

"Um-hmmm." She stared off at the window, either at her reflection or into the night. Maybe the caribou had more of wallop than she cared to admit.

"And the lamb in blueberry wine sauce? I got the impression it's Giselle's favorite. I think what the kitchen staff whipped up is what Giselle might call 'the usual'."

"Um-hmmm."

"I suppose it's a little heavy for two in the morning. We won't want breakfast."

"Um-hmmm." She still wasn't listening to him.

"You know I'm madly in love with you."

"Um-hmmm."

"Madison."

"Um-hmmm."

"Madison!"

Her eyes came into focus. She frowned. "I'm listening."

"No, you're not. You're a million miles away. Were you by any chance thinking of me?"

She glanced down at her hands and twisted the gold band on her ring finger. "I was thinking of someone I knew a long time ago."

"That guy. That other lieutenant." The fine dinner heaved in his stomach. Here they were alone and for the moment relatively safe in a beautiful city—a beautiful, romantic city—and Madison was lost in thoughts of a man from her distant past.

"Yeah." She smiled sadly. "That other lieutenant. He gave me this ring as a promise he'd come back for me one day. He said that when he did, he'd make it real."

"He never did." Jon's words came out a little too acidic. He swigged his drink.

"Not yet. I mean, no. No, he never did."

"How long since you've heard from him?" He remembered the letter on her kitchen table, addressed to Tim Sandusky and returned to sender.

"Almost seven years."

"Sev—" He swallowed the word. She'd been pining for the guy all this time and without a single word from him? "When was the last time you talked to him?"

"When he gave me this ring." She twirled it again. "He didn't want to leave me. He was forced to. He was...." She changed her mind about what she had nearly said. "He was...special."

"Special enough to put your life on hold for him all these years?"

She met Jon's gaze. "Yes."

"Madison, you're holding onto the past. The guy's probably already married with a bunch of rug-rats underfoot."

She flinched. *Oh shit. She flinched.* Jon sucked in his breath. He'd pushed too far. Madison never let her wounds show. Ever.

"I'm sorry," Jon whispered. "He must really have been special to you." A god, he added silently.

"He was my first real love."

Jon finished his drink. It burned all the way down but didn't warm the chill inside him. "Will he be your last?"

"I always thought so."

"You don't sound so sure."

She smiled, not quite so sadly this time, then shrugged. "If Owen Plummer's a time traveler, then maybe I could go back and change the past."

"What would you change? That you met that lieutenant?"

"No!" she answered too quickly. "No. As painful as it was to lose him, never having known him would cost me too much. I don't expect you to understand."

"I might, you know. Understand."

Roxie had been right that day in The Facility. She'd told him he was more of a fool than she was to love someone who couldn't love back.

"If I could change the past," Madison said, "I'd change the night Tim and I were caught together. That's the night my life fell apart. If that hadn't happened, if the rumor mill hadn't been so cruel, if the Air Force hadn't sent Tim off to Iceland, he would have stayed. We would have married and spent the rest of our lives together. Things would have been so different."

"Think so?"

"Definitely." She frowned, and he knew she'd never thought otherwise.

"You think your life would have been perfect if you'd married him?"

"Maybe not perfect, but easier."

"Or maybe not easier but different. Madison, there will always be troubles, no matter which path you take. You might have married him and been divorced several years by now. Then you'd look back on your time with him miserably. As it is, you've elevated the guy to sainthood. Wasn't there anything bad about him?"

She twisted the ring. "I'm sure there was."

"You don't remember?"

"No."

"Have you changed since then? Since he left?"

"Oh, God, yes. I was a trusting kid. I had no clue how to play the political games at work. I let people walk all over me. That doesn't happen now."

"So you've changed."

"Doesn't everyone?"

"Doesn't Tim Sandusky?"

She pushed back in her chair and stood. "What are you getting at?"

"That Tim Sandusky isn't the same man you were in love with. Just like you're not the same woman he fell in love with. You're hanging onto a future with a man who no longer exists. You're—whew!" Where was he getting this stuff from? He could almost smell his mother's herbal perfume.

The phone rang. Jon turned too quickly and knocked over his empty glass.

"Someone's calling for Giselle," Madison whispered. She didn't move.

"If you could fake them out, pretend you're Giselle, no telling what kind of information you could get."

She shook her head frantically. "I can't. I'll never be able to pull it off."

Of course not. She didn't speak French that well. She wasn't good at it, so she wouldn't even try.

Not him. He was a lieutenant. Everybody knows lieutenants can't do anything right, so if he tried and failed, no one would be the wiser. But if he tried and succeeded....

"I guess it's time for me to play the tramp." He leaned across the bed and snatched the phone off the hook. He'd explain in English that Giselle was asleep or in the shower or somehow not available and do his best to get a name and phone number, maybe a message. "Hello?"

"Jonathan?"

He sat bolt upright. "Mom?" How did she *do* that? He detested her calls out of the blue like this.

"Where are you?"

"Mom, you're the one who called."

"Yes, honey, but I don't know what number I called. I was having a dream about your friend and a man from her past and I was explaining to her that he's not the same—"

Oh, Christ. Jon stopped listening. He didn't want to hear how he was channeling for his crazy mother. Probably more of her astral projection shit.

"And then I woke up and dialed a number in the dark, and you answered. Where are you?"

"Quebec City."

"Yes. I see it now. You're with The Falconer."

"Mom," he wailed. Madison watched with amusement from across the room. She busied herself with perusing Giselle's closet. "Yes, Mom. I'm with her."

"Good. No matter what you do, don't let her out of your sight again."

"Why?" The hair on the back of his neck stood at attention. Worry prickled all the way down his spine. "What's going to happen?"

Across the room, Madison stopped stroking a black velvet cape and looked up. To be such an otherwise stable person, she had a much easier time believing all this weird psychic stuff than he did, though at the moment, he didn't doubt his mother's abilities in the slightest.

"The Universe is watching out for you," his mother said. "You and The Falconer. One day, she will save the human race. That is her destiny. And yours is to keep her alive. Protect her." Her voice dropped to a whisper. "No matter the cost."

"You mean Project Andromeda? She's already done that." Now if he could only talk Madison into taking the disk and herself back to Eglin and safety.

"No, Jonathan. There are many ways to save the world. She will do this again and again."

"Reincarnation?"

"No. In this lifetime. In her past lives, she ultimately could not save her people. You must make sure she lives out her karma this time. Without you, she'll sacrifice too much. She'll get herself killed before she can live out her destiny. Her soul is awakening now. Don't let her fail."

Madison re-hung the hooded cape in Giselle's closet, closed the door, and then sat down on the corner of the bed. She folded her hands in her lap. Should he tell her what his mother had said?

"Sure, Mom. I'll take good care of her."

"Take care of yourself, too, Jonathan. I was worried about you at the Villa. I don't want to lose you."

"The Villa?" His mother had always claimed a psychic link with him. Any time he'd been hurt or in trouble during his childhood, she'd come running to protect him. "You're the one who called Giselle Villemaire."

"I try to stay out of your life. I try not to meddle."

"It's okay, Mom. Meddle away! You saved our hides with that phone call. What the heck did you say to Giselle to make her toss her purse to Madison and jump out the window?"

Curious, Madison inched closer to him. She could hear only one side of the conversation but enough to understand.

"I told her exactly how she would die and exactly how she could escape that future."

"And she believed you just like that." Giselle had believed something the way her cheeks had drained to a pale white.

"She believed because I told her something from her childhood."

"Smart, Mom. All kids are afraid of the dark. Or the boogie-man under the bed. Shoot, the monster under the bed was probably afraid of her."

His mother didn't speak for a moment. Jon could feel himself being dragged into deeper waters. "Don't judge her too harshly. You don't know what she went through."

"No, but I know what she put Madison and me through."

"She was only five years old. Her family home was on fire. She and her mother were trapped in her attic bedroom. They had a chance for escape but Giselle wouldn't leave without her kitten and her kitten wouldn't come out from under her bed. Giselle dallied too long and the fire trapped them in the attic. Her mother smashed a window and dropped Giselle out onto a porch canopy. Without the kitten. Giselle's mother didn't make it."

"God." For a brief moment, Jon actually could see the pajama-clad little girl with a sleek curtain of black hair sitting in the grass and crying for her lost kitten and not yet understanding she'd lost her mother. She'd learned a hard lesson early in life. No wonder she'd given up her precious disk and leapt out the window at the suggestion. She'd lived through adversity once, and if she didn't dally, she would again.

"You believe me."

Jon blinked, amazed. "Yeah, Mom. I-I guess I do."

"Good. Then believe this: without you, The Falconer will die before she can fulfill her destiny."

CHAPTER SIX

He drank too much.

Madison stared at the overturned glass. She'd never seen Jon drink anything more than a couple of beers at the Officers' Club after some long, boring Commander's Call where the General du jour imparted his words of wisdom for making the Air Force work "smarterfasterbetter." Except for Jon's passion for protecting her, he seemed to take most things in moderation. Especially touching her.

Not like Tim. Tim had been particularly talented at touching. He'd done nothing in moderation. Every moment had been lived as if it were his last. He'd tangled her in his web of passion and she'd willingly given herself up for the brevity and intensity of the moment. He'd transformed her from a quiet child into a creature of life. He'd been change personified, showing her something new and different and exciting with every hour they spent together. Tim had loved her, but he'd never protected her. In his wild passion, he'd stripped her to the bone and unwittingly left her vulnerable to the jackals.

He drank too much. She'd forgotten. *Tim drank too much.*

And wasted too much money. It took money to buy all those first times and all those moments of passion. The weekends at Grayton Beach and in the mountain retreat of Highlands, North Carolina; the picnic lunches in the park on Tom's Bayou; the candlelight dinners overlooking the Gulf at sunset; the romantic balloon rides over the desert while TDY in Arizona; the flowers and wine and pleasures of the flesh. All had cost money, and Tim had freely spent it. Much to Madison's discomfort, he'd never kept a penny of savings. Seize the day, he used to tell her. *Carpe diem.* Everything he made, he spent on living for the moment.

She'd hated that about Tim. An alcoholic spendthrift. Yet, for almost seven years, she'd forgotten. Jon was right: life with Tim Sandusky—and raising a child with him—wouldn't have been all roses.

"Still thinking about him, huh?" Jon asked, bounding up from the bed and then crossing the room to the window. He glared out at the pin pricks of city lights beyond the St. Lawrence River. He looked so young and yet so fierce.

"So what else did your mother say?"

"I told you everything." His jaw twitched with the lie.

"I heard you mention reincarnation." Madison sat cross-legged on the bed and leaned forward. She couldn't stand it, the way he withdrew from her when he was angry. It shouldn't have mattered, but she longed to make him happy. She owed him that much.

"I don't remember."

"I don't really understand it, you know. I've heard about karmic debts. If you do something bad to someone in this life, then in the next, you have to make it up to them. It's the old 'what goes around, comes around' on a cosmic scale?"

Jon shrugged. Either he was really mad or really hurt.

"The way I figure it, I must be spending this whole lifetime making up for something awful I did in my last life." She must have been a murderess on a grand measure. What else could she have done to deserve losing Tim, losing Delilah, losing hope? What kind of karmic debt would she owe Jon for standing by her through thick and thin, or did he owe her for something long ago?

Jon squared his shoulders, careful to keep his back to her but still able to watch her in the reflection of glass if he wanted. Even now, even angry and hurt, he didn't turn completely away from her. No, he'd been there all along. Throughout the long hours of the Project Andromeda source selection. Ignoring the rumors and character assassination to the point of fighting for her dubious honor. At her side, changing diapers for a stranger's child when the burden of new motherhood left her paralyzed from memories and lack of sleep. Behind her when she marched back to work amid the slanted looks and ugly whispers. Gallantly in front of her when Giselle and her uninvited guest threatened Madison's life. With her all the way to Quebec City, even when his absence from work could mean his career.

She couldn't let any of this hurt him, damage his career with the Air Force or his reputation. She had to keep him safe, but for now she had to keep him alive.

He was too good to her. She didn't deserve him.

"Jon? What are you doing here?"

"There's a madman with a gun after us, remember?"

"No, what are *you* doing here? Why you? Why are you here with me?"

He shifted on his bare feet. His eyes glinted in the mirror, watching her though he still pretended to gaze into the night. "Just the wrong place at the wrong time, I guess."

"I don't believe in coincidences."

"Okay, then. My mother would call it Fate."

"Maybe. But why *you?"* She couldn't make him understand. Probably a mistake for her to push it, but she had to know. "Why are *you* here with *me?"*

He turned to face her and crossed his arms awkwardly. "I don't know what you mean."

"I think you do. Why me, Jon? Why not Miri or one of the girls down in the Fuzes Branch or the cute college girls who stop by the gym after classes? They're more your age and style."

He cocked his head. A lock of blond fell into his eyes. "What makes you think I'm interested in someone my own age? Why would you think any of those women are my 'style'?"

"Because you're young and cute and idealistic, and you should be with someone who can love you back. Not running all over North America with someone like me."

"Maybe I like running all over North America with someone like you," he said softly.

"What is it? You miss your mother? You always wanted a big sister? *Why me?"*

Jon took a deep breath and settled onto the edge of the bed. Leaning on his elbow, he made himself comfortable. The tiniest hint of a smile played with the corner of his lips. "Why not you?"

She reached inside herself for the truth. "Because there are easier women to get to know. And there are far easier women to love."

Jon rolled onto his back and stared up at the ceiling for a long while. She thought he'd chosen not to answer, or that maybe he didn't have an answer. When he swallowed the third time, she realized he was gathering his courage.

"Not for me," he finally said. "When I first saw you, it was about six months ago. You were sitting in a briefing on chemical weapons. Must have been fifty people in the room, and I think you were the only one who wasn't an engineer. I didn't know that then. The lights had been dimmed so we could see the view graphs better, and you sat there, so relaxed, in the back of the room while some GS-12 who didn't know his ass from a hole in the ground briefed the Colonel and about a dozen visiting dignitaries. Otto had come down with the flu a few hours earlier, his substitute was making a fool of the entire Lab in front of the VIPs, and it was too late to cancel the briefing."

Madison nodded. She vaguely remembered that fiasco. One of many.

"You were wearing a white suit," Jon continued. "You had your hair pinned up on top of your head but this one strand had wriggled its way free and you sat there, looking like an angel, but twisting that lock of hair around and around your index finger." He demonstrated on an imaginary lock of his own hair. His blue eyes took on a faraway gaze as if retelling a fairy tale. "You were almost smiling. And I couldn't take my eyes off you. And I knew right then I wanted to be close to you. I wanted to find out who you were and if you were single and see if there was a spark between us."

Madison swallowed a smile. She remembered the briefing, too. She remembered Jon, the bright-eyed lieutenant who had pretended to frown at the conference room's polished table when in fact he'd been stealing glimpses of her in its reflection. His face had been a little flushed as if he'd been caught perusing a photo-essay of scantily clad women. The only thing that had distracted her from his lean good looks was the absolute awfulness of the briefing going on around them.

"So why didn't you come over afterward and introduce yourself?"

"I would have, but you surprised me. The General had asked a question. Otto's substitute couldn't answer it. Then he asked another question and Otto's substitute stuttered and fidgeted and looked like he wanted the ground to open up and swallow him. The tension in the room was so thick, you could have sliced it with a knife. And then you spoke up."

"It was no big deal." Another day, another dragon to slay.

"You were the only person in the room who wasn't an engineer, but you got up and finished the briefing yourself."

And that was largely the reason Otto hated her. Her insistence on knowing what kind of technology she was supposed to negotiate had left her more knowledgeable than Otto's hastily chosen replacement. She'd made Otto's empire of engineers and scientists look stupid. After all, she was a mere contracting weenie, not a fabulously intelligent technical type.

"I guess I lost my nerve," Jon said, studying an unraveling thread in the brocade bedspread. "The way you took over the podium like a raging angel. An ordinary woman might have turned me down for a date, but I got the feeling that you'd probably castrate me if you didn't like me."

She laughed. "So you became my shadow instead."

He lifted his gaze, the lock of blond still dangling between his eyes. "Can you blame me? Tell me the truth: would you have gone out with me if I'd asked?"

"No. But not for the reasons you think."

"Because of appearances."

"Because of appearances. Yes. I wanted to be with you, but I couldn't. Jon, if it weren't for appearances, I would have pursued you a long time ago."

It was late at night. God, it was late. She was too tired to care what she said. Too weary to worry about how he might think of her tomorrow. And given that tomorrow she might be a cold-blooded killer if that's what it took to stop Owen Plummer from hurting her family, Jon wouldn't mind about a little thing like blatant honesty from a half-drunk and fully-exhausted woman like her.

He reddened. His breaths quickened. "Really?" he squeaked, then cleared his throat. "I mean, really? You...you wanted me, too?"

"Yeah." She could have leaned forward and kissed him. She didn't. "I wanted you. You were very sexy. Very pleasing to the eye."

"You know how it is with all the sexual harassment awareness stuff these days. I couldn't say what I wanted to. I kept hoping maybe you would. You were so kick-ass. I had this fantasy where we were, um, involved. Purely physical. That's all. I didn't have to worry about repercussions because you wanted the same kind of relationship, no strings attached. But then everything changed."

"It did?"

"I've spent almost every waking hour by your side, hoping something would happen. And it did."

No, it didn't, she wanted to say. She'd made damned sure nothing had happened between them.

"I watched you take on the world, Madison. You throw this impenetrable wall up around you and don't let anything get through to you. But I saw the cracks. I didn't want to. I didn't mean to. But they were there. I'd been in lust with you, but then I started to fall in love with you. With the real Madison, not the L. Madison Steele in your signature block."

"You saw the real me, huh?" she joked. "If you know what's good for you, you'll keep your mouth shut."

"Forget the tough guy image. I know you. I know there's a vulnerable side."

She shifted on the bed. "I don't want to get into this."

"I'm already into it with you. They say that sometime during our sleep, we let the masks we put on for the rest of the world fade and we let our true faces show. Back when I was helping you with the Cashwell baby, that first night I heard you crying in your sleep, you pierced my heart."

Madison let out a shaky breath. He was so wonderfully candid—probably a side-effect of his youth. Most men she knew wouldn't be caught dead displaying their hearts. Jon had a way of opening his own and crow-barring his way into hers, too.

"Do you...do you still want me?" he whispered low enough that if she said no, he could lie and claim he'd asked something else.

The old yearning she'd banished long ago stirred low in her stomach. She'd wanted him the moment she had first laid eyes on him. Right now, she wanted him even more.

Tim had been the heat beneath her winter. Warmth and passion. Somehow she'd always thought of him as summer, even though they'd fallen in love in early autumn and he'd been banished before the last spring freeze. When he'd left, her life had turned to winter. A barren, cold place where she was bent on survival and no time for the frivolity of magic and sunshine.

Jon. He wasn't summer to her, but maybe a little bit of spring. The thaw had begun.

Madison twisted her ring and gave it a gentle tug. What was the point of wearing Tim's ring when he hadn't cared enough in seven years to come back and claim her? Jon was right about that, too. She wasn't the same woman she'd been back then. That woman didn't exist anymore. She was no more the woman Tim remembered than Tim was the same man she'd fallen in love with. That Tim was dead. He had to be. Because if that Tim were still alive, he would have come for her long before now.

She pulled harder at the ring. She'd worn it for so long, she wasn't sure it would come off at all. If she pried off the shackle Tim had left on her finger, Jon could overlook the hurt of playing second lieutenant to her first. She kissed the tips of two fingers and pressed them against his lips. "Don't go anywhere," she whispered.

He closed his eyes and smiled.

Madison scurried into the bathroom and turned on the faucet marked "C." It took a spurt of steam for her to remember that "C" stood for *"chaud"* instead of "cold." She reversed the motion and turned on the "F" faucet, which spewed out freezing cold water.

She soaped her knuckle and pulled harder. Outside, Jon waited for her with his chiseled cheekbones and thin lips, with his slim hips and broad shoulders, with his gray-blue eyes of curiosity and fire, with his slender hands. And she was keeping him waiting.

Madison yanked on the ring until her knuckle turned white. It was almost as if her bones had grown around the ring as a tree trunk grows over a wire meant to support its structure and makes the wire a permanent part of its whole. Tim was a part of her past and her past was a part of her. She could no more erase Tim from her life than she could cut out her heart. Wrenching the ring from her finger wouldn't change anything except to give her another scar, a physical one.

She rinsed the last of the soap from her finger and dried her hands. Outside, Jon waited. Anticipation fluttered in her stomach. Tonight might be her last chance with him. If things went badly with Owen Plummer, there would be no second chance.

Rubbing her fingertips over her cheeks, she wished the dark circles would disappear. Her jaw still bore a slight yellowish bruise, courtesy of Dr. Frick. Her long hair, her beautiful hair Tim had loved, needed brushing and re-braiding. Her face badly needed a wheelbarrow's worth of make-up to give back the youthful glow that waned after nearly twenty-four non-stop hours. During the sleepless nights with Bronwyn Cashwell, Jon had seen her at her worst. Maybe one day, he'd see her at her best. It wouldn't be tonight.

She turned out the light and tiptoed back into the bedroom. Amid the dimness of distant city lights, she could see that Jon hadn't moved. He lay quietly atop the brocade bedspread, eyes closed, breathing softly.

Fast asleep.

She'd waited too long.

Madison kissed his forehead and tasted salt. She stood by his bedside and watched for a long time, memorizing the tired peace in his face, the curve of his eyelids, the smell of his skin after a travel-weary day. She filled her brain with enough of him to last the rest of her life, even if Owen Plummer put a bullet through her skull in the morning and her brain ceased to function. Given that, maybe she should concentrate on filling Jon's head with memories since he might keep his head longer, keep her memory alive along with himself.

Who the hell did she think she was?

She could wake him up with kisses and intentions of seduction. In a few days, he'd return to Eglin with a headful of sweet memories and a pair of empty arms. He'd struggle through every day and wonder as he pulled the sheets over him at night, whatever happened to his lover and when would she return? If she slept with him now, he'd spend the rest of his life pining for her.

She'd do to him what Tim had done to her.

Madison crossed to the window, pulled back the curtain, and stared out at the distant lights. She laid her brow against the window pane and shut her eyes tightly. In a moment of weakness, in the stillness of what she'd refused to recognize as love, her eyes stung. Hot tears seeped from under her lashes.

Sniffling, she backhanded the tears and steeled her spine. L. Madison Steele cried for no one.

Especially not herself.

CHAPTER SEVEN

In this dream, as in so many others, Madison lay naked under him, moaning his name. Jon knew it was a dream, but he couldn't drag himself away from it. He ached for her touch, even when it wasn't real.

"Jon?" she whispered against his cheek.

"Don't talk." He laced his fingers through her wild mass of curls, anchoring her head to the pillow. She arched against him, exposing her throat to his kisses.

"Jon—"

He cupped her free hand over her mouth and sank into her body with a fevered groan.

Jon, she said with her mind, *wake up.*

He opened his eyes and blinked. A cold sunshine filtered through heavy curtains into the museum-quality room. Giselle's suite.

"Madison?"

He brushed his hand over the patterned brocade bedspread beside him. No warmth. Madison hadn't slept there. At least not recently.

Jon sat up and banged into a headache. He fell back to the bed and waited for the pounding to go away. Too much caribou wine, he decided. The dirty dishes from last night's dinner sprawled across the antique table on the other side of the suite. The last thing he remembered was Madison sitting on the corner of the bed, twisting that damned ring, and looking at him as if he were a piece of candy. He'd been drunk enough to tell her how he felt about her. He must have fallen asleep in mid-sentence.

"Madison?"

He swung his legs over the side of the bed and stood uneasily. The door to the suite had been locked but the chain dangled, still swinging slightly. For whatever reason, she'd gone out, and recently.

The clothes she'd worn yesterday lay precariously on the floor by the open armoire where Giselle kept her unusual wardrobe of nothing but black. Empty hangers jangled against each other. Jon could smell Madison's scent in the air. She hadn't been gone long.

"No matter what you do, don't let her out of your sight again."

Lydia Colter had tried to warn him. He hoped to heaven Madison had slipped out for a bucket of ice or to arrange breakfast. He glanced at the dainty chock on the night stand. No, not breakfast. Lunch, maybe.

It was nearly 11:00 a..m. Giselle's rendezvous had been scheduled for noon. He'd slept all morning. Some protector he was!

He plucked a handful of keys from the pocket of his jacket. The keys to the rental car, plus Giselle's keys to the Villa, the Metropole, and the Chateau. Madison needed those keys to go anywhere beyond walking distance, and she needed the room key to return. Instead, she'd left the keys behind, left them where Jon couldn't miss them.

A sliver of silver in his jacket pocket caught his eye. With a dread sinking into his gut, Jon reached for the curved edge. Even before he touched it, he knew she'd left the Project Andromeda disk with him for safekeeping.

She wasn't coming back. She'd lied. She'd left him.

Jon stalked to the phone and, with only a moment's difficulty, dialed the OSI's office at Eglin. "Austin Wait, please," he grated out. "It's Jon Colter."

"Why aren't you back here with that disk?" Wait yelled without bothering to ask how the weather was or if Madison was alive.

"Madison's gone."

"What?"

"She's gone. I woke up this morning, and she was gone."

"They took her. Goddamn it, I knew this would happen!"

Jon's gaze settled on an empty spot on the wall of knives. The sickle she'd admired last night was gone. If she couldn't take Willpower with her, she'd take the next best thing, a replica of an ancient weapon that seemed to call her name.

"I think she left on her own. She left the disk with me."

"You've got it?"

"Yeah." Jon turned it over with his fingers. "You've got to help her. She would never have left the disk behind if she weren't in real trouble."

"Listen, Colter, and listen good. Get on the next plane back. I want that disk in my possession by nightfall."

Obviously Wait hadn't heard him right. "As soon as I find Madison—"

"Now!"

"But what about Madison?" She could be in danger. She could be dead.

"Your job is to get that disk back here. With or without Madison Steele. We cannot let that information get into the wrong hands."

"I agree, but I can't." He wouldn't leave Madison behind. All Wait cared about was getting another feather in his professional cap. The job was more important than the people he sacrificed. If Madison died in the process, that was too damned bad for her. "Can't you send someone to pick up the disk?"

Wait cursed long and loud. "Where exactly are you?"

"The Chateau Frontenac in Quebec City. Giselle has a suite here.

We figured this place would be as safe as any to spend the night."

"You're calling from her suite? Get out of there, Colter. Get out now."

"Giselle's in custody. It's not like she's going to—"

"She escaped."

Jon dropped the disk. He picked it up with shaky fingers and tucked it into his pocket. He couldn't imagine anyone getting away from a pitbull like Austin Wait. "When?" he asked lamely.

"During the night. We had her in the hospital with a guard at the door. She had two arms in casts and a wrapped ankle, but she still managed to get away without anyone knowing. Someone thought they saw a man matching Owen Plummer's description, but you know how eyewitness accounts are—twelve witnesses see twelve different things."

"You think they're on their way back here?" Madison had planned to substitute herself for Giselle and meet Owen Plummer at noon. If Plummer didn't show at rue du Tre'sor, maybe Madison would hurry back to the suite.

"Possibly. Look, this line's probably bugged. The whole suite's probably bugged."

Jon swallowed hard. What had he said aloud to Madison that he didn't mind the whole world hearing? He'd told her how he felt about her. He'd provided deadly ammo for anyone trying to get to Madison through him. Giselle had taken great care to prevent electronic eavesdropping on the Villa. He crossed his sweaty fingers that she'd done the same here.

Wait sighed as if none of it made any difference. "The man at Giselle's, the one who killed Beatrice Harper and tried to kill the rest of you, his name is Tremaric. He's one of the Sleeping Dogs."

Giselle had double-crossed them by selling Project Andromeda to two other bidders. The same group responsible for occasional acts of bio-weapon terrorism.

"Listen, Colter. There's an Interpol agent in Montreal. I trust him. Get to Montreal and call me. I'll put you in touch when I hear from you."

"But what about Madison?"

"You can't wait for her. Get to Montreal and get rid of that disk. If they don't already know you have it, you've got a chance."

"But Madison—"

"Colter, if you don't move now, you'll die. Go! Now!"

He clenched his jaws. "I won't go without Madison."

"If it will make you feel any better, I'll come get her myself. Now go!"

Jon dropped the phone into its cradle. He turned too fast. His head spun and he lost his balance, bumping into the other armoire, the one that shelved Giselle's state-of-the-art computer system. The blank screen sprang to life, courtesy of a screen saver deactivated by the sudden bump.

Jon collapsed into the desk chair and stared at the screen. The sentences emblazoned black on gray might yield some clue. He clicked on the "back" button, then again, then again. Madison must have stayed up all night playing with Internet search engines. The keywords *time travel* had spawned several dozen hits, leading her to a long file: *The Book of Enoch.*

It would only take a minute to see what she'd found. Only a minute.

CHAPTER EIGHT

"How many times do I have to kill you?"

Madison froze at the whisper. The man was right behind her, close enough she could feel the warmth of his cheek on hers through the hood of her black velvet cape. With her left hand, she pulled the hood closer to her throat. With her right hand, she gripped the wooden handle of the razor-sharp sickle. It fit well in her palm. She took a deep breath.

"Don't turn around."

She didn't.

Quebec City seemed extraordinarily clean, both of litter and crime. Here in the crowded, narrow alley known as rue du Tre'sor, the morning sunshine seeped between the striped canopies to the gray cobblestone floor. Artists, perched on step stools, pointed to their spotlighted sketches and paintings of Quebec's castles and battlefields and jabbered on in French to bewildered tourists. With so many people elbowing their way through the alley, Madison felt safe. Even with Owen Plummer pressing against her back.

"What do you want?"

"You know what I want."

She clutched the cape at her throat. Even in Giselle's long, black sweater, black leggings, and black ankle boots, she felt the chill of an autumn breeze on her cheeks. "There's a nice selection of postcard paintings of the old Citadel fort over there," she said. "Would you like me to recommend one?"

He grabbed her right arm, and Madison gave a little cry of pain. His grip went to the bone. The chill of a blade touched her cheek in warning.

"Let go of me or I'll scream."

"I'll slit your throat before you open your mouth."

Not without a fight, she decided. She was right-handed. She didn't know if she could stab him in the heart with her left hand, but his grip rendered the better choice of hands useless. She discreetly released the hood of her cape and changed hands. The hood fell to her shoulders, catching on the thick braid at her neck.

"You're not Villemaire. No wonder you're not—I said, don't turn around!—no wonder you're not dead. What are you doing wearing her clothes?"

Madison studied their shadows on the wall. He seemed taller than she remembered. If she could twist around and plunge the sickle below his rib cage and upward. Oh, there would be witnesses, but Delilah would be safe. Freedom—life itself—would be worth it to keep her daughter out of the hands of a time-traveling hit man like Owen Plummer.

"Who says they're her clothes? I've been told I look good in black."

"Good. You can be buried in it. I know her clothes. That cape was in her closet."

Madison writhed sideways and caught a glimpse of his face. It wasn't Owen Plummer. A shudder ran the length of her spine. The man who'd shot at them. The one who'd chased Jon and her to the airport. She steadied her breaths.

"You should have slept in her bed," he continued. "That would have saved me the trouble of this conversation."

She'd left Jon sound asleep on top of the covers. "And if I had?"

"I dusted Villemaire's sheets with bath powder. The kind that absorbs through the pores. Virtually untraceable in an autopsy."

Oh, God. She'd been briefed on different kinds of biological weapons, including the more innovative variety. She had to get back to Room 402. Back to Jon.

"Let's take a walk," he whispered. "I hate crowds."

"I kind of like them myself."

He squeezed her arm again, sending a shooting pain all the way to her fingernails. If he got her alone, he'd kill her. Still, his grip gave her no choice. If she screamed for help, he'd slit her throat. She'd die either way, but she'd buy time first.

He guided her harshly out of the busy alley and onto the cobbled sidewalk. Enough people roamed the street to make escape possible, particularly between the little sidewalk cafes that had seemed so romantic last night when she hadn't had a killer escorting her. Pigeons fluttered out of the way as Madison and the man pressed toward an opening in the wall.

An underground parking lot. Or maybe an alley leading to another street or the service entrance of one of the quaint inns or restaurants. In any case, dark and damp and built of gray bricks and mortar. Too much like an Old Quebec tomb for her taste.

Madison walked faster, aiming her steps at a small park beyond the whole in the wall. The family picnicking on the grass near the statue of a war hero provided an air of security. Instead, the man pushed her into the cold shadows. She stumbled and fell into the wall rather than catch herself with her left hand and betray the sickle in her fist.

"Give me the disk."

"What disk?"

Without warning, she elbowed him in the stomach. His knife clattered across the cobblestones. The blade was new and shiny, maybe two inches wide. He'd traded in his gun for a knife, probably the fastest weapon he could buy in a strange city. She turned to run.

He shoved her cheek against the wall. The stones were gritty, icy. Her cheek stung. His huge hand squashed against her temple. She couldn't even see him. "I know you have it."

"Maybe Giselle's got it."

"I downloaded her computer while she was in the States. She didn't have it then. My friends in the OSI tell me she didn't have it when she was picked up. That means you've got it."

Friends in the OSI? Who? Austin Wait? The man was lying. He'd say anything to frighten her. That was his negotiation style.

"If I give it to you, you'll kill me in this...this alley."

"I could kill you and take it off your body." His hot breath on her ear sent chills down her neck. "Or I could slit your wrists and fuck you while you bleed to death and then take the disk off your body. Which would you prefer?"

"How about 'none of the above'?"

"Yes," he said. "Good choice. Blood on my coat will attract attention. We'll do this the quiet way."

He released her arm but slammed her entire body against the wall with his and held her there. The breath knocked out of her, Madison nearly dropped the sickle. He was so much bigger!

He snapped a leather glove onto one hand and drove his fingers deep into her mouth. He dug his thumb into the indention between her throat and the artery that throbbed with every heartbeat. She would have bitten his fingers off if she could have, but all she could do was gag and pray he wouldn't dislocate her jaw.

He wrapped his other arm around her, a thin vial in his fist like the kind the cosmetics clerks at the mall give out as free cologne samples. With his thumb, he popped off the plastic stopper.

"Drink it," he commanded.

Madison fought to turn her head, but the gloved fingers triggered her gag reflex. The liquid was clear but the rotting smell told her it wasn't water.

"Come on. It'll be quick, baby. I promise."

She tried to tell him to go to hell, but she gagged again.

"One drop. That's all it will take. Just pretend it's sweat on your upper lip and it's rolling down into your mouth and you swallow."

"Nnn—-" She tried to squirm out of his hold. Something hard pressed into her lower back. Either a gun or an erection. She preferred the gun.

"Don't worry, baby. I'll even make it fun for you. As soon as you swallow, I'm going to push you up harder against that wall and pull those leotards down and stick it in you real good. You'll be coming as you're leaving this world." He laughed. "Should be a lot of fun for both of us as long as I remember not to kiss you."

Madison let her whole body go limp. Let him think she'd given up or given in. Hell, let him think she couldn't wait to die in convulsions he could confuse with orgasms.

He must have felt her relax. His grip eased.

In a fury, Madison stabbed backward with the sickle, through the cape, not particularly caring what she hit, but hoping....

CHAPTER NINE

"And it came to pass when the children of men had multiplied that in those days were born unto them beautiful and comely daughters. And the angels, the children of the heaven, saw and lusted after them, and said to one another: 'Come, let us choose us wives from among the children of men and beget us children."

Jon stared at the computer screen and gulped. It couldn't be! He'd spent his whole life telling himself his mother was a raving lunatic, yet the black type on the gray background, a translation of one of the Dead Sea scrolls, substantiated his mother's wild rantings about reincarnation, angels, and—worse—interdimensional time travel.

He closed the file and stomped the red button on the surge protector. Maybe he'd get a chance to read all of *The Book of Enoch* when he returned to Eglin. Jon slipped on his shoes, then his jacket. He threw dirty clothes into the canvas bag and wrapped it over his shoulder. Once more, he patted down the keys in his jacket pocket and the disk in the button pocket of his pants. He had to leave. Now.

A knock thundered at the door.

Too late.

He fumbled with the latches on the window. With a huff, he managed to open the window wide enough to squeeze through. He poked his head out the opening.

Please, please let there be a fire escape.

Sunlight blinded him. No fire escape. Nothing to grab onto outside but the guttering leading down from the steep roof. He dangled one leg out the window in search of a firm footing. He dropped the canvas bag of clothes out the window and watched it grow smaller in the distance.

"Jon!" More pounding. "Open up!"

"Madison?" Grabbing an antique chair for balance, he pulled back his foot. The chair went over with a tumble. The slats of its back crunched beneath his shoes as he lurched for the door. "Madison!"

"Jon? Open up!"

The latches wouldn't turn fast enough. He fumbled with the chain, nearly tearing it out of the wall. He gave the door knob a desperate jerk.

Madison fell through, almost into his arms. Wild eyed, breathless. Her cheek scraped and bloody. Shaken as he'd never seen her.

"You're all right," she gasped out. "Thank God. You're all right."

He reached for her damaged cheek. "I've got to get you out of here."

A gloved hand punched through the open door. It seized Madison's throat. She lost her footing.

In an instant, Jon recognized the man from Giselle's villa. Tremaric. One of the Sleeping Dogs.

Jon grabbed the door jamb. With all his strength, he kicked the son of a bitch's knee cap.

Tremaric howled and let go. Madison tangled her boot around his, tripping him as she pulled away. The gloved hand caught her long braid and jerked her back hard. Her head hit the doorjamb with a thud.

Instinctively, Jon slammed his shoulder against the door. It closed on the braid and almost on the gloved fingers. He bolted the door. After what seemed an eternity, he managed to get the chain into place as if it would do more good than the other locks.

The door shuddered under a blow from the other side. Jon leaned against it and prayed.

Madison was pinned like a dog on a tight leash. Her chest heaved under the black cape. He imagined her heart raced like a trapped animal's. She closed her eyes tightly to shut out the pain.

"There's another way out," Jon said. "We can go out the window and down the gutters. I know you're not afraid of heights." Even before he'd seen her on the fire escape the night Roxie had died, Jon had never known Madison to be afraid of much of anything.

She shook her head, wincing at the movement. She couldn't move.

The door shuddered under another blow.

"You've got the disk?" she whispered.

"Yeah."

"Then go. Take it and go. And Delilah—" Opening her eyes, Madison clutched at his sleeve. "—Swear to me you'll keep her safe."

Like he'd kept Madison safe? He should never have taken his eyes off her.

"Hang on," he said. "I'm going to open the door. When I do, you run for the window."

"No. You can't. He'll come through."

"If he's got a gun, it won't matter much anyway. He'll shoot us through the door."

"He won't risk shooting the disk."

"You sure?"

Madison swallowed. "No."

"Then I'm going to open the door, and you're going to run."

"You can't take the chance. Just take the disk and go. I'll keep him here."

"Now you look here, L. Madison Steele. Whether you like it or not, we're a team. I will not leave you. I will never leave you. I'm not your old boyfriend, Lieutenant Tim or whatever his name was. I will be by your side for the rest of your life. For the rest of eternity if that's what it takes to keep you safe. Now, I'm going to open this door, and you're going to run for the window. Got it?"

"Wait. There's another way." She held up the sickle. Giselle's sickle. Blood ran down the curved blade and onto her hand, staining her fingers strawberry red.

Good God, she'd stabbed someone! Tremaric, he hoped.

"My hair. Cut it off."

"But—"

"Do it!"

Jon sawed through the braid, strands of blonde frizzing away from the blade as he sliced through it. Free and in a dead run for the window, she tugged him along and took back the sickle, tying it to her wide black belt, and tucked it inside her cape as if she'd done the same many times before. He had a feeling she had.

The door shook. He felt it in the floor.

"I'm not sure the gutter will hold both of us," she told him as she leaned out the window. "You go first."

"No, you."

"You've got the disk. I've got the sickle. Now go!"

Keeping his eyes on Madison, he obeyed. He both climbed and slid but didn't look down until he reached the bottom. Military boots weren't meant for scaling French castles, but they'd do in a pinch.

Madison fared almost as well in Giselle's black boots with soles fit to hike in. The black cape flew out behind her as she used her boot-clad knees to slide most of the length of the gutter, interrupted occasionally by a rivet or clasp. She jumped off before she hit the ground.

"Let's go!" she commanded.

Snatching up the canvas bag, Jon followed, amazed at her strides. She doubled back through the main entrance to the courtyard where she'd parked the night before. By the time he dug the car keys out of his pocket, Madison stood on the passenger side of the car, anxiously pumping the latch to no avail.

Once inside, he jammed the keys into the ignition and steered in a lopsided circle until they could clear the other cars. Tremaric appeared at the stone doorway. Pressing one red hand into his thigh, he limped forward, reaching inside his coat with his other hand. Something hit the back fender. Jon punched the accelerator and peeled out of the courtyard at a dangerous pace.

"I missed," Madison murmured as they sped out of the city.

"What?"

"I-I hooked him in the thigh. Muscle, I think. I hurt him pretty bad, but I missed the femoral artery."

He ventured a glance in her direction. All color had left her cheeks. Her fingers trembled as she clapped her hands to her neck. The braid was gone, leaving a jagged mess of curls and one waist-length tendril that had escaped both braid and blade. Her face contorted like an amputee's suffering phantom pains.

"It'll grow back," he said. If he could keep her alive, it would.

"He tried to kill me." Her frown deepened. Her cheeks scrunched in anger.

Jon smiled. Tremaric had tried to kill her and she was offended. Better than being scared witless, he supposed.

"You're lucky he didn't. His name is Tremaric. Austin Wait says he's one of the Sleeping Dogs."

"You talked to Austin?"

"I'm sorry. I had to get help somewhere."

She stared through the windshield, squinting into the sunshine. "Dogs."

"What?"

"Dogs. Giselle had a file on her hard drive."

"Giselle escaped. Plummer may have been involved. Wait wasn't sure."

Madison didn't seem to hear him. "The file had been erased. That-that goon erased it. *Dogs.doc* was the name of file. I think it may have been about the Sleeping Dogs. And that means the other files...." She turned to stare at him. "*Time.doc* wasn't a utility file. It was about time travel. Enoch's Gate. The Sleeping Dogs know about Enoch's Gate."

Jon floored the accelerator. The black Cadillac coming up fast behind him might have been a coincidence, but he had a feeling, oh, a feeling he couldn't shake. He couldn't explain it, but he could feel the coldness creeping up behind them. Like Death.

"Can you read French better than you can speak it?"

She nodded. "Reasonably well. I can't comprehend it fast enough to communicate."

"Can you read road signs?"

She shrugged. "'Rue' means 'street.' Lessee.... Uh...depends. Why?"

"We're going to Montreal. It's a couple of hours west of here. There's an Interpol agent who'll meet us there. We'll be crossing the St. Lawrence. There's a big bridge up ahead."

Madison straightened. "I see it."

"You'll have to help me look for my turn-off. Don't look back, but

Tremaric's on our tail. We can't screw up."

"Okay. Yeah. I see it." She squinted at a sign emblazoned with a French word and *Montreal*. "You need to get in the other lane."

The bridge loomed ahead, its arches of metal high against a blue sky. An elaborate trestle ran parallel to the bridge. Three lanes of traffic moved with them, three moved against them, plus turning lanes. Behind them, Tremaric closed in.

"Great," Madison muttered under her breath.

"What's wrong?"

"I never can remember if *droite* means 'left' or if it's *gauche*. Go back to the lane you were in."

"Christ." He checked his side mirror and ignored the blasts of horns as he crossed two lanes of traffic.

"There. Get in the turn lane."

He edged his way into the lane. In the rear view mirror, a black Cadillac did the same. It stayed consistently two cars behind, mirroring his moves.

"I had this little ditty in high school so I could remember on tests. Let's see. 'I *droite* to the right and I *gauche* to the left.' Or was it 'I *droite* to the left, and I *gauche* to the right'?"

"Madison!"

"Don't turn! Go back to where you were!"

"Goddamn it." At the last possible moment, he veered out of the turn lane and into the solid wall of traffic in the on-going lane. He couldn't bear to look. A bus beside him honked furiously but let him in anyway. No wonder foreigners looked at Americans as such idiots. "Will you make up your mind?" he yelled at Madison.

She slumped down in her seat and gazed out the passenger window. The black Caddy hadn't made it out of the turn lane. Traffic beside and behind it had forced it to turn and head in the opposite direction they were going. Madison's screwed-up sense of direction hadn't cost them anything and had probably helped. It would take precious, long minutes for Tremaric to turn around and find them again. The Sleeping Dog was headed into the rural Gaspe' Peninsula, and they were headed toward Montreal and safety.

"Sorry," he said, reaching to pat Madison's knee. "Sorry I yelled at you. Women aren't as good at a sense of direction as men are."

"It's not my sense of direction that's goofed up. It's my ability to remember foreign languages I haven't thought twice about since high school."

"Maybe it's both."

"No, it's definitely my language skills." She sighed heavily. "Montreal is to the west, and my sense of direction tells me we're headed east."

CHAPTER TEN

"Why are we stopping?" Madison asked.

Jon steered toward an exit ramp. He hadn't said a word in the two hours since he'd realized they were indeed traveling east, parallel to the St. Lawrence Seaway. She'd stared out at the flatlands and the hint of hills ahead as well as the distant dark line of mountains on the opposite shore. His jaw set, his eyes straight ahead, he had driven like demon. No wonder men under the age of twenty-five suffered such huge insurance premiums.

"Jon? Why are we stopping? Talk to me."

Please, God. Anything but the silent treatment.

"Gotta get gas."

An unobtrusive sign announced the next town, Riviere-du-Loup. It seemed quaint enough. A nice spot for a picnic under different circumstances. Not that it mattered. If Madison had been able to tell her right from her left, they would have been in Montreal in the time it had taken to reach this small, riverside city. They could already have contacted the Interpol agent Jon had mentioned and gotten the Project Andromeda disk and themselves to safety. Even if she hadn't managed to find Owen Plummer and stop him before he hurt the people she loved.

"I'm sorry," Madison said again.

Jon answered by veering silently into a combination gas station and convenience store. If only he'd hum a Rod Stewart song. Perhaps then she could get a grip on what was going on inside his head.

"Jon? Aren't you going say anything?"

"Watch for black Cadillacs." He slammed the driver's door and headed for a pump that looked like something out of the 1950's.

With a sigh, Madison leaned her head against the passenger window and hid her face behind one hand. A month ago, she wouldn't have cared if he spoke to her or not. A week ago, she would've told herself it was for the best. Not now. Though she'd tried not to, she'd come to depend on Jon. His youth, his innocence, his warmth fed the lifeline to her. She needed him.

And then, for a split second, she stood in a cemetery somewhere, three fresh graves at her feet. A hint of rain in the air. The smell of carnations. An unusually warm day for November.

Then the vision vanished, as quickly as it had come, leaving with it the ache of dread in her bones. The vision had been nothing more than a flash of memory, yet in that brief second, she knew she'd lost Mama, Daddy, and Delilah to the Sleeping Dogs. And that Owen Plummer had somehow been involved.

Terror caught in her throat. She clutched at her chest. With a desperate grab, she found the door latch and pulled it open. She tumbled out onto the stained sidewalk, gasping, choking. The cool air hit her face, then sunlight. The awful weight in the pit of her stomach dissipated though a twinge of sickening remained.

"Madison?" Jon bolted across the asphalt from the store exit to the pumps. He dropped to the cement beside her.

Instead of answering, she coughed and sputtered.

"Here, here, drink this. I got some juice for you." Bottles clinked inside the brown bag in the fold of his arms. He pulled out a small bottle of orange juice, shook it up, twisted off the lid, and held the bottle to her lips. "Drink."

She gulped down the cold liquid. Perspiration stung on her forehead. She turned her head to decline the rest of the juice. "I'm okay."

"What happened?" The color drained from his face as he tried to guess. "Did Tremaric inject you with anything?" Jon took her jaw in his firm hand and tilted her face upward to his. He studied her face, concern in his eyes. She thought his chin trembled.

"I'm okay. That bastard didn't inject me with anything. He did try to make me drink some kind of toxin, but I got away first."

"Did he touch you? Did he spill any toxin on you? Some toxins can be absorbed through the skin. You don't know how deadly those things can be."

Oh, she knew. "If he had, I wouldn't be talking to you now."

"You're sure you're okay?"

She nodded. "Jon?" It seemed silly now. "For the past couple of months, my dreams have been really wild. Especially these last few days."

He drew back, barely enough for her to notice. "What do you mean by 'wild'?"

"Sometimes the dreams are s-o-o-o vivid. Disturbing. I try to tell myself they're dreams, but they seem like something more."

Jon shrugged and tucked the bottle of juice back inside the paper bag. He didn't look her in the eye. "You've been under a lot of stress. Sometimes that affects dreams."

"It's not just dreams. Not anymore. Sometimes it's like I'm there. And sometimes it's more like a memory. Little flashes and glimpses. I'm getting it more and more."

He rose, uncapped the gas tank to the little red wagon, and shoved the gas nozzle into the opening. Invisible vapors wavered upward. Fresh petroleum assaulted her nose. "You're tired," Jon said. "Did you sleep at all last night?"

"A little. The dreams woke me."

"What kind of dreams?" His voice broke.

"I was leading an army. Thousands of men. Tens of thousands." She leaned against the cool metal of the car door. "You were there, too, Jon. My right-hand man. My best friend."

The hardness melted in his face. Jon winked at her from the gas pump as if to say "Why, naturally!" She wouldn't tell him she'd seen him in this same dream before. She wouldn't tell him Jon had died, that she hadn't been able to save him.

"One of my men had betrayed me. Stole this green rock I took with me into battle. Chrysoprase, I think it was. It brought out the power in me. This man, he was a trusted soldier. A general, maybe. Not as trusted as you, but I was really pissed at his betrayal. So I hunted him down and dragged him back for justice." She shut her eyes against a flash of memories. "There were these two trees. Big trees. I had my men tie their tops to the ground in such a way that their trunks overlapped. The man who betrayed me, I had him bound head to toe to where the trees crossed. I walked over and looked him in the eyes and I said, 'I will always be the better man.' And he looked at me and his eyes were so filled with hate and somehow I knew that he was really Beatrice and he swore he'd have his revenge." She opened her eyes. With the light in her face, it was hard to see.

Jon stared at her as if he'd heard the story before. Or been there.

"I gave the order. Two of my generals drew their swords. They cut through the ropes, and the trees flew apart." She shut her eyes and exhaled slowly, seeing again the flourish of leaves and bone and blood. She'd stood over the carnage, triumphant and angry and wounded. Execution could not suffice for betrayal.

Jon was quiet. Too quiet. He replaced the hose and turned back to her, taking his time.

"When I woke up, I'd been asleep maybe an hour. After that, I couldn't sleep."

"No wonder you're having such weird dreams. You've slept less than an hour in the past day and a half? Lack of sleep can cause dementia, you know. You'd better be careful before you start hallucinating."

"No. No, no, no, Jon. This is different. It's not weird dreams because I'm tired. I've been tired before. I've never had nightmares like these. Why would I dream this kind of stuff?"

He leaned against the fender. "Your dream is perfectly reasonable if you think about it. Beatrice was one of your right-hand people. You depended on her, you trusted her. She betrayed you. That breach of trust translated into a mutiny from one of your soldiers."

"But the gore. How could I have ordered that?"

"You didn't. It was just a dream, okay?" He flicked her chin affectionately. "Think about what's happened to you in the past week or so. Roxie's death. Austin Wait babbling on about incidences of biological terrorism. Giselle Villemaire and Tremaric pointing guns at you."

"And Owen Plummer."

"And Owen Plummer," Jon agreed. "Lack of sleep. From babies being abandoned on your doorstep. Having your clearance pulled. Getting shot at. Then seeing Beatrice up close and personal in the bushes at Giselle's villa. Why wouldn't you have violent dreams? Why wouldn't anyone?"

"But that was all violence done to me. I'm not the violent type."

"You stabbed Tremaric in the thigh, and you don't think you could be violent if you had to be?"

Of course she could be. She would have to be to protect the people she loved. Self-defense. All justifiable. "I may be a fighter, but I'm not an executioner."

"No? You're holding yourself responsible for the whole Project Andromeda situation, including the way Beatrice took advantage of you. You think you could have stopped it all, and because she's dead and Roxie's dead, it's somehow your fault. It's a wonder you didn't dream you were executing Roxie, too. That's how you feel, isn't it?"

She cringed. "That makes sense, I suppose. I wish all my dreams made that much sense. Jon? Do you think I might be psychic?"

He glared at her. "Not you, too! I've heard this from my mom all my life. You're tired. That's all. After a good, long nap, you'll be as sane as the rest of us."

"But how else can I explain all these weird dreams? I don't even know what chrysoprase is. And the flashes of things that feel like they're going to happen."

"For what it's worth, my mom says we're all a little bit psychic. I don't buy that, though. I think we use only 8 percent of our brains to calculate all the possible outcomes we're likely to encounter when we make a decision and the other 92 percent is unexplored territory. We have a gazillion thoughts below the conscious level in that part of our brains and when something actually does happen, we think we've thought of it before. And maybe we have. If we've thought of all the possibilities out there, then yes, we do know the future. We may not know which future, but we know it."

Madison blinked back the image of the three graves in Georgia. "Don't get me wrong. I don't want to have psychic visions. I don't want to know the future. Knowing that bad things are going to happen takes the joy out of living."

"Who says they're going to happen? There are many possible futures. If you have the chance to glimpse one that's bad, won't that give you the information you need to change course and keep the bad from happening?"

"God, I hope so."

The vision of the graves had something to do with Tremaric and the Sleeping Dogs. They were responsible somehow. An act of revenge, maybe. Owen Plummer was a part of it, though how she couldn't guess.

She'd foiled the plans of the Sleeping Dogs. In time, Project Andromeda might render useless their fledgling biological terrorism attempts. She'd kept an international terrorist group from America's best defense against biological weapons. Her. A rank amateur. A little farm girl from rural Georgia who'd lost her innocence to a gypsy-hearted man determined to celebrate first times without any regard for the consequences. She knew only one way to keep Tremaric from taking revenge. She felt it in the pit of her stomach. Only one way to save her family. Both Tremaric and Owen Plummer had to die.

Whether she did the killing herself didn't really matter. Jon would probably do it if she asked him to, but she couldn't destroy his youth like that. This was her fight, and she'd never been good at delegating.

What would it be like to kill a man? She could tell herself it was self-defense. It was. Defense of herself, her daughter, her parents, the civilized world. She'd hit a dog one night while driving to and from graduate school classes. At the time, she was eight months pregnant with Delilah. The road had been a lonely stretch, the dog a stray. She'd decided against stopping, but it was too late. She'd already heard the crunch of bone beneath her tires and seen the upturned, jerking legs in the red glow of her taillights. The guilt lingered for days. Maybe for years, since she did still think of it now and again. But for men bent on striking down innocents, whether with their laser guided guns or e.coli-infested hamburgers in school lunchrooms, she had less compassion than for an injured cur.

What could she do? The American courts of justice too often let killers go free. International opinion was too easily overcome by hatred for whichever side had retaliated last. No one would stop such men. That was the problem. Men like the Sleeping Dogs had access to the cruelest of weapons—strange viruses that lay dormant inside vaccinations for childhood diseases, micro-organisms that thrived on sweaty palms and paper money, flesh-eating bacteria designed to spread quickly through daycare centers—yet everyone would turn their heads and refuse to believe such senseless hatred existed or that anyone could be capable of such horrors. Even after the body count rose, people would still turn their heads as if not seeing it would make it less real. The realities of biological warfare were too awful to believe, so the world of innocents would either convince themselves of some elaborate hoax or pretend the media had, for once, failed them.

No one else would act. No one but her. L. Madison Steele had to be the one, no matter the personal cost.

"Madison?"

"Huh?" With Jon's strong grip, she pulled herself to her feet. "What's wrong?"

"You zoned out on me. You weren't having another, um, vision, were you?"

"No. Just thinking. Exploring all the possibilities."

"Good. The sooner I get you back in the car, the sooner you can take a nap and get this psychic crap out of your system."

She eased back into the car, careful to stow the bag of juice and cola bottles at her feet. Jon was there for her. For now. For as long as it would take.

She twisted in her seat to watch him circle the car. Then she saw the black Cadillac on the horizon.

CHAPTER ELEVEN

Jon punched the accelerator as he turned the corner. The little red wagon was barely small enough to fit into the alley. The Cadillac behind them turned too quickly and tore off its right headlight. Jon watched in the mirror as the oversized car backed up and tried again, failed again.

In the past ten minutes, they had already shot through a series of alleys, nooks, crannies, and backroads. Definitely better to deal with Tremaric here in the small city than out on the two-lane highway which was apparently the only paved route through the Gaspe' Peninsula.

Madison sat beside him, pale, wringing her hands. Thank God she wasn't like girls he'd dated in the past. If so, she would have been a blithering idiot. Hysterical. Screaming, "I don't want to die! I don't want to die! Watch out for that curb! Be careful of that stop sign!" and generally getting on his nerves.

He floored the gas pedal. It wouldn't take long for Tremaric to figure out where the alley led to and take an adjacent street to the one they were on and cut them off.

They spun out onto another street, narrowly missing an oncoming car. He overshot the road, hit the curb, and bumped back onto the asphalt. He swerved again before regaining control of the car. The little red wagon grazed a yellow road sign with the word *chutes* written in black.

Chutes. Tunnels. Alleys. Sounded like a good enough hiding spot to him.

A small electrical tower loomed a block ahead. Another yellow sign waited at the next intersection, this one with an arrow pointing to the right.

"What does 'chutes' mean?" When Madison didn't answer, he glanced over at her. "'Chutes.' What does it mean in French?"

She shook her head. "I have no idea. The only kind of chutes I can think of are laundry chutes."

He glimpsed the black car in the rear view mirror. "I'm going to lose that asshole if it's the last thing I do." He hoped it wasn't.

Jon swerved right at the intersection, then a quick left. At the next yellow sign, he took another right. The pavement seemed to drop off underneath them as the road curved sharply around into a U-turn. He slammed on brakes. A few more feet and they would have gone through a wrought-iron fence and into a ravine of smooth rock and splashing water. A fine mist settled on the windshield.

"Waterfalls," he said over the dull roar. "I guess that's what 'chutes' means."

He slammed the car in reverse and parked in the shadows near the edge of the small cliff overlooking the gully. A killer driving into the parking lot wouldn't see them there, not until he was on their bumper. Jon waited and held his breath. If Tremaric found them there, they'd be safer in the car trying to make a quick getaway and get past him.

The route they'd followed had taken them off the beaten path. Maybe Tremaric assumed they'd turned back toward Montreal or at least back to the main thoroughfare through Riviere-du-Loup. Madison sat and wrung her hands but didn't speak. "What would you like to do?" he asked as politely as if he'd asked her to share a cocktail with him after work at the Officers' Club. He hated to come right out and say, "Tell me what the hell to do."

Madison reached for the door handle. "I can't stand this. I can't stand staying here like a sitting duck! Let's go!"

"I think we'd be safer here in the car. This place is kinda, well, secluded. I don't think I would have found it if I hadn't come this way by accident. I think we're safer here than back out there."

"Okay, fine! We'll stay here, but let's at least get out of the car. I've got that cooped up feeling, like I'm in a cage or something." She shivered. "You know I hate to sit still."

She was out of the car before he was. By the time he reached the iron fence, she was holding on tightly to the top rail and leaning over into the rise of mist. Delicate droplets sparkled on her cheeks and in her hair. Glancing once over his shoulder, Jon slipped his arm around her.

"Madison? I'm worried about you."

"I feel...a little...a little sick."

"Can't blame you for being wobbly."

She heaved in a deep breath. Gripping the railing with bloodless fingers, she rocked back and forth. "I'm nauseated. Sick to the pit of my stomach like a swallowed a brick. Oh God, I think I'm going to be sick!"

Jon tossed another glance over his shoulder. They shouldn't be staying in one place too long. He cuddled her against him, rubbed her back a little, and finally let his hand rest on the small of her back. He had to fight to keep it steady. "You're going to be fine, Madison. Everything's going to be fine."

"Are you so sure?"

"Yes," he lied. "Positive. What I want to know is how Tremaric found us at that gas station. Last time we saw him, he was headed for Montreal. It should have taken him twenty minutes or so to turn around and head our way. How did he know we took the exit at Riviere-du-Loup? He wasn't behind us when we turned. I know how to make sure I'm not being followed." His father had taught him that back in high school during his summers at the militia's camp.

"How did you pay for the gas?"

"Credit card. I checked out a map back at the gas station, and there's not much ahead but trees and mountains. I figured we'd better save our money since we don't know quite where we'll end up."

"Credit card, huh? Then there's a record. Maybe Tremaric's a time traveler, too. It's real, you know. People can jump around in time, in different times."

He nodded. "Enoch's Gate."

"Last night after I had that dream about Beatrice, I couldn't sleep so I started messing around with the Internet on Giselle's computer. You won't believe with I found."

"The Book of Enoch."

She turned abruptly. "How did you—"

"You left the computer on. I checked the cache files."

"Did you read it? *The Book of Enoch?"*

"Scanned it mostly. I didn't have much time."

"Then you know what it was about."

"Yes." *The Book of Enoch* was a Dead Sea scroll found in 1947 in the cave of Qumran. The church fathers had elected to keep its contents hidden. Not the first time that had happened. In 325 A.D., the Church fathers had elected to omit reincarnation and human divinity from the Bible. The fact that the ancient manuscripts had been tampered with was confirmed in 553 A.D. by Pope Vigilius and the Second Council of Constantinople. The Church found its followers easier to control if they had but one chance at salvation. Even at its least disturbing, *The Book of Enoch* was a threat to over 1600 years of organized religion.

"Enoch didn't die, remember?" Madison laid an unsteady palm on his chest to balance herself. "He was taken up into heaven and stayed for a while and then he came back to teach everything he'd learned before he was taken up permanently. What he brought back with him was lessons about reincarnation and time travel. He said that there were portals in heaven. Gates. He could go through one and be on the other side of the stars. He could move through time and space through those gates. Jon, that's what Enoch's Gate was all about."

The project the Kennedy Administration had had Owen Plummer working on. Top secret project.

"Think about it, Lieutenant. Kennedy wanted to put a man on

the moon in ten years' time. With Enoch's Gate, they could travel anywhere they wanted. Time or space. Austin's sources said that Plummer was talented beyond his time. Maybe he was. Plummer must have gone back to the early '60s and allied himself with the Kennedy Administration. Would have made sense. That was during the Cuban missile crisis. If Plummer was a good American, he would have done whatever he could to help us out in the cold war."

"What makes you so sure Plummer wasn't in his own time back in the 60's?"

"Because no one knew about Enoch's Gate then. That's something that's come to light in the late 1990's. Many of those scrolls found in Qumran are still being translated. Plummer must come from a time when Enoch's Gate has been accessed. He's come back to change history."

"I didn't have a chance to read the entire file on the scrolls. Just the highlights."

A smile tugged one corner of her mouth upward. "You don't think time travel is a highlight?"

Reincarnation. That's what he'd considered the highlights. Enoch's explanation of angels reincarnating among men. "Didn't you see the part about reincarnation?"

"Oh yeah," she answered non-chalantly.

He laughed, a little of his nervousness slipping away. "You know, Madison, you're funny that way. I grew up around a woman who talked about reincarnation and past life regressions and psychic experiences and witchcraft. If you ask if she believed in ghosts, she'd say yes without thinking about it. I always found her wild theories impossible to believe. But with you, I would have thought that as analytical as you are, you'd demand proof before accepting such odd beliefs."

She shrugged. "Sometimes, I guess, you have to go by gut instinct. For some reason—and in spite of my Baptist upbringing—those ideas don't seem so odd to me. It's almost as if I've been there before."

"I guess I'm like the guy who has to climb the mountain to look for the truth. And when I get to the peak, you're already there. You have been all along."

Her grip tightened suddenly on the railing. She held on as if she might float up and fall over the side even though the laws of gravity would have to fail her first. "Oh, God. Oh God, I'm going to be sick."

He rubbed at the stubble on his cheek. "Did you have breakfast this morning?"

"A bite."

"Maybe that's making you sick."

"I don't think so." She clutched at her stomach.

"Was the juice okay? Maybe it was rancid."

"Juice was fine. It's more like a repulsion. I haven't felt this nauseated since I was three months—" She stopped short and clamped her hand over her mouth.

Since she was three months what? Pregnant? His knees ached and nearly buckled. *Pregnant?*

"Since I was three months into my graduate program and...and forgot to study for a major exam."

She didn't look at him. She wouldn't look at him. She was hiding something again, damn it.

Madison tilted her face back, eyes searching the base of the little cliff covered with yellowing shrubs and green ivy. He followed her gaze to the top, to where the water tumbled over the edge of the rocks into the ravine below them. A lean man stood silhouetted against the vivid blue sky. Feet apart, 60's style suit jacket flapping in the breeze, thoroughly modern gun in his right hand.

"Plummer," she whispered. She fumbled for the sickle secured to her waist, though what she thought she'd do with it or what use it was against a weapon with laser sites, Jon couldn't guess.

Owen Plummer touched something on his wrist. He stepped back. Then he shimmered out of existence.

CHAPTER TWEL VE

She wasn't sure what time it was. The drone of the rental car's engine and the sunshine on her face made it seem as if hours had passed while she slept. Jon was at the wheel, singing softly, "You're in my heart, you're in my soul...." She could smell his scent in the cramped car. She longed to sleep in his arms instead of curled up in the passenger seat.

Opening her eyes, she blinked into the light. Jon didn't notice. He stared intently at the road. Unaware of her surveillance, he pressed his cheek against his shoulder, first on one side and then the other. Then he curved his shoulders back until his spine cracked. He let out a contented sigh.

"Back hurting?" she asked.

"Hmmm. You're awake."

She stretched like a cat. Giselle's sweater was a little too long on her. If she didn't sit on the hem, the sleeves swallowed up her hands, even though she'd cuffed them several times. She'd shed the Cat-Woman boots on the way out of Riviere-du-Loup, but to be really comfortable, she longed for an old pair of jeans and a t-shirt. Jon's T-shirt especially, warm with his scent. At the last rest stop, they'd washed out the clothes in the canvas bag and let them dry in the sunny back seat.

"Have I been asleep long?" she asked with a yawn.

"Maybe an hour."

"Any sign of the black car?"

"None. Go back to sleep. You need your rest."

She shook her head and gazed out at the roadside. The landscape had changed. The St. Lawrence on the left had widened until she could no longer see the distant Canadian mountains in the haze. The occasional seal sunned on the rocky shore, sea spray squirting up from the rocks with every wave. The flatland had turned to autumn-forested hills and small cliffs disturbed only by quaint farmhouses and barns.

"I had the strangest dream."

The corner of his mouth quirked upward. "Who'd you dismember this time?"

"No, no. A good dream." She'd stood over the green hills in some ancient place and held her arm out to one side, just above her head. It wasn't her hand though. It was a man's hand, with the wrist and hand bound in dark cloth. Maybe leather. A magnificent falcon swooped out of the cloudless sky and landed on her wrist. It was more like a childhood memory than a dream. She had such a sense of pride in her bird.

She closed her eyes, seeing it all again. She must have been thinking of Delilah and her sparrows. Jon had joked about Madison being a mighty falconer and she'd turned his teasing into a dream. "Jon? Do you know anything about falcons?"

He gulped. "I've met a couple of falconers through my dad's group. Part of their survival-of-the-fittest paranoia. The falcon's been a symbol of power for many generations. The Egyptians called Ra their 'falcon-god of the heavens' because he could soar higher into the celestial realm than any other god. What do we call our F-16 fighter jets these days? Falcons."

"But why is a falcon so revered? Why not some other bird?"

"According to my dad's friends, falcons were very important to nomadic tribes in ancient times. The tribe depended on the falconer and his bird to find and catch the food they ate. It was a position of great responsibility. If the falcon—or the falconer—failed or died, the entire tribe would starve."

Madison nodded and turned to stare out the window. She didn't want to talk. The weight of the falconer's burden lay heavy on her shoulders, and she understood. His people depended on him. Every life in his tribe rested on his skills alone. The position was as noble as that of any self-sacrificing contracting officer intent on saving her people, no matter the cost.

"What else are you dreaming about?" Jon asked with apprehension. "Am I in any of these dreams?"

"No," she lied.

"Good." He sighed his relief.

"These dreams are different. I've never had dreams like these."

"Different how?"

"Usually my dreams are mish-mashes of what happened during the day or things on my mind or things I want to happen. In the past few days, they've been more about places I've never been and things I've never done. People I don't know. Or at least they don't look like people I know even if they are."

The other dreams had been more like a medley of memories, either of past or of future. In one dream, she had been trapped inside a burned-out church in what she thought was Italy. She was a man, a soldier, a leader of a rebel faction. She had to protect the children around her. Some were wounded. Some she recognized as engineers she'd worked with in the past few years, ones she'd helped get promoted. One of the wounded children was her father. She had to save them, but in the end, she couldn't. Her lone rifle was useless against Mussolini's men as they stormed the arched window over the altar.

In another dream, she was a woman riding the wilds of Scotland on her black horse. Her black cape and long hair flew out behind her as the wind struck her face. She raised her broadsword and ordered her men to follow her.

She must have had an affinity for weapons. She remembered spinning a sickle, large and fierce with a cord tied to the handle, over her purple-hooded head and under a cloudcast sky. It was meant for cutting herbs, for practicing Druid magick to honor the waning moon, and at the moment in her dream, for defending Avalon against invaders. She let go the cord and the blade sailed to its target.

A small dagger, more streamlined than the sickle she'd carried in dreams and reality, appeared in a different dream. Instead of tucking the dagger into her belt, Madison had slipped it into her garter under a ball gown of white organza. Her mother, who somehow was Lydia Colter, chastised her for the calluses on her hands and for not taking better care of herself. Madison couldn't make the woman understand. What were calluses compared to Southern soldiers dying so far from home? Without a word, she laced the hood of her black velvet cape under her chin and walked away. If she was successful, General Lee would have the information to defeat the Yankee invaders. Virginia would have its freedom.

"Would you prefer I dreamed of you?" Madison asked.

"I'm not sure. I guess it depends on what I'm doing in the dream. What are you usually doing in these dreams?"

"Fighting. Always fighting. Trying to protect my people." She preferred dreams in which she was unarmed. In the past few days, her dreams had armed her with rifles, swords, daggers, sickles, and even a razor-taloned falcon.

"I can't believe I'm saying this, but we should get my mother to regress you. Given your martyr complex, I wouldn't be surprised if you were Jesus."

She sniffed indignantly at the blasphemy. "Oh, I don't think there's any need to worry about that. And I'm not interested in being regressed." Not that she was worried about discovering she was Jesus in another lifetime. She was more concerned with finding out she'd been Attilla the Hun or Vlad the Impaler. "I prefer to be known for who I am in the present, not who I was in the past."

Deep in thought, he caught his lower lip between his teeth. "Normally I would agree, but if there is such as thing as reincarnation, like in *The Book of Enoch,* then my mother may be right about a few things."

"Like what?"

"Like you're really the same soul given a different set of preordained circumstances in each lifetime. You learn certain lessons from each incarnation, she says, and you carry those lessons and new strengths and new debts with you into subsequent lifetimes. You have access to the strengths of those previous lifetimes even if you came into this lifetime not realizing how strong you are."

And if she had access to those strengths, she might be strong enough to kill to protect her daughter.

Madison closed her eyes and settled back into her seat.

CHAPTER THIRTEEN

Progress came more slowly now.

Without the rolling hills on the right and the Quebec mainland visible on the distant left, the road seemed narrower as if carved into the side of the steep cliffs overlooking the rocky St. Laurence that widened into the Atlantic. The steeper the hills, the more winding the road, the slower the speed.

The faint smell of burning brakes lingered in the air. In most places, Jon was lucky if he could manage 35 mph. The road snaked its way around the cliffs and through tiny fishing villages in the coves. Every few miles a yellow highway sign offered a bizarre warning: the black caricature of a car on a cliff-lined road with a wave from the sea rising over it like the hand of the devil.

Thank God, it wasn't foggy or stormy today. His mother would have said the sky was a cool, healing blue. She believed that colors affected the body and spirit and that shades of indigo could calm the most frazzled yuppie. Jon tended to disagree. Madison's eyes were a deeper hue and they did nothing to relax his body or his spirit. If anything, they incited his soul to riot and his body to recklessness.

Madison whimpered from the passenger seat. She'd slept fitfully for the past hour. Fighting with the seatbelt, she drew her knees up to her chest and hugged them. She pulled Giselle's black, bloodstained cape tighter around her.

He wanted to wake her, but she needed sleep. Rest, anyway. But this wasn't rest. From the deep furrows on her forehead, she wrestled with demons far worse than Tremaric or Plummer.

Jon shot a worried glance at the rearview mirror. They hadn't seen anything of Tremaric or Plummer since Riviere-du-Loup. His shoulders ached from driving for so long, but he dared not stop now. He couldn't become too complacent. Best to put as much distance as possible between Madison and the bad guys.

"No," Madison whimpered. "No, no, no."

Jon started to tap her knee to wake her but stopped. She needed sleep. On the other hand, if he woke her, she could free herself of this nightmare and land in sweeter dreams. He patted her leg.

"Don't take my baby," she murmured, twisting away from him.

Poor Madison. All those nights of rocking the Cashwell baby had taken their toll. She'd been willing to risk everything for that baby. Her. A woman reputed to be the Ice Princess of Eglin. The kid must have stirred something maternal in her, the way she'd taken to the child like a mother tigress. As much as she doted on both a stranger's baby and her little sister, it was a wonder Madison hadn't found a guy to marry to have a baby of her own. She had all the qualities that would make an excellent mother: logical, independent, intelligent, stable. In short, nothing like his own mother.

He laughed out loud. The prospect of a bunch of little Madisons running around was almost scary! He could picture them now: curious blue eyes, analytical minds, stubborn. Sort of like Delilah Steele, except with blonde hair.

"What's so funny?" Madison roused up from her seat. She blinked and rubbed at her eyes, surprised to find wetness on her badly scraped cheek. Discreetly, she smoothed away the tears.

"You."

"Me? What? Was I telling jokes in my sleep?"

"Not exactly." Crying. Crying in her sleep again. "What were you dreaming about?"

"I don't remember. Any sign of Tremaric or Plummer?"

"No. I think we've lost them. We're going to need to stop for the night eventually."

"Good. I want to call my mom."

"I don't think that's a good idea." He checked the rear view mirror again. "Calls can be traced."

She shuddered visibly. "What if someone's already gotten to my family? I have to talk to my parents. I have to find a way to convince them to take a vacation with Delilah."

"What makes you think your family's in danger?" After all, he and

Madison had the disk. Both Tremaric and Plummer certainly knew that or they wouldn't have both shown up in Riviere-du-Loup.

"Just a hunch."

"So you want to U-turn back toward Montreal? Meet Wait's contact?"

"No. I don't know that we can trust Austin. Not anymore."

What? The man she'd chosen to turn to for help instead of him? Madison had changed her mind? "Look, I can't stand the arrogant son of a bitch, but Wait's our best chance of getting back safely."

"Maybe not. Tremaric has a contact in the OSI."

"And you think it's Wait? Geez, Madison! We've relied on his information for everything. If we can't trust Wait—"

"We're on our own. We've got to get the Andromeda disk back to Eglin."

"To who at Eglin? The OSI?"

"No. I don't know." She shook her head furiously, the mass of short curls bouncing on the back of her neck. "To somebody higher up in the Government."

"And who in the Government do you trust right now? Gavin? Otto? Mr. Smith? Col. Kildee? Everybody in our chain of command's got his own agenda, and we're not necessarily part of it." For a moment, he sounded like his dad, spouting about agendas and trust and the Government.

They sat in the sad truth for a mile or two. Finally, Jon broke the silence.

"Too bad we can't dump the disk. Or hide it."

Wearily, Madison rested her forehead in her palm. "We could hide the disk, but it could be found. We could destroy it, but likely it could be salvaged with high-tech equipment. At least some part of it." As far as she knew, there were no approved destruction devices for CD-ROMs other than burning it at an EPA-approved facility. Chemical destruction worked only for certain types of CDs, she didn't know which ones, and it was a slow and messy process. Sanding wasn't approved because of the variable depth of the laser cut in the master disk. Whatever the destruction process, it had to consume the disk until the particles were less than .25 mm in any direction, or else the Sleeping Dogs might recover exploitable information. "This is one job I'm not qualified for," Madison continued. "This is national security we're talking about. We can't just get rid of the disk. There are procedures."

"Screw the procedures, Madison! If the Sleeping Dogs catch up with us, they've got the disk, whole."

"They may already have the disk. Beatrice might have made copies."

"Nah. I doubt it. Beatrice was smart enough to know that if the OSI ever ransacked her house searching for evidence and found anything, her frame-up of you would have fallen apart. She planted evidence in your office where it would be found and tipped off Security that it was there. She didn't care about what Project Andromeda meant for our troops. It was all a game to her." A dangerous game of greed and revenge. In the end, Madison's two-faced employee had lost the gamble to someone far out of her league. The Sleeping Dogs didn't have time for bit players like Beatrice or patience for game players like Giselle.

Madison pounded the dashboard with her fist. "I've got to keep that technology out of their hands. You don't understand how important this is, Jon. These people could destroy every living thing on the planet."

Jon picked up speed along the winding road. "You're like everybody else. You think this kind of terrorism is something new. When germ warfare comes to mind, you think of some Dr. Frankensteinish mad scientist toiling away in his lab with his microscope and computers." He'd learned differently on his visit to Iraq with Otto. "Chemical and biological warfare have been around for eons. Check out ancient mythology. Remember Sophocles and Euripides?"

"Not really. It's been a long time since I had a World Lit class."

"They were Greek writers from a hundred years before Alexander the Great. They retold old myths about some very modern weapons." He peered quickly into the mirror before continuing. "Legend has it, Deianeira was abducted by a centaur. Her husband, Heracles—or Hercules—wounded him. Before dying, the centaur urged his captive to mix his blood with oil and keep it hidden from air, water, sun, and heat to be used as a love potion if her husband should ever stray."

"Let me guess: he strayed."

"Eventually, yes."

"Figures."

"Save the editorials, okay? He strayed, so she made him a special tunic and treated it with this mixture of centaur blood. According to Sophocles' version, once Heracles put on the tunic and began to sweat on it, it burst into flames. The treated cloth clung to his skin so he couldn't get it off without pulling off chunks of skin. He tried to put out the fire in a stream, but that only made it worse. He died a horrible death. Now what does that sound like to you?"

She grimaced. "Sounds like he got what he deserved."

"Madison!" Jon rolled his eyes. "Doesn't it sound like napalm?"

"Or an overactive imagination."

"Then there's Euripides' villain, Medea. When her husband left her for another woman—"

"Ah! I think I'm detecting a common thread here. Kind of like a mythological *Fatal Attraction?*"

He ignored her. She was in a rare mood, probably thinking of that Tim person again. "When Medea's husband left her to marry another woman, Medea sent her rival a gown treated with a magical substance not to be exposed to air, water, heat, or light. When the woman put on the gown, it melted on her skin—and her skin with it. Same fate as Heracles."

"Maybe the weapon was figurative. You know, the adulterers all perished."

"No. Euripides and Sophocles were writing these stories at the same time. Centuries later, alchemists call it the 'recipe for fire.'" Jon chewed at his lower lip. "When I went to Iraq with Otto, I got a rather detailed in-brief about the history of chemical and biological weapons in the ancient world. Ancient Greece and Rome tortured both criminals and Christians to death by making them recreate Heracles' fate. Persia had petroleum-based weapons as far back as the fifth century—*B.C.*, Madison. The Byzantines used what they called 'Greek fire.' They sprayed enemies and their ships with it and it clung to everything it touched and nothing, not even water, could drown the flames. Petro-chemicals were banned every couple hundred years as being too immoral to use, even in war." He squinted against the memories of photographs of melted flesh. "But they always came back. And they're still out there. Even today. Naphtha, maltha, sulfur, petroleum. Some of these chemicals are common enough anyone can get them."

Madison wrapped her arms around her chest and hugged tight. "What would the Sleeping Dogs do with that kind of technology?" she whispered, clearly not wanting an answer.

"Biological weapons been used for centuries. The earliest recorded case was in 1347. Tartar forces under Kipchak khan Janibeg were attacking the Genoese city of Kaffa. When the plague-infected invaders started to lose the fight, they lobbed diseased corpses over the city walls. By the time the city fell, along with most of its population, those who had escaped spread the plague across the hemisphere. Some believe that's how the Black Death got its start—as an act of biological warfare."

Madison covered her mouth. "Hundreds of thousands died because of that one instance." Twenty-five million, all told.

"Even during the Civil War, Southerners killed livestock and dumped the carcasses into lakes where they knew Northern troops would drink and become ill. We're so afraid of what the Iraqis have buried inside their bunkers, but Madison, anybody anywhere has access to bio-weapons. All it takes is a fast-food hamburger, a little dirt, and a Mason jar, and you can make your very own botulism. Believe me, I've seen it done."

His jaw stiffened at the thought of it. His father had insisted that one day the Government would take away the right to bear arms and people would have to defend themselves somehow or be helpless pawns to martial law. Jon had seen the walls of Mason jars in a bunker in

Montana. He'd watched his father make toxins in a matter of days. All it would take was one drop on the lips or down the nose. A child's squirt gun would be deadlier than any machine gun.

"In the earlier centuries, people moved on foot and horseback and by ship. Plagues took years to spread across the nations. These days, death is only a plane ticket away."

Madison let out a moan. "How in God's name do we stop this? How, if everybody has access to it?"

"We don't. We join the club. That's what Andromeda's all about, right? Staying one step ahead of the other guy. And if we know how to neutralize biological weapons, then we'll know, too, what the next step is so that we can have more powerful biological weapons."

"The trade-off studies."

"Yes." The Cameron Institute had won the Project Andromeda contract with the understanding that they would perform trade-off studies on cost, effectiveness, and any unique features before proceeding to the second phase. "Unique features" could cover anything deemed beneficial to the Government, including offensive rather than defensive measures.

A movement in the mirror caught his eye. A distant car, dark in color, took the last curve a bit too fast. Jon watched the mirror uneasily.

"Do you think the prophecies are right?" Madison asked. "That we're going to destroy the world as we know it before the first decade of the new millennium is over?"

Jon lost sight of the car as he rounded another curve. He glanced from the road ahead to the mirror and back. "I don't know if we'll destroy it, but I think we can certainly change the world as we know it."

"Do you think the Year 2000 will be the end of time?" *Aught-aught*, as the military called the last year of the millennium.

"Maybe. Or it could be it'll seem like it with all those computers going nuts trying to figure out how to reset their clocks."

Jon studied the mirror, expecting to see the black car round the cliff a quarter mile back. Instead, it zoomed around the last curve behind him. Definitely the Cadillac and definitely coming up fast.

"That's a wishy-washy answer," Madison continued, oblivious. "Half the prophecies say our future is dark, and half say it's bright. So which is it? They can't all be right. "

"I think it may be both. Hey, Madison?" The car was closing fast.

"Yeah?"

"Hand me that bottle of cola."

"Sure." She dug around in the bag at her feet and brought out the oversized bottle. She started to twist the top off for him.

"Don't."

He took the glass bottle from her and wedged it between his knees for safekeeping. The black car was coming up too fast. The Caddy was built like a tank. If it touched Jon's rear bumper, their little red wagon would shoot straight out over the narrow road and into the rocks twenty feet below. Tremaric's sturdy face came into focus in Jon's mirror.

"What are you doing?"

"Tremaric at six o'clock."

Madison twisted in her seat and cursed. "How did he find us? I don't get it. Faster, Jon!"

"I can't go any faster and not get us killed." His dad had never taught him to drive on the sides of cliffs, and this obstacle course was worse than usual.

"He going to ram us!" Madison shrieked.

Jon rolled his window down as fast as he could, keeping a tight grip on the steering wheel with the other hand and leaning into a hair-pin curve. The little red wagon didn't have the same responsiveness as his motorcycle, but then, neither did the Cadillac.

Jon hung the bottle out the window, waiting, waiting, waiting for the exact moment. He spun out of the curve and picked up enough speed to see the Cadillac's grill in the mirror. Then with the precision of the god of engineers, he aimed the bottle up and back and let go.

Tremaric's windshield shattered into a thousand prisms. The car grazed the cliff, then overshot the next curve, leaving a trail of rubber and pebbles as it dipped and then dropped over the embankment and onto the scattering of rocks rising from the river.

Jon peered into the rear view mirror as he drove into another twist of highway. Thanks to his handiwork, the Cadillac now lay askew on the rocks, though whether it was steam or sea spray boiling up from its hood, he couldn't tell.

Madison clenched the armrest with white knuckles. He knew how she felt, how the weakness in her knees set in after the danger had passed, how the moment of relief actually hurt. Slowly, the color came back into her cheeks.

"You're wrong, Madison," he said. "They can all be right. All prophecies bear themselves out truthfully. It's all in the interpretation."

CHAPTER FOURTEEN

The lights of the city were nothing short of a miracle. Gaspe', a jeweled city nestled between the mountains and the sea, wasn't very large, but it represented something Madison and Jon hadn't seen for hours: civilization.

Early in the day, when the road had been straight and the peninsula flat, Jon had held the pedal to the metal, easily surpassing speeds of 85 or 90 mph and leaving Madison peering behind them for both Sleeping Dogs and Canadian highway patrols. By dusk, the only scenery was a solid wall of rock to the right and a solid wall of sea to the left.

Jon had wanted to spend the night in one of the one-story motels in the occasional fishing villages lurking in the coves between the cliffs. In spite of his stiff back, Madison had insisted they press onward to some place better populated. If Tremaric found another set of wheels during the night, how long would it take him to swing by the rare motels in search of two Americans who didn't understand French?

By nightfall, they'd followed the road into the mountains and through hairpin curves. Signs warned daredevils not to climb the frozen waterfalls clinging to the cliff's edges. Sunset muted the autumn colors, and the beauty of the mountain forests faded along with their hopes of finding a safe place to spend the night. They'd passed the outskirts of a national forest and seen most of it at 15 mph or less while they desperately watched the strip of road for the invisible line between pavement and ravine.

At 10:00 p.m. and sputtering on gas fumes, they'd rounded the corner and seen the lights of Gaspe' across a wide bay. Both had sighed. For hours, Madison had joked, "Home is just over that mountain," a line out of Delilah's favorite cat-and-dog-trying-to-get-home movie. The joke had worn thin, as had the conversation. With the lights of Gaspe', it seemed home really was just around the corner. But the bay was wide and it took another hour to reach the town.

They found an out-of-the-way motel on the hillside. The night clerk didn't understand English, but she did comprehend the meaning of cash, particularly American dollars. She gave Madison a key and bridged the language gap by leading her to the screen door and pointing out a diner across the parking lot. For all Jon's worries that the French Canadians hated Americans, Madison found them reserved but welcoming and as clannish as her cousins back in rural Georgia.

Madison didn't waste time to check in. The hunger pains were too severe, the aches in her bones too deep. She headed across the parking lot, Jon in tow. A few dozen men milled around the steps to the diner. Most of them wore work clothes and hard hats. The women with them dressed like cheap hookers. Madison clasped Jon's hand in hers and led him through the crowd to the door.

Inside, Madison showed her room key to the cashier and, in dismal French, ordered the nightly special. The cashier pointed out the buffet line and the free T-shirt bonus, one per family, proudly advertising the best little diner in Gaspesia. They found a booth in the back of the diner, shoved a low-burning candle in a jar to the far end of the table, and in complete silence finished their glasses of iceless colas and plates of Canadian spaghetti served on paper placemats advertising historic sites on the Gaspe' Peninsula.

On the way back across the parking lot, Madison's feet dragged the ground, kicking up loose stones. The room was a far cry from Giselle's suite at the Chateau Frontenac. The door didn't close quite right, even after Jon wedged the straight chair under the door knob, locked the deadbolt, and secured the chain latch. The room smelled of mildew and stale smoke. The carpet was uglier than the orange-purple stuff back in the office, but it matched the spread on the lone double bed. Across the room stood a single lavatory, the pipes underneath exposed. Next to it was the permanently ajar door to the bathroom.

Madison smiled. It wasn't much to look at, but they'd paid for it without using a credit card, it was in a rowdy section of town where Tremaric was less likely to look, and they were safe. At the moment, the dump seemed like paradise.

Jon limped over to the wobbly dresser and checked the deeper drawers. "What are you looking for?" Madison asked.

"Blankets. Pillows." The drawers were empty. "There's only one bed. I guess I'll take the floor."

Madison grunted. "We slept in the same room last night, on the same bed if not in it. It is possible for me to show a little restraint and not attack you."

He shrugged, then collapsed onto the bed. Hours of driving had left his face drawn, aged him by ten years. Of course, she'd aged ten years, too, holding on for dear life to the handrest while he negotiated hairpin curves with a maniac behind them.

Jon stared up at the stains on the ceiling. "It might be okay if you didn't show restraint. Just once. I'm not him. I'm not the man who left you."

Madison picked at her fingernails. "I know."

The more Jon tired, the braver he was with her. She supposed it took strength to be patient with her. Bone-weary from all the driving, Jon let down his guard and pushed back, whether she liked it or not. All those days and nights in The Facility, he'd dutifully followed her orders and lapped at her ankles like a puppy dog. When he was truly tired, he talked back, argued, told her things she didn't always want to hear. Fatigue brought out in him a strength she needed.

She kept thinking of a lighthouse they'd seen on the rocks jutting out from the peninsula. From the wear on the stone exterior, she could tell that storms frequently crashed into the lighthouse's foundation and often crashed over the lighthouse itself. Yet the building weathered every storm, thrusting out a beacon of safety to those in treacherous waters when its own waters were no less dangerous. Regardless of the forces pounding against it, the lighthouse never wavered from its responsibility.

God, she was tired of being the lighthouse! Inside she felt like a lost child on a deflating raft. Where was safe harbor for Madison herself?

"If you're done in the bathroom, I think I'll go soak in the tub," she announced, tugging off the cat-woman boots. "I'd like to wash the road off me."

Jon didn't answer. Madison didn't look up as she crossed the room. She shut the bathroom door behind her as much as possible and turned on the *chaud* water. A few minutes later, she stepped out of Giselle's clothes and into the full tub, sinking all the way up to her bare neck, which felt strange in the absence of the long hair Tim had loved. She'd left the bar of soap on the lavatory. Rather than give herself the chance to see the probably pained look on Jon's face, she lathered with the complimentary bottle of shampoo on the tub rim. Bubbles prickled on the backs of her arms. She'd longed for this all day.

Among other things. She longed, too, to hold Delilah in her arms again. To see Disneyworld through her child's eyes over Christmas holidays. To pick blackberries with her next spring. To take enough time off from work to plant a garden of blue flowers with her. Tim had loved blue flowers. So did Delilah.

Madison longed to see Tim again. To find out why he hadn't kept his promise to return. To tell him in person he had a daughter and see if it made a difference. To find out if he could still make her melt.

And then there was Jon. Madison yearned to taste his mouth again. To ride on the back of his motorcycle at breakneck speed with the wind in her face. To wish on shooting stars and open her eyes to find his arms around her.

Maybe it was too late for any of it. Life wasn't an inexhaustible well of experience. Tomorrow would bring with it a danger that seared to her bones. She would meet Owen Plummer again. And Tremaric. And maybe Death.

If not tonight, she might never again make love to a man. She'd thought she had at least forty years left of life. Even if she made love a scant once a year, that was forty more times. Stolen from her. She'd run out of times.

The last man she'd slept with was Ben, a divorced bartender in California. He was sweet enough, plus he played by her rules. Rule #1 for him was don't ask too many questions. Rule #1 for her was never get involved with men at Eglin. She had lovers in a handful of cities where she visited defense contractors on a regular basis. A man in every port, so to speak.

On her last visit to San Diego, she'd landed in early evening and headed straight for the hotel bar. She'd ordered her trademark Absolut Screwdriver, and Ben had looked up from the other side of the bar. His smile faded with surprise, then returned.

Every day after her meetings at the contractor's plant, she hurried back to the hotel. As entertaining as he was, Ben had been a bit distracted. On the last night, Ben had rolled off her and said, "Don't think any of this means anything."

She hadn't. That was Rule #2 for both of them.

He'd met a woman, he said. He wanted to remarry but first he had to know if he could be faithful to her. And, on that last night of his tryst with the woman he knew as Lorelei, when he was fully sated, he decided it was time to make a commitment to someone else. Was she upset? he wanted to know.

No. Not at all. Though she admitted she was a little sad at the prospect of losing her San Diego liaison.

Like any man, Ben hadn't believed she could accept his decision so lightly. Then, on the off-chance Madison might not accept a severance, Ben had listed all her physical faults and personality flaws to cement their parting.

She didn't want the last time to be with San Diego Ben. She wanted it to be with Jon Colter.

She opened her eyes. Jon stood in the doorway, staring down at her in the sud-filled tub. She grabbed a thin white towel and pulled it over her breasts.

"I...sorry. I didn't hear you splashing around any more. I was worried." He'd changed into his fatigues, the ones that had dried in the back seat. And he'd shaved.

"I must have fallen asleep."

"I couldn't." His face reddened. He couldn't seem to find an appropriate spot to set his gaze.

Madison held her breath. He was such an innocent, such an innocent, and she wanted so badly to corrupt him.

Jon turned to flee the room but stopped. He pulled his back straight, then pivoted to face her. All evidence he'd ever smiled left his face. His eyes turned a dreamy blue serious as he knelt on the cold floor beside the tub and took the damp washcloth from her. Without a word, he wet the cloth again and gently began to dab at the scrape on her cheek. She barely felt the sting.

"This won't work," she whispered. "You're twenty-three. I'm almost thirty."

"So? When I'm ninety-three, you'll be almost a hundred. And life will be over before you know it's begun."

He pressed the warm cloth again to her cheek. Its heat made her want to close her eyes. He dropped the cloth into the tub and caressed her battered cheek, smoothing the wound with his thumb. Leaning forward, he lightly kissed her lips and drew back, leaving her wanting more.

"Shhh. I'm not done yet."

God, she hoped not!

She curled one hand around his neck to draw him closer. He unfurled her fingers and laid her palm over her heart. "Don't touch me. Let me touch you."

In his slender hands, he scooped water from around her neck and dampened her hair. He raked his fingers through her curls until he sculpted her hair to her neck and temples. As if they had all the time in the world, Jon washed her hair without ever lifting both hands from her skin.

Madison whimpered under his magical touch. He touched her like almost no one else. She should have let him touch her a long time ago. She should have begged him to touch her. "Hmmm. Don't stop now," she said as he finished rinsing her hair.

"Like I said, I'm not the guy who left you." He stood and wiped his hands.

She gazed up at him from the tub, no longer careful to hide her body behind the useless towel. She was his for the taking, she told him with a not-so-subtle tilt of her chin.

"I hope you liked that."

"Very much," she admitted in a throaty voice.

"Good. I just wanted to show you what you're missing."

CHAPTER FIFTEEN

"What the hell is that supposed to mean?" Madison slammed the bathroom door behind her before Jon could settle himself onto the bed. Her face beet red, she stood in the doorway, one hand on her hip and the other clutching a thin, white towel to her chest. One nipple peeked out. She would have been really pissed if she'd known.

"It means," he said, cradling the back of his head in both palms, "that to be such a smart woman, you can be pretty stupid sometimes."

Her chest heaved. Water from her scraggly hair dripped onto her shoulders and ran down into the folds of the towel. She looked as if she'd run for miles rather than from the next room. "I am not stupid," she huffed out.

"Then what would you call it? You work from daylight to midnight making things happen at work that no one else would dream of. That's what you do, Madison: you make things happen. I doubt there's anything in this world or beyond it that you can't do. So why can't you let go of the past, stop worrying about the future, and give yourself some pleasure in the present?"

Stunned, she lowered herself onto the edge of the bed and bowed her head. "You've come to mean so much to me, Jon. I'd never do anything to hurt you."

He grinned. "Hurt me. I can take it."

She frowned up at him, then let her gaze run down his body. The corner of her mouth twitched upward. "You think you can take it, huh?"

She laid one palm on the knee of his fatigues. He'd been waiting all his life for her touch. She slid her hand up his leg. Anticipation made him want to crawl out of his skin, but instead, he kept still and plastered a grin onto his face.

She caught his zipper between her thumb and forefinger. Inch by agonizing half-inch, she tugged the zipper down to its base. His body yearned against the restriction of his briefs. Still, he didn't move as she reached between the gap of his briefs—taunting, teasing, tantalizing—and slowly pulled him out.

Oh, Christ.... He shut his eyes. He felt first her breath, then her lips, then the heat of her mouth.

Oh, Christ.... He opened his eyes to make sure he wasn't dreaming. *Oh, yeah. Definitely a dream.* The sight of Madison, completely naked, straddling him for an intimate kiss, waving her ass in the air, searing him with the gaze of an apostle of truth. Oh, she was definitely a dream. Jon unfolded his hands from behind his neck and wove his fingers through her wet tangles, anxiously helping along the motion of her bobbing head.

With an angry scowl, she broke free of him. "Don't hold my ears," she scolded. "I know what I'm doing." She seized his hands and pinned them to the pillow. Her nipples grazed his T-shirt. He wasn't grinning any more. She searched his eyes for a moment as aware as he was of where their bodies lined up. With the slightest wiggle of her hips, her body found his. All expression left her face. Only her eyes widened in acknowledgment. She sheathed him slowly to the hilt. She closed her eyes and tossed back her head, leaving her throat vulnerable to him.

He dared not move. She felt like home. Jon moaned aloud. *Ah, Judas H. Priest!* He'd wanted her for so long. Wanted this for so long. He couldn't believe he was finally, finally inside her. He felt their union with an ancient passion. As if this were a time to offer sacrifices for such intense joy. He had to put some happiness back into her face. If it took all night, he promised himself, he'd make her smile.

***

Exhausted, Jon rolled over and picked up his watch from the night stand. Four in the morning. Madison hadn't let him sleep a wink. He guessed it was true what they said about women at her age being at their peak. Or maybe she was making up for lost time. She probably hadn't made love in seven years. One thing was for sure: he'd driven all thought of Lt. Tim What's-his-face out of her mind.

Virtually purring, Madison cuddled against his chest. He could tell by the fullness of her cheek that she was smiling. She looped her little finger through the gold ring in his left nipple. Hell, he'd had a few surprises of his own, though by now she was intimately familiar with an array of touches that elicited a response via the gold ring.

He stroked Madison's arm, savoring the feel of her skin against his. He caressed the curve of her breast, lingered at her navel, then rested his hand at the underside of her belly. The dim light from over the lavatory caught the shimmer of the soft, silvery engravings on the inside of her hip bones. He frowned. They looked a little like...stretch marks. With his thumb, he smoothed the silver markings. And he knew. *He knew.*

"She's yours," he whispered.

"Hmmm?" Madison roused from her reverie. "What did you say?"

"Delilah. She's not your sister. She's your *baby.*"

Madison jerked away from him and sat up. She grabbed the sheet and covered herself with it as if he'd stripped her down to the bone. "What are you talking about?" she demanded. Before he could answer, she spat back, "You don't know what you're talking about! You don't know what you're saying!"

He raised on one elbow. "I think I do. Don't run away." He reached for her but she wrenched her shoulder out of his reach. The rejection stung. After the way they'd loved each other all night, how could she withdraw from him now? How could she cut him off like this? For damned sure, he knew her better than anyone else in the universe. "Madison?"

Her face hardened. "Leave me alone."

"I won't tell, if that's what you're worried about."

"Won't tell what? There's nothing to tell."

"Don't be defensive with me. I'm on your side."

"Nothing to be on my 'side' about. You're mistaken."

"I don't think so." He'd never seen her so defensive—and he'd seen her defensive over a lot of things. "It all makes sense. All the little things you've said. Delilah is yours. Yours and that—" Distaste fluttered in his stomach. "Yours and that lieutenant's."

Jon pressed his back against the headboard. If he'd ever had reason to fear Madison, it was now. The kitten purring in his arms had turned back into the mother tigress, and she would kill to protect her young.

"You...you can't prove anything. Not anything," she sputtered. "What kind of evidence do you have?"

Evidence? This wasn't a court case! Had she forgotten all the tender, heart-felt promises he'd made in the night?

"In the car this afternoon, you were crying in your sleep. You said something about someone taking your baby away from you."

She blanched. "I...I told you I'd been having bad dreams. Weird dreams. Why on earth would I be dreaming about a baby?"

"Other than Bronwyn Cashwell, I couldn't think of a good reason."

"That doesn't prove anything." She paced from one end of the bed to the other and back again. And again.

"True. But your mother's too old to have a baby."

"So? Technically, she was too old when she had me, but Toby came along close to ten years later. Delilah's not her natural child. She's adopted."

"That makes even less sense. Why would people the age of your parents adopt a baby? Considering their health, they'd have to have good damned reason."

"They're very generous people."

"Maybe. Except that Delilah looks like you but with dark hair. Tell me: did Lt. Tim What's-his-face have dark hair, too?"

Madison answered with a glare.

"He did, didn't he?"

"Leave it alone, Jon. *Leave...it...alone.*"

He was too tired to care. He wanted the truth and he wanted the quickest route to it. "The rumors are all true, aren't they?" What was it Mac had said? "You were a COPPER CAP trainee at the time. You and that lieutenant suspected fraud on the missile program you were both working on. But your contracting officer—Beatrice Harper—wouldn't do anything about it. So you took it up the chain of command, but they wouldn't do anything about it either. They papered over it and tried to pressure you out of the Government by working you to death."

Madison steeled her jaw and looked away.

"But it didn't work. You took everything they threw at you. That lieutenant, he helped you. You spent a lot of time with him. You fell in love with him. And maybe him with you."

"Stop it," she whispered.

"Then one night, you and the lieutenant were working late. Just you and him. And you...." How did the joke go? They had 'violated the clean desk policy'? "You and that lieutenant got, um—" he closed his eyes to say the words—"caught in the act." He opened his eyes. Madison's back was still to him. "They couldn't have planned it any better, could they? That was exactly what those people needed. If it hadn't been that, they would have found something else. You know they would have. Maybe it would have been a trumped up security violation or time clock fraud or whatever reason it would have taken to fire you on the spot. As it was, they had a scandal they could lord over your head to keep you in place. And for the lieutenant, they sent him as far away from you as they could. Isn't that right?"

"Stop. Please." Her shoulders shuddered under the burden of memories.

"And after he got shipped out, you found out you were pregnant. Didn't you?" It had to be after the lieutenant had left that she'd found out. Had to be. The way Mac had told it, she and what's-his-face hadn't been lovers before then, and he'd been packed off to Iceland almost in a matter of hours. God. Did Delilah's father even know their little girl existed? If Madison hadn't heard from him since he'd left....

"It must have been really hard for you to drag yourself into work after that, what with the scandal and all. People watching you to see if you'd crack. You probably didn't know whether to pretend nothing had ever happened and let them make up wild stories or to admit everything and have them crucify you. I can understand why you asked to go on long-term-full-time training when you found out you were pregnant. The last thing you needed was more scandal."

Madison's shoulders sank in defeat. She collapsed onto the corner of the bed, her head in her palms. "I couldn't let anyone know. It wouldn't have mattered if I'd been an engineer or worked in personnel or scrubbed toilets for the janitorial service. But I was in *Contracting.* You know how it is in contracting. It's such a fishbowl. We have to be morally, ethically, legally above reproach. At least when it suits the powers that be for us to be that way." Her voice crackled with bitterness. "More than anything else, I wanted to be a contracting officer. I knew I had the backbone to stand up to Congressmen and four-star generals. Not that many other people do, you know."

He knew. Even during his short tenure with the military, he'd seen the subtle and not-so-subtle pressures from defense contractors, Congress, and plenty of engineers for the folks in contracting to step over the line. Madison had the reputation of being a hard-ass on legal issues.

"But I could stand up to the pressure," she continued. "I could watch out for the taxpayer and get the best deal for Air Force at the same time. I was really good at what I did, but to be a contracting officer, I had to meet a certain list of criteria. One of those criteria was character. It didn't matter that the people who held me up for public ridicule had skeletons in their own closets: affairs, drugs, kick-backs, stealing change from the offering plate. Unlike theirs, my scandal was public. It was too easy for people who didn't want to fight me as a contracting officer to point to my character and say that because I'd had a love affair with a guy I worked with, that I didn't have a good enough character to be a contracting officer. Didn't matter that we were both single. It was a convenient excuse for all the people who disagreed with me for fighting against the system like I did on that missile program. I had to do what was legal, ethical, and—most importantly to me—what was right. It's hard enough, you know, how they used Tim against me, but if they'd known about the baby, they would have found a way to kick me out of contracting on the basis of my lack of—" her face twisted—"lack of moral character."

"So you went out of state for a year to get your master's degree. Good enough excuse to use to hide."

"I wasn't hiding. I was protecting. I thought long and hard about having an abortion so I could keep my job. I made an appointment with a clinic in Pensacola. That day came and I didn't keep my appointment. When it came down to it, I knew that my baby was probably all I would ever have of Tim. So I talked to Mr. Smith about doing the best thing for my career. I didn't mention the baby, of course. He agreed that getting out of the fray for a while might be good." She sniffed. "I don't know that he thought it would be that good for me, but he acknowledged that all my coworkers were spending their time at the water cooler and not at their desks. So he approved my training plan and I headed to graduate school for the next year. I lived with my parents out in the middle of nowhere, where no one but the doctor who delivered me knew what was going on."

"Your parents were really upset." The gun. Willpower. Her dad had said she didn't have any willpower. Given Buford Steele's religious slant, it must have been almost as hard for him as it had been for Madison.

"Daddy and I had an agreement. He and Mama would raise Delilah as their own. I would send them money every month. Half of everything I made, before taxes. I would make sure she was taken care of financially, but I would never have any say in the way she was raised." Her shoulders trembled again. "She would know me as her sister, never as her mother."

"Madison." He scooted to the end of the bed, circled her with his arms, held her quivering body close to his.

"They take real good care of her. They really do. They love her and care for her and show her how to grow things on the farm. They send her to music lessons and take her to Sunday School, but it's not enough. I think we've all done Delilah a disservice. If you look at the prophecies and what they say will happen to the world, I should have been teaching her so many other things. Instead of sending her to piano lessons so she can play *Nearer My God to Thee* at the church recital or dressing her in crinolines, we should have been teaching her to use a gun and fight. In a society of survival of the fittest, an inner city gang kid will be better equipped than all the middle class kids who take ballet lessons and soccer once a week. I didn't let my daughter be raised on the streets to know what guns and knives are. Maybe Delilah would stand a better chance in an Armageddon-ridden world if she had more of a survivor's instinct and hadn't been so well loved. But what can I do? I gave up my right to her."

"Why?" Jon pressed. "Why did you give her up? You could have gotten a different kind of job. You don't have to be a contracting officer. Your father would have let you out of your agreement if you'd told him after Delilah was born that you were going to take her back and raise her yourself."

"I had plenty of time to reconsider. Plenty. She was born a week after I finished my exams. I took two more months of leave. I had lots of vacation time saved. I wanted to stay with her until she was sleeping through the night before I left her with my mother. And all those nights I stayed up rocking her."

Madison's voice broke. She raked in a shuddering breath. "All those nights, I had lots of time to reconsider. But I didn't really know anything about babies. One night when she was two months old, she was colicky, and I rocked and rocked and rocked her and walked the floor with her. Nothing I could do would stop her from crying. My mom got up about three in the morning and picked her up, and Delilah quieted right down, and I knew then that anybody else in the world could raise a baby and quiet it when it cries." Madison sniffed. She didn't like doing things she wasn't good at.

"I felt like everybody else in the world could be a better mom than I could, but nobody else could do as good a job for the Government as I could. Nobody else could negotiate contracts as well. Nobody else could stand up to the politicians' pressure. Everybody else caves in when things get rough. Not me. I realized a long time ago that it didn't matter what I wanted personally. 'Service before self' they kept telling me. The people of America needed me, and they needed me as a contracting officer—not as an unemployed, unwed, welfare mother. So I did what I thought was best for everybody: I gave up my little girl, and I went back to work."

Jon swallowed hard. Best for everybody but her.

"I'm the best there is at what I do. Everybody knows that. Everybody."

Jon sighed. He'd joked about Madison's god complex, but he'd been closer to the truth than he'd realized. She'd sacrificed her own child to try to save the world.

"Everybody knows," she continued, "that if there's a problem, they can always come to L. Madison Steele and L. Madison Steele will fix it for them. L. Madison Steele, the pillar of stone. The night Tim and I got caught, I showed weakness for the last time. I learned that night that any time you show people your wounds, they will move in for the kill. So no matter what's happening around me or what I really want or how hard it is, I have to be the strong one. Everybody else can get down on their knees and beg for God's help or have a nervous breakdown or disappear on stress leave, but not me. No! I have to be the strong one." She turned her gaze toward him. Tears pooled in her eyes. "Just once," she whispered. "Just once, I wish that I could be the weak one."

"Ah, Madison." Madison, the woman of steel, who cried in her sleep because that was the only time she dared let it out. "Just for tonight, let me be the strong one."

She laid her head against his chest and sobbed.

CHAPTER SIXTEEN

Thursday, 7 October 1999, Gaspesia, Quebec

"Let's stop up here," Madison suggested. She hadn't spoken all day. If she didn't have good reason to now, she wouldn't have broken her silence yet.

Morning-afters were awfully uncomfortable, even in the best of circumstances. She'd bared her body, heart, and soul to Jon last night. She couldn't help but wonder if it had been the right thing to do. The sex had been wild and wonderful and cathartic. She hadn't known many men who could keep up with her. Including Tim. She supposed there was something to be said for younger men. Their engines did seem to rev up rather quickly, no matter how many times they were kick-started during the night.

"Are you hungry again?" he asked. "It's nearly noon."

They'd overslept and gotten a late start. Back in Gaspe', they'd settled on brunch at the hotel diner instead of breakfast.

"No, but I'd like to stretch. Maybe look at those rock formations down there." Off the coast, a huge rock jutted up out of the water. She'd seen it in a dream during the few hours she'd slept last night. Maybe it meant that this was where she would meet Tremaric or Plummer. Maybe it was where she and Jon would part ways, and she would send him home alone while she stayed behind to take care of business.

"Sure. I'd love a good stretch, too."

He wouldn't need such a good stretch if he'd let her drive once in a blue moon. Instead, he'd insisted he'd been "trained" for such duty. Fine. It gave her time to think and look at the quiet coastline scenery. The magnificent rock was visible from miles away. They kept close to the jagged coastline. The little town of Perce' seemed to be built around the rock rather than any other industry.

They reached the point nearest the rock at a public park, complete with a few eateries, antique shops, and public restrooms. Even before Jon could kill the engine, Madison writhed out of her seatbelt and opened the passenger door, which he'd confessed annoyed the daylights out of him.

She clasped the sickle close to her belt as she scanned the parking lot. Of the half-dozen cars, none of them bore any sign of evil. So far today, they'd seen no sign or Tremaric or Plummer, yet she had a feeling no matter how fast she ran, she'd meet both men again. No need to go looking for bad guys to murder her. They would come to her. Both of them. Today. How could she know that? *How?*

Wearing orange life jackets and black scuba gear, several college-aged kids—Jon-aged kids—bounced out of the restrooms. They laughed and flirted as if the world would go on forever. Then they crawled into a small motor boat and headed out toward the rock. Madison made her way down the walkway, barely aware of Jon behind her, and out to the edge of the pier. She watched the boat for a long time. The kids slowed down at a narrow opening in the rock, like a keyhole, then sped through it. A few minutes later, they emerged on the other side. Madison wished she could get a closer view, too. She climbed down from the pier and crunched across the tiny beach.

High above sat a house on top of a cliff. The surface of the cliff was dead even with the rock. At one time, the rock must have been joined to the cliff and poked out into the ocean like a sturdy finger. The part around the knuckle had collapsed into the sea, probably thousands of years ago.

Madison took in its beauty and crunched a few feet closer to the rock. She glanced down at her feet. Unlike back home on the Gulf of Mexico, not a grain of sand sparkled on the beach. This beach was nothing but pebbles from the size of her little fingernail to the size of her hand. Some larger. Smooth rocks like river stones. They were even more beautiful where the clear water washed over them.

She glanced over her shoulder to where Jon stood guard at the edge of the gate. Several times, he flipped a pebble off his elbow and caught it in his fist. When he saw her watching, he stopped, waved timidly, and pulled his jacket closer around his neck.

Madison tugged off the cat-woman boots, then the socks, then rolled up the leggings to above her knee-caps. She tiptoed into the ice-cold water. Bending, she picked up an eclectic selection of stones for Delilah. If Madison was lucky, she'd take them back to Delilah herself. If not, Jon could.

"You'll make yourself sick that way," Jon said in a maternal voice. He shuffled up behind her and stood out of the ebb of the tide. "I'll get those for you if you want. My boots are made for all kinds of inclimate weather and turf."

"That would spoil the fun." She backed out of the water. She couldn't feel her feet, only a deep ache against the water's biting cold. "Here," she said, pressing the stones into his hands.

He frowned at the damp pebbles of gray and brown. "What am I supposed to do with these?"

"Take them back to Delilah for me. In case I don't make it."

He stared at her. "Give them to her yourself."

"You've got pockets. I don't."

Jon unceremoniously dumped the rocks into his jacket pocket. "I'll carry them back home for you, but you can give them to Delilah yourself."

"Don't you want to pick some up, too?"

"What for? Ballast?"

"Souvenirs." She stopped cold. Her breath froze in her chest. "We've had this conversation before."

"I don't think so."

"Maybe it wasn't you. But it was somebody and...I told whoever I was with to pick up the stones on the ground and fill their...pouches. The men were complaining about how heavy their packs were, and I told them not to be stupid. Fill their packs and they'd be sorry. Don't fill them and they'd be sorrier." The roundness of the pebbles stung under her bare feet. The feeling was coming back again. "Except they weren't pebbles washed in by the sea. The stones were...rubies?"

Jon shook his head. "I've heard that story, too. No. I read it. Ancient history. Hey, you're not going kooky like my mom, are you? It sounds like you're remembering past life stuff."

"Kooky? I don't do kooky."

She was looking right at Jon, yet seeing someone else. A young man, black hair, jagged cut, a scraggle of beard, eyes that gleamed an amber brown. He stood before her, ceremonial sword in his hand, and swore an oath to love and protect her, in the center of a circle of stones. She could hear herself laughing in a different voice, telling him in a language she didn't know, that she didn't need his protection, only his love.

"Madison? Are you okay?"

She spun around, trying to shake off the vision. And then she was back in Georgia, standing over three graves. She rubbed her temples. Her head ached.

"Madison?" Jon wrapped an arm around her shoulders.

"I keep seeing things. God, why am I seeing things? I'm not psychic. Oh, God, Jon, make it stop!"

"Wh-what are you seeing?"

"The past, the future, the—" She squinted at the rock jutting up out of the ocean, out to where the college kids laughed and admired Mother Nature's handiwork. The rock trembled, slowly at first, then faster. The edges slivered and broke away, splashing into the deep water around the boat. In a final death throe, the rock shuddered and vanished beneath the waves. Madison shrieked and covered her mouth.

She blinked. The rock was still there, still solid.

Then she stood in the middle of the 405 freeway a few miles north of Tijuana, Mexico, looking northward at what had once been San Diego, what had once been Los Angeles, what had once been California. The stench of dead fish and children was more than she could stand. She floated forward to where the highway gaped and crumbled over a cliff into the encroaching Pacific. Nothing of the American west remained, save a handful of islands.

She covered her face and writhed away from Jon's touch. Poison. She felt like poison. She wouldn't contaminate him with the horrors she saw. She stumbled into the stinging cold water, unable to see it for the barrage of images that flashed behind her eyes.

"Oh, God. Oh, God. Jon, make it stop. *Make it stop!*"

The swollen waters of the Atlantic lapped against the thirty-eighth floor of the Marriott Marquis in New York City. The Great Lakes succumbed to years of rain and emptied into the Mississippi, flooding a third of Texas and all of Louisiana. Along the upper Mississippi, heat and water gave rise to swarms of mosquitoes and fevers that defied powerful, state-of-the-art antibiotics.

She tried to shake the images from her brain. Jon reached for her, touched her. She lurched away, stumbling deeper into the freezing waters.

Thousands of Japanese buried alive in an ice cap. Great Britain, Great Britain and her beloved Scotland and Wales with all their history and stone circles, vanishing forever under the seas. Skies darkening until the stars no longer shone. Nuclear reactor cores melting in the absence of electricity to cool them. A United States without a government, broken geographically and constitutionally, salvaged only by a network of underground militia groups and reverting to thirteen colonies. And Owen Plummer, standing on the edge of what had once been Washington, D.C., tears of guilt streaming down his pale cheeks.

"No!" Madison shrieked. "No! Oh, God! Make it stop! Make it stop!"

Water hit her face. Icy, mind-numbing water. She fell head-first into the lagoon, catching herself with her elbows against the pebbles and sputtering as Jon dragged her upward. She clung to him, sobbing into his chest.

"Shhh. Shush, now." He tried to help her walk. She couldn't feel her own feet in the freezing water and nearly fell again. Jon carried her ashore and crushed her against him. "It's all right. I've got you."

The flashes of places and emotions withered away, leaving a desperate emptiness gnawing at her. She pressed her damp cheek against his jacket and clutched at him. Her frozen feet thawed, ached, but the feeling returned.

"Tell me what you saw. Was it the end to the world?"

"N-no. But you would have wanted it to be. I-I don't know what's happening to me!"

"It's not you." Jon untangled himself from her and backed away. His face paled to an ashen white. "It's...me."

She took a fledgling step toward him. Wind whipped around her with a cold shudder. She reached for him. He was the only anchor she had.

"No!" He sidestepped her touch. "Best thing for you is to stay away from me!" His face contorted in agony. "Ah, damn it to hell, Madison! You're not seeing visions of the Apocalypse. *I* am."

She shook her head, quite sure she'd witnessed the end of the earth as she knew it herself. How could she ever forget the flashes of horror worse than any Bible-thumping evangelist's favorite fire-and-brimstone sermon for a tent revival? She'd seen prophecy herself, with her own mind's eye.

"This has happened before, you know," Jon said. With Madison's every step closer to him, he backed up another step. He bumped into the low stone wall that separated the shore from the parking lot. "Not with me. With my mom. My parents. I can't let it happen to you and me."

Madison closed the gap between them and laid a cold hand over his heart. "Let what happen?"

"My parents are separated, but they really loved each other. Still love each other. They've never loved anyone else and will never love anyone else. But they can't be together."

"Why not?" She slipped an arm around his waist and laid her head against his shoulder.

"My mom wasn't always a dabbler in New Age psycho-babble. When she married my dad, she was a corporate lawyer. He was a banker type. Love at first sight. Real straight arrows, both of them."

He stared off at the rock as if he expected it to shatter at any moment. Madison studied his face. From his wild descriptions of his parents, she wouldn't have guessed they'd once been ordinary people.

"I was born five months after they married," Jon continued. "Mom always knew when I was hurt or in trouble, but she thought it was the same maternal instinct every woman has. It wasn't. She started having visions and feelings. Sometimes people died in her dreams and then in real life. She didn't know she could change the future by warning people. She stood by and let them die because she didn't know she had a choice. The visions scared her, so she shut it off."

"Can a psychic do that?"

"Lowered her antenna, she said. She decided one day she wasn't going to have any more weirdness in her life. Then my dad started seeing things. Bad things. Really bad things. It split them up, Madison. My mom's gift...curse...split them up."

"But you said she shut it off."

"She thought she had. The Universe aimed these signals at her and she refused to receive them, she said. So she deflected them onto the person closest to her, physically and emotionally. My dad." Jon shook his head. "It took years for them to realize what had happened. I got caught in the middle of it. I was barely a teenager and the last thing I needed was a nutcase for a mother."

Madison could see it must have been tough on him. Along with all the other ills of adolescence, both parents had dropped out of the corporate rat-race to live extreme lives, Lydia Colter in particular. No wonder he'd had such confused feelings for his mother.

"My mom got some help from so-called spiritual counselors who helped her get a handle on her talent. She eventually moved to L.A. and immersed herself in witchcraft and magick. That was her way of dealing with the visions. As much as she and Dad loved each other, they never got it back together again. He stayed on in banking for another year, but his heart wasn't in it. One day, he and a couple of other bankers were at a farm auction when a guy from an out-of-state militia group tried to recruit him. Dad sold his stock, emptied his bank account, took the cash, and moved to Montana to join a paramilitary survivalist group. And that's how he dealt with the doomsday visions."

"How did you deal with them?" Madison asked, but she already knew. He'd made fun of them. He'd ridiculed his mother as a wacko, a kook, a New Age nut. If he didn't give her visions credence, he didn't have to face them.

Jon sighed and peeled Madison off him. His back to her, he crunched through the rocks along the wall's length. "I think I may have inherited my mother's intuition for such things. I've been telling myself it's coincidence, but the feelings are stronger. More frequent. I kept telling myself that this insanity can't be hereditary, but I think maybe it is. I've been shutting out the messages from what my mom calls 'the Universe' and what your father calls 'God.' I've been deflecting them onto you. The harder I try to shut them out, the more violent the messages."

Jon was psychic. Not Madison. All the times he'd ridiculed his mother's wacko talents, he'd been guilty of them himself and in deep denial. And for that, Madison had suffered the worst of the prophecies firsthand in her mind.

"You're psychic." Certainty blew in from the Atlantic behind her.

He gave his head a firm shake. "I can't accept that. I won't."

She swung him around to face her. Madison aimed her index finger between his eyes and shook it hard in his face. She'd been given access to the future and she didn't want it. He had to accept his talent, whether it was a gift or a curse or both. Because seeing again what she'd seen today would drive her to the ends of the earth to get away from it or it would drive her mad.

"Accept it, Jon—and be quick about it!"

CHAPTER SEVENTEEN

He tried hard. Really hard. But like a too-tired muscle, his mind stiffened and quavered against the idea. He couldn't accept his mother's fate as his own. He wasn't a loony fortune-teller who could see into the future or divine the past.

It was Madison's turn to give him the silent treatment, though he wasn't entirely sure her cold shoulder was intentional. The two-lane highway had straightened out, veering away from the coast and the barely visible New Brunswick coast across the water and back toward the mountainous interior of the peninsula, back toward Montreal and civilization. Madison hadn't spoken since they'd left the Atlantic waters. She hovered, part of the time shivering from when she'd fallen into the icy water—even though she was now dry and warm in the T-shirt he'd worn with his fatigues a day ago or more. Everything was a blur.

Discreetly, he patted the disk in his jacket pocket. They hadn't stopped for a bathroom break since Bonaventure. He knew he'd had the disk in his pocket then, yet out of habit, he reached for the hard circle over his heart at least once every ten minutes. They hadn't seen anything of the Sleeping Dogs in nearly twenty-four hours, but his stomach turned queasy every time he thought about Tremaric. Jon had to get Madison and the disk to safety at Eglin. Or maybe not to Eglin. Not if Austin Wait had anything to do with the Sleeping Dogs. Maybe to Montana. His father's group could be trusted to keep her safe, if the need ever arose.

Madison let out a ragged sigh. "I understand now why your dad had to get away from your mom."

Jon sucked in his breath. "Don't say that."

"Then stop the car right now and let me out."

"With Tremaric and Plummer on our tails? Madison, we're in the middle of nowhere. By nightfall, we should be able to make it back through the mountains to the St. Lawrence River. If we can keep up the pace we have for the past few hours, we can be back in the States—easily—by midnight. Worst case, by dawn."

She turned on him, her blue eyes wavering behind tears. "By then I will be stark, raving crazy! I can't stand the death images. I can't! The harder you push them away, the harder they hit me. I try to sleep and I dream about how the world will be when Delilah's grown up. So I try not to sleep, and I dream of myself in a far-off land a long time ago and of things I did and people I killed. I see their faces, and some of them I know. Then I forget who they are and who I was and who I am. God, Jon. Will you please, please, please let the messages in and stop throwing them back at me? Accept it, will you? You've got your mother's abilities. Whether you like it or not."

"I can't. I don't know how." He'd denied it for so long. How could he admit now—to Madison or himself, or especially to his mother—that he had the same curse he'd ridiculed his mother for? How could he damn himself the same way he'd damned his mother? "I don't have the slightest idea how to let the messages in. I'm too good at keeping them out."

"Then try!"

He gripped the steering wheel and slowed down. The road stretched out like a long, flat ribbon, with high mountains rising above the valley in a carpet of green and yellow dotted with red. A country creek bubbled along on the left side of the road, occasionally dipping behind a copse of scraggly trees. They passed a small, covered bridge and a dilapidated barn. No houses. No cars. From all appearances, he and Madison were the only two living creatures on the face of the earth.

"All right," he said. "All right. I'll try." For her sake he would.

He tried to visualize himself as a receptacle for messages from the Universe. Instead, he saw himself as fly paper. Maybe something would stick. He hated this.

He tried to be open. He tried to—what was it his mother called it?—"tap into the universal stream of energy."

Nothing. Nothing except a brief flash before his eyes.

He stared straight ahead. He saw the highway, the mountains, the creek. Yet at the same time, he saw a flash of memory, the same way he might see what was real here and now and at the same time remember exactly how the auditorium looked, the mums smelled, and *Pomp and Circumstance* sounded on his high school graduation day. Except that the flash was clearer than memory.

Madison in the body of an athletic young man. Not too tall. Blond hair, blue-gray eyes. Madison on the inside. Jon could tell by the eyes, recognize her by the soul. She wore a helmet and gripped a sword. Surrounded, outnumbered, fighting like a demon, determined to protect the empire she'd built and keep her people safe. She wore a chrysoprase pendant around her neck. Jon knew her name.

"Um, Madison?" His forehead suddenly felt cold and clammy. He could barely feel his hands on the steering wheel. She blinked at him across the wide expanse of car seat. He untangled his fingers from the steering wheel and reached to clasp hers. He'd never seen a vision before, not anything he could honestly call a vision. God, all this stress was messing with his head. Stress and lack of sleep. "Madison? Do you know who Alexander the Great was?"

She shrugged. "Of course. He was, um, some historical figure, wasn't he?"

If Jon could have made his knees stop trembling, he would have smirked. "Is that all you remember?"

"It has been a while since World History 101."

"Not for me. I minored in history in college. Because I liked it, not because I had to. My mom always talked about historical times, ones she learned about first-hand through her past-life regressions with clients, and I thought the historical trivia she came up with was interesting and you couldn't find it in textbooks, so I read a lot about it on my own. More to prove her wrong than anything else, but I sort of accidentally got sucked into liking history myself. Madison? The stories you told me earlier about the Beatrice's execution dream and the memory of telling men to pick up the rocks? Those things really happened—over two thousand years ago."

"Then how could I have dreamed them? The rocks...I definitely remember being in a dark alley or canyon or something."

"Like you said, I've been deflecting the future and the past onto you."

"That's not possible. You're saying I was Alexander the Great?"

Two weeks ago, he would sooner have believed that little green men wandered around on Mars. But now, now he'd seen it himself. Felt it. "I could see you as Alexander. He was the greatest conqueror of all time. Expanded Greek civilization into a vast empire, greater than any other in the history of mankind. He was responsible for spreading democracy as we know it."

She started to say something but coughed instead. She coughed several times as if she'd choked on her own breath. Finally, she regained control and shook her head. "I'm not a world conqueror. The things I saw in my dream, that couldn't have been me. How could I possibly have been that ruthless?"

"No, you are not Alexander the Great. But you were." He'd heard his mother talk about it often enough, about reincarnation, about lessons the soul must learn. "If what I've been seeing and what you've been seeing are real, then your soul spent time as Alexander the Great, a man born to be leader. A man who had incredibly good fortune in his life, one miracle after another."

Madison laughed. "Incredibly good fortune? You think this guy was me?"

"No. I don't. But if what my mom says is right and there is such a thing as reincarnation and you once shared the soul of Alexander, then maybe that soul was born into this lifetime as L. Madison Steele. Maybe that ancient soul came into this world in the late twentieth century into a strict Southern Baptist family in a small Georgia town. What if that soul came back as a shy country girl without a lot of confidence in herself as Lorelei but plenty under the facade of L. Madison Steele? What if, instead of one bit of good luck after another, that soul faced adversity, time and time again? No, you're not Alexander, but I can definitely see the two of you sharing the same soul: you're every bit the warrior he was."

Madison frowned and leaned back in her seat. "It wasn't that long ago you were telling me how ridiculous all this was."

She was right. So right. These were things he didn't want to see, didn't want to know. He needed to live in the physical world and not the twilight edge of the spiritual goobledy-gook. His mother had found help and so could he. Lydia Colter had turned to New Age therapists to get a handle on her gift. For him, he would find someone, too, who could help. Maybe an exorcist.

"Oh, Jon, stop it! Stop it!" Madison pressed her thumbs against her temples. "You're shutting it off again. God! Stop it! Pull over, pull over. I'm getting out."

"I can't pull over here. Tremaric is—" He gasped. The Sleeping Dogs were close. He slammed his foot against the accelerator. "We've got to hurry."

"Pull over! I've got to get away from you. Don't you understand? I can't stand this anymore. I can't stand to see the future! Let me out now!"

She reached for the door handle and unlatched it. She was always jumping out before he came to a complete stop. He grabbed her arm and pulled her back. "Are you nuts? I'm doing eighty! You get out, and you'll kill yourself!"

"I don't care! Let me out of the car! Pull over now!"

"There's no place to pull over. Tremaric will see us."

Maybe a quarter mile ahead lay a long, narrow, light gray shed across the creek. Another covered bridge. It was far enough off the right-of-way that Tremaric wouldn't see their car if they pulled inside and waited. Jon slowed down with a screech and fishtailed onto the gravel road. Not another car was in sight as they entered the shade of the bridge, but he could feel Tremaric presence. A small sign hung over the wooden arch: Routhierville.

God, please don't let me die in Routhierville.

He pulled to the far end of the covered bridge so that another six inches would have put the hood of the car back into the cool sunlight. Madison unstrapped her seatbelt and tumbled out into the chilly shadows. She looked ridiculous in his Government-issued T-shirt, borrowed leggings, and hip-high black boots, but her face had never looked sadder.

Nervousness gripped Jon's throat. He'd let go for a moment and had accepted a feeling. Tremaric was coming. He was close. The last thing Jon and Madison needed to do right now was stop.

He stepped out of the car, slamming the door behind him. Madison hunched over on the opposite side of the car from Jon. She rubbed her temples and shook her head as if her ears rang.

"Come on, Madison. We've got to go."

"Go on without me. Just...just go away. Stay away from me. Take the disk, but I'm not going with you."

"Yes, you are." He rounded the trunk of the car and started to lay a hand on her shoulder, but she pulled away.

"Jon, I cannot live like this. Don't show me all the bad things in the world that I can't do anything about. I'd rather not know the future, so I'll have some hope of being able to stop the bad things when they happen. But don't take away my hopes." She peered out between the slats of the wall, toward the creek. It gurgled beneath the bridge.

"I'll try. I'll do it your way." He leaned against the fender of the car. A rough bump of mud irritated his palm. He glanced down. They'd stuck to the highways and paved back roads. He didn't remember going through any mud. No. Putty.

His back to Madison, he knelt at the fender and picked at the bump with his fingernail. Back in Quebec City, when they'd left the parking lot inside the Chateau, Tremaric had limped out with his thigh bloody from Madison's wounding and hobbled after the car. He'd struck the rear fender with his fist before Jon and Madison lost sight of him.

Jon peeled the putty off the fender. He turned the lump over in his palm and pressed it between his finger and thumb. He held up a tiny button, about as small as a watch battery, and squinted at it. Damn it! Tremaric had slapped tracking device on their car. That's how he'd been able to find them before they'd left Quebec City, and how Tremaric had found them again at Riviere-du-Loup and again on the cliff side. He'd lost them for a while in Riviere-du-Loup because Jon had parked between a power station and a waterfall. Last night, Jon had left their car directly outside their motel room in case they needed to make a quick getaway. If Tremaric's car hadn't been badly damaged when Jon's bottle had smashed the windshield and forced him onto the rocks, Tremaric certainly would have found them by now, maybe even killed them in their bed while they made love. Tremaric had had enough time to get a new vehicle. Maybe new weapons.

"Madison?" She covered her ears and ignored him. "Hand me that piece of wood at your feet."

She shook off the crippling visions and knelt to retrieve the wood. Tentatively, she handed it to him. "Wh-what is it?"

"Tracking device. Courtesy of the Sleeping Dogs. That's how he's been able to find us so far. He wasn't tracing phone calls or credit card transactions. He was tracing *us.*"

Her eyes widened with realization. "Then he'll find us. He...is...going to find us." She nodded with certainty as if she'd seen it already.

"Not if I can help it." He pushed the putty and the metal button into a crack in the wood. It was a piece of board, possibly left over from the construction of the bridge or dropped off the back of a pickup truck. The wood couldn't have weighed more than a pound. Once he dumped it into the creek, the wood and the tracking device would flow downstream quickly, and Tremaric would follow it, not them. That would buy them a little time.

Brakes squealed outside on the highway.

"Tremaric!" Madison whispered, even before they saw the black Bronco turn the corner and burst onto the bridge like a shadow within a shadow. The running lights had been bashed in for stealth. The man behind the steering wheel was tall and imposing. Definitely Tremaric.

Jon let down his guard for a split second and saw a flash of truth: he himself lying helplessly on the ground, Madison on the ground in front of him, and over them...a stone-faced Plummer aiming his gun between Madison's eyes.

"I think—" Jon said, his throat closing up—"we've run out of time."

CHAPTER EIGHTEEN

"Get in the car!" Madison shouted. She heaved in a rejuvenating draw of oxygen mixed with the scent of Jon's T-shirt and came alive. Her feet, her hands, her tongue—nothing seemed to move fast enough.

The Bronco bore down hard, the racing of its engine almost but not quite drowning out the creaking of boards under its tires. They'd never make it to the car in time. Never. Time was against them. Even if they could get inside the car, Jon would never get the car cranked and out of the Bronco's way before it collided with them.

Jon was too busy looking ahead and didn't see, couldn't have seen, how fast the truck was coming. Madison flattened herself against the wall. "Jon!" she shrieked. "Get out of the way! Jon! No!"

Jon held the driver's door halfway open. He glanced desperately in her direction as if seeing her would somehow save her. He couldn't find her in the cold shadows.

The Bronco rear-ended the little car above the bumper. The trunk collapsed like tin foil. The car lurched forward into the light, spun it sideways, over the dirt bank, into the creek. Madison ducked as the Bronco squalled past her in the car's path.

"Jon!"

He slumped against the opposite wall. He'd let go the car door, but the blow had hurled him backward into the wall. No. She would not let this happen. She would not let it end this way. Alexander would not have given up without a fight, and neither would L. Madison Steele.

The smell of burning rubber and metal against metal made her jerk her head up. The Bronco had locked bumpers in the collision and the little car tumbled forward into the creek, taking the Bronco with it. Tires spun on gravel and dirt. Tremaric's truck was as disabled as their rental car. There was no escape now except on foot.

"Jon? Jon?" She scooted over next to him and tapped his cheek. *Oh, God, the Universe, Whoever's out there—please don't let him be dead!* She needed Jon's strength. His youth. His passion. She'd never asked for help easily, but she couldn't do what she was born to do without him. "Jon, come on. Get up."

He opened his eyes. Pain glazed over them as he struggled to focus on her. He lifted one hand to his heart and pressed it against his jacket pocket. A smile flitted across his lips.

"Come on, Jon." She held back the tears so close behind her eyes. "Come on, Lieutenant. Get up. That's an order, Lieutenant. On your feet!"

He grabbed her shoulder. She strained to help him up. "Can't. Can't focus. Head hurts." He patted the jacket pocket against as he stumbled forward. "The disk. I'll stop Tremaric. You take it and run."

"And leave you here? Not in this lifetime. Not ever."

"I thought you wanted to get away from me." He forced out a laugh, then grabbed the wall to steady himself.

"I never wanted to get away from you, just the nightmares. I wanted you to accept who you were. Now come on. Come on!"

They limped into the light. They'd never make it this way. Tremaric was still trapped inside the Bronco, but she could hear him kicking at the door.

She saw a barn in the distance. Several hundred feet. Further up the mountain, a farm house. Directly ahead, deep woods crawled up the mountain. Madison nudged at her belt. At least she still had the sickle. Forget that old saying—this was not a good day to die.

Jon stumbled and went down onto the gravel and grass.

"On your feet, Lieutenant! Get up!"

She pulled him up by the scruff of his collar. Madison let him bear his weight on her. She almost went down herself. Half-running, half-limping, they headed for the woods. At this rate, Tremaric would shoot them both in the back and take the disk off Jon's lifeless body. She heard rather than saw the truck door burst open behind them. She paused for a split second, then pushed Jon forward. His weight was more than she could bear. He collapsed. She fell to the ground with him.

"Come on, Jon! Come on, Lieutenant! Get up."

"Can't. Go without me."

"Never." All those lonely years she'd endured only to find a man like Jon in front of her and the face of death behind her. She raked her hand through Jon's blond hair and felt the dampness. Fresh blood soaked her fingers.

"Go," he pleaded. "You've got to get away." He clasped her hand. "I love you, Lorelei. I always have. Don't let it be for nothing."

Madison swallowed hard. What a cruel joke. Somewhere out there, a Higher Power was laughing at her.

A vice-like grip encircled her arms, pinned them to her sides. It pulled her up backwards to her feet. Tremaric! She dug in her heels. She stomped at his feet. A cold blade pressed into the skin at her Adam's apple. Her own blade. Tremaric would kill her with the sickle she'd intended to use to kill him.

She'd been through worse, she told herself. A negotiation gone wrong, a scandal, something had to have been worse than this, and she'd lived through it. She'd given up her own child and lost the love of her life, yet she'd had the strength to go on. She would get through this, too.

"I want that disk," Tremaric hissed in her ear.

"Yeah, and people in hell want ice water."

He jerked her backwards to remind her that she didn't have a power base in this negotiation. "You know," he said, easing the stinging tip of the blade across her cheek, "I wouldn't mind carving you up before I yank out your throat."

"No!" Jon gasped from the ground. He patted his jacket pocket unconsciously. "No! I—"

Madison glared down at him to shut up. He wouldn't though. He'd give up the disk and all the children of the world to save her. And Tremaric would kill her anyway. Or did Jon think Tremaric was a man of honor?

"Okay, okay," Madison conceded. She glanced down at Tremaric's leg, bandaged and bloody where she'd stabbed him a day ago. He hadn't changed the pants. The leg looked nasty and sore. A perfect target. "I'll give you the disk, but you've got to turn loose. I can't get it like this." She relaxed in his tight grip.

"Oh, no, you don't. We're not trying that again. You tell me where the disk is, and I'll get it myself."

Her cheek stung. Something wet ran down her face and dripped off her jaw onto her dark T-shirt. "If I tell you where it is, you'll kill me."

He laughed. "You were dead the moment you messed with us."

"Us? Who's 'us'?" She had to keep him talking. Had to buy time. Find a way. She couldn't do that if she was dead.

"You don't have a need to know."

God, he talked like a Government puke.

"Stop stalling. I only have to keep one of you alive long enough to find out where the disk is. Which one's it going to be? You? Or your boyfriend? Choose."

She wouldn't beg for her life. Wouldn't show fear. That's what he wanted. That was his power base. Only one way to topple a power base like that: take it back from him. Take the initiative.

"So how long have you and Austin Wait been pals?"

"Who needs Wait? I've already got people inside the OSI. Wait's as good as dead."

Too bad Austin wasn't there to defend himself. "If you expect us to forfeit our lives, at least tell me why."

"I don't owe you an explanation."

"Don't you?" The moment wasn't right yet. "Aren't you at least going to tell us why the disk is so important to you?"

"No."

Didn't all murderers confess their crimes to their victims in a few minutes of catharsis before their victims became victims? Wasn't that how it happened on TV? This wasn't buying any time. Any time at all!

"You mean you'd kill us without telling us why you're doing this?"

"That's right."

Any moment now.

"What kind of terrorist are you? I thought terrorists always wanted everybody to know what their causes were."

He chuckled. "Who said I was a terrorist? I get paid by the same United States Treasury you do."

Madison clutched her hands together in a double fist. The moment was right. "You mean to tell me you're—"

Wham!

She brought her fists back hard against Tremaric's leg. Caught off-guard, he wailed and let go.

"Run, Madison!" Jon shrieked from the grass. As if she'd leave him behind.

Instead, she spun to face Tremaric. The butt of her fist readied to shoot out and jam the bones of his nose upward into his brain.

He caught her wrist.

"Stupid little bitch! Enough games. I want that disk." His upper lip curled in contempt. He wielded the sickle before her eyes, then let its point prick the indention under her chin and lift her face to his.

She couldn't die like this. She had to reach deep down inside and find a way to beat him. The disk was still her responsibility. She wouldn't let a terrorist steal Government secrets that could put an end to his reign of biological terrorism. Lydia Colter had to be wrong: all those past lives she'd tried to save her people and failed. Madison couldn't fail this time. The world depended on her.

"I have to know why."

"You don't have to know anything except where that disk is."

"I have to know why you would destroy the lives of so many people."

She locked gazes with him and time froze around them. It was more than her own impassioned reflection in his cold eyes. It was a glimpse of truth.

Then she saw it: the cover page of a contract she hadn't signed. A contract for a cool $10 million, dated late 1969. A classified contract with two barely legible signatures at the bottom, one representing the U.S. Government and the other, The Cameron Institute.

In her mind's eye, she flipped through the pages of the contract, ignoring the boilerplate legalese until she came to the classified Statement of Work, which specified tasks to be performed by TCI. Phase I, as with most Government research and development contracts, was a study, this one to analyze the bio-weapons of both friendly and unfriendly nations. In Phase II, TCI was to design a microorganism capable of destroying the human immune system. Phase III involved testing on human subjects.

Then she saw the stack of contract folders, some of them housing classified reports to a special Congressional committee and some modifying the contract to extend it from five years to ten to give TCI ample opportunity to study the effects on the test population.

A long time later, maybe late seventies or early eighties, she saw the faces of men she didn't know. Men seated on one side of a long table. High level bureaucrats. Or maybe they were Senators—she couldn't tell. One scientist with a bucket of vials and a TCI insignia on the pocket of his white lab coat fidgeted on the opposite side of the table.

"We appreciate your cooperation," one of the men in black said to the professor.

"Did I have a choice?"

"No."

The entire project had been classified, with personnel operating at different levels of security. Supervising scientists had access to their subordinate's knowledge, and their supervisors had access to theirs but not each other's. For ten years, they had been operating in the blind, all of them reporting to this man, who in turn reported to the council. To the Sleeping Dogs.

Madison shook her head to clear her vision. The sickle's tip pricked her skin and stung. She frowned at Tremaric. He wasn't a terrorist. Not in the traditional sense. He was an enforcer for an organization inside the Federal government. One with its own agenda.

"We're still testing it," she heard the professor say. "What do you need samples for?"

"That'll be all." The chairman of the group stood to leave, but Madison caught his thoughts as he turned.

At last...a way to cull the bad apples and weaklings...a way to make America strong again...before it's too late....All the junkies and fags and niggers...let their vices kill them off....America belongs to better stock....

Madison gasped. "AIDS," she whispered. "My God. The Government took out a contract to develop its own bio-defense program, and you people took it from TCI and let it go—on purpose."

"You know too much," Tremaric growled.

"You'll do the same with Project Andromeda."

They'd already laid the groundwork with odd outbreaks of E.coli and Ebola near national defense centers to make it seem like a foreign threat. They'd do it again. To "clean up America." They'd blame it on terrorists but the same little group of insane government gods who had condemned hundreds of thousands of Americans to a slow death over the past two decades would also unleash botulism, anthrax, plague, flesh-eating bacteria—all of it and worse—on the rebellious, the indigent, the old, the unworthy. With the AIDS contract, they'd demanded the results directly. Three decades later, amid the advent of Internet and the Freedom of Information Act, the Sleeping Dogs couldn't afford such outright demands. Easier to employ information brokers to steal it from another Government agency and blame it on terrorists. Talk about the Government's right hand not knowing what the left hand was doing!

"Why?" she croaked. Why condemn millions to the long, agonizing trauma of AIDS? They'd intended it for the poor, the tired, the hungry nipping at the heels of Liberty but the lab-inspired disease had gotten away from them. She felt their guarded reasons, their almost nobility. They were "pruning" the country for the good of posterity.

Tremaric tapped the underside of her chin with the sickle. "The disk. I'm losing patience."

He was the same as the men he worked for and the generation before him. Except Tremaric wielded knives and carried out the dirty work. Determined, intelligent, self-righteous. He'd already pigeon-holed Madison as a trouble-making slut. She didn't fit neatly into the secret Government's expectation of the perfect citizen. He wouldn't hesitate to kill her once she'd given him what he wanted.

"When hell freezes over," she murmured.

The sickle's point bit into her skin. She could tell he wasn't the kind of man who was used to asking twice. No, he was the kind of man who carried out orders and expected his orders to be carried out. Whether or not she was in his chain of command.

It was all legal, perfectly legal. She saw it in his eyes. A federal law that allowed open-air testing of biological agents on any American population—without their knowledge, let alone their consent. Sometimes over San Francisco. Sometimes over tiny Panama City Beach in Florida. Perfectly legal because one obscure little Congressional committee had to be notified. Perfectly legal because one local "official" had to be notified thirty days in advance of the dusting. A high-ranking Federal employee at the nearest military base, perhaps. Or a dog-catcher.

Madison blinked, opening herself to the Universe, to Jon's refused talents, to the messages of truth and terror. There was more to it than that. More to it than a secret Government council ordering the unleashing of bio-warfare germs on the general populace and studying the rates of cancer and sinusitis. They'd joined forces with the Department of Health. The Department of Defense's bio-warfare program would have its uses in peacetime, uses that involved vaccinations normally given by the Department of Health. A joint endeavor memorialized in the U.S. code of law.

Tremaric dug into his pocket and extracted another vial of toxin identical to the last. He thumbed off the cap.

The truth hit Madison like a thunderbolt between the eyes. The vaccination she'd received before going overseas last time. The mandatory flu shots Jon took yearly on base. They were all part of a mass experiment. What better way to track the demographics of different diseases and immunization effectiveness? What micro-organisms were being introduced in routine vaccinations?

Who knew what was really pumping through her veins? Hers and Jon's and millions of other U.S. citizens? Or the millions of school children who were vaccinated before their first day of school.

Oh my God! What was in the shots the county health department gave Delilah before she started the first grade?

"What have you done to my baby?" she shrieked. She grabbed the sickle by the outside of the blade. She twisted it out of his grip. Pain ripped through her hand. "What have you done to all of us?"

She knocked the vial out of his hand. Where it dropped, grass wilted.

With the other hand, she lurched for his throat. She wanted to kill him. She had to kill him. She had a duty to the children of America to rid them of at least one Sleeping Dog.

It didn't matter how much time she had to rot in jail. It didn't matter that she'd probably never see Delilah again or that her parents would hang their heads in shame over their wayward daughter. It didn't matter whether she fried in the Florida electric chair or burned in hell. Tremaric would never relegate another American child to be a statistic waylaid by his oh-so-noble cause.

She'd ring his arrogant, judgmental neck. And then she'd seek out every other Sleeping Dog and do the same to each and every one.

Madison kneed his injured leg once, then twice. He doubled over in pain.

"Madison!" Jon yelled from the ground. "Run! Run!"

Tremaric regained his steeliness for a moment. He raised his leg and his booted foot shot out hard against her chest.

She flew backward. Twisting. Falling. Falling. The ground came up hard to meet her.

Madison raised up on her elbows, opened her eyes, and blinked. Jon lay a few feet away in the grass. Blood colored his blond hair. He reached out for her.

She shot a glance over her shoulder. Tremaric had retrieved the sickle—and the vial. At least a few deadly drops remained.

"You made your choice," Tremaric snarled. "Your boyfriend gets it first."

"No!" On her elbows, Madison pulled herself forward. Her hand hurt like hell. Her chest hurt to breathe. She threw herself on top of

Jon. To get to her lieutenant, Tremaric would have to go through her.

Static crackled in the air around her. A shiver shot down her spine. The hair on the back of her neck stood up as if lightning were about to strike her. Bile rose in her throat. She swallowed.

The air in front of her seemed to waver and take form. Owen Plummer! A few feet away, draped in his 1960's garb and a very modern gun in his grip, he trained his eyes on her. He raised the gun and pointed it at the bridge of her nose.

Madison whimpered and scooted backward on her elbows. What chance did she stand against a monster who could appear out of thin air? She turned her head slightly. The red laser site blinded her. The beam sprayed across her forehead. A little higher.

He squeezed the trigger.

She heard a sickening thud behind her and swallowed the vomit creeping up in her throat. Daring to take her gaze off Plummer, she glanced tentatively over her shoulder. Tremaric lay where he'd fallen, staring without sight at the afternoon sun. A neat hole no larger than her thumbnail marred his high forehead. A ribbon of scarlet slid down his temple and dripped onto the dirt beside his cheek. She sucked in her breath and held it. Her own fate was not far off.

She peered up at Plummer. His hand, still extended straight out in front of him and gripping the gun, lowered an inch as if the weight of his weapon was more than he could bear. The red beam angled down at her own forehead. Was he here to finish Tremaric's dirty work? Take Project Andromeda for his own greedy needs?

"Don't." Her command came out as a whimper.

She opened herself to Jon's gift, hoping for more messages from the Universe, but none came. Nothing except the nausea in the pit of her stomach.

Plummer's chest heaved suddenly, and he covered his mouth as if he might throw up. He lowered the gun. "I would never hurt you, Lorelei. You have too much left to do."

"Who are you?" she demanded. She didn't trust the temporary promise of safety. "Why have you been stalking me?"

The corner of his mouth turned up in amusement. The slightest shimmer of a twinkle lit his ice-cold eyes. "Stalking you? Hardly."

"Hiding outside my house. Following me all over town. All over Quebec. I call that stalking, and you don't?"

"No." He holstered the gun, then raked his hand through his sandy brown hair. Except for the stoniness of his face, he could've been any Joe who worked for the Government. Any scientist.

She had so many things she wanted to ask. About time travel. About Enoch's Gate. About what the future really held for Delilah. Even for her and for Jon.

"You can call it stalking," Plummer said. "I call it watching over you."

"I don't need watching over."

He nodded over her shoulder at the dead man. "History will prove you wrong."

"Then you are from the future."

She started to get up, but he held out his palm to stop her. "The future will come, whether you prepare for it or not. Only those of us who are mad can save the world and know we've saved it." He blanched and stepped backward, swallowing furiously, struggling with his own nausea. A side-effect of time travel, she guessed. Whatever portal from heaven had brought him here had caught her in its field and twisted her insides into a nervous knot. "You have a mission, Lorelei Madison Steele. You've got a world to save. Today was only the first time."

Jon grabbed her good hand and squeezed. His mother had said she'd save the world time and again.

"Wh-why me?" She raised onto her knees and shook her head. "Why do I have to save the world?"

"Because that's the way Delilah Steele has written history. She's a beautiful woman. And a wonderful child. She loves you very much. You should spend more time with her."

Madison's heart filled up. Her daughter would be a beautiful woman one day. In spite of all the visions of doom and gloom Jon had deflected onto Madison, her baby did have a future—and one that included a man Madison knew as Owen Plummer.

"Who are you?" Besides a watcher, protector, guardian.

"You really don't know, do you? I'm your angel."

Angel? Like the angels reincarnating in *The Book of Enoch?* Reincarnating and traveling through time?

"You mean, God sent you to...?"

Owen Plummer laughed and touched the button on his watch. "I...am...*not*...that kind of angel."

The air around him crackled and shimmered. Owen Plummer faded into nothingness.

And then the time-traveling hitman who'd been her guardian angel was gone.

PART IV

THE ARMOR OF LIGHT

While ye have light, believe in the light,
that ye may be the children of light.
These things spoke Jesus, and departed,
and did hide himself from them.
—*John 12:36*

CHAPTER ONE

Thursday, 21 October 1999, V alparaiso, Florida

For months, Jon had dreamed of getting Madison Steele in bed. Here. Her bed in a tiny house surrounded by blue flowers and shadowed by fighter jets in a landing pattern. He'd yearned to get her into bed not once, but on a regular basis. Now that she was accommodating, he was, well, handicapped in his efforts. He'd relished the thought of being invited into her bed. Of how the sheets would feel as he slept by her side. Somehow, real life never quite lived up to fantasy. Madison sighed and rolled off him, though whether it was a sigh of contentment or boredom, he couldn't tell.

"Sorry," he muttered. He fell back against the pillow and turned his cheek toward the open window. In the glow of waning candlelight, a restless breeze fluttered in the curtains.

"Sorry?" Madison nearly giggled. "For what?" She dipped her head for a gentle kiss against his bruised chest. Anything harder and he would have screamed. Her frazzled hair tickled his chin, one long tiny braid on the side reminding him of its former glory.

"I don't feel I'm doing you justice. You deserve so much more."

"Don't be silly. I never asked for an acrobat." She kissed the space between his eyes—probably the only place on his body that didn't hurt. "You've got to give yourself time to heal."

So he was impatient. Who wouldn't be? In the two weeks since Tremaric had rear-ended their rental car and sent Jon flying into the wall of the covered bridge, the bruises had nearly faded and he'd managed to stop limping. A mild concussion and a few broken ribs were nothing compared to Madison's bandaged hand or the cut on her cheek.

The worst of his own injuries weren't permanent, but his broken collar bone would keep his shoulder in a halter for the next month and prevent him from literally sweeping Madison off her feet and carrying her to bed for several months. The injury wasn't so bad, except that it wounded his pride. Especially when he bedded Madison.

Madison reclined beside him and stared up at the ceiling. Her eyes glittered in the candle glow. She wove the fingers of her good hand through his and pulsed a little squeeze. He tried to open his mind to hers, in case he could hear what she was thinking. If he really had inherited his mother's talents, the Universe chose not to reveal any secrets. Not yet.

"What are you thinking?" he asked.

"About the future. Owen Plummer came back to us from the future. He's seen it. He's seen Delilah all grown up. It means we do have a future. In spite of the Tremarics and the Sleeping Dogs and how long it might take me to stop them." She smiled and sighed again. "This is the closest thing to peace of mind I've had in a long time."

For good, he hoped. Probably because she now had someone to share her burden with. "You should be relieved. You got the Project Andromeda disk back. The Sleeping Dogs didn't know they were tangling with Alexander the Great. They'll have to find some other way of getting Project Andromeda."

"And I'll have to find some other way of getting the Sleeping Dogs. Who knows what other pies they have their fingers in."

She lapsed into silence. They didn't need to talk. She felt wonderful beside him. Maybe in time she'd come out of the closet and let their co-workers know she had a relationship with her favorite lieutenant. Maybe by Christmas she'd be willing to wear the chryoprase necklace he'd found in an antique store and secretly put on layaway. Meanwhile, he'd readily share her secrets and share her bed. His body spent, his mind exhausted, Jon closed his eyes. Vaguely aware he was humming "My Heart Can't Tell You No," he let himself dream of a future with her.

"Jon?"

He opened his eyes to slits. "Hmmm?"

"I haven't had any more visions. Does that mean that you've...?"

"Accepted it? I suppose I can accept all the psychic mumbo-jumbo as easily as I can accept time travel. You have to admit it's all rather unusual." On the other hand, so was L. Madison Steele.

"In spite of what Plummer said, it's still hard to get all those glimpses of the past and future out of my head. I think it's going to take some time before I can accept it all."

He tried to nuzzle against her but winced instead. Maybe in a few more weeks, he'd be able to hold her the way he wanted.

"Jon? How could your mother have seen the same things I've

seen and still be so calm?"

He remembered the pain and frustration. His mother didn't like to talk about those times. "She dreamed about people dying. People who were important to her. Within a day or so of the dream, people did die. After her father died, she shut herself off from the premonitions. Then Dad began having them. After Dad left her, she had another dream." Jon sniffed. "It was about me."

In the past, he'd laughed off the story. Just a coincidence, he'd told his mother. Making jokes had been so easy.

"I was on a puddle-jumper bound for Montana to see my Dad. Tiny little plane. The kind where they wind up the rubber bands to make the propellers twirl. We taxied to the runway, and then we taxied back to the airport. My mom had called the airport and told them they had to get me on a plane back to L.A. Some wild and crazy story. Matter of life and death and all that. Mine, but she didn't tell them that part. She'd had a premonition that the plane was going to go down. I was really peeved. We had words. I swore I'd never speak to her again. I found out later that the plane had gone down—pilot error."

"So your mother changed your future." Madison bolted upright in bed. "She used the visions to change your fate. And so can I. I can keep those things from happening. Even if no one else knows what I've done."

Jon nodded to himself. What was it Owen Plummer had said?

"Only those of us who are mad can save the world and know we've saved it."

"Tomorrow," he whispered. He tugged her closer. "Save the world tomorrow, Madison the Great. Tonight, love me."

CHAPTER TWO

Madison closed the front door of her house behind her and tiptoed out onto the doorstep. She flipped on the porch light. The bricks felt cool and rough against her bare feet as she eased herself down to sit on the top step. She stared up at the stars. The same stars had looked down on her and generations before her and—God willing—generations after her. For the first time in her life, she felt as if she belonged. As if she'd found her purpose. She'd wasted so much time getting there.

She plucked a leaf of ivy from the brick wall behind the steps and twirled it between her fingers. She half-expected Owen Plummer to appear again out of thin air, but she hadn't seen anything of him since he'd saved her life and Jon's in Quebec. She didn't have an explanation for Plummer except that he was a time traveler. Certainly that was why she felt the awful nausea in his presence. The effects of time travel. Yet, there was no record of him or Enoch's Gate except for what little they found on the Internet or Austin Wait had extracted through his own resources. Nothing proved anything that had happened on the Gaspe' Peninsula. Just one dead man, a badly battered lieutenant, and a contract negotiator with blood on her face and hands. The Interpol agent from Montreal had met two of the three in a tiny hospital where only French was spoken and had taken the Project Andromeda disk and its rescuers back to safety at Eglin. Madison had only her scars and to show for her efforts. Scars and a sickle that had mysteriously appeared on fireplace hearth the night after her return to Florida. She'd last seen that sickle lying in the grass near the covered bridge of Routhierville. A memento from Owen Plummer.

As for Giselle Villemaire, information broker and connoisseur of ancient weaponry, the woman had disappeared without a trace. With or without the help of Owen Plummer. Maybe he was her angel, too. Or maybe Lydia Colter's warning had done some good and straightened out her wayward soul.

Too late for Beatrice. Beatrice Harper's funeral had come and gone. As if blaspheming her murder victim, Beatrice had been buried in the same cemetery as Roxie Daniels. Gavin was still away on a month-long TDY to an executive management course in Hawaii. At least there he could mourn Roxie's senseless death without having to trouble his wealthy wife with his despair.

Madison had no idea what else was happening at work. She'd taken the past two weeks off to recuperate while Security reinstated her clearance. It would be weeks before she could sign her name again. Honestly, though, she would have gone in to work if she'd been allowed on base. Jon had been put on quarters in lieu of spending time in the base hospital, though he'd elected to stay at her house and have his calls forwarded there. The rest of it was likely politics as usual. When she did return, people would repeat rumors and vague assumptions of what had happened in Gaspesia. She'd tell them she could neither confirm nor deny anything and for them to go on about their small-minded business.

As for Madison, she'd recover. Any woman who had the soul of Alexander could do no less.

Toby would be home at Thanksgiving. She'd help him come up with some excuse so their parents wouldn't know that Jolene still faced trial for kidnapping and months or maybe years of therapy. It helped, too, that a witness had come forward to say someone, vaguely described but definitely a woman, had been seen thrusting Baby Bronwyn into Jolene's arms near the bus station. The authorities believed the real kidnapper might have been Beatrice, though now, there was no way of knowing. Madison would talk it through with Toby during a long walk down the country roads. Then she and Toby would stay up late and eat chips and play cards at the kitchen table and talk about the secrets of the Universe.

Maybe Madison would even drop by the Democratic Headquarters and visit with little Bronwyn Cashwell. The thought of holding someone else's child no longer tore at her heart. And if she thought hard about it, she could remember holding Delilah the same way and remember without pain.

A car door snapped shut on the other side of the darkened street. Madison squinted into the shadows. Austin Wait stepped into the circle of light that extended from the porch into the night. "Hi."

"Hi yourself," she said.

He stopped at the outer edge of light, looking both mysterious and sexy in a James Bond sort of way. He smiled. "I'm surprised to see you out here this late at night. Did you wear Colter out?"

She ignored the insinuation, partly because it was true. "You're surprised to see me out this late? It's almost midnight. Isn't a little late for housecalls? And don't you dare say you were in the neighborhood."

"You're right. I did come by for a reason. Something I wanted to give you. I changed my mind and was about to leave when you came out."

Her curiosity antennae perked up. "Something for me? What is it?"

"How's your hand?" He motioned at the heavy bandages on her palm.

"Better. Healing."

"And your face?"

She rubbed one knuckle across the medical tape on her cheek. "As best as can be expected. What were you going to give me that made you change your mind?"

Austin took one reluctant step into the light and dug into his inside coat pocket. He retrieved a small stack of envelopes in varying sizes and secured by a double twist of rubber band. Austin inhaled deeply.

"I've wracked my brain trying to figure out whether to give these to you. I went through Beatrice Harper's desk, including her locked file cabinets, looking for anything related to Project Andromeda, Villemaire, Plummer, the Sleeping Dogs, anything. I didn't find what I was looking for, but I found these."

He tossed the stack to her. She caught them on her knee. She hadn't seen the handwriting in seven years, but she knew it so well. Tim. Without looking at them, much less reading them, she pressed the envelopes to her chest."

"They've all been opened," Austin offered. "They're all addressed to you. Apparently Beatrice Harper stole them from your in-box at work. The letters from Major Timothy Sandusky stopped coming a year ago."

reer, and Tim had been promoted to captain and later to major. All the time she'd had faith in him and wondered if she were really a fool, Tim had been writing letters to her work address. She'd changed home addresses but work had been the constant. In seven years, she'd never received a letter from him, no matter how many she'd written, and all the letters she'd sent to his old address had come back "return to sender."

She expelled a long breath and looked up at Austin. "Thank you. I'll read them later."

He shook his head. "I don't understand you. I thought this would either tear you up or you'd tear into the letters to see what they say. But you act like it's nothing."

There was nothing she could do about the letters. And if she could do anything, she wasn't sure she wanted to. The old wound had only now begun to heal. Why open the wounds again when she finally had a chance at happiness?

"I waited for these for so long." She thumbed through the addresses. Rejavik, Iceland. Denver, Colorado. Tucson, Arizona. Los Angeles. She'd been TDY to three of those cities in the past seven years. Tim might have been on any street corner and she'd never known to look up and see him standing there in all his wild passion and longings. Madison glanced up. "I can wait a while longer."

Austin laughed and shook his head. He closed the gap between them and leaned against the porch railing. "You never cease to amaze me, you know?"

"Good. I wouldn't want to be boring."

"Considering what we've been through, are you ever going to tell me the truth about the 25K you squirrel away every year?"

"No."

"Didn't think so. You don't have to. I already know."

Crap. She didn't like the idea of the OSI knowing all her secrets. "You do?"

"Yeah. You send money to your elderly parents once a month to help take care of them."

"Who told—"

"Colter. Don't worry. Your secret's safe with me."

"I thought it was safe with Jon."

"I understand you'd want to keep something like that hidden. Given what a hard-ass you've got to be on the job, I suppose something like that might make people think you really do have a heart." He winked at her.

"You won't say anything?"

"Nah. Consider it my way of thanking you for telling me about Tremaric's telling you he had a man inside the OSI. I'll be looking a

Good. She'd need all the help she could get to find out who they were and expose their agenda. Austin Wait was a good man. He just didn't know it yet.

"Austin, there's something else I want you to do."

"Uh-oh. Might've known you'd want a favor."

"How much vacation time do you have?"

"Tons. Why? Ready to ditch the Kid Colter and spend a few days with me?"

Madison smiled. The offer was tempting, but for the moment, one man was enough for her. "I want you to go see your kids," she said. "People like you and me, we spend so much time saving the world that we forget to save ourselves. Maybe it's time people like us did something for ourselves for a change."

Austin twisted his jaw to one side and then the other, mulling her suggestion. Finally he nodded. "You're right. I think I'll do that. And what about you, Lorelei Madison Steele? What are you going to do for yourself?"

"I'm going to take a few days off this Thanksgiving and Christmas, even if I have to take them as sick days, and I'm going to spend a little time with my parents and take my little...*sister* to Disneyworld."

"Sounds pretty tame for a wild woman like you, Lorelei. You sure you don't want to go up to the mountains with me later this week?"

"I'm sure. There's something else I plan to do for myself."

He raised his eyebrows expectantly. "What's that?"

"Goodnight."

With a devious smile, she nodded to Austin, rose, and went back inside to wake the man in her bed—the one she'd given access to her heart.

§

Watch for the exciting sequel,
Breach: Book 2 of The Lorelei Files,

and look for more New Age fiction at
www.spilledcandy.com

Discussion Questions for Reader Groups

1. What is the difference between religion and spirituality? How does the course of events in ACCESS cause Madison to question her childhood teachings and open the door to a new spirituality?

2. How does taking care of an abandoned baby force Madison to face her past? How does the baby paralyze her ability to act? Do you consider Madison a good mother?

3. As an unwilling protector, Madison takes the role of hero while Jon takes the traditional heroine's role. Other than age, how else are the usual hero/heroine roles reversed?

4. What would Madison's life be like if she had married Tim? If she had never met Tim, what would her life be like now?

5. How is Jon willing to sacrifice for Madison? How does Madison sacrifice for Jon? For Delilah? For her country?

6. Who is the better match for Madison: Jon or Austin?

7. How did Jon's early home life create the man he is? How does his relationship with his mother change during the course of the story?

8. How do Jon and Madison's past life relationships mirror their current relationship? What evidence do they discover that reincarnation is real?

9. Owen Plummer, a recurring character in the series, is identified as a time-traveler. Do you think he comes from the past or the future? How does he travel through time? Why do he and Madisoin experience simultaneous nausea?

10. What if anything is admirable about Giselle? About Austin?

11. How is Delilah like her mother? Her father?

12. The laws and Congressional testimoney featured in ACCESS are genuine. What non-conspiracy theories do you have that explain the need for these laws? What are the dangers of these laws?

13. How can all prophecies be true? Though we can't change our pasts, how can we change our own futures? Our country's future? Our planet's future?

Order Form

Dear Spilled Candy,

I'd like to order the following:

____ print copies of **Access**
at $12.95 each for a total of ....$_____

____ disk copies of **Access**
at $4.95 each for a total of ....$_____

Postage and handling $3.00

Sales tax (Florida residents—7%) $_____

Total amount enclosed $_____

Please send check or money order (US funds) to:

Spilled Candy
P O Box 5202
Niceville FL 32578-5202

____ Yes, I'd like my books autographed! Please use my name as shown below.

____ Yes, I'd like my books autographed, but not for me personally. I've attached a separate page of instructions, including any special occasions (ie, "Happy Birthday to a great critique partner!")

Name:______________________________

Address:____________________________

City/State/Zip:________________________